MW01530970

Living the Sacred Story

Living the Sacred Story

✦

A Journey into the Landscape of the Bible

Bonnie Glassford

iUniverse, Inc.
New York Lincoln Shanghai

Living the Sacred Story
A Journey into the Landscape of the Bible

iUniverse, Inc.

For information address:
iUniverse, Inc.
2021 Pine Lake Road, Suite 100
Lincoln, NE 68512
www.iuniverse.com

Some names have been changed to protect the privacy of individuals.

ISBN: 0-595-28320-9 (pbk)
ISBN: 0-595-65761-3 (cloth)

Printed in the United States of America

Contents

Introduction

I am a woman of very average means who undertook a longed-for but otherwise ordinary journey that led to extraordinary understandings. The first time I travelled into the Biblical landscape, I was forty-six years old. Although I had recently graduated from theological school with a Masters in Divinity, and so presumably had some maturity in my understanding of the Biblical text, my mental images of the lands of the Bible were still largely those formed in Sunday School. Throughout my early years, I was influenced by pictures of a European looking Jesus surrounded by little blonde children in puffed sleeved dresses or short trousers. These westernized impressions were later reinforced by trips to art galleries, where I saw nativities and other events from the Hebrew Bible and the New Testament depicted within, or outside of, Italian and French towns.

Of course, there is much in our culture that transplants the stories of the Bible into the context that we know best. In some ways that is useful because it brings situational relevance to the story. There is also a hazard in it, however, because we can forget that the Bible is a product of the ancient Near East, completely formed within the Near Eastern mind and culture, and originating in ancient times. Developing a new and more accurate set of background images helps us to understand the intent of these stories. For this reason, one of the most valuable benefits, for me, of living in the Holy Land was that of replacing my old impressions of ancient Near Eastern life with a set of more relevant ones.

I arrived in the Holy Land with a complete set of these old images, and by two years later my impressions had been drastically changed. This process of change led to a surprising discovery for me—that the landscape of the Bible is not only a backdrop to some familiar stories embedded in our culture, but is also an internal, psychic landscape that we carry around with us. Talk to any priest or rabbi about a moral or situational problem, and you are likely to hear a number of references to that internal landscape, to the point that it becomes a picture language that can be used to talk about our human life in a way that makes it easier for us to understand. The Biblical landscape is part of the stuff of our life; it is helpful to have it as accurate as possible.

Another benefit of going to the Near East was the deepening of my spirituality. I might have known that before. People do not go to Jerusalem for the same reasons that they go to Paris or New York. They go to Jerusalem out of a deeper yearning. Meeting other people in Jerusalem is seldom an occasion for mere acquaintance. People there are willing to "go deep" at once and to dispense with the usual small talk. That, of course, is exactly what happened to me. In my encounters with other people on the same journey, I also encountered my own ideas and all the prejudice, doubt, fear and misunderstanding that went along with those ideas. My hope is that the reader will sense the growth that followed, and will be assured that just as it is alright to have a firm and solid faith, it is also alright to struggle with our doubts. It is from such struggling that deeper faith emerges.

Bonnie Glassford
Vancouver, B.C.

Acknowledgements

I would like to thank the members of my co-op community who supported me in this project and who believed in me, especially Dan Fawcett whose encouragement, support and fundraising helped keep the vision alive. I also thank Emma Smith, Father Denis Keating, Lyndon Grove, Jean O'Clery, and Bianca Dalpiaz for reading the manuscript in its various stages, for encouraging me, and for providing insightful feedback.

My deep gratitude goes to the people of the Biblical landscape for their friendship, their steadfast presence in a difficult environment, and their superb hospitality. I am deeply grateful to the Sisters of Our Lady of Sion for hosting me in the Holy Land and giving me not only this opportunity, but also their love.

PART I

1

The Journey Begins

Often through ordinary things and ordinary events we glimpse the divine. I am sitting on the window seat watching a downpour of rain soak my overgrown back garden. It is dense and green, close and sensuous, with the earthy smell of wet topsoil and spring, and the intensity of colour that a grey sky lends the earth. It is at once an ordinary garden—and Paradise.

Everything begins with the ordinary. For many years of my life I parented a challenging teenage daughter and struggled to pay the mortgage. Eventually this phase of my life was over. That brought a bit of sadness, but also and a good measure of liberation. I was able to take time from my government work to complete a degree at the theological school. Throughout my lifetime, I had been more or less a person of faith, a Christian, and in more recent years I had attended church more regularly than before. That experience was very fulfilling, but I still felt that I wanted more knowledge of the Bible and an opportunity to deepen my spirituality. Theological school was a good starting point to accomplishing those ends. Now, with my studies completed, and even though I still had financial limits, I could travel to places that were important in the ancient world.

Still accustomed to all faces of thrift, I had to be parsimonious with vacation time from my civil service job, so I actually planned to work on the day of departure, to take a late evening flight from Vancouver to Amsterdam, and to carry on to Istanbul the next day. Too cautious to strike out on this entirely solo, I booked a series of four adventure tours that would take me to Turkey, Syria, Jordan and Israel. The group would spend a bit of time hiking or walking, not just sitting in a tour bus, and the entire trip would last about six weeks. I had only the vaguest notions of what my destinations were like. They could reveal their mystery to me on their own terms.

It was hard to know what to take with me. I stayed up until two o'clock in the morning, frantically sewing a few items that turned out somewhat bohemian looking. I arose at five for work, planning to go to the airport after my shift. My

3

baggage consisted of a small backpack for hikes and daily use, and a big sports bag that was so heavy I could barely lift it. This was a mistake; one learns to pack lightly. My houseguest helped me to the morning train with all this gear; a tall, strong colleague met me at the train and helped me to the office.

"What have you got in here...a headstone?" he asked. Concerned about not being able to obtain vegetarian meals, I had packed instant food, plus a few guidebooks, but when I tried to lift the bag, it felt as though I had the Encyclopedia Britannica in there. A third friend dropped by the office on his day off, and drove me to the airport after my work. It took, I reflected, three men just to get me to the plane; how was I going to get all around the Near East with this stuff, acquire mementos along the way, and then make it back home?

When I arrived in Turkey late the next night, I was a bit scared. The airport seemed small and dark, and it appeared to be populated by swarthy, inscrutable men. Everything seemed eerie, as in a black and white movie. I felt visible, vulnerable, and more than a little alarmed. It was after midnight. Finding my own way into the city at this hour could be dangerous. This was Terra Incognita—the unknown land. It was night and, in my mind, danger lurked everywhere. Someone was supposed to meet me here, but where were they? Finally, to my relief, a sign held above the heads of the crowd bore the name of the tour company, and a pleasant, smartly dressed young man and an attractive woman with long dark hair helped me to get my baggage out to the car. These were my first Near-Easterners, so I looked at them with great interest. They were handsome and congenial, and in their presence I was relaxed. They spoke English to me in the car, but I was tired and my little bit of remaining consciousness was employed in seeing what I could from the car window. I was in Istanbul, and I was full of wonder. From this moment I was in not a new world, but in a very old world, even though we were driving a modern vehicle through a city of fifteen million people. I noted that the Turks drive on the right-hand side of the road as we do in North America. The driving conventions were familiar—at least when they were observed—and I decided that if I had to, I could probably drive in Istanbul.

The waterfront was a mysterious sight as we drove past, and I sensed it would be equally dignified during the day. My two hosts left me at the hotel in the old Sultanahmet district of central Istanbul and I thought it wonderfully exotic. The hotel staff was friendly and welcoming. Kathy, the Australian roommate the company had arranged for me, had already checked into the hotel room before I arrived. She too had decided to arrive a day earlier than the commencement of our tour in order to sleep in and get her bearings. A moment before sleep I thought happily about where we were. This room was within walking distance of the ancient centre of old Constantinople. There would surely have been buildings in this district in Justinian's time. I felt that pleasant thrill of being in the presence of something very old; this was the very thing that I had come here to experience.

Breakfast the first day: what would it be? Food is a great item of interest to the traveller, as much as the sights and the people. The hotel dining room was set up for groups, with long tables covered in white tablecloths, yet there was something very oriental about the room. The ceramic tiles decorated in blue and saffron, the patterned skylights that looked a bit like stained glass, and the wooden screening with its cut out shapes of minarets, all contributed to the suggestion of the Kasbah. The breakfast was a buffet that consisted of a lot of foods I would normally associate more with lunch than breakfast. There were dried apricots, dried figs, halvah, green olives and black olives, sliced luncheon meat, French bread, sweet rolls, cereal, boiled eggs, orange juice, cordial, tea and coffee. I am a vegan, a strict vegetarian who does not eat animal products, not even egg or anything containing milk. Throughout the Near East there was often very little for me, as these were traditionally herding cultures and heavily dependent on meat and dairy products. I had brought my own powdered soya milk so I was able to have cereal, but this was the last place that cereal was available for a long time on the trip. One cereal vaguely resembled corn flakes but became mushy very quickly, and there were also what appeared to be crispy-toasted wheat berries. We were delighted to see American-style coffee that first day but it, too, became something of a rarity as the weeks progressed, and I often wished I had brought some coffee and a small kettle or boiler.

Our tour was not due to begin for another day. My first real day in Istanbul was to be spent visiting the Topkapi Palace at leisure. The little winding streets on the way were picturesque as Kathy and I passed deteriorating mosques, hundreds of street vendors, carpet shops, and porcelain wares. There was even a European-style shopping district with Georgian buildings where high-priced goods were being offered, mainly carpets and exquisite blue porcelain. Although the roads were narrow, the sidewalks were wide and made of lovely, small paving stones. The streets of Istanbul seemed very European, but that was just Istanbul. The rest of Turkey had a much more eastern flavour.

Our first shock on approaching the palace was the intense pressure from street vendors to buy their wares. Souvenir books, cards, scarves, hats and currency were the main offerings, although there were some storefront vendors of carpets and porcelain that tried to pressure us into their shops. Competition is fierce and the vendors really have to hustle in order to make a living, so they are very persistent, omnipresent, and can be very annoying. The next shock was the sight of guards armed with military-style weapons outside the crenellated front of the palace. We were definitely not used to this—Kathy from Australia, I from Canada.

The Topkapi Palace is organized with one court inside another, and that inside another. The grounds are like a gentle park, with wide footpaths and large trees. There are a few gardens, but the landscapes seem informal in contrast to the stately gardens in the palaces of England and France. At the heart is the Harem. I had always thought the Harem was a part of the palace where the sultan kept hundreds of beautiful women, and that he could jump into their midst and ravish them in wild abandon any time he wanted, but I learned that that was not so. The Harem was merely the private apartments of the sultan and his family, and although the sultan may have had a number of wives, his relationships with them were very formal, and were usually controlled by his mother. The Queen Mother was an extremely powerful person. Wives and sons of the sultan were often in danger of being killed by another of the wives who wanted to be the mother of the next sultan. There was plenty of palace intrigue in the sultans' days; but the palace has now been a museum since the fall of the Ottoman Empire and the coming of the national hero, Ataturk, in the 1920s. The rooms and chambers are now empty but for a few costumed mannequins, or else have been converted into museum exhibits. In the large room where the sultan entertained personal guests, there was a low seating area with plenty of cushions, and this arrangement was enclosed by what resembled a larger version of a tester bed, so that the seated people could draw the curtains around them and keep out the draft. Nearby was a small, bronze fountain that was always running to ensure that the servants could not overhear the sultan's conversation. Perhaps the most memorable feature of the Harem was the great quantity and distinctive patterns of blue tiles. They were everywhere at the palace but there seemed to be a greater number and more beautiful designs within the Harem. The royal family enjoyed plush interiors with beautiful textiles and stained glass windows.

The administrative areas of the palace are now devoted to fabulous museum exhibits. The exhibition of the Sultan's Portraits contains rare books and calligraphy, and although Islamic law forbids any picture of the Prophet Mohammed, there is a beautiful, framed illuminated text describing him. The museum of holy relics contains the tooth of the Prophet and a hair from his beard, as well as his sword and bow, and a piece of the skull of John the Baptist who is revered by Muslims as the prophet Yahya. Adjacent to this museum room is a beautiful room, which is actually a mosque in which an imam recites, or rather sings, the text of the Holy Quran all day.

The treasury contains dazzling items of almost incredible richness. The Spoonmaker's diamond is a huge set stone weighing 86 carats and is surrounded by 49 brilliants. It is so dazzling that everyone's flash photos of the stone showed a thick band of refracted light shooting out of the diamond. There is a pair of solid gold candlesticks of about a metre in height and studded with gemstones. Various jewellery worn by the sultans and their families, and by Ataturk's family, is on display.

After visiting the Harem and museums we went to the attractive cafeteria to choose from among the very appetizing offerings. Lunch for vegetarians was a tomato and cucumber salad and a kind of rice-flour pudding with chickpeas in it, some ersatz orange juice, and a small cup of strong coffee. We sat out on a lovely treed terrace overlooking the port and reflected on all we had seen. Today we had been in the presence of items holy to millions of people in the world, and we felt contented and sanctified. We looked out onto the port of Istanbul where deep-sea vessels awaited discharging their cargo, but the most interesting sights were the many mosques dotting the embankments, where domes and minarets stood out high above the trees and announced the presence of faith.

Winding our way back to the hotel meant evading extremely persistent carpet-sellers. We met with our tour leader, a lively and attractive young New Zealand woman universally known as "Poz," and we had our first glimpse of our fellow travellers for the portion of the tour through Turkey. The travellers were tired and did not venture far. Kathy and I decided to explore the district and find our dinner. There were plenty of restaurants in the Sultanahmet district. The convention is that the food is on display in the window and the proprietor stands outside the place and promotes his business, meaning that he tries to lure you into the restaurant. We selected a place where the various dishes were about a dollar and a half per portion: cooked cabbage with tomato and rice, plus sixty cents for the worst Turkish coffee imaginable, and I think forty for bread. The atmosphere was not bad; we sat at small round tables with short upholstered stools, about one foot or so off the ground. Outside the restaurant, on the sidewalk, the rubbish was piled up and a scruffy little grey and white cat was trying to get into the bin for a meal, a poor little refugee in the midst of a street lively with discos and loud music.

On our way back to the hotel a young man in a suit, accompanied by two young associates, placed himself in front of us and said, "I have been waiting for you! Come with me and I shall take you to my magic carpet!"

We were thoroughly taken aback. The fellow reminded me of characters in cartoons of the 1930s and 40s who are depicted as men in suits but with wolf faces. It was night, we were in an unfamiliar culture, there were few other people around, and this encounter was just a bit alarming. He won us over. This charming man recited Australian poetry, imitated accents, and generally was so very entertaining that we caved in and went to his shop. We learned that he was married to an Australian woman, and he and the two younger men were intermittently answering the phone, making arrangements for the woman to go to Cyprus that night to renew her visa. He has a Turkish name, Gali, but he is usually called Charlie, and everyone seems to know him. We went into his shop for apple tea, and he talked and talked, a little about carpets, but about everything. The two younger men, plus one or two others, joined us in our role as Charlie's audience. During our visit an old man, homeless and wandering the streets because he had been displaced by his hostile tenants, came in from the cold to sit and have tea. Charlie welcomed him in, and it was this gesture that won for Charlie a soft spot in our hearts. It was a very pleasant interlude, and we were not pressured into buying a carpet by the picturesque and cordial Charlie.

The routine on tours is that you rise early, place your bags outside the room, and have breakfast as a group. That first morning, after a thoroughly terrible sleep, I joined our group and met our tour guide for the day, Gokar, a very young man, slim and fine-featured with pale skin and dark hair. He was a real beauty, with honest and lovely eyes, but probably would not be considered attractive by North American standards because of his long nails and nicotine-stained fingers. He was, however, a fountain of knowledge. In Turkey all tour guides must be Turkish, must pass a government exam, and must wear their certification I.D. whenever they are working.

The Roman hippodrome was once a place where sporting chariots rumbled around, but now it was a ruin into which the landscaping of the modern city had crept. Some of the space was now a historical park. Gokar had begun talking about the Byzantine history of the city, when a well-dressed but belligerent fellow started arguing with him, in Turkish, about the facts of Istanbul's history. At first some of us thought he was part of our group, but when it dawned on us that he was merely an intruder, we became irritated and asked him to leave. Gokar was patient throughout this, and looked down most of the time to avoid eye contact, but defended his argument calmly. No sooner had we convinced this antagonistic fellow to leave, when a police officer on a motorcycle ran into a commercial vehicle on the street beside us. There was no real damage, but the officer was very embarrassed. Istanbul was certainly not boring.

The hippodrome had been a great outdoor arena and racetrack at the centre of old Constantinople. It still displayed its three columns erected in ancient times, and the Kaiser Wilhelm memorial. Emperor Constantine built the hippodrome as a theatre for grand scale sporting events, and decorated the site with monuments, such as the three decorative columns, that were the spoils of his various campaigns. One of the columns was an Egyptian obelisk, originally built to commemorate the victories of Pharaoh Tuthmosis III, but now called the Obelisk of Theodosius. Its base rested on the Roman pavement about six feet or so below the present road level. An area around the obelisk has been hollowed out so that visitors can view all of the details of the monument. On its side was a Byzantine relief of a crowd of arrogantly stylish citizens viewing a chariot race, providing us with a peek at the lives of the upper classes of the day. Another monument was called the Ormae Sutun obelisk; it had been sheathed in bronze in its heyday, but was now stripped and rough surfaced. The third was the Serpentine Column, so called because it consisted of three huge, bronze, intertwined serpents that at one time supported a large golden bowl, now missing.

Close to the hippodrome was the Blue Mosque, more properly called the Sultan Ahmet Mosque as it was built by Sultan Ahmet I in an effort to surpass the Aya Sofya. The interior of the mosque seemed lighter and whiter than in pictures, and it was very huge and difficult to photograph without a wide-angle lens. Also, the lights hung down very low, and had wires visible up to the ceiling. The interior finish of blue and white tiles gave it its nickname of "Blue Mosque." It was stunning. Gokar described the prayer practice by referring to the carpet. The beautifully patterned and multi-shaded blue carpet was set out in rectangles just large enough for one person to kneel upon comfortably. It was usually one rectangle per person except on holy days, when the mosque was so packed they had to double up. He told us that the reason for the separation of men and women during worship was the need for concentration in prayer. He said that if an attractive woman walked by when he was saying his prayers, it destroyed all concentration, particularly if she was wearing a mini-skirt. The women in our group snorted with contempt at this account, but the poor fellow was just telling the truth from his own perspective. After the mosque I bought some slides of the interior, although heaven knows, buying something just encouraged the vendors to come on more strongly. Once you had a proven record as a potential customer, they were like vultures.

At last we were ready for the Aya Sofya, or Hagia Sophia, or St. Sophia, the remarkable structure that began as the emperor Justinian's great church in the sixth century, served a long term as a mosque, and was now a museum. Feelings of awe at the antiquity and endurance of this wonder of architecture engulfed us we walked toward the red stone monument. On the way into the church, as I shall call it, were the remains of the Theodosian predecessor of the current build-ing—just enough pillars and footings to create an interesting garden. Inside, there did not seem to be anything holding up the huge dome, and that was, of course, the great architectural accomplishment of its construction. Unfortu-nately, during its time as a mosque, the building was relieved of most of its inte-rior decorations, because they were considered by Islam to be images. Now, apart from the incredible openness of the interior space, the inspiring age and excellent condition of the building, and the remains of a few mosaics and icons, the build-ing was very empty, dark and somewhat sad.

The nearby Yerebatan Saray was the old underground cistern that used to sup-ply the palace precinct with water. What was visible from the outside was a little old stone building just large enough to serve as an entrance, but inside, under-ground, it was huge. There were 336 pillars, live fish swam in the water, and the cavern was surrounded by walkways. A few pillars were of particular interest. The pillar of tears had teardrops carved all over it, and it was traditional to tell it your sad stories. Two other pillars had Medusas on the base, but one Medusa had been installed sidewise, and another was completely upside-down! This odd way of installing the carvings was a response to superstition; it was meant to reduce Medusa's power.

On the way out I decided to buy a few books, and when I emerged from the shop, the group had left me behind and had gone somewhere for lunch. Reason-ing that they would have to go to the Topkapi Palace some time that afternoon, I went to the palace and waited for them. It was raining, but I had my fleece jacket and an umbrella with me, so I was warm and dry, and I had brought granola bars and some other snack food with me. I settled onto a raised pavement in front of the palace gift shop and turned my attention to some serious people watching. There were all kinds. Although it was mid-October there were still plenty of European and North American tour groups, but the really interesting people were the Turks themselves. The men were dressed in a style that would have gone unnoticed in parts of Europe, and would simply be considered somewhat conser-vative in North America—all except the Kurds, that is. The baggy trousers, espe-cially baggy in the behind, were the trademark of Kurdish men that distinguished them wherever they went. The garb of the women, on the other hand, would have stood out anywhere in the west. Occasionally a woman veiled in black *hijab* would be visible, but very rarely, as the veil was discouraged by the secular Turk-ish government. The veiled women might even have been visitors from another country. Many Turkish women modestly covered their hair, but with beautifully patterned silk scarves in gentle dusty colours, sometimes enhanced by gold. They also covered their clothes, but with beautiful, long, tailored coats in the same dusty pastel colours as the scarves. It was a different look, but it was a refined and fashionable look. I watched a dense parade of humanity walk by and into the palace, plus I got to talk to a few cats who were not exactly strays but unofficial residents of the palace, who were tolerated as long as they kept up the work of rodent control.

My group finally arrived, just around the time I was getting truly bored. We toured the Topkapi, this time taking in some exhibits we had missed the previous day: the clothing, the porcelain exhibits, and the Baghdad kiosk. I was impressed by the sultan's costumes and resolved someday to make myself a replica of a green tunic with buttoned cuffs and chartreuse trousers. I thought I would leave out the pointy shoes.

Near the blue mosque is the Sultan Ahmet mausoleum, where the sultan was buried, along with many of his relatives. Throughout Turkey we saw similar burial mosques of important or holy people. Inside the Sultan Ahmet mausoleum were the cloth-covered tombs of about two dozen persons, the largest tomb being that of the sultan, and beside him that of his son, the subsequent sultan. These Muslims were buried on their side, in fœtal position, facing Mecca, so the tombs appeared short and wide to our western eyes. The sarcophagi were peaked at the top, draped with prayer rugs, and they had a turban at the end where the deceased person's head rests inside. The mausoleums, although not places of worship, hade the status of mosques, and so we always wore long trousers or a skirt, and we had ready a scarf and long-sleeved shirt, so that we would not have to miss these sites. Poz carried around a large piece of thin, batiked cotton that she could wrap around herself as a sarong; thus she could wear shorts, but still be instantly ready to enter a mosque.

We rested our feet then had a glass of wine within the hotel. The group went out together for dinner at the Vitamin Restaurant: soup, fried rice with fried noodles, and sautéed cabbage. After so much vigorous sightseeing, I ate much more that I needed to eat, and I shared a small bottle of wine with the two other ladies at my table. That evening, in the room that I was still sharing with Kathy, I had no difficulty getting to sleep.

◆   ◆   ◆

We had the exotic Istanbul breakfast and then got into our tour bus, which was only about half full, so there was plenty of room for us to stretch out or to store baggage on the seat. Our driver was Regep (Reh-JEEP), an attractive young man who was positively obsessed with cleanliness in the bus. We had to wipe our feet on several carpets before climbing aboard, and Regep was constantly fussing around, tidying up, washing the coach, cleaning the aisle. We all wanted to marry him. We set out for Gallipoli, or Gelibolu as it was known in Turkey. Outside Istanbul we were able to see the style of new housing being built. Many of them were A-roofed, almost reminiscent of Swiss chalets, and most were made of masonry block. Even concrete buildings were faced with some kind of tile or brick. There were also houses that, oddly, had a larger floor area on the second floor than on the first. The natural vegetation around Istanbul was mixed forest: coniferous on the higher hills, deciduous lower down. By the side of the Aegean Sea we looked through the olive groves, and down the steep cliffs that fell into the turquoise and deep azure water.

Our tea stop was Tekirdag, where we saw plenty of people in agricultural vehicles. In fact, we saw this everywhere—people came from the farm into town on the tractor, or in a vehicle drawn by horse or donkey. They drove right through the streets of town among the cars. The people in the towns and countryside all seemed vigorous, healthy, and hard working, and the cultivated land was teeming with produce. Turkey, Poz informed us, was a self-sustaining country having no net import, and indeed, the entire countryside was burgeoning with productivity. We were in Gallipoli by lunch. I got something to nibble on and took in the bank.

The bank was small and crowded, decorated in a style that appeared to date from thirty years before. The walls were covered in wood panelling, which made the interior seem dark. About a half-dozen tellers sat behind a long, undifferentiated counter. There seemed to be no specialization; customers just lined up in front of one of the employees, no matter what business they wanted to transact. Service was incredibly slow, but the employees were able to respond to me in English sufficiently to transact business. I was not bothered by these differences from our competitive institutions in North America, but rather observed that people there generally were more patient than we were. Still, I reflected that such subtle differences might be something that visitors should know of beforehand.

The battlefield at Gallipoli was now a national park. There was a museum at the Kabatepe end of the park, near where the Anzacs from Australia and New Zealand were actually supposed to land, and the entire vast area was dotted with cemeteries and memorials. Instead of landing at Kabatepe, however, the Anzac forces drifted about a mile out of their way to Gallipoli, and that was the miscalculation that led to the terrible slaughter that ensued. Nothing could prepare the traveller for the experience of visiting Gallipoli. New Zealanders and Australians, familiar with every moment of the conflict because they are taught it in school, were not the only ones moved by the sight of so many soldiers' graves. The haunting magnitude of what happened in that place spoke to each traveller in a different way.

At the top of the deadly rift known as Ammunition Gulley was the highest point of Australian penetration, called the NEK. There we began our exploration of the park. The conflict at Gallipoli had taken place near the end of the First World War, and the political chaos of the day had kept the War Graves Commission from carrying out its task for several months. As a result, most of the dead were not identified. Each cemetery featured a list of names of those identified, and cited a much larger number buried there whose names remained unknown. The Turks, too, had raised a memorial to the unknown soldier. Among the displays was the statue of an old man in a fez, representing the old order, and a little girl in modern European dress, carrying a bouquet of flowers, representing the new. The fez had been banned in 1922 as part of Ataturk's program to bring Turkey into the modern world. A small square in the corner of the memorial was an open-air mosque.

Finally we went down to Anzac Cove to see the bottom of Ammunition Gulley. High above on the steep hillside was a geological prominence called the Sphynx, the landmark that the Anzacs used a reference point. During the attack, the New Zealanders had gone around the Sphynx to the left, and the Australians to the right. Poz, herself a New Zealander, sat with us on the beach and read aloud an account of what happened that day. For many in our group there was a renewal of national pride. For myself, I could not imagine anything that made worthwhile the horrific experiences, and the terrible slaughter of young men, that took place at Gallipoli.

Daylight was almost over when we caught the ferry across the Dardanelles. We watched the sun set on the little town of Eceakat (EH-cheea-kat) as we sailed away from it. A row of shops was illuminated, and the dome and minaret of the little mosque was silhouetted against the pink and navy blue sky. The landing place on the other side was called Çanakkule (Cha-NA-koo-lay), and there we had dinner at a waterfront restaurant where we could share with one another our reflections on what we had seen that day, and we noted the great range of perspectives expressed. One young man of our group, who was himself an Australian soldier, was moved to tears when he spoke of the Gallipoli experience. We retired to the Anzac Hotel, a mid-town place right beside the town clock, which bonged every quarter hour and tried to drown out the traffic noise below.

Alas, the Anzac hotel did not serve American or European-style coffee; I really missed it, as I am such a coffee addict. We had a meagre breakfast with strong tea, and set out for Troy. I have to admit that my previous knowledge of the Troy site did not come from the archaeological journals. I had studied the very poetic accounts in Homer's Iliad in high school and university, but that, of course, was then and this was now. Most of my more recent impressions came from the detective adventures of Vicky Bliss in Elizabeth Peters' novel *Trojan Gold*, or else from C.W. Ceram's *Gods, Graves and Scholars*, which contained a layperson's account of Heinrich Schliemann's quest for the Trojan treasures. But Troy was romantic and engaging all by itself, and revealed itself through the travellers' experience of the site. The first thing we saw at Troy was a large wooden horse, a modern-day photo opportunity for tourists. This was great fun, and, laughing, we climbed up the steps, right inside, and had our picture taken waving from the upstairs windows of the horse. This, of course, was not the romantic, evocative part; in fact, whenever I encountered tourism promotion such as this, I regarded it in a humorous light, I took delight in it, and I did not allow it to impede my enjoyment of the antiquity of the site. The Trojan horse had been put there as a playground structure for children of all ages, and so I thought I may as well join in and play.

Our guide to the site was Mustafa, a local man completely obsessed with Troy, who knew every trench, every artifact, and every hypothesis, and who, if things were different, would probably have loved to be an archaeologist himself. He had published a beautiful coffee-table book that was for sale in the Troy gift shop and elsewhere. Heinrich Schliemann excavated the Troy site from 1873 to 1890, and secreted from the country various artifacts, including some axes and a trove of gold items known as Priam's Treasure. The artifacts disappeared from Berlin during the Second World War, but turned up in Moscow's Pushkin Museum in 1994, after the Cold War was securely over. We gazed on the site where these treasures of Troy had been found. Mustafa led us around and described each discrete section of the ruin in terms of the ten known cities of Troy, although there were 46 or more different building phases identifiable. The entire site seemed to be accessible to visitors. There were enough information signs and bridges over the excavations that visitors could enjoy the site, yet it could function as a place of archaeological study as well.

We went back to the motorway and had a chance to view the countryside, overflowing as it was with Çanakkule's principal crops of cotton and tomatoes. People in Asia Minor did not live on their properties as westerners do, with the farmhouses isolated from one another. Rather, they lived in the village and went out to their land each morning to work. We passed many trucks and donkey-drawn carts carrying families out to the fields. Groups of women in kerchiefs and long skirts were picking cotton and tomatoes, and eventually the crops were piled up alongside the road to be picked up by trucks and taken to market.

As the fields and buildings passed by our coach window, the housing changed in style to large tracts of row housing with terra cotta roofs. All had solar water heaters and solar panels on the roof. There were mixed trees and lots of olives. Our lunch stop was Bergama, the modern little town at the foot of the acropolis of ancient Pergamum. Pergamum was famous for its library, which was later plundered by Marc Anthony to replace the books lost in the burning of the Alexandria library during Rome's attempt to invade Alexandria. Anthony presented the Pergamum books to Cleopatra as a gift. The very name Pergamum is bookish, as it is related to the Latin word for parchment, *pergamen.*

In the main part of the modern town of Bergama is an ancient building that began as a temple to the Egyptian god Serapis, and in the second century of the Common Era a basilica was added on the site, probably the centre of worship for the developing Christian community. The cobblestone main street was lined with the usual single-story buildings with shop fronts, banks, the occasional carpet display, and several long, open-air cafes. I had a pide (PEE-day) for lunch, a kind of thin Turkish pizza that is normally not vegetarian but they made me one topped only with tomato sauce.

This was the first time in my life that I had been in a place mentioned in the Bible, and I was in awe. I felt as if the cover of a huge, imaginary book were opening, and I could walk inside. Pergamum is familiar as one of the seven cities of Asia Minor that St. John the Divine mentions in the book of Revelation (Rev 1:11 and 2:12). In the book, John wrote scathing, accusing letters to the Christians of Pergamum, probably the very Christians who worshipped in that old ruined basilica, accusing them of following a false teacher. We went up to explore ancient Pergamum, known locally as the Acropolis. As with many other ancient cities that have modern counterparts, the old city is high on a hill, at some distance from the modern town site, and surrounded by cultivated land. I climbed up to the Roman military barracks at the far end of the site to see the town as the Roman soldiers saw it. As I saw it, of course, the ancient town was in ruins, dominated by the great standing columns of the Temple of Trajan. As the ruins are perched so high on a hill, it would have been difficult for the local people to quarry the site for their own buildings, and so there is much remaining. Locals are reverent of any place that has been a site of worship, and bits of tissue paper and cotton are tied to the shrubbery as votive offerings. Below you can see the great theatre; it appears very steep, as if some of it might have slid down the hill at some moment in history. The major artifact from the site, the Altar of Zeus, is now kept in the town museum.

We went on to Selçuk (SEL-chuk) and checked into the Kale Han Hotel, a sprawled-out wooden building that made us feel at home. Although the rooms were small and not luxurious by North American standards, the hotel was quaint and pretty, with antique furniture and lace dresser scarves, so that being a guest there was a bit like visiting my great-grandmother's house. The courtyard of the hotel had a well-maintained pool and deck chairs, a flower garden and large pieces of rustic pottery.

Our dinner spot was a restaurant by the beach: really just a big, smoky hall with a lot of men watching football on television, but the food was good. After dinner we went to a carpet handcraft centre next to the restaurant, where the proprietor gave a carpet demonstration explaining the knotting, dyes and styles of carpets from different regions of Turkey. A couple from Washington D.C. bought a lovely hall runner for their home for U.S. $600, but most of us were not in a position to make such a purchase, and would have wanted more time beforehand to study Turkish carpets, as the American couple had done.

Selçuk in my mind was a locus for the persistence of the feminine face of deity, although the vigorous efforts of St. Paul, and the later influence of Islam, have until recently obscured this history. The native Anatolians worshipped a fertility goddess called Cybele, or Kybele, and Ephesus was the centre for her cult. Those early people were not Greeks or Romans, but were from farther east in Asia Minor, and they left behind some intriguing statuary that was now in the Ephesus museum. The statues of the goddess appeared to have a large number of breasts, but scholars have argued that these large spheres on her torso were really bulls' testicles, or perhaps honey sacs, as bees are also depicted. If bees were really important here, they may have given the city its name: the Greek word for bees is *apasos*, which may be morphologised into Ephesus. Bees were the symbol of productivity or fertility, and thus their possible connection with the mother goddess. Still, I found it all a somewhat strange argument; after all, if you are going to have a mother goddess, chances are she will have plenty of breasts, whether in size or in number!

When the area became the Greek city-state of Ionia, the cult of Artemis, known to Romans as Diana, gained ascendancy and the great Temple of Artemis, or Diana, was built. All that now remained of the temple was a single pillar and a few foundation stones on the ground, but in its heyday it was one of the seven wonders of the ancient world. In the first century of our era, the worshippers of

Diana were tremendously loyal to their beloved goddess. The book of Acts tells of how St. Paul ran afoul of their sensibilities and got into a terrible conflict with the local artisans. Paul was arrested, and many believe he almost lost his life over this issue.

In 700 B.C.E., the Lydians came to Ephesus. In 600 B.C.E., Crœsus was the king of Lydia, with his capital at Sardis, and he minted the world's first coins. As he was fabulously rich, he probably had a lot of those coins himself. Later the Persians came, then Alexander the Great. Alexander rebuilt the temple, but by then its importance was waning and the great Temple of Artemis was eventually destroyed. Many of the stones were used to build the Isa Bey mosque in the 13th century, and most of the treasures of the Temple are now in the British Museum.

In Selçuk there was so much of interest, ancient and modern. I shared a taxi with four others and went to Meryamana, the house that was believed by many to be the final home of the Virgin Mary. It had been a first century house, ruined down to its foundation stones, when the belief in the Virgin Mary's occupation gained enough momentum that the house was rebuilt as a place of pilgrimage. The approach to the rebuilt house was a stone walkway, and a bronze statue of the blessed Virgin welcomed the visitor to her home. A community of nuns lived on the property and maintained the place. As we came up the walk, we could hear people singing the English hymn tune of Abbot's Leigh, and then we saw that they were hearing Mass at an outdoor chapel beside the little house. It was evident in the faces of the worshippers that this was for them a holy place that gave them great joy, and allowed them to feel close to Mary.

We went back to town to the Ephesus Museum, where a lot of the artifacts from the Ephesus site and from other cultures that occupied the area were displayed and were very well interpreted. The well-known statues of Kybele with all the "breasts" were there, as well as statues of the emperor and empress, grave items, lamps from throughout the centuries, and wall paintings. I lost my companions at the museum and so set out up the road from the museum on my own, past the ruins of an old Turkish bath, or hamam, erected 1372, a kind of large brick beehive complex with escape holes for the steam, and now apparently occupied by chickens. I then went up to the Isa Bey Camii mosque, built in 1307. Inside the door, a man was giving out booklets and information, and he assured me it was all right to wear shoes inside the mosque, as all the carpets were roped off. I was interested in buying a guide to the mosque, but the man was almost reluctant to sell me one, assuring me that he was not a businessman but a holy man. In the end I concluded that he was more of a businessman than he claimed as he persuaded me to pay almost five dollars for a very small booklet. At first I thought the mosque was built on the site of former places of worship because it contained Greco-Roman features. What had happened, however, was that the builders had quarried the Temple of Artemis, located just a few yards down the road, to obtain and recycle the beautiful dressed stone as a building material for the mosque. Thus the front of the mosque is built almost entirely from bits of the Temple of Diana, and very little is left of the temple itself.

Next I went on foot up to the St. John Basilica, now also a ruin. Ephesus was closely associated with the Beloved Disciple, who was traditionally held to be St. John the Evangelist, and the story was that he brought Mary, the mother of Jesus, to this town after the death of Jesus; thus, the emperor Justinian built the huge commemorative basilica overlooking the town. The church was, in fact, so large that the visitor can forget that everything visible there was all inside the church walls. This was especially true now that nature was taking over parts of the ruined interior of the church. A gravesite within the ruin was marked as the grave of St. John, and nearby a plaque marked the visit of Pope Paul VI in 1967.

After visiting the basilica, I once again became separated from my companions and set out by myself. I sometimes wondered why I had even paid for a tour since I did not seem to be firmly attached to it. Along my way, I passed a very old, tiny, old mosque, perhaps fifteenth century. These little mosques are very usual in the towns, and seem close together—for convenience, I supposed, so that men working during the day do not have to go far to observe the five daily prayer times.

When I was passing the museum a carpet-seller came out and asked me where I was from. By now, I was thoroughly tired of this line and tried to escape. He trapped me with guilt by calling out, "What's the matter? Don't you like Turkish people?" I had to go back, of course, so we got into a big conversation and he persuaded me to have apple tea with him. He was a stocky man, balding, a 35-year old Kurdish carpet seller from Hakkari in Eastern Turkey, and he was working in the family business with his mother and two brothers. We talked about the different cultures in which we each live, and about how they have formed our ideas of right and wrong. He then persuaded me to return later in the evening and have dinner with him. His name was Ibrahim.

On the way back to my hotel, I didn't know what to think. I could be grabbed as a hostage to promote the Kurdish cause. Or there might be an offer of marriage, with the real prize, for him, being a visa to Canada. At the very least I might be forced to buy a carpet! I began to worry about this quite a lot and decided to give Kathy his business card, with the idea that if I did not return within a reasonable time, say midnight, she would send out the cavalry. By the time I returned to my room I had talked myself into a state of alarm. I had lunch at the hotel because people there spoke English and I knew I could make my dietary needs known. Soon it was 3:30 pm—time for Ephesus.

Our guide was Nejat, a fellow who appeared to have a hip disorder and got around the fallen stones amazingly well on his crutches. Like most local guides in Turkey, he knew and loved every little stone and every feature of the site. He told us that the city of Ephesus had been home to about 250,000 people. You work out the population of ancient cities by the size of the theatres; the theatres were built to seat one tenth of the city's inhabitants. Nejat also told stories from the Bible because of the city's association with Paul, with the Beloved Disciple, the Virgin Mary, and Luke. Behind the shops, in a section not currently open to visitors, is a grave believed to be that of the gospeller, Luke. It is possible to imagine what the city was really like from the great quantity of excavated remains, and it was large, as large as a modern city. It was the first lighted city in the world. On the paving stones of the sidewalks there are square holes in the pavement where the posts for torches would have been placed, each with four more holes around it by which the four chains holding up the post would be secured to the ground. A row of bulls carved in stone overlooked one of the streets, perhaps the very unfortunate fellows whose testicles were now suspended from that lady in the museum!

Examples of different kinds of building columns were on display: Doric(crowned with a circle topped by a square), Ionic (with horns), Corinthian (with leaves), and Composite. We could also see that ceramic drain tile, exactly the same as the drain tile in use today, was used by the Romans in constructing the sewer system. There was plenty of evidence of the arrival of Christianity. A cross was visible on the side of a cornerstone, and crosses were typically carved over the doors of Christian homes. On the pavement was visible the spider's web pattern, a secret Christian symbol made up of the letters of ICTHYS and rendered so that it looked the same from all directions. This word, Greek for "fish," is an acronym of the Greek title "Jesus Christ, God's Son, Saviour." There had been a famous school of medicine at Ephesus, and a lot of the surgical instruments were now on display at the Ephesus museum. Many of these instruments were exactly the same as their modern counterparts; forceps, for example, have changed little since Roman times. There is a huge, upright building stone with the medical symbol, the caduceus, on one side and Hermes, or Mercury, on the other.

As Roman emperors were worshipped as gods, there was a Temple of Domitian, and another of Trajan, where we saw the carving of a foot with the heel in the form of a round ball: the foot of the emperor Trajan controls the world. Based on this image, some believe these ancients were aware that the world was round, and that only the later Semitic influence, brought by Christians, put an end to this concept. Hadrian's temple was built around 120 C.E., and remained buried for several centuries until it was excavated and reconstructed starting in 1956. The front keystone of the arch over the door bore the head of Pike, known to Romans as Fortuna, and the inner one the head of Medusa. As well, Amazons are depicted on the frieze—powerful images of the feminine. The newest excavation at Ephesus revealed a long mosaic floor and a row of arches that could have been shops. The large building formerly had been thought to have been a brothel, and was now believed to be a large residence of fifteen rooms. The beautifully restored Library of Celsus was a high point of our visit; it was impossible to be unaware of its image, since posters, postcards and other images of this library were seen everywhere in Turkey. The elegant façade of this library with its two tiers of porches was frequently depicted on the front cover of books.

The Agora, the marketplace of Ephesus, was a long, colonnaded avenue and the shops were in permanent stalls on either side. The colonnade down the centre of the pedestrian walkway was still there; it appeared to have been a covered market, although it was certainly in the open air now. The shoppers were all gone, replaced by tourists and pilgrims. St. Paul the apostle lived in Ephesus for a time, between two and three years. We know that Paul was a tentmaker who had to sell his tents from time to time to support his vigorous ministry as an itinerant preacher in those first years after the crucifixion and resurrection of Jesus. Was it here in this lovely marketplace that Paul sold his tents? Or had he gotten himself into so much trouble with the local artisans and merchants by that time that he could not share their commercial area? Surely Paul spent some time in this marketplace, if only as a customer, and stayed in one of the houses in the city. He spent some time in jail in Ephesus, when his friends, Priscilla and Aquilas, risked their heads to save him, as recounted in the book of Romans (16:3-4). Again, I experienced a feeling of strange awe at walking in the actual landscape of the Bible, and seeing the remains of the shops and houses that were familiar to this important New Testament writer.

While in Ephesus, Paul wrote some letters, probably including the letter addressed to his little church community at Philippi, which is now the Letter to the Philippians in the New Testament—and amazingly, we are still reading that letter today. Paul mentions in his second letter to Corinth that he escaped capital punishment in Ephesus. Whatever the exact details of what went on in Ephesus, the experience was for me just as it had been in Pergamum—a great thrill to be in a place mentioned in the Bible. I could imagine the frail figure of Paul, his face intense, beetling through the marketplace purposefully, arguing with any who tried to oppose him, encouraging all who heard his gospel. I connected with his need to carry on the tent-making trade to support his ministry, as I, and so many others today, must work at worldly jobs in order to support ourselves so that we can continue our ministries. Not only is this not such a new way of "doing church"; it is a very old way of doing church.

We saw two theatres. The first, smaller theatre we passed was the senators' council chamber, probably the one mentioned in the book of Acts as the place where Paul was brought before the city fathers. On this occasion, the local artisans accused Paul of destroying their business by speaking out against worship of Diana, or Artemis, whose statues were the principal souvenir item offered in Ephesus. The larger theatre, beyond the library, was the actual performing theatre where artistic or sporting events took place. The excavations of the site were extensive, and we had a real sense of what the city was like in its prime, even though only about ten percent of it has been excavated. There was plenty more scope for discovery. We saw our fill, then trudged, exhausted, along the old Roman road leading out of town.

After we left the Ephesus site and were driven back to the hotel, I prepared for my mystery date with Ibrahim. I found him sitting outside his shop, talking with his brother. The shop had just closed at seven, and they said they had had a good day. They had sold one carpet and one killim, a heavier folk-art mat less expensive than a carpet. Ibrahim suggested we go to a restaurant in the municipal building, fifth floor. The elevator was out of service, so we had to go up the stairs of this otherwise very modern looking building. I ordered aubergine dishes, which are usually excellent throughout the Mediterranean, although I found these ones to be very salty. It was a starlit night, and after dinner we took a romantic stroll the short distance to the ruins of the Temple of Artemis. It was unnerving walking by the Jandarmara and seeing it guarded by a young man with a serious military-style weapon, but the young man was a local person and Ibrahim greeted him in Turkish. Armed guards and army were very usual sights for the local people, but I did not like it at all. Selçuk seemed a quiet, country place with no apparent threats to security; no need for such guns. Still, military presence is very available as all young men in Turkey do mandatory service time, so all these young conscripts were to be put to some use. The Jandarma was a police organization with jurisdiction outside of the cities, where no city police were present.

We walked and talked, exploring the dark streets with their mysterious ruins: the Artemisian, the basilica of St. John, the citadel. We stopped periodically, and eventually we visited an outdoor café for a glass of wine. Where we sat we could see a litter of kittens playing on a display of carpets at another carpet seller's, and the owner of the shop did not stop these little characters in their play, but actually encouraged them to run up and down the carpets by dangling a cat toy in front of them. Ibrahim walked me up near the castle, past a "no pedestrians" and "do not enter" sign, to the citadel, then down the hill. He begged me to stay a few days and get to know him. He suggested we could marry—this was no surprise. "Will you marry me" seemed to be a very local greeting with which local gentlemen hailed us foreign visitors. I promised to write to him, although later I found I could not put my hands on his business card among my papers. It was a very romantic and pleasant interlude. Ibrahim referred to our meeting as a sweet accident. No hostage taking, no marrying, no carpet—all completely benign. I *could* possibly see him again—but where is that card with his address and telephone number? Nowhere to be found!

I arrived at the hotel near midnight. It was a good thing I had not had to depend on Kathy to send out the cavalry because she was in a dead sleep. Later that night I stayed up in the charming lobby decorated with antiques, writing in my diary, until a Clint Eastwood look-alike in cowboy boots, a hotel employee, wanted the sofa beside my table. The hotel was full and he said this was the only place available as a sleeping space for him. Kale Han was very charming, but it was not the Ritz.

◆   ◆   ◆

The next morning we left Selçuk. We drove past the Temple of Artemis to get a last look at what little remained of it, then continued our coach journey to Pamukkale, about three hours. The nearest big town was Denizli, of which we saw very little, but it appeared very industrialized, with heavy vehicles parked everywhere. In the quaint, touristy town-site of Pamukkale, we went to Mustafa's restaurant—we seemed to meet a lot of fellows named Mustafa—where the portly proprietor entertained us with witty impressions of the various nationalities that frequented his restaurant during the busy season. The Australians fared the worst from his sardonic tongue. There was no impression of Canadians; I have been told that Canadians seem bland to other peoples, and perhaps Near-Easterners found us too boring to be considered funny. I ordered the leek soup with carrots and rice. The people that ordered the chicken sandwich or the kebab sandwich had the best bargain: the sandwich was made with half of a large French bread.

Adjacent to the calcified falls of Pamukkale was the ruined city of Hieropolis, of which the most visible feature was the extensive necropolis. This city of the dead consisted of acres of first century tombs, graves and funerary buildings, including a few tumulus tombs and a large number of Greco-Roman crypts. We spent the better part of an hour exploring crypts and tombs, near which a young entrepreneur of about ten or twelve was on hand with his three camels, offering a photo opportunity or a ride through the necropolis.

The spa at Pamukkale was built right on the ruins of the Roman spa, which meant that the stone debris under the warm mineral water were really the pieces of the Roman building that previously occupied this site. This was the best thing all day; we were actually sitting in our bathing suits, immersed in the healing water, right on the Roman ruins. The water was warm and bubbly, and it was stinging to our skin, but in a stimulating way. It was magnificent. A stocky European woman in a plain black swimsuit, and with a grey Prince Valiant hairstyle, emerged beside me and grinned. Carried away by the exotic and historic surroundings, she exclaimed "Cleopatra!"

By this time I was, as usual, hopelessly separated from my tour group, so I went down the street to the calcified falls by myself. It was something of a disappointment as it was quite dried up, due to the nearby development of hotels that divert some of the water for their own use. The calcium pools and the shiny white rock surrounding them look like snowdrifts or ice fields. They are very beautiful, but really dangerous. An unlucky traveler could easily ruin her trip by falling and breaking an ankle!

After the day at Pamukkale, we drove into the dry and sparsely inhabited countryside to our quite posh hotel, where I sat out on the balcony to watch the sun setting over the rolling hills. I became so engrossed that I failed to hear my room-mate, Kathy, pounding on the door of our room for ten minutes, trying to get back in after her swim in the hotel pool. After an aperitif, our group proceeded to the elaborate buffet—a lively scene with so many groups present. We sat at long tables with white tablecloths, and it could have been anywhere in the world, except that some of the food was typically Middle-Eastern, especially the desserts, which included such Arabian specialties as *boormah*—honey-soaked shredded wheat. After dinner I caught up my diary and sipped wine in the room, and hoped that Kathy was all right since it was one o'clock in the morning and she had not come back.

2

Paul's Landscape

At six a.m. Kathy came in, solidly wrecked but claiming to be fine; nothing a little sleep wouldn't cure! We had breakfast and got into the coach, and the party-goers, including Kathy, joined us. They were somewhat under the weather and immediately went to sleep in the coach. We travelled for a long time through vast expanses of agricultural land with lots of open spaces ringed by hills. The beautiful Lake Egirdir (Eh-YEER-deer) was an exquisite blue, light coloured with a hint of aqua, a colour slightly reminiscent of the glacial lakes in the Rockies. The word *turquoise* came from this region: Turkish blue. The tea stop was a café with a shop and a lovely toilet. As we progressed farther and farther east in Turkey, toilets became of increasing concern, and perhaps this is a good place to talk about Turkish toilets.

The toilet in the tea-stop had a row of cubicles, some with European-style W.C.s and some with the flat porcelain toilet *à la turque* on the floor. At this café, the Turkish toilets were very clean and well serviced; there was even toilet paper, whereas usually throughout the Middle East we had to carry our own toilet roll. The doors of the cubicles were beautiful natural wood, stained a deep pine colour, and the walls of the common area were wood-panelled. Pretty ceramic and glass decorations with the blue and white "evil-eye" motif adorned the walls. As well as a row of beautiful, clean hand basins, there were chairs and a table-ledge before a huge mirror, where the ladies could do their hair and make-up. This was the nicest toilet we encountered in Turkey.

So much for the *de luxe*. The usual facility was a clogged up, unflushable installation with the running water turned off, or else with water running out of the tank onto the floor. European-style water closets often had a cracked seat that did not really fit onto the base. A great many toilet facilities were unfit for use even by the most adventurous and desperate. Middle Eastern people, we learned, did not use so much toilet paper, but rather cleaned themselves with a water hose that was always available, either installed in the wall, or as part of the W.C. As the drainage systems could not handle the mountains of paper thrown down the W.C. by North Americans and Europeans, there was usually a basket in the bathroom for the used paper, and the attendant emptied it as part of the clean-up task.

Our lunch stop in the apple-growing region was the town of Egirdir itself. The country roads were lined with great piles of apples, accumulated directly onto the ground and waiting to be picked up and carried away by large trucks. One of the main industries in Egirdir was military training for Turkish men. As we approached the town, we saw a huge Turkish flag and patriotic message painted onto the side of the hills. It was a reminder of duty to which the men woke up every morning, and which they saw each time they went outside.

In Egirdir itself, I consumed some time getting money changed at the bank, then I joined the American couple who had bought the rug in finding something to eat. I had a traditional dish of white beans in a thin tomato sauce, served on rice, and a spicy lentil soup, plus "Nescafé." The coffee choices almost everywhere are Turkish coffee, which is a thick mixture of fine coffee grounds and water, served in a tiny cup and usually flavoured with cardamom; or instant coffee, which, regardless of the brand, is always called "Nescafé." This was my best vegetarian lunch so far in Turkey, and cost L.350,000, or just under four US dollars. The toilet was the weak point of the café. We had to exit the building and go two doors down and one floor up into the *pension* to a room that had not been cleaned in this quarter-century, where a barely flushing W.C. leaked water onto the indoor-outdoor carpet. It was unclear whether this was the Men's or if it was unisex. There was a sign that said "Men" on the wall of the corridor, and men seemed to be going in when I was coming out, but there did not seem to be a corresponding facility for women.

Next we perused a small shopping centre, or bazaar, that was housed in a Seljuk-style building that was probably at one time a caravan stop, or *caravan saray*. People in Egirdir were conservatively dressed, mainly wearing a European, tailored style of clothes. Most women had their hair covered. Navy and other dark colours seemed to be preferred. All of the children in Turkey wore the same school uniform: a little azure-blue dress with a frilly white collar for girls, and tailored-style navy sweater with grey short pants for boys. We saw plenty of school-children everywhere, especially in Egirdir. We got back into the bus and resumed our journey along the beautiful, turquoise-blue Lake Egirdir. Even though we were not exhausted, I dozed in the bus, perhaps because I had got a bit of "Turkey tummy," and I made a mental note that there would be no more fruit and vegetables for me.

Our afternoon drive to Konya was long and broken only by a tea-stop at Bey-sehir (BAY-sheh-HEER), a typical small town with a sturdy bridge built by the Ottoman Turks. By the time we reached Konya, it was late in the afternoon, but we had some time to go exploring before dinner. The city was lively and interesting, relatively unspoiled by tourism. Outsiders were rare enough to evoke interest from passers-by in the street. A delightful group of young schoolgirls sought me out and practised their English with me, pleased with the opportunity to try out their new language skills. Their English, which was now taught in all Turkish schools, was very good.

The bazaar, much of which was indoors, was extensive and well stocked with attractive goods. Some of the items of interest were the long, tailored overcoat worn by the Muslim ladies, and the beautifully decorated silk scarves to cover their hair. The most popular colours were the muted or dusty colours of pink, blue and sage green, but neutral colours such as black, brown, beige and taupe were also available. The costume was so lovely that we were all strongly tempted to buy a coat, and they were very affordable at around sixty to eighty U.S. dollars. Ultimately, we decided there was probably nowhere we could wear these coats and not look out of place, particularly in the case of the Australians with their hot climate, so no one bought a coat. The bazaar and the sights at the Aladdin Hill, at the town's centre, provided easy-going sightseeing for us.

Food choices in Konya were very limited for the strict vegetarian, but I was able to find the ubiquitous green beans and tomato dish with rice. It was not bad, but experienced through a veil of Turkey tummy. Some of us walked to the Alad-din Hill then went to our hotel, the Sifa Hotel, for the night. The bathroom in our room was clean and deluxe by Turkish standards, but there were still a few problems. Unlike the one pictured in the hotel brochure, the layout of fixtures was not human-engineered. The basin, which stuck out very far from the wall, was installed directly in front of the European W.C. so that one had to sidle around the sink to gain access to the W.C. I am a bit shorter than average, and anyone taller than I would have had trouble navigating in this bathroom.

In central Konya was the Mevlana Museum, former monastery of the Whirl-ing Dervish sect of Sufism. Every day, a pilgrimage of faithful still queued up in order to be in the burial place of their thirteenth century spiritual leader, Çelalad-din Rumi, whom they call Mevlana, meaning "the Guide." The burial chapel was a richly coloured and solemn oriental interior, and Mevlana's tomb was draped in olive green. The tomb of Mevlana was the largest and most prominent feature of the museum, but the monks of the order were also buried in Mevlana's mauso-leum, and the beautifully illuminated manuscripts that they created are on display nearby. As in the Sultan Ahmet Mausoleum, the monks were buried in foetal position, on their sides, facing Mecca. The tombs were decorated with prayer rugs, and a white turban posted at the end of each tomb marked where the head was located. The faithful visiting the tomb seemed joyful, but also overcome with emotion, and many people were in tears. The dervish liturgy, which consists of whirling in a ritual pattern with the right hand palm up, the left hand palm down, certainly is meant to induce trance. The liturgy was now illegal, outlawed by Ataturk in his desire to create a secular state, and the monastery was opened as a museum in 1927. The whirling was still being performed once a year, but as a cultural icon only. Still, Mevlana's faithful followers were keeping alive the spiritual core of the sect, and the very ecumenical writings of Mevlana were becoming popular throughout the western world under his personal name of Rumi.

The sixteenth century Selimye Camii mosque was right next to the Mevlana museum. The mosque was still in use, and visitors were required to donate to the restoration fund. As with many mosques, the furnishings were very spare. A poor fellow on the middle of the floor inside the mosque, an amputee, asked me for money, pointing to the place where his legs used to be. Encountering people begging for money in a culture with no safety net posed a real problem, as I would have liked to give something to all of them, but of course I did not have the resources to help everyone that I met on my journey. Clearly, this fellow was limited as to what work he could do, and it was likely that his own family and community were his main resource. But of course I could not communicate to him that my own resources were limited, and there was no one nearby to translate. A woman carrying a young child later approached me on the street for money, and in that instance it was difficult to discern whether or not she was a professional beggar or in real need. In any case, I was surprised to note that there seemed to be fewer people on the street asking for money than in my own city, even though the social services in Turkey were not extensive. The family organization in Turkey, however, was very strong and served as the main support for the needs of all family members, especially those with limited earning power.

Konya was the centre of the former Galatia, the area to where St. Paul wrote the letter to the Galatians. The modern town of Konya derived its name from its old Roman name, Iconium, as it is called in the New Testament. There was very little sign of Christianity today, as Konya was a Muslim area, and fairly conservative. Women were generally veiled in their beautiful *jilbab* coats and *hijab* scarves; even foreign visitors were required keep their knees and shoulders covered, and couples did not walk hand in hand. There was a wonderful covered bazaar, very clean, with a great variety of shops. During the coach trip, Poz had been playing some Turkish popular music, Refet el Roman, and this and similar music was available in the bazaar. In my quest to buy some of the beautiful scarves that the Turkish women wear, I found two elegant silk squares for a total of about sixty U.S. dollars: one a dusty sage green and ivory with large, rich-coloured flowers and painted over with gold, and the other Wedgwood blue and ivory, with smaller motifs and a finer gold over-painting. With a young Australian companion from our group, Melanie, I walked to Aladdin Hill in the centre of the town. There we found the ruins of a castle, the historic Aladdin mosque, and gardens.

By the time we left in our coach it was slightly after noon. Our new driver was Sefir. Poz had fired Regep for arguing with her in front of passengers. It was very sad to see the last of our little housekeeper, but he was apparently on warning for this, so the firing was necessary, and Regep went back to Istanbul in disgrace, graciously saying his goodbyes to all of us as he trundled off with his baggage. In the afternoon we passed the big caravan saray by the side of the road in Sultanhani. The caravan sarays were built by the Seljuks to encourage trade. There was no charge for merchants to stay at the caravan saray with their goods and camels, but they paid an annual fee for membership in this service. The caravan saray looked a bit like a castle, walled all around a big open space in the centre. We were able to visit and to explore a very well preserved caravan saray at AgziKarahan (Ah-zee-kara-HAN), our tea-stop. The saray was built in 1239, and was the largest feature of the little village that it dominated. While we were there, Poz called us into the enclosure and said she had something to show us, which turned out to be two birthday cakes for a woman in our party. It was a high point for the lady, as she exclaimed, "A birthday in a thirteenth century caravan-saray—what more could you ask for?"

This area was cold in winter, and it does snow, so the villagers had been getting ready by storing fuel. They had compressed animal dung into wheels about eight or ten inches across, and piled these up into structures like giant beehives, which they then covered with fresh dung. There were hardly any trees in the area, but the villagers gathered and made use of whatever sticks they could find.

The landscape was dotted with other caravan saray ruins, not so well preserved as Agzikarahan. After Nevsehir (Nev-she-HEER), we began to see homes burrowed into the soft rock that was typical of the Cappadocia (Ka-pa-DOHK-ee-a) region. Our afternoon tour was the underground city at Kaymakli, where we were guided by a local gent named Mustafa; it did seem a coincidence that most of our guides were called Mustafa.

The underground cities were systems burrowed into the soft rock, and the surface of the walls had become hard after long-term contact with air. Dwellings were originally hollowed out by the Hittites before the Common Era, but the area became a convenient base for Christians in the sixth and seventh centuries, and so elaborate underground building plans were developed. Here, the vulnerable minority could hide from invaders and hostile armies, with enough food and water stashed away with them to last a long time. Four or five thousand lived here for three months or up to a year when the enemy was present. A stone was rolled in front of the door from the inside, but it was impossible to move, or even to see, the stone from the outside. The 90-metre ventilation shaft was well hidden, and there was a secret tunnel where there was always a guard who could advise when the enemy had left. We descended down into five of the eight levels; below that there was no electricity. The temperature was always even, cooler than outside in summer, warmer in winter. There were hidden communal kitchens, meaning that smoke was routed out secret vents so that the enemy could not see from where it was coming. The pillar in the centre was the focal point around which the builders developed the city, and this plan of construction is cited by archaeologists as evidence that the cities were planned beforehand, and not simply added onto as they went along. The ancient underground city of Kaymakli was opened as a museum only in the twentieth century, but the villagers certainly knew about it and stored food there throughout history.

Our accommodation in Avanos was called the Sofa Hotel. It was very quaint and beautiful, consisting of four old houses joined together, two of which had been burrowed into the tuff, but it was so complex we could not distinguish the plan. The hotel was decorated with vines, geraniums, bits and pieces of pottery and other local bric à brac, and the general effect was absolutely charming. We went into nearby Goreme (GOR-em-ay) to the also quaint Sedif Restaurant for a very nice dinner, especially the stuffed peppers and stuffed grape leaves. As with many restaurants in Turkey, the largest part of the restaurant was out of doors, with an open canopy covered in grapevines. Although it was October, the weather was still summery enough for us to enjoy sitting out in the air for our meal. It was an informal atmosphere, even humorous, as terrified pussycats ran under the tables with Turkish children in pursuit, calling "Kitty, kitty!"

After our night in the charming Sofa Hotel, we set out in the coach to explore Cappadocia. The so-called fairy chimneys of the region were formed when boulders from the volcano or other geological activity sat on the surface of the volcanic tuff that comprised the local rock. When the tuff was eroded away by the normal process of weather, the tuff under the boulder was protected from that erosion, and formed cylinders with boulders atop, similar to the formation that we call "hoodoos". Some of the volcanic tuff was eroded into valleys of sharp ridges similar to the badlands in Wyoming. The rock was quite soft and could easily be burrowed into, so all of Cappadocia had become honeycombed with hollowed-out rock dwellings.

The trail that wound among the cliffs of fairy chimneys was an awesome landscape for us, and we began walking along the trail. On one side was a mixture of crops that maximized land use: tomatoes and peppers between grapevines, with the occasional lone fruit or olive tree. On the other side of the road was a valley. The cone-shaped hollow dwellings carved right out of the rock looked as if they should have had a gnome sitting outside the front door. Some of these homes have been in use since 2000 to 3000 B.C.E., hollowed out by the Hittites in Bible times. In the 1960's, the Turkish government banned this kind of troglodyte life-style and emptied all the rock houses. There were people in the fields around them, however, as this land was still cultivated. We saw people harvesting a crop that resembled a casaba or a cantaloupe. Water for the rock dwellings and for irrigation came from underground wells.

We hiked all morning until we came to the little village of Cauvsin, our teastop. We passed the old cemetery with the short, squat, over-ground tombs, all of its population facing Mecca, and all with a headstone and footstone, although the modern trend is to leave off the footstone. At one of the outdoor restaurants, we had apple tea, but it was the signs on the toilet doors that were the items of interest; one cubicle featured a little painting of a high-heeled shoe, the other a smoking pipe. Outside the café, little children approached us boldly and asked for bon-bons, which we did not have. Some of our group went up into the hill to explore the ancient Hittite condos that overlooked the village.

We drove to the high village of Uchisar, where there is a hilltop outcropping called the Castle, actually itself a natural formation now riddled with tunnels and windows. We climbed to the top, and Poz had implied it was an easy climb for even the most feeble, but in actual fact there were 161 steps, and I was a bit winded. The panoramic perspective obtained from this height made the ascent worthwhile, however, and we delighted in an enthusiastic pursuit of landscape photography. Besides the usual offerings of pottery and carpets, the local people in Cappadocia sold elaborately decorated knitted gloves for which the region is known. These gloves were absolutely covered with multicoloured designs, and thus very economically made use of every little bit of yarn. At the little gift shop at the castle, I bought a pair of these village-knit gloves for my daughter, a thoroughly elaborate pair of gloves of many colours, dominated by hot pink, and knitted in various geometric designs. At one dollar, they were a real bargain.

Next stop was a wine tasting at the Duyurgan Wine House. The wines of the region, although respected by Turks, we found to be quite astringent, and definitely an acquired taste. After sampling the white and the red, I jointly bought a bottle of the red another woman of our group. The wines were all blends, but there was a choice of vintage. Ours was six years old, and it came to U.S.$5: not dirt-cheap, but a bargain for the vintage. The newer wine was around $2.50. We had lunch at the same restaurant as before, the Sedif, and since there had been something of a scarcity of vegetarian cuisine in most places, I was fortunate here to be able to eat as many stuffed peppers and stuffed grape leaves as I could hold. The local people also made wonderful fresh flat bread, like very thick pita.

In the afternoon we drove to Zelve to see the open-air museum, which consisted of three very extensive valleys of dwellings. The first valley was closed to visitors, as part of the face of the rock had fallen down, and so it was considered dangerous, but you could spend hours or even days exploring the other two. Zelve was a monastic community, so the monastery is still there, as well as churches. All of these dwellings, as with the neighbouring communities, were emptied in the 1960's. They were like cave dwellings, and it was hard to believe that they were in use right into the twentieth century. Heritage housing is highly prized in some western cities, but these ones were literally ancient.

We stopped briefly at the Valley of Fairy Chimneys to gaze in awe at these wonders of nature, and then went to visit the Sirca Pottery works in Avanos. Our guide was, of course, named Mustafa. He was a very engaging Turk, probably in his early 30's, and very comfortable talking with a group and telling the story of the Turkish potter's craft. His cousin, Ibrahim, demonstrated the pottery making. There was an expression in Turkish that even a blind man could find his way to Avanos by the pots and broken shards. Pottery has been made in this area since the Hittite period because of the excellent clay, and everyone makes pots. Today, children in Avanos start learning the potter's trade at about the age of twelve. Ibrahim demonstrated making a teapot. It only took him a couple of minutes, including deftly making the handle and a perfectly fitting top, using only the kick-wheel. We were served apple tea or regular tea, and someone was selected from the group as a "student," as a bit of fun and to show how difficult it actually is to make pottery in this way.

The Avanos pottery designs were colourful and elaborate, and the particular pottery work that we visited was licensed to sell replicas of national treasures found in museums. The Ottoman style designs consisted mainly of charming scenes from the life of the sultan and his household, and the Seljuk style were mostly blue and white designs, and very rich. They might depict, for example, white flowers and leaves on a solid background of blue, and a variety of different blues were available. Our hosts took us to their "exhibition room," really the gift shop. I love crockery and wanted to buy some pieces, but there was so much to choose from it was hard to make a decision. With Mustafa's help I chose two round platters: one Ottoman miniature of the sultan and his ladies, with a lot of bright yellow and turquoise in it; and one Seljuk type of white on royal blue. They gave me two trivets, similar to the decorated tiles in the Topkapi palace, at no charge. The bill came to a little over two hundred dollars.

The next item was the Turkish bath, the hamam. The one we went to in Urgup was a lovely old nineteenth-century building, but it was no longer a traditional hamam, because to accommodate the needs of tour groups they accepted men and women together. In a traditional hamam, there would be men's times and women's times, and in the big towns and cities the hamam would have a women's room and a men's room, both operating at the same time. Because men and women bathe together at Urgup, everyone wears a sarong, a large piece of checked cotton like a tablecloth. Wearing our sarongs, we first poured water all over ourselves, and then lay on a big marble slab in a room full of steam to open our pores. We were in there for quite some time, periodically pouring more water over ourselves. One by one we were called into the next room by the masseur. He massaged us all over, or at least on any spot where the sarong was not, getting out all the muscle knots, and not all that gently either! Then he sat each of us on a marble step and exfoliated our skin with a loofah glove. I think I lost several pounds just in dead skin, and noted with disgust that I appeared to have been carrying around more dead skin than live. Finally, the other bath worker washed our hair, soaped us all over, and rinsed us off. After that a few people went back into the steam room, but the rest of us dried off and floated out of the building clean, relaxed and in a state of bliss. It was heavenly.

Meanwhile, Colorado Wally, who had not been interested in the Turkish bath and so sat in the pub, met us at the corner and led us to the establishment where he had been waiting. The proprietor came out and shook Wally's hand; it appeared they were already old friends, and old Wally was talking a real line to convince the waiter he was a 94-year-old Polish traveller with a harem. He offered the waiter his pick from among us!

Next item on this busy day was the Turkish folklore show. Normally I dislike these shows as they are often very contrived, put on only for tourists, but this was a small town affair and quite authentic. The young people in the dance troupe danced literally for hours, plus a belly dancer put on a terrific show. The music group was composed of a lot of completely unfamiliar instruments. There was a small drum, one guitar-type that looked like a small bandura, one "oboe," one accordion, a zither, and something resembling a tabla. As well, a leader with a large drum led the dance troupe. The dance troupe, consisting of four couples, went through several changes of costume and danced throughout the entire evening. The girl who threw knives with her teeth was a spectacular piece; young and sweet, she came out into the spotlight in a red and white oriental costume, took the large knife upright in the underbite of her teeth, and gave her head a brief flick. The knife shot across the stage onto a slanted board set up for the purpose. Also amazing were the fellows doing the competition-style dancing, somewhat similar to Cossack dancing, moving mainly from a squatting position using what must have been incredible thigh muscles. The meal was quite good, too. This all took place at the Sarikaya Restaurant in Avanos: Sari means "out of," and Kaya means "rock," and indeed, this was a spectacular troglodyte experience in a building burrowed out of the rock.

The next day, during a full day of driving through eastern Turkey toward Adiyaman, I thought once again of poor old St. Paul trudging on foot through Turkey on his way from Syria to Greece, challenged as he may have been by his mysterious ailment, to which he referred, in his second letter to the Corinthians, as a "thorn in the flesh." I began to have a greater respect for the poor old missionary, and have since become increasingly respectful of his accomplishments. As we headed east, settlement became increasingly sparse, and the toilets grew worse. We went through some rolling hills with evergreen forest, and then cultivated fields reappeared: cabbages and sugar beets, and finally we saw chili peppers being dried by the side of the road. We were slightly delayed at a place where a large truck was overturned, and farther along we saw another truck whose load of cotton was spilled into the ditch. We were intrigued by the gypsy or nomad villages of small tents, close together, all partially covered with plastic. We got to the Hotel Bozdogan in Adiyaman at seven, and only had time for a glass of wine before dinner at seven-thirty. After such a long day of travel, we had gained a new respect for the driving distances in Turkey. This was a big country!

The next morning, we were to head to Mt. Nemrut at ten-thirty. I had left my toothbrush, toothpaste and flat sink stopper at the last hotel; sink stoppers were not usually provided in the Middle East, so it was a good idea to carry along a one-size-fits-all plug or flat rubber stopper. I had to go to the store before leaving the hotel, and got the toothbrush and toothpaste and something to take along for lunch. Kathy had stayed up late and had had a restless night, so I picked up some lunch for her also. Sefir had a day off with the big bus, and we hired three smaller coaches for the trip to Mt. Nemrut. It was quite a distance to the mountain, but an even greater distance from the bottom to the top of the mountains we were ascending. The first noticeable site we passed was the Septimus Severus Bridge, built by emperor Severus, who reigned from 194 to 211 C.E. His bridge was still in use, thanks to the expert engineering and building techniques of the Romans, but to ensure our safety the driver wanted to drive the coach empty over the bridge, and the passengers were asked to cross on foot. The coach picked us up on the other side. It was beginning to rain and people's rain gear began to appear. From the bridge we could look into a canyon and see three rock dwellings, buildings actually, perched at different levels and dating from all different periods.

The morning tea place was a little indoor-outdoor cafe with what must be absolutely the worst toilets in Turkey. They were so awful that we could not go inside, but most of went by turns behind the rocks at the back of the toilet, and someone directed traffic. We sat outside on the patio, even though it was raining, as there was a bit of shelter and I had my umbrella, with which I sheltered Wally and myself. Farther down the road, we again saw rock dwellings, and on top of the cliff was part of the ruins of a fourteenth century castle of the Mamluks, the mysterious people conquered by the Ottoman Turks, and the remnants of whom became reabsorbed into the Egyptian people.

Arsameia was the ancient capital of the Commagenes, and the Arsameia ruin, at the top of a long, high road, was a cave and tomb site with a large relief of Mithridates I Callinicus, the founder of Commagene, shaking hands with the god Heracles. The district was remote and unpopulated, but at the Arsameia site was the only house for miles around, with a "cafeteria" where we could buy soft drinks or water from the family. The boy spoke some English, so I started talking to him. He was the youngest, and the last one still home, of a family of twelve children. His poor, dear mother, a wizened and overworked looking soul, was so happy that I was speaking English with him that she tried her best to communicate with me, complimenting me on the fleece jacket that I had made the night before the trip. I told the boy his English was so nice and his mother was very kind, and when I went to leave the mother gave me a hug and a kiss—universal language!

We drove back, through unpopulated hills, then past fields and a very few houses. The fields were beautifully cultivated, and included some tobacco, but the houses were all in very poor condition. I was amazed to see so many Massey-Ferguson tractors, and I assumed that these were imports from Canada, as Massey-Ferguson was a Canadian company, although the company also manufactures in Europe. The drive up Mt. Nemrut was long and the road very steep, winding around to reduce the incline. The road was built in concrete sections filled with small asphalt blocks. This kind of road surface was much less slippery and provided a better grip for vehicle tires than a sheet of asphalt ever could. There did not seem to be any sign of human habitation for hundreds of miles, either in the valley below, or in the untreed hills beyond.

When we reached near the summit, it was very cold and windy, and we came to a building with a heated café lined with carpets in one part, adjoining another part that contained the second worst toilets in Turkey. Six people decided that weather conditions were too terrible, and they remained back in the café and played cards. The rest of us ventured up the mountain. It would be hard to describe accurately just how uninviting it was. There was a terrible wind-chill factor; the mountaintop was enveloped in a cloud, and it was trying to rain. I was wearing my fleece jacket with a nylon K-way overtop, the hood tied around my head, and cotton in my ears. I was not especially cold, but at that altitude, with the wind blowing, it was very hard to catch my breath, and the wind was giving me an earache. Kathy, who seemed to be developing asthma, became unable to breathe and, frightened of this, she slumped onto the footpath and started crying. After she recovered a bit, a young Australian couple, Samantha and Jason, helped her back down to the shack. Jason came back up the hill but Sam stayed with Kathy, who was now in the care of the Washington D.C. lady, a physician.

We were on our way to see the remains of the Antiochus memorial, of which all the gigantic stone heads had fallen from the statues to the level below, leaving the decapitated stone giants seated on their thrones on high. We thought of the Shelley poem "Ozymandias," with his "two…trunkless legs of stone." It certainly seemed that this could be the site the poet's traveller was talking about in that poem, although there were more than two, and these were headless trunks instead of trunkless legs!

Fortunately King Antiochus, the chap whose tumulus we were going to view, had had the entire mountaintop covered in coarse stone, and had built some stairs in places. When we finally got to the big stone heads, I was a bit disappointed because it was so foggy we could not see the full site, and the seated figures were obscured by fog. It was so cold that my electronic camera started acting up, and I had to take pictures with the old rangefinder. On the other hand, it was certainly atmospheric! Poz appointed Phil and Mark, the two Australians whom we called "the boys," to bring up the rear so she would know when the last people came back. The boys looked a bit miserable, wearing shorts in this terrible atmosphere, but wrapping themselves in blankets. Then, predictably, Phil, Mark and I got separated from the group. It is unbelievable, but I can even get lost at the summit of a bald, uninhabited mountain with only one road. Finally the three of us became disoriented and went back to the top for a while, winding around and around the plateau of the tumulus, and panicking a bit in the dense fog before realizing our error and finding the way back to where Poz was. All of us who made the trek up were proud of our accomplishment, and the six card sharks in the shack were most congratulatory. "Well, I *am* impressed!" said our Washington lady.

We were all pretty quiet on the way back as everyone was quite exhausted. We had had to eat our picnic lunches on the bus because of the rain, so our nice hot dinner at seven-thirty was particularly welcome. Before dinner, Fran and I finished our bottle of wine that we had picked up at the wine tasting. After dinner and late into the night, I sat at a table in the hallway of the hotel so as not to disturb Kathy, and I worked on my diary so that I would not get too far behind.

◆   ◆   ◆

Abraham's Territory

Our next day's destination was Sanliurfa, known to the locals and to history as Urfa. En route was the Ataturk Dam over the Euphrates River, part of the enormous South-East Anatolia Project, or GAP Project, and the fourth largest dam in the world. The project was expected not only to irrigate 1.6 million hectares of now semi-arid land, but also to provide cheap hydro-electricity for the people of Eastern Turkey and to encourage industry and employment. The dam, of course, was huge. What the guides failed to mention was the devastating effect this loss of water flow might have on neighbouring Syria. A very moving feature was the sculpture beside the viewing platform that commemorated the twenty-five lives lost in construction of the dam. Each person was named and the dates given on the memorial.

My first view of the Euphrates, so important in the Bible, made me a bit sad as the effect was so high-tech, and so uninspiring. What was more inspiring was the thought of the antiquity of cultures that have depended on this river, and the role that the Euphrates plays in the Bible. In the creation story at the beginning of the book of Genesis, the river that flowed from the Garden of Eden was mentioned as having four branches, of which the Euphrates was one. Abraham gave the river to the people who lived around it, and the Bible lists the names of their nations, in Genesis 15. But none of this faith history was visible in the massive concrete project. Only the ongoing human dependence on the old river connected us with that ancient past.

In Urfa, the central feature was the fishpond. In Islamic tradition, Urfa was the birthplace of Ibrahim, the Muslim equivalent of the Judaeo-Christian Abraham. The tradition was that the local tyrant, the evil Nemrut, threw Ibrahim onto a funeral pyre for destroying pagan gods, but Allah turned the fire into water, and the burning logs into beautiful fish. The fat and pampered carp in the present day fishpond are the sacred descendants of those fish. It was quite a moving experience seeing the fishpond and hearing the call to prayer from so many nearby mosques, surely the densest concentration of mosques in Turkey. People beside the pool were friendly and curious, apparently unaccustomed to seeing visiting westerners. Some children were selling fish food by the pool, and some others walked along beside us. Even members of the army were curious and stopped to listen to Poz's speech, although they could not understand a word. I got separated from the group, as usual, and got mixed in with a group of local ladies, who were saying something about my hair. I thought they were telling me to cover my hair, but I realized later they were just interested in the colour—a light blonde not common in Turkey. Although I could not understand most of what they said, I heard the word "Alleman." Understanding that they were guessing I was German, I said "Alleman Yohk—Kanada!" They were completely delighted with my feeble attempt to speak their language.

Sanliurfa's castle had been developed atop a high hill over several cultural periods, but it was now just a ruin. There were so many mosques between the fishpond and the castle that the call to prayer that we heard from atop that hill was a wild cacophony of loud and competing *muezzins*. Tunnels had recently been excavated below the castle and visitors could now go through them. We entered the tunnel and descended 172 steps to the street below. On the way to Ibrahim's Cave, we picked up some of the delicious bread rings that were sold in the streets throughout Turkey for around ten cents.

The cave is a very sacred site for Muslims, and a lot of pilgrims were going inside to view the cave and to sample the healing water. Women went in one side and men the other, as only men were allowed to enter the sacred cave, and women could view it from a separate viewing platform enclosed by a grille. The men and women could not see each other's sections inside. There was not much to see from the women's side, and it was difficult to take pictures because of the dark, and because some of the faithful disapproved of photography. The cave was very built-over, and with the heavy bronze partition in place it was very difficult even to recognize that it was a cave at all. There was a courtyard outside enclosed by mosques, and beyond that was a major theological school, then the bazaar. I went with two other ladies, Fran and Alice, into the bazaar and once again we all became thoroughly lost. The bazaar was very extensive and, as was usual in Middle Eastern bazaars, organized according to commodity. This was very different from the western retail plan, which avoids having shops selling the same commodity located too close to one another. In the East, proximity and competition sharpens mercantile practice and makes it easier for the customer to shop. We wound around the fabric section, house wares and shoes, ultimately lost and unable to exit the bazaar, until finally a boy led us out of the bazaar and into the street. There were lots of kebab places on the main street, but the severed sheep's head on the sidewalk would have, I thought, put off even the staunchest of meat-eaters. We located some lentil soup, the best deal in Turkey.

People in Urfa were most friendly, and very unaccustomed to foreigners. A young woman, her hair hidden by the white scarf, started talking to me and said she was a student at the university. This was a bit of a first, as women in the eastern parts were very reserved, so we had spoken mainly to businessmen. Young Turkish men and boys were also very interested in chatting to us; they often joined us as we walked along. At any rate, this charming university student pointed us toward the museum, so we went. Inside was an interesting mix. Immediately inside the door was a relief carving of a soldier from Harran in the Assyrian Period; a cuneiform inscription belonging to King Naboned from the Babylonian period in Harran; and a mosaic nail—a really big one, eight to ten inches long, made of stone, dating from 3400-3200 B.C.E., the Chalcolithic age, and found in the Hassek Hoyuk dig in 1986. But the museum exhibits seemed to be plagued by insects and, sadly, were deteriorating.

It was pouring with rain. Later, in dry clothes, I joined some of the group for a beer, of which the most popular brand throughout Turkey was Efes, the Turkish name for Ephesus. Although I did not usually drink beer, this product was so nice and so refreshing that I thoroughly enjoyed it. In the markets of this neighbourhood there was baklava, a half-kilo for three dollars, beer sixty cents, and wine approximately seventy-five cents for a bottle of red. The bottle itself without the wine would be worth more at home! There were loaves of hot French bread for fifteen cents, and fresh figs for about fifty cents a bag. I sat in my room writing and nibbling fresh green figs until dinner. The restaurant across the street featured the local specialty, kebabs. I had lentil soup—my own plus Melanie's—cold, fried potatoes, aubergines and warm rice, and I shared a bottle of wine with some others. It was our last evening with the travellers doing only the leg of the tour that led through Turkey. Tomorrow they would be going back to Istanbul, my roommate Kathy among them.

The town of Harran, our morning stop, may or may not be the Biblical place to which Abraham went on his journey. Perhaps it was a different Harran, but in any case, there seemed to be reminders of Abraham throughout this region, and people in Harran were almost living in the style of Abraham's day. Harran did not receive a great many visitors, so when our coach pulled in, a large group of mothers and children appeared. They were intrigued with us, and with the fact that we are intrigued with them. The town was surrounded by the remains of a wall. The houses appeared to be made of adobe, and the old beehive houses, so called because they resembled larger versions of the old-fashioned straw beehives, were often adjacent to the new house, and were used to house animals, and to store feed and straw. I began talking with a group of mothers with children, and the children managed to obtain all of my chewing gum and a bit of change. I obtained a lot of photographs—and an amazing tour guide who turned out to be my most colourful new friend of the whole trip.

Huseyin was at that time 20 years old and obviously smart. He had listened to the speeches of tour guides that had come to his village, had learned the talk, and could emulate their methods. Of course, while I was talking to Huseyin, I saw my tour group walking off into the distance, and I experienced a moment of panic, but Huseyin told me not to worry; it was a small village and there was no place for them to go. He took me to his home to show me the beehive houses attached to the house. In one beehive there had been a hearth; this was the kitchen. The next one was much larger and was filled with straw; a third was fairly empty and probably housed animals at night. Two incredibly skinny cows and several chickens were in the yard between the new house and the beehive houses, which, according to Huseyin, had been occupied by the family until twenty or thirty years ago. His family's beehive houses were 130 and 140 years old respectively. Next I met Huseyin's mother and father who were sitting on the porch outside of their house with their daughter, eating delicious sesame flatbread. There was no cooking facility inside the house, and meals appeared to be prepared and eaten on this front platform. Huseyin's mother had very gnarled skin and her face was decorated with blue henna tattoos from the lips down, Bedouin style. She had a very pretty face, although she appeared more aged than she likely was. The mother had very dark eyes, but Huseyin's father had startling blue eyes. I had also noticed a little blond-haired, dark-skinned child in the village, who perhaps had European genes. Inside the new house were two rooms and a toilet, and Huseyin showed me the wool-filled quilts that his mother had made from large pieces of leftover cloth. Huseyin was the only person I met who spoke English, and he told me that Arabic is usually spoken here, although Turkish was the official language so everyone also knew Turkish.

Huseyin and I took our leave and headed toward the castle in an effort to catch up with my group. On the way, we passed by Huseyin's aunt's house, where a pretty girl was outside sweeping, a girl of perhaps fourteen or fifteen. She was trying to talk to us but Huseyin was hurrying on. I said, "She wants to talk to us," but he became stern and purposeful, and said, "We don't have time!" Then he revealed, "I don't want to talk to her. She wants to own me." Meanwhile the sweet girl was gesturing to me that she intended to marry Huseyin. Fatmah, as I later learned her name to be, was perfectly charming. She was taller than I and very slim, and wore a long green dress made of a silky, flowing fabric, a pink cardigan, a bead necklace and sandals, and her beautiful long, dark hair was covered with a white scarf. I told Fatmah that her news was nice, and everything seemed agreeable, but when I mentioned this to Huseyin he said, "I don't want her!"

Huseyin took me up to the castle and started to give me the tour guide prattle. The castle was built on three floors, and had been occupied by the usual waves of conquerors. The first floor was now below ground level, the main floor included the ruins of a church and of a mosque, and the upper floor was a caravan saray. We went to the top floor, where the rest of the group was already, and took pictures of the village from that perspective. Next we all climbed down, including Huseyin and numerous children that wanted to come along, and we headed down the road, I once again listening to the continuing saga of Huseyin. We passed his aunt's house again, and the aunt came out to pester Huseyin for cigarettes, so in my photos the dear auntie has a ciggie hanging out of her mouth. This would not be seen in other parts of Turkey, nor in the rest of the Muslim world. The folks in Harran, however, are a different people from the rest of the country, apparently Bedouin who have settled down and mixed with Circassians and other peoples. Although they have Muslim names they do not appear religious in the least, and in fact have their own values. Huseyin's aunt asked me what became of my husband and I told her we were no longer together. I had by then been single for a long time, but Fatmah and her older sister came to the window and expressed great indignation on my behalf. I was touched, and I appreciated their support and their friendly concern. Then they started telling me the story of how the older sister's husband had left her with five babies to go off with another wife—all this in rapid, indignant Arabic with a few words of English, but I got the drift. I felt sad for the poor girl, and it did seem it was a family disaster.

Huseyin and I left again to view the ruins of the first Islamic university, or Ulu Cami, 8th century. The police had followed us to the castle, and by now we had picked them up as well. Our arrival was a village event, and the police, who seemed to have nothing else to do, had followed us in their ancient white *Polis* van to the ruined university and there they allowed us to take their photo. There was also a group of archaeologists working at the site who said to Huseyin, in Arabic, "What are you up to now?" They apparently knew him quite well, and considered him to be a character. We all trekked back to the castle where a local entrepreneur called Ibrahim had a tea place set up. He showed us how to wear the Arab kufeeyah, and sold the silk, hand-made and block-printed escarps for ten dollars.

By now I had heard most of the story of Huseyin's life and was beginning to feel like the Dear Abby of Harran. Fatmah had already talked to her father, who had talked to Huseyin's father, about the possibility of Huseyin marrying Fatmah. When his father asked him about it, Huseyin just said no. I expressed astonishment that he had refused so flatly to his father, and wanted to know how his dad had responded.

"He said 'No problem,'" Huseyin replied. "My father is democratic," he added proudly. It was later revealed that the girl Huseyin really wants is in Poland—a fifteen year old Polish girl that has now visited Harran three times on her own, according to Huseyin, and he is obsessed with her. He would be going into the army in a few months for a year and a half, and when he finished his service she would be 17 or 18 and they could get married. That was his plan. I had my doubts about the whole thing because of the differences in their lives and cultures, and told him how much I liked Fatmah, but he was not listening.

As we were marching back to the coach, Huseyin started asking us for a shirt. I did not have one, but I gave him the K-way jacket I had with me, another member of our group gave him an AmEx t-shirt, and I promised to send him a shirt and any other clothes I could. We departed on the coach, waving to everyone. I thought sadly that in the other places we visited in Turkey, people were living as if it were a hundred years ago. In Harran, they are living as if it were a thousand years ago. It would all change very soon with the coming of the GAP project.

Beyond Harran there began to appear a lot of carcasses of animals, picked over, along the road and in the fields. We stopped for lunch at quite an elaborate development with two large cafeteria restaurants and three gift shops, all situated very near a bridge crossing the Euphrates River. The vegetarian options were, as usual, limited, but there were rice, bulghur wheat and salad, with utterly the thickest Turkish coffee so far. The Euphrates River flowed past here in a much more natural state than at the GAP dam, here appearing much as it must have in Biblical times: a quiet blue river tufted with green patches of reeds. The drive back to Gazi Antep seemed long now, and we dropped off the nine departing passengers who were going back to Istanbul. It was raining and we were all tired, so most of the faithful remnant just stayed in the coach for our quiet drive to the Syrian border.

Suddenly we stopped. A tank rolled out of the olive grove and, passing in front of us, turned down the highway in the direction from which we had come. Then came another, and another, with other military vehicles as well. We all sat there open-mouthed, as more and more tanks and vehicles came out of the olive grove, around fifty in all. We all wanted to take pictures of them, but that would be folly, and I actually wondered for a moment whose tanks they were. We were still in Turkey, so I fervently hoped it was the Turkish army out on manoeuvres, and fortunately it was. Still, even though it was perfectly in order, the orchard tank parade was, to the Canadian eye, something of an alarming sight.

Pergamum: one of the seven cities of Asia Minor mentioned in the Book of Revelation.

The Agora at Ephesus: did Saint Paul shop here?

Paul's trial before the Ephesus Council may have been in this theatre.

The Trojan Horse—a toy for all ages. Bonnie at top left window.

The Fairy Chimneys of Cappadocia.

Huseyin and family at Harran.

3

The Road to Damascus

It took almost all day to get across the border from Turkey into Syria, what with a baggage search, the increased security arising from an incident the previous day, and the usual Middle Eastern delays. The Customs office reminded me of those small government offices built in the forties and fifties, still in use but outdated, minimal—or like the waiting room of an old bus station. We spent most of the day draped on chairs in the dingy border crossing, staring at the portrait of then Syrian autocrat Halfez Assad and his late son, Bassel, who had been killed two years before in a car accident. This was a traumatic event for the ruling family, thus for the nation, and Bassel's picture was still on display everywhere. In the political climate of Syria, if any members of the populace were relieved at the news of Bassel's demise, they would be well advised to keep that opinion to themselves.

When at last we were in our new coach in Syria, the collector of Customs came aboard, apologized for the delays, and welcomed us to Syria. Our new tour leader, Rasha, was an Egyptian woman who spoke perfect English. Married to an Englishman, she had spent considerable time in England and America, and thus had a window on what her clients' lives were like. The guide was a young Syrian woman, Abir, who would be accompanying us throughout, unlike in Turkey where there had been a separate guide for each site. We drove into Aleppo—busy, colourful and exotic—to our hotel for a buffet of hot and cold dishes with magnificent salads and plenty to eat. I was actually too tired to do much else and too cautious to wander outside after dark. My new roommate was Poz, joining us as a regular group member.

So there we were, in Aleppo, a city that changes your definition of the word "antique" once and for all. That first morning we went on foot to the National Museum, where Abir gave a synopsis of Syrian history from an Arab perspective, and opened our eyes to the notion that there were views of history quite different from those taught in Western textbooks. The museum encompassed really ancient history, from 5th millennium B.C.E. up to the Greek or Classical period. The displays were mainly archaeological pieces from the nearby tells. Items from Tell Haleb, which was the original Aleppo, and from Ebla were of great interest ever since the finding of the Ebla cuneiform tablets was reported in the mainstream press in the 1980s. Those very tablets from 2300 B.C.E. were on display.

Also from the tell was a frieze with an attached strip held on by nails, an important artifact because it tells us that they *had* nails in the 4th millennium B.C.E. In fact, there were some really huge nails, about eighteen inches long, foundation nails from Tell Haleb. There were clay amulets, idols, evil eyes, fertility figures, and domestic animal clay figures. The patriarch Sargon founded Akkadia, which was the ancient name for this region, and these Akkadians were mentioned in the Bible as neighbours of the ancient Israelites. Israelites, by the way, is the ancient name for Hebrew people in the Bible, before the word "Jew" came into use, and is not the same as the term "Israeli," which denotes citizens of the modern state of Israel.

Sargon was king for fifty-six years, and he attributed all his success to the goddess Ishtar. In the museum were giant statues of the god Habab and the goddess Ishtar seated together, and they must have been worshipped together, rather than in separate temples, as other couple deities had been. The goddess has a cup of wine in her hand and appears confident and relaxed. In fact, many female figures in the museum appeared powerful and free, just as Ishtar did in that gigantic representation. The Mesopotamian sphinx, too, was depicted in ancient Syrian sculpture as female, whereas the Egyptian one was male. The whole collection was of incredibly ancient pieces in excellent condition.

The streets of Aleppo were filled with small vehicles that were almost museum pieces themselves. Syria at the time still traded very little with the west and there were limits on importation, so it was difficult for people to obtain recent-year vehicles. The taxis were mainly yellow and were at least ten years old. Most vehicles were also very tiny. This national collection of old beaters gave the streets a picturesque appearance, but I am sure the citizens would have happily gotten rid of their old, unreliable jalopies in favour of something new.

In central Aleppo is the Great Mosque, where tradition says that Zechariah, the father of John the Baptist, was entombed. The mosque was built in 715, and the minaret rebuilt in the eleventh century. There was also a caravan saray across the road; in fact, there were a hundred and fifty old caravan sarays in Aleppo, such a busy trading centre it was and is. There is a line about it in *Macbeth*: the husband of the woman eating chestnuts had gone to Aleppo, "master of the *Tiger*," an English trader presumably.

The citadel of Aleppo was a huge twelfth century fortress on the hill, never taken by force. The Arabs built it as a defence against the Crusaders, on the ruins of the former Byzantine fortress, which was in turn built atop the city's ancient acropolis. Construction was carried out under the direction of Ghazi, the son of Salah al Din (Saladin). The security was ingenious: there was a hidden drawbridge, and the front entrance was sidewise so that the door could not be opened by a battering ram. The entry way wound around two or three more gates, all visible from an upper guard post. We were surprised to encounter the tomb of that old dragon-slayer, St. George, who was loved by the early Syrian church; his legend was familiar in the Middle East, and a bit of imagination was needed to discern the historical kernels of the story. The dragon could represent a force of evil, whether the Roman emperor or Satan himself, and the princess rescued by St. George was likely the Christian church. We went into the water cistern, used as a prison even in this century during the French mandate, and then viewed the area where families lived; it was not only soldiers who lived in this citadel, but the king and military families. The citadel was a self-governing area with its own laws, its own mosques, everything. The hamam, the bathhouse inside the citadel, was particularly interesting as it was large and complex, and Abir talked about hamam culture, and about the special baths taken before a wedding. The girl had weddings on the brain. She was twenty-four, the usual age for Syrian women to marry, and thus three-quarters of all she talked about was weddings and marriage customs. Some of it was quite funny. She did an amusing imitation, for example, of a prospective mother-in-law testing the candidate bride by visiting early in the morning to catch her unawares, or testing the girl's teeth by having her crack open a walnut.

We had tea and juice at the tea place, and outside I met a happy party of schoolgirls around ten to twelve years old. Some had their heads covered in the cotton scarf usually seen in Syria, and some wore the national school uniform, which resembled khaki army fatigues and was indestructible. Some wore both, and that was a charming sight. Whereas in Western Turkey children came up and demanded to have their picture taken, then asked for money, in Eastern Turkey and in Syria *we* were the novelty, and people, including children, came up and asked to take *our* photo on *their* cameras! The Syrian girls and I took pictures of each other.

After all this we travelled to the countryside to St. Simeon's monastery, site of the original old pillar-sitter. Rasha had brought us a picnic of chicken or falafel pitas and bananas, and soft drinks or Turkish coffee were available. In Syria as in other countries in the Middle East, "sandwich" meant some kind of filling wrapped in a large pita bread.

The monastery itself was built around the pillar where St. Simeon sat for most of his life. As long as I have known the story of St. Simeon, I have thought him extreme. My memory of the story was that he had sat atop the pillar to purge the desires of the flesh, but what Abir was saying was that Simeon had become known as a teacher, and because so many people came to hear him, he had to sit on top of a platform so that he could be seen and heard by all the pilgrims. Perhaps my Christian teachers had left me with a distorted picture of the old saint, whereas the reverent narration of a young Muslim woman brought this ancient Christian to life for me. Whatever the truth about Simeon may be, the remains of the pillar were still there, only about the size of a boulder now since so many pilgrims throughout the centuries had chipped away bits of it as souvenirs. The ruins of the huge church were there, with a lot of parts extant, probably because it was built on a somewhat remote hilltop. A beautiful feature, very noticeable on this building, was the Syrian capitals. These top pieces were, or had been, perched atop pillars resembling the classic Corinthian pillar, but were much more beautiful. It was important to the Syrians that the leaves carved on the capitals appear to be swaying in the breeze, and this gave an overall fluid appearance to the rosy coloured building stone. The effect was stunning. St. Simeon was originally buried beside his pillar, and later his body was removed to a niche outside the mausoleum of the monastery, where it remained for three days. Then it was placed in the mausoleum, eventually in the churchyard, and ultimately moved to a mausoleum in a part of Istanbul's Aya Sophia not open to the public, where it remained. After that, it became the convention for the bodies of deceased monks to remain first in the little niche outside the mausoleum for three days, and then to be buried in the mausoleum itself.

We drove back the same way, past beautiful new housing developments built in the same style as the older ones, thus preserving the character of the city, even improving it. The local stone was that beautiful rosy-sandy colour that gave the city a rich and civilized appearance. The higher-priced buildings featured lovely carving along the rooflines and the balconies. Meanwhile, Abir chatted about the Aleppo merchants who have been famous for millennia for their trading acumen. Even today, if you go shopping in Aleppo, the merchants will relieve you of all your money, but they will make you feel happy about it and will make you feel you have really received something good.

We split into two groups, an ice-cream group and a hot chocolate group, and set out to find our treats. The main streets in Aleppo were wide, and although the signage wais in Arabic, the city layout was not unfamiliar, and the restaurants were neutrally decorated and could have been anywhere in the world. I ordered a coffee, and afterwards Rasha helped me buy a toothbrush, as it was very difficult to do anything without some knowledge of Arabic.

In our room, I listened to Poz and Rasha play the guitar and swap songs. Our dinner was again a huge spread of buffet salads and hot food. I did quite well at the buffet, but even so, the cook made me a special vegetable stew with rice. This country is fairly friendly to vegetarians, as tabbouleh salad, falafel, humus and rice are standard.

After dinner I went to a "pub" with some of the group. We set out on foot, winding around picturesque little fourteenth century streets with their exotic and antique sights. It was all new to us, and it was fun just to see street signs and posters in Arabic, even if we could not understand any of it. The so-called pub was near the Armenian church with the statue of the old bishop outside. To get to the pub, we went into a beautiful old courtyard and down the steps into what used to be the water cistern of the house, which the Armenian owners have now decorated with relief wall carvings. This certainly evoked a secret and subterranean atmosphere. I had a local beer, which I think was called Al-Shark, that was like raw product, no hops, and six percent alcohol, but they bring you a huge bottle of it for a hundred Syrian Lire, or about two and a half dollars. The stuff was so bad I could not finish it, and even the halest Australians had some trouble getting it down. "The boys" pronounced it to be terrible, but managed to finish theirs. We returned to the hotel about eleven at night and retired in anticipation of the six-thirty wake-up call.

Next day we left Aleppo. At least it was not raining as it had been the previous day, although it was a bit dull. We could see people heading for work: in very ancient cars, on foot, or waiting for the ancient and eclectic buses. There were more ladies in the black *chador* here covering their hair and bodies, although it was rare to see someone with her face veiled. The beautiful *hijab* coats and scarves that we had seen in Turkey did not seem popular in Syria. Here, there were more white cotton scarves, some of them decorated with fringes. The houses were all masonry; the new buildings were built of block with stone facing. Like Eastern Turkey, Syria had been less altered by tourism than elsewhere, but Abir talked about the traditional morning and evening routine of Syrians, now changing due to westernized work patterns. And of course, Abir and Rasha played tapes of the songs and chants at a Syrian wedding.

Far into the countryside, on our way to Salah al Din's castle, we came to a little village and learned that our coach would not be able to go up the mountain;

we would need minibuses instead. Rasha hired two very rickety and frightening minivans, and up we went, crying "Excelsior!" We entered the castle by what used to be the secret entrance, where a huge natural pillar of rock obscured the opening in the mountainside. Crusaders built the castle in 1100, and in 1188 it was taken by Salah al Din, known to readers of Sir Walter Scott as Saladin, but it was only recently that it had begun to be called Saladin's castle, in order to assert that it belonged to Syria and not to the countries of the former crusaders. Just walking in that place stirred the imagination, as we were walking in the very place that those medieval warriors of both sides had walked, the people who also walked the pages of Scott's romantic stories. The site was almost vacant, apart from one other group who had departed ahead of us, so we had the castle to ourselves.

Departing proved difficult. We exited through the same secret gateway in the rock and set out down the mountain, when the van ahead of us began experiencing real problems. It was making horrendous noises on braking, and the crew got out a couple of times to look at the vehicle's rear end. As we were on a very winding road, on a steep incline, beside a real cliff, this was pretty scary. Our half of the group left the ailing van there on the mountainside and careened down the cliffside road to the village below, shrieking all the way. Our van driver then went back up the mountain to transport the others down. Mr. Toad's Wild Ride in the mountains of Syria! We were glad to see the coach.

We drove on for about an hour to Ugarit, the archaeological site near the Mediterranean coast. Although the city of Jericho also claimed to be the oldest city in the world, Ugarit may have had a better claim by a comfortable margin. We were the only people around for miles, other than the townsfolk, but basically we had the site to ourselves so it was quite wondrous. Abir guided the tour at Ugarit. The site was discovered in 1920 when a farmer found a statue from the second millennium B.C.E. When the site was excavated, five discrete layers were found at Ugarit, with evidence that five different languages had been spoken. The world's oldest alphabet was found here, as well as the oldest song that modern people can figure out how to sing. The song itself was reconstructed by musicologists from the notation, which showed which string to use, along with the words. As the song was in the diatonic scale, the musicologists then knew that the diatonic scale was used in the second millennium B.C.E. Thirty thousand clay tablets were also found; the oldest were written in cuneiform, then evolving into Ugaritic. They had been written within the Royal Palace precinct, where there was a water pool for making the clay tablets and ink. The alphabet, forebear of our own alphabet, was created around 1400 B.C.E. by these people, who were a Canaanite branch group.

We wandered the little streets between what once had been walled buildings, now only a few feet high. By now we were getting used to the ancient Middle Eastern idea of the common loo, and indeed, Ugarit also had a public together-ness loo. Plumbing bits on display included water tanks, all one piece, with con-duit running away from them. On the pavement and walls, many building stones were joined together in a J-shape, a construction technique that seemed to hold forever. The main street had shops on both sides, empty now because the gold and other artifacts were removed to the museum in Aleppo. The very amazing thing about Ugarit, this city more than four thousand years old, was that there was still a certain familiarity about it. The streets were a bit narrow, and there was an enclosed feeling, since the streets were walled on either side; still, we could eas-ily distinguish the shopping district, the wealthy residences, the cemetery and so on. This city is the ancestor of our city planning.

There was one house there of which, incredibly, we knew the name of the owner. It was the writer Rabano, whose washbasin, library and tomb were still recognizable. In Phoenician times, a red-orange dye was made in Ugarit, extracted from a mollusk by a method that was very smelly, and so the operation was located outside the town; in fact, the word Phoenician is derived from a Greek word referring to the dye manufacture. As these people were Canaanites, the god Ba'al, bad-guy god of the Old Testament, was worshipped in the temple. In Ba'al's temple in Ugarit there was still an ancient anchor on the floor, an offer-ing to Ba'al left there millennia ago by one of the sea-faring Phoenicians. Our lit-tle group was alone at the excavation. We sat within what was left of the temple of Ba'al and played a tape of the oldest song in the world, and we watched the sun go down over the ancient ruins of Ugarit. Those moments were a time machine, in which antiquity whispered its evocative language in the charged air that caressed every hair on the backs of our necks.

The hotel in Latakia, the Palace Hotel, was far from being a palace, and we decided to have dinner at a seaside restaurant called Spiro's. There was no vege-tarian entree, but that did not matter as I absolutely stuffed myself on dolmades, humus and *chips*! Everyone was delighted to see the chips, or French fries, as it had been a few weeks now that western food had been rare. The folks were tired and trudged into the hotel, but the crew went looking for some dessert, and I went along. We took the huge coach, just for the five of us. The driver, the Egyp-tian fellow Magdi, Rasha, Abir and I went to a modern and tidy fast-food place for Arabian sweets with Turkish coffee. On the way back Abir, Rasha and I played an Arabic pop song over the sound system of the bus, and we danced up and down the aisles while the driver bounced around in his seat. These girls were a riot.

The next morning we packed up and proceeded to Krak des Chevaliers, a crusader fortress built in 1110. It had taken 80 years to build, covered three hectares, and was on a hilltop near the sea, but out in the countryside. It was taken by the Arabs in 1272. The castle was extremely well preserved, mainly because it was inhabited until 1920 by the descendants, presumably, of the original servants and staff. During the French mandate of Syria, the French fired and evicted everyone, and built the village of Krak des Chevaliers beside the castle to house the former castle residents. The castle was restored in 1936 and was considered the best example of a crusader period castle in the world, due to its excellent state of preservation.

Krak des Chevaliers was meant for soldiers, not families. The interiors were so huge it is easy to imagine the crusaders with all their horses and military gear inside. It was built with an inner castle and outer castle, all fully defended, and surrounded by a valley below called the Christian valley. One tower was called the Tower of the King's Daughter: there was no king's daughter, but the idea was that the tower was to be defended as if the king's daughter lived in it. Outside the Great Hall of the castle there was an exterior wall that resembled a gothic church with its pointed arches, although it was not a church at all but a dining room. There was an outdoor meeting place called the Round Table, redolent of Arthur, where the crusaders held their conferences in the sun. In bad weather they had to meet indoors. There was also the inevitable communal loo, but not as sanitary as the ones built by the Romans—alas for the loss of Roman engineering technology in the western world! Below we could see the village of Krak des Chevaliers and the Mediterranean beyond.

We had a "sandwich" lunch at the castle then drove to Homs. Eventually we left the treed region of Syria and went into the desert. At first much of the desert we passed was reforested, as the area had originally been treed but the vegetation was killed by climate change and goats. After an army checkpoint—and there are a few of those in these parts—we entered the real desert. A few beehive houses dotted the sand, but they were now unoccupied because this is a military zone, and we could not stop or get out of our vehicle in this region. After the beehive houses, there was nothing except a road, power lines, and desert. If we had continued straight on that road for 850 kilometres we would have arrived in Baghdad, in Iraq. But that would be pointless—the border was closed, as Syria had at the time no political relations with Iraq. We turned off.

◆   ◆   ◆

Some distance down the road we got out and strolled through the desert, about a mile or two, with the sun setting behind us, before carrying on by bus. When we entered Palmyra it was dark, but some of the ruins were illuminated. We wound around the remains of the ancient city, its tall pillars still standing proudly under the full moon, and the Ninevah Song, another piece reconstructed by musicologists, was playing on the coach's sound system. Vegetarian options at the Palmyra Tourist Restaurant were very good: wonderful fresh salads, humus, dolmades, vegetable stew, a mountain of rice fried with peas, pistachios, pine nuts, fried almonds. There was dessert and Turkish coffee. We took full advantage of the wonderful food.

After dinner, a trio of us scrambled over the ruins of Palmyra to take some night photos. We passed a long line of sellers of fresh dates, all seemingly competing for the same stragglers as they were, to my eyes, all selling the same wares, and there had to be at least a dozen tents in the row. In the cool desert night, our little group climbed around the stones to get the best advantage of the columns, the illumination and the full moon.

It occurred to us that we would never be able to do this elsewhere in the world, as such a national monument would be fenced-off and under guard. Palmyra just sits there in the open desert: mysterious, waiting, dignified, ancient. We wandered among the tall, moonlit columns, and strolled slowly and quietly back to our rooms. I was grateful to have had to privilege of visiting this ancient beauty in my lifetime.

The next morning, the sky was slightly overcast as we made our way to the ruins of Palmyra. The ancient city stretched itself proudly across the desert, alongside a lush oasis, miles away from any other settlement. Silently and nobly guarding its ancient stories, Palmyra was itself a queen, gorgeous and in excellent condition, holding court over the desert. The soft rosy-beige colour of the stone had a lot to do with this effect, as well as the natural preservation resulting from the city having been buried in the sand for so long. The brave Queen Zenubia was the heroine of the Nabateans' story. They were contemporaries of the Romans, but not always allies. As with her counterpart, Cleopatra, Queen Zenubia had the courage to stand up to the Romans, but in the end it was to her peril, and they destroyed her. The huge Temple of Bel (not Ba'al) was a highlight. Animals were sacrificed here, so there is a big sacrificial altar with conduits for blood to run off it. The carved dragon on the wall of the bank (they had a bank!)

brought to my mind the story of Bel and the Dragon in the biblical apocrypha, in which the god Bel and his temple were central to the narrative.

Palmyra, situated by the oasis, was sometimes called "Palm-area" by English speakers, but the Arabic name was Tadmor—"lost in the sand." There was a long, colonnaded street as in Roman cities, but unlike in Roman cities, the street was not straight but deliberately bent for aesthetic purposes. The pillars with their palm branches carved in the capitals were like the ones we saw at St. Simeon's: like Corinthian ones but carved with the palms or leaves swaying. The visual appearance was entirely more fluid than that of a Roman city, and it was very beautiful.

After thoroughly exploring the Palmyra ruins, we went to the Palmyra museum, where the main displays were the items found in the ruined city and in the tombs nearby; in fact, a lot of the museum pieces were funerary. Each prominent Nabatean family had a statue of the family group in their crypt, and when family members were buried in the tombs, their bodies were placed in the wall as if in a chest of drawers, with an effigy at the end of their "drawer." Some of the family groupings and other statuary were on display.

A little outside of the ruined city was the Palmyra necropolis, consisting of overground tower tombs, and underground crypt complexes. There were two tombs open, one of each kind, and we went to both. The tower tomb was absolutely terrifying. We climbed up and up a spiralling stone staircase, and in places we could see through the risers of the steps to the ground floor many, many feet below. The effect was not helped by the total darkness inside the tower. I arrived at a lookout about two-thirds of the way up, and by then I knew I could go no farther because I was dizzy and terrified by the open height. After looking out of the view window, I started back down, clutching the wall all the way. When someone started coming up the stairs toward me, I held out my hand to signal them.

"Stop! Wait there! I'm coming down," I said in what I hoped was an imperious voice.

I heard a scream from somewhere above, and later learned it was Elsa, a woman of our group, who had become completely unnerved. She later recovered herself, although she shook for some time afterward and was very quiet in the coach for the rest of the day. The underground tomb was more congenial. It was called the Tomb of the Three Brothers, but an inscription over the door invited others to pay the money and be buried with them; it was a commercial operation. The tomb was divided into three rooms, with the same spaces for "drawers" as in the overground tomb.

After a break we set out to climb Mt. Zenubia, a desert hill with a crusader-era castle or citadel perched on top of it. Our tour leaders assured us it was an easy ten-minute climb for the feeblest and most out-of-shape octogenarian, or so they implied. There is no truth in advertising. It was a bloody hard trek, and I ended up with Wally and his wife, Mary, encouraging me, or we encouraged one another. Colorado Wally was certainly the elder statesman of our group, but the only way I, twenty or so years his junior, could make it up the hill was to follow him and to place my feet in the same spots he placed his. Within the castle walls at the top we heard the strains of Flemish language; a Belgian tour group was already exploring the courtyard of the medieval castle, and a young Flemish woman in our group immediately gravitated their way. Their presence was unusual, because there seemed to be so few tourists anywhere in Syria. After a brief exploration of what remained of the castle, exhausted, I took the coach back down.

Later we shopped for shoes in the small bazaar, where the ladies paid about five dollars for camel leather sandals. In the date market, after a couple of tries at communication, I bought a half-kilo of dates for a hundred and fifty Syrian Lira, equal to about two dollars. The kiosks were stretched along the main road, and were constructed as one huge, long tent with partitions along the length. Within and in front of each of the stalls, the vendors had strung their bunches of dates. The dates on display were of various varieties, and ranged in colour from light yellow, through red, to brown. I was invited into a kiosk for tea by Mahmoud, a young Bedouin date-seller. We were restricted by our language differences, but he cordially offered me tea, we exchanged addresses, we got our picture taken, and I promised I would come back for another visit at nine that night unless it rained.

I was now getting seriously sick with Middle East tummy so I rested at the hotel, where I had the cosmopolitan experience of watching on television the National Geographic special, in English, of the railways of India, carried through NBC in the desert in Syria. It seemed indeed to be a small and cosmopolitan world. We had a free night for dinner, and I went with Rasha's group to the same place as the previous night, since we had had such excellent food there. This time, I asked for much smaller servings, but it was to no avail. A large tureen of lentil soup was followed by a mountain of fatoush salad, and another mountain of rice, peas and nuts. To be on the safe side, I ordered 7-Up.

After dinner, I convinced Rasha to go with me to Mahmoud's tent-kiosk in the date market as an interpreter. Through Rasha, I learned that Mahmoud was seventeen years old, finished eighth grade, and lived in Palmyra. The date sellers were Bedouin, but had stopped wandering and had settled in the town, living nine months of the year in a house, and the three months after the date harvest in their tent-kiosks. Mahmoud's cousin appeared on the scene to join us and said that he was the person who had sold me the dates that afternoon. We chatted for some time, and four others from our party appeared and shared in the tea. We all had a grand old time nibbling dates and drinking tea, and finally we took our leave. It was different and it was fun. I promised to write to Mahmoud, but it was a rash promise that I never kept. Afterward, when I had arrived home, the prospect of having letters translated into Arabic just seemed a bit daunting, and I could not accomplish it.

My sleep was by now interrupted periodically by bouts of Middle East tummy. Still tired, I joined the group for our journey to Damascus. One more drive through the date market where we waved goodbye to our date-seller friends. One more drive past the beautiful and stately ruins of Palmyra. The drive to Damascus was mainly through desert. I was really not feeling well, and by the time I arrived in Damascus I was experiencing chills.

Our exploration of Damascus began outside the citadel, another relic of the Crusades. Beside the citadel was the entrance to the Al Hamidiyyeh Souq. There was a large equestrian statue of Salah al Din outside the souq, the covered market, as that hero of the Arab world spent his last days in Damascus. The souq was enormous, and everything in the world was sold there, especially clothes and spices. While our group was queuing up to buy shewermas for lunch, we were delighted to meet some girls who heard us speaking English and asked where we were from. They were Lebanese and were visiting Damascus on a shopping trip, but they had lived in Canada for fifteen years during and after the sixteen-year civil war, and had recently returned to Lebanon now that it was safer to do so. Some members of the group had chicken shewermas for L10 each, or roughly twenty-five cents, and some people had four or five of them.

When we left the market, we saw that the superstructure over the entrance was actually a ruined Roman building, quite a large one. It was, in fact, the remaining structure of the Temple of Jupiter, built in Roman times. Worship of the Roman god was still practised during the time that Saint Paul lived here, and the presence of that temple in Damascus, especially after Paul's conversion experience, must have dismayed him greatly. Again, I found myself gazing at something that Saint Paul himself had seen during his sojourn in Damascus. It was an indescribable feeling—that of sharing in the physical landscape of the New Testament. I found it hard to speak of this, and we turned our way down the street to "Saladin's" mausoleum.

There were actually two tombs in the Saladin mausoleum: his original one, and the newer, more elaborate one that had been commissioned by Kaiser Wilhelm II. It is an important man who needs two tombs! The group then carried on to the Omayyad mosque, part of which used to be a Christian church. One of the minarets of the mosque was called the Jesus Christ minaret, as local Muslims believed that Jesus Christ would appear there on the judgment day. The women in our group donned instant jihab—black, hooded tie-up capes for our visit inside the mosque, and we looked exactly like what we were: tourists wearing temporary cover-ups. The interior of the mosque was huge but almost shabby. The carpets were not notable, and there was very little decoration. A prominent feature of the mosque was the enclosed tomb that putatively contained the head of John the Baptist, known to Islam as the prophet Yahya.

By this time I knew I was really sick with the local infestation, and was not going to make it through the day of touring. I went out of the mosque, and Rasha took me to the main street, where she negotiated with a taxi driver to take me back to the hotel for SL30. It was a good thing he took me to the right place, because if I had had to tell him anything it would have been hopeless. Almost no one in Damascus spoke English, and I did not know a word of Arabic. I lay in the room, fevered, for several hours, chilling and aching everywhere. Once I woke up, convinced that all my teeth were abscessed because they all hurt so much. Everything else hurt too, however, so the abscesses turned out, fortunately, to be imaginary. It actually occurred to me that this might be cholera, but I was too sick to crawl out and tell anyone about my fears.

I woke up later, sweating and with a big headache. Once the headache was under control I went up to the restaurant to eat something: lentil soup and most of a plate of rice. Then back to bed. I woke up feeling much better. At breakfast, we waited a long time to be served. The staff did not want to bring the breakfast until the whole group arrived, and nothing would convince the waiters that the entire group would never be all assembled at once. I waited an hour for breakfast, while members of the group straggled in one at a time. A half hour after this, we left, although I still had not had any coffee. This was a disaster for me, as I was truly a caffeine addict.

Our outing was to the National Archaeological Museum, another national, a very extensive institution, which contained large structures brought from ancient sites. There was, for example, an entire underground tomb from Palmyra, as well as a very old synagogue. There were a lot of items from Ugarit, including the world's oldest alphabet. There was also a particularly extensive collection of early glass.

Roaming around in the major parts of Damascus was as safe as, or safer than, it would be in any western city. Poz and I, with a few others, went to an outdoor Handicrafts Market where a movie was being made, then back to the covered Souq al Hamiddiyeh. Some of the traditional local crafts were attractive as souvenirs, and I bought a small, lidded box inlaid with mother-of-pearl, plus about a dozen little shells, dipped in gold metal to create charms, all twelve for about three dollars. We found the famous olive oil soap of Aleppo, nine large bars for about two dollars. Lunch was a huge falafel with parsley, tomatoes, chips, and everything else, all for about fifty cents. Then we entered the Christian district, looking for a place mentioned in the New Testament, the street called Straight.

The destination on the street called Straight was St. Anania's Church, with its small, Roman period house in the excavations below. Tradition has it that this house was Anania's house, where St. Paul stayed during the blindness that he suffered after his visionary experience on the Damascus road, as written in the book of Acts. This little house had an authentic feel to it, and it had been kept as unadorned as possible to maintain the dignity of the experience. The rooms were tiny and the house was built of small, dark stones resembling rubble. If this was indeed the place of Paul's convalescence, he and his friends were living in very close quarters. Again, I thought about Paul and the tremendous rigours he had had to endure in his travels spreading the gospel. He had never been my favourite, but the more I retraced his footsteps, the more he rose in my estimation.

After we roamed around a bit, we went back into the souq, where my comrades did their serious shopping for boxes, tablecloths and spices. We returned to the hotel in time to meet the others for dinner. Dinner was at the Al Kamal Restaurant, and once again I had lentil soup and rice, but this time with a heavenly plate of chips. Our dessert stop was certainly unique. On the front window of the restaurant was a mock-up of the Pizza Hut logo and the words "Pizza Hat"! When we went inside, we found it had nothing to do with pizza, but rather was an ice cream parlour with Arabian sweets. It seemed that the Syrians wanted very badly to have all the fast food and other trappings of the western world, perhaps because they knew that their neighbours in Jordan had all these things. I had coffee, and the others had thoroughly splendid looking sundaes.

One of the things we continued to notice in Syria was the slightly greater number of veiled women, including a lot more women completely veiled in the black *chador* than in Turkey, although even in Syria it was really not normative. In Damascus, there were more women with their faces veiled as well as their hair. We watched a family with three such modest ladies in the restaurant to see how they would handle eating with their faces veiled. Two of them moved the veil, or lifted it just a little, so they could eat. The third had an active little baby with her and the baby had managed to rip the veil from his mother's face.

At the time of our visit, we noted how inexperienced Syrians were in catering to western tourists. Our hotel, for example, was a beautiful building, but with inadequate and unwashed bedding, poor housekeeping and breakfast service, and no toilet paper—and since most of us were by now really sick, toilet paper was the first thing on our minds! Although in Syria the merchants in the bazaars were very competitive, the service mentality in the hospitality sector was not part of the culture, and this made tourism in Syria very difficult. Because of government restrictions, this kind of service infrastructure was developing very slowly. In some ways, this made Syria a good destination as there were still few tourists, but the tourists that did go there would be well-advised to be patient, tolerant, and hardy.

At the next day's breakfast, there were still communication problems, as the hotel staff still expected we would all arrive in the dining room at once. We arrived one at a time, however, and the dining room service was not set up for this. As a result, it was a bit late when we set out, close to nine o'clock. By this time cranky, and all sick, we drove to Bosra, a city of the ancient Decapolis—the "ten cities." Bosra was particularly interesting now because it was an archaeological site, but with people still living right in it. I was intrigued with the recycling of stones, which in Bosra meant that people took apart the Roman buildings made of black dressed stone, and built their modern little houses right on the site of the Roman city. Bits of the past were embedded in the houses, where the capital of a column might be built into a wall otherwise made of regular blocks. The appearance of Bosra was really intriguing; the little cubic houses of black basalt were built right along the Roman colonnaded street, and the entire town was now still undergoing archaeological excavation. A few of the Roman buildings were relatively intact. The bath, for example, still had its original Roman roof, the theatre was considered the best Roman theatre in the world, and there was a fortified citadel.

Touring the citadel was to be our last site visit before departing from Syria. Travel had been difficult in Syria, but the rewards had been incredibly great. The entire journey had been worth it just for the opportunity to see the proud city of Palmyra, and to meet some of her Bedouin residents. Strolling through the streets of the ancient city of Ugarit, and visiting the temple of her Phoenician visitors, were memories I would guard as gems. Walking down the street called Straight, following in the footsteps of the intrepid Saint Paul, had been profound. Never again would I hear with the same ears the story of Paul's dramatic conversion on the road to Damascus. All of these places were now a part of my inner imagery—forever.

Off to the border, where we had lunch at the cafeteria, then anyone whose tour finished here, plus Abir and our driver Aboul, were left behind, and we went on to Jordan. Some had left during the night, and Poz had actually moved out of our shared room as soon as I had become really sick on that first day in Damascus. When we arrived in Jordan a great cheer went up. Many of the group members had been quite ill in Syria, and they had lost patience with the difficulties of the Syrian hospitality sector. They had missed out on some of Abir's narratives, although we all appreciated her great knowledge, and heaven knows she was certainly a lively thing. She was young, however, and it was not easy for her to place herself in the traveller's shoes. Maybe she was simply well suited to her craft: more of a guide than a nurse.

Krak des Chevaliers

The Altar of Baal at Ugarit. The three-holed stone is a ship's anchor.

The Temple of Jupiter in Damascus is now the entrance to the bazaar.

◆　　　◆　　　◆

Compared with the antiquity of Syria, Jordan appeared pristine and ultra-modern. Magdi, the handsome young Egyptian that had accompanied us throughout Syria, was now our tour leader, and we met our new Jordanian guide, Reyed. Shortly, we arrived in Jerash. It, too, was another city of the Decapolis, but not the black basalt colour of Bosra; rather, it was again the rosy-buff coloured stone, and very beautiful. The name Geraso would have been used in Bible times. In one New Testament story, for example, Jesus healed a possessed man known as the Gerascene demoniac. The man may have been from around Geraso, now Jerash. This beautiful city was first built by Alexander the Great then rebuilt by the Romans. It had been, and still was, one of the loveliest cities of the ancient world. The colonnaded street drew the visitor into the heart of the city, with its circular forum enclosed by well-preserved pillars. As the city's history spanned Roman worship and then Christianity, monuments on the major streets included the pre-Christian Temple of Artemis as well as a second century cathedral. The remains of a lovely fountain now sat high and dry in the city, and our group spent some time examining the splendidly engineered Roman columns, built with enough "sway" to survive a minor earthquake. Competing with Artemis were three later churches, all lined up alongside one another, one of which had a well-preserved mosaic floor. There was a theatre, this one made from the beautiful buff stone, and although very lovely, was not as well preserved as the one at Bosra. Reyed explained to us the difference between a Greek amphitheatre, cut right into the hillside, and a Roman theatre, for which the Romans developed free standing building technology so they could put up a theatre anywhere. The Roman theatres generally had a wooden stage.

We had been telling Magdi and Reyed that we needed to go to a supermarket, but the two men, not understanding the idea of "supermarket," instead took us to a corner store right outside the hotel. At the Hillside Hotel—newly renovated, modern, clean, everything worked—we were completely happy. We needed a bit of rest and pampering after the more rigorous travel we had experienced in Syria. In addition to comfort foods, we could now watch comfort television: there was a news story on CNN about Hallowe'en in North America, but of course there was no Hallowe'en in the Middle East. After a pleasant chat with Nabil, the Public Relations manager of the hotel, I joined my companions for dinner, where the chef himself brought out a special vegetable soup for me, with rice and chips. We had not really seen anything of Jordan as yet, but we all thought it was wonderful.

Next day's breakfast was exquisite; the hotel was exquisite. Toast for the first time in over a month! Everywhere else, bread at breakfast had meant pita, which was good, but because we were ill, we were tired of it and needed comfort food. The persistent symptoms of my illness turned out to be, in the end, resistant even to the medication that the group eventually bought in Jordan. I decided to try penicillin instead, as I had some with me. I began to feel better as soon as I started the penicillin, and got steadily better as the course of the prescription progressed. Even with my splendid immune system and great resistance to illness, this was the only way that I was able to overcome the infestation.

On leaving Amman, we could see that the west part of the city was beautiful, and accordingly, property was very expensive. Everything was ultra-modern and lovely, but it was sad that the old culture was changing so rapidly. Fast-food chains had made inroads in Jordan as there were such restaurants as Subway, and a big playtime McDonald's was opening. The city had grown so much that the original seven hills of Amman were now twenty-one hills. Buildings were in the Arab style: square or rectangular-looking with a flat roof—no need for a sloping roof as there is hardly any precipitation; it is all near-desert. The sandy-white limestone visible everywhere was brought from the West Bank. One of the new ultra-modern villas, we were told, could cost five million US dollars. This was the rich west side, however, whereas lower income people lived on the eastside. There were refugee camps where Palestinian refugees still waited, having at first lived in tents for several years following their arrival, but having by now moved into minimal housing built by the UN and the Jordanian government.

We took the motorway south, past Tel Hisbon. What appeared to be a hill, a natural feature, was actually the unexcavated site of the old Ammonite city, from whose people the modern city of Amman derives its name. Our destination was Mount Nebo, known locally as Siyagha, the place which tradition identifies with the site from which Moses was allowed to view the Promised Land. According to the book of Deuteronomy (Deut 34), Moses was to lead his people to their land, although Moses himself was not to enter it. From the viewpoint on Mount Nebo, there was a vast panorama of arid land and faraway habitations. What we saw was likely not very different from the view Moses might have had on that day around 1250 B.C.E. The Dead Sea was off to the left, then a distant oasis that was Jericho, with Jerusalem beyond. In the distance was the land of milk and honey, but that part of the Jordan valley nearest Mount Nebo remained mainly undeveloped. On the summit of Mount Nebo stood the sculpture known as The Bronze Serpent. The sculpture combined the image of the crucifix with the bronze serpent that Moses held up on a staff to cure the Israelites of their snakebites (in Numbers 21:4-9). Incorporating the serpent as it did, the piece was also very reminiscent of the caduceus. A Franciscan church was built at the summit, housing beautiful ancient mosaics, remnants of previous churches on the site, but with modern stained glass windows depicting scenes from Moses' life. It was exhilarating to stand on that spot, and to remember Moses and his long journey leading his people to the Promised Land. What Moses saw was the vast potential of the land. It was a land of scruffy, rocky terrain, ideal for goat pasturage—hence the milk. There were thousands of wild flowers, as well as an oasis of date palms—hence the honey. Thus the Promised Land was, too, a land of promise.

In the heart of the agricultural region en route to Amman is the town of Madaba, meaning "a meal". There, covering most of the floor of St. George's Greek Orthodox Church, is the very famous mosaic map of the Holy Land that has provided archaeologists with details of ancient cities. The little oval depiction of Jerusalem, for example, clearly shows the colonnaded route of the Cardo, its pillars depicted as flat on the ground rather than in perspective. Numerous other, familiar features of Jerusalem are also visible, such as the Holy Sepulchre. All of the Christian cities of the ancient Near East were represented on this map, and the depictions were both charming and informative.

In this region, we were in the territory of the Biblical Moabites. A little farther along was the Arnon Valley, or Wadi Mujip as it was called in Arabic, a huge dry valley with a precarious road carved along the cliff. We got out of the bus for a better view. This road, the King's Highway, was mentioned in the Bible (in Numbers 20:17; 21:22 and Deuteronomy 2:27). It was a well-known road that, even in ancient times, ran from Damascus to the Gulf of Aqaba. Later, it became part of the Roman road network, and was still basically the road in use today. When he was leading the people of Israel into the Promised Land, Moses passed through here and promised the Edomites and Sihon that he and his group would stick strictly to this road when passing through their host's lands. The road is pretty terrifying, and John, the Australian dentist in our group, pointed out that our lives were completely dependent on the cardiac health of our middle-aged, stocky coach driver. We stopped to photograph a black basalt Roman ruin that was a traders' station, like an early caravan saray, with part of the Roman road visible beneath it. As with many archaeological sites, the excavation was right beside the road, and integral with the community living all around it.

Eventually we came to Karak castle, a Crusader fortress that had been conquered after three years of assault by Salah al Din, in response to the murder of his sister, who had been taken to that castle as a captive. There was also a small, but very good museum on the site, with neolithic tools, ancient burials, bits of pottery, and various displays, including a large panel on Gertrude Bell, the eccentric and fortitudinous Englishwoman who trekked around the Middle East by herself in the nineteenth century. Tall, red-haired and assertive, she must have been a curiosity to the local Arabs and Bedouin.

We pressed on in our coach. When we stopped for coffee, a handsome Bedou man was allowing children to sit on his camel's back for a ride. The man wore the traditional long, loose white shirt, or *thawb*, with the red and white checked kuffiyeh over his head. He laughed aloud to encourage the child riding the camel, and to set the little fellow at ease. Of all the domesticated beasts, camels must have the worst personalities, but this one seemed very well trained, and relatively cooperative.

Afterward, instead of watching the scenery, the travellers began watching a movie on the bus, and when there was a lull in the movie action, we watched the sun set. After a couple of hours of travel, we reached the Petra Diamond Hotel, somewhat out of town but clean and reasonable. Our spirits were good because we were anticipating the next morning, when we would go on our exploration of the mysterious and breathtaking lost city of Petra. After a supper of beautiful salads, chips, rice, and abundant vegetables, with lamb chops for the non-vegetarians, we received a briefing from our leaders, Magdi and Reyed, and then retired.

The next day we went by coach to a point near the Petra site. After the entry gate, we walked down a long footpath, with horses and donkeys beside us on a parallel path, to the opening of the canyon, called the *siq*. At the entrance to the site, everyone was required to pay for a horseback ride and the assistance of a Bedou horseman, even if we did not use the service, because provision of the equestrian service, maintenance of horses, and the extensive horse hospital, all provided employment for the Bedouin. To see these expert horsemen riding camel or horse was a real treat. Still, most of our group chose to walk the entire way instead of taking a camel or horse. After a long walk, we came to a narrow opening at the end of the siq that revealed a wonderful courtyard, with the incredible façade of the Treasury opposite, the enormous building carved in the rock face. What a sight this must have been to the "discoverers" of Petra, after it had become forgotten by the outside world. All of these huge and wonderfully beautiful buildings, built right into the stone, were titanic, mysterious, awesome. We halted our march to take in the sight.

Petra was much more complex than we had previously thought, as it was an entire city that continued along the canyon and contained a great many monuments. The original Nabatean buildings, tombs in fact, as well as the Nabatean people, were later taken over by the Romans in 106 C.E., so Petra also contained an entire Roman city. The city was completely breathtaking and beyond the imagination. One of the tombs was coloured a beautiful rainbow of vibrant colours, and appeared to have been painted. Our guide, Reyed, however, said to us, "This was just painted last week by a real professional painter from Amman." We must have all looked blank, and after a few seconds of our confused silence he added, "The painter is God."

It was about ten-thirty or eleven in the morning when we started up the 850 steps to the hillside façade called the Monastery, really another tomb. Marjorie, an Australian woman of retirement age, told us she had been awake all night worrying about the 850 stairs, probably imagining a straight-up staircase going to the sky, with nothing on either side but a sheer cliff. It was not like that at all. The steps were built into the side of the mountain and sloped around. Nowhere was there just a sheer drop on either side, although there was a cliff with a narrow path opposite us, and a fearless troop of goats passed by us and went around by that path! The 850 steps were a tough climb in the hot sun, though, and as I was out of shape I am sure I was completely flushed. I poured water on my face and head periodically. Melanie was also having a slow climb, and Magdi stayed near us to ensure we made it. At the top we sat opposite the Monastery and just gazed at it. A daredevil was on top of it, climbing and jumping around. Reyed told us that the daredevil performed these stunts several times a day, and would not take any money for it. In the U.S., Canada, or any European country, he would be arrested at once—never mind tips! After a while the young Australian couple went up the steps to the roof of the Monastery also, and waved at us from their high vantage point.

I became a Desert Police groupie. These are the Bedouin who patrol the desert, on horse or camel, mainly because they know their way around, and are the people best able to survive in the desert. They are present throughout Petra, vigorous and very romantic in their uniforms of army fatigues and kufeeyah, looking rather like young and outdoorsy versions of Yassir Arafat. After the long trek back down the 850 steps, we stopped in a tent-restaurant. The Bedouin operate these places, as well as the souvenir stands and their horse/donkey/camel ride businesses. Boxed lunches were offered for 3 Jordanian Dinar, equal to about five or six U.S. dollars, but I had my own lunch, which, thanks to the penicillin, I was now able to eat without hazard. Then we had the afternoon to do what we liked, exploring around the site. A lot of people climbed the 550 steps to the high sacrificial altar, with its association with Ibrahim's near-sacrifice of his son, according to one Muslim tradition. I had had enough stairs for one day, so I perused the two museums, viewed the Roman part of Petra that included a Roman theatre and colonnaded street, then trudged slowly back to the entrance gate. The two kilometre canyon seemed like two hundred kilometres going back, and by the end of the footpath I was dragging my knuckles. Back at the hotel we had time to watch "Indiana Jones and the Last Crusade" before dinner. This was fun, as part of the movie was filmed in the Treasury building in Petra.

When I woke up, it was St. Winifred's day: my birthday. I actually forgot until I heard the radio in the hotel kitchen, by coincidence, playing Happy Birthday. A birthday immediately following the amazing experience of being in Petra. What a landmark! We drove back to Amman, a three-hour drive, and this time we took the desert highway instead of the King's Highway that goes down and up the wadi. Back at the Hillside Hotel, most of our group was too tired to explore Amman, but I wanted to go to the National Gallery, and I decided I would do it anyway.

The gallery closed for lunch, then re-opens at three. Nabil put me into a cab, instructed the driver in Arabic where he was to take me, then handed me his card with the phone number and all the information in both Arabic and English. The taxi driver dropped me in front of a lovely gallery with gardens on either side of the walk; then he departed. Inside, an employee handed me a program and indicated the price. But the list was, to my surprise, a program of works for sale, their names and prices enumerated on the program. I was horrified. I was in the wrong place! No one spoke English; even street signs were in Arabic; I had no idea where I was; and I could not imagine trying to communicate all this to another taxi driver. The attendant called in an expert, a young man who spoke perhaps six to ten words of English, and I tried to speak to him. In the course of our alleged conversation, he let slip a word of French. Aha! Here we were on safer ground, to our mutual great relief, and we were able to communicate quite effectively in French. There were times when it was good to be Canadian. The young fellow walked up to the upper street with me and showed me how to get the *service,* a white Mercedes that operated as a kind of shared taxi, and took up to five passengers. I made it to the National Gallery, and very cheaply too.

The gallery did not look so much like an institution, but more like a large house, and was built in the pale buff-coloured, flat masonry style visible everywhere in Jordan. Only the main floor was available for viewing, as the rest of the gallery was being readied for a forthcoming Dutch exhibition. Considering that Jordan was a fairly wealthy country, the gallery was very small, with works displayed on two floors that would be similar in scale to the gallery in a small to medium-sized town back home. Muslim tradition, however, forbids the depiction of human beings and animals, and I wondered if perhaps public support of the visual arts did not have the same value as it did in the western world. There was a good sampling of Middle Eastern pieces, including some interesting sculpture, mostly ceramic, and there were even paintings done by women. Some of these pieces even had the veil and the lack of freedom for women as their theme.

After the gallery I went back to the hotel and made myself beautiful for dinner. Everyone was very subdued after the Petra day, and perhaps getting fed-up with travelling. Quite a few were also still sick, or relapsed. After dinner I played cards with Sam and Jason, Melanie and the "boys" before staring at CNN long into the night.

Next day we set out early. We knew that procedures at the Israeli border would be lengthy, as there was a high alert. We passed near the Dead Sea and arrived at the Allenby Bridge, which was the border with Israel, where we waited a long time to be invited to cross. All personnel of the tour company had left us by this time, and the Jordanian coach driver was in a rage over the tip he had been given by the tour leader. He raged at us on and on, but we were unable to communicate with him, and tips and gratuities were to be handled by the company so we were not in a position to get into an argument about it. When we crossed the bridge into Israel, and we entered the Customs Hall with our baggage, about one third of our group was given an extremely thorough search. First the baggage was put through an image-enhancing X-ray machine, and then a few passengers were taken aside for a personal search. I was the first to have my baggage examined. It took an hour and a half, and they looked at every seam of everything. I really do not know what they could have suspected to be concealed in the elastic of my two dozen or so pairs of knickers that they merited such scrutiny. It was the most thorough examination I had ever witnessed. In view of this painstaking thoroughness, a few members of our group asked me why I had "so much stuff"! I asked myself the same question.

Bedu rider at Petra.

View from Mount Nebo: what Moses saw when he viewed the Promised Land.

4

Entering the promised Land

Once we were actually in Israel, or in this case Palestine—meaning hours later—we continued along the hilly, arid lands near the Dead Sea, and viewed the remains of Jericho, the ancient oasis city whose destruction over three thousand years ago was described in the book of Joshua in the Bible. We would be accompanied by a British tour leader, Annie, and an Israeli guide, Rachel.

Jericho was a patch of green on a vast expanse of surrounding dry ground. High hills perched above the pretty town of green shrubs, market gardens and date palms. People came here to see the tel, that pile of ancient layers of past habitation so prominent in the Biblical epic. Even though it was exhilarating knowing we were walking along the very walls that in the Bible fell down at the sound of the trumpet, we found the excavations at Tel Jericho not easy for the visitor to interpret. What could be seen was a small part of the city wall, excavated to the third millennium B.C.E. level, with very minimal signage and interpretation throughout the site. It was very difficult for us to imagine the battle of Jericho, with Joshua and the Israelites, taking place here on this arid platform pocked with excavated areas revealing the strata. One of the most visible features was the base of a very ancient tower, perhaps four to five thousand years old. The purpose of this building was disputed, as some scholars believed it to be a silo, some a fortification. Besides this, large, well-preserved patches of the brickwork of the ancient walls could still be seen.

For over a hundred years scholars have been digging up Jericho and trying to piece together the elusive history hidden within this mound. They have constantly debated whether or not anyone was actually living here at the time when Joshua and the Israelites arrived. The site was originally surveyed by the British engineer Charles Warren in 1868, and more vigorous excavations were carried out by the German team of Ernst Selling and Carl Watzinger from 1907 until 1911. These two concluded that the site was uninhabited during the period of Israelite conquest, a conclusion that did not sit well with contemporaries who expected to hear confirmation of the Biblical narrative. The British archaeologist John Garstang excavated from 1929 to 1936, and reached the very different conclusion that the archaeological evidence and Biblical narrative were not divergent, basing his findings on the discovery of a section of wall that had been destroyed during the Late Bronze Age, the period identified with the exodus.

Kathleen Kenyon excavated at Tel Jericho from 1952 to 1958, making use of more modern, improved archaeological methods that came into use in the 1930's. She published her findings, among other places, in a 1958 book entitled *Digging Up Jericho*, and a subsequent one, *Excavations at Jericho*, in 1960. She was unable to find any evidence of habitation during the period of the Israelite conquest. That, of course, does not really prove anything. It does not mean that no evidence is possible, nor does it necessarily mean that the site was uninhabited during the period of the Israelites' arrival in the land. It only means that Dr. Kenyon did not find any artifacts or detritus of people who may or may not have lived there at the time. At any rate, it was generally agreed that Jericho was the oldest known human settlement, perhaps dating from 8000 B.C.E. The conquest of Palestine by Joshua and his Israelites was some time within the 1400 to 1250 B.C.E. range. This was the best we can say archaeologically at the moment—apart from acknowledging that we read the Bible as a record of faith, and not as an archaeological report.

These ancient remains of Jericho, also called locally Tel es-Sultan, are situated within the present city of Jericho, surrounded by market shops, Arab-style housing and a lush oasis of palms. When we visited, the Palestinian security forces were training nearby and we could hear the sounds of their voices as they underwent their exercises. In the dry, desert distance there were higher hills, one with a monastery atop. This was the Mount of Temptation, traditional site of Jesus' forty days of temptation in the wilderness, and the monastery is the Greek Orthodox Monastery of the Temptation, or the Forty Days, open to visitors and now even more accessible by way of a cable car, although the cable car was not that day a part of our itinerary. The entire area was a montage of history, all visible at once. Then came Jerusalem.

Entering Jerusalem is a profound experience for any Jew, Christian or Muslim. The traditional stop is at the Mount of Olives, which faces the side of the ancient walled city with the Golden Gate at its centre, and that gate is in front of the exquisite Dome of the Rock. We stopped at this Mount of Olives viewpoint and gazed at the Old City, spread out in all its quiet serenity and sagesse. It was a sunny day, and the deep ochre city walls looked warm and secure as they held the compact little city in their embrace. The words of the old spiritual, *Oh, What a*

Beautiful City, resounded in our mind's ear. Did I believe in love at first sight? I certainly did, for I fell in love with Jerusalem at first sight. I was later to learn that the Old City is far from quiet, and its serenity is sometimes assailed by commerce, conflict and downright weirdness, but nothing of this could ever diminish my lasting love for Jerusalem.

Many of the points of interest were visible from the Mount of Olives viewpoint, where visitors found themselves atop an extensive Jewish cemetery that extended to the valley below. This almost met up with the extensive Muslim cemetery on the other side of the road. The graves of faithful Muslims extended right up to the city wall in front of the now bricked-up Golden Gate. Beside us on the hill, we could see the various churches associated with the traditional sites of gospel events: the churches in the garden of Gethsemane, where Jesus prayed on the night of his arrest; and the Dominus Flevit church, traditionally where Jesus wept over the fate of Jerusalem. These thrilled us deeply; but the experience was marred by Wally's discovery that he had been robbed of 180 shekels that he had just changed and had shoved into his pocket. The professional pickpockets were two young Palestinian men that operated as a team, pretending to sell postcards.

On an orientation walk near our West Jerusalem hotel, we did little except to change some money and to explore the Ben Yehuda Mall. That first night, this was enough, as we were tired and emotionally overloaded. The Ben Yehuda Mall was not a covered mall in the North American sense, but rather a wide cobblestone street with no vehicular traffic other than military vehicles. Throughout Israel, and particularly in Jerusalem and Tel Aviv, we became accustomed to sitting at an outdoor café and having army trucks drive back and forth, with soldiers bearing military weapons and watching the action. We gave the shops a casual perusal, and even visited McDonalds. The sign in English actually said *McDonalds*, but in Hebrew letters read as *MacDavid*, which appeared to indicate a kosher McDonalds. The non-kosher restaurants read *McDonalds* in Hebrew as well as in English lettering.

Our dinner, however, was at Abu Shanab's, one of the cheapest, best places in the Old City. The sidewalk leading up to the Jaffa Gate offered a picturesque approach along the walls of the Old City, and the restaurant was up a small street near the gate. The meal was good: about two and a half dollars for a baked potato with a plate of salad, and a glass of wine was under two dollars. The place specialized in wholesome, ordinary meals such as pizza, stuffed potatoes and salads, and the décor was warm and pub-like, with lots of natural wood. Night fell during the meal, and on our walk back to the hotel the Old City seemed to us very ancient and monumental with its stone streets and buildings illuminated. A row of palms lined part of the city street, and great streams of traffic hurried by, in contrast to the silent solidity of the old city walls.

Now that we were in Israel, we could wallow in some indulgences of North American life: a thoroughly western breakfast, including the first corn flakes since our Istanbul hotel. I ran back to the room to get my soya milk mix so that I would not miss this treat—breakfast for vegans had been a bit sparse until now. We were ready for our walk by eight-thirty. Rachel distributed maps, and we all walked over to the Old City and entered by the Jaffa Gate. This entrance to the Old City is right beside the intersection of two busy vehicle thoroughfares. All kinds of people were coming and going through the Jaffa Gate, but the most interesting to us were the *haredim*, the religious Jews, still dressing as they did in the old *shtetls*, the Jewish villages of eastern Europe, as a symbol of their identity. Right outside the city walls, we could see the first Jewish neighbourhood to be located outside the Old City, designed by Sir Moses Montefiore in 1865—complete with its windmill. This neighbourhood had undergone redevelopment, and now featured an upscale modern housing development known as Yemin Moshe, presumably meaning Sir Moses Montefiore, but suggestive also of the original Moses of the exodus.

Inside the Old City was a network of narrow streets that comprised the colourful bazaar. Hundreds of little shops along the roof-covered streets were packed full with exotic clothing, souvenirs, art and everything else. As we headed to the Jewish Quarter, in the general direction of the Temple Mount, we turned onto the cobblestone street that was the Cardo, the ancient main Roman road that extended from one end of the Old City to the other from Roman into Byzantine times. It still did, in the sense that the narrow, medieval road still in use was built overtop of it, and parts of the ancient colonnaded street were preserved in situ, and were on display. Almost the entire Jewish Quarter had been demolished in the War of Independence in 1948. Until 1967, the city was under Jordanian rule, but since the Six Day War in 1967, there had been considerable excavation, redevelopment and change. Because it had been substantially rebuilt since 1967, the present Jewish Quarter was almost all new, but built in the ancient style using the same beautiful off-white buff stone. The ruins of the old Hurva synagogue, for example, were a poignant reminder of the war of 1948; only the floor area and one rebuilt arch remained and were maintained as a memorial to the old synagogue.

At last we arrived at the Western Wall, including Robinson's Arch and the portion of the wall that was being newly excavated. Here, we were in the presence of something subtle and real—the remaining part of the Second Temple. The Wall was not the wall of the Temple building itself, as that had been completely destroyed by the Tenth Roman Legion in 70 CE, but rather it was the exterior western wall of the courtyard that formerly enclosed the Temple precinct. When we went into the Western Wall plaza, we passed through metal detectors, and on our way into the Temple Mount, our bags were opened and checked. There seemed to be police and army everywhere that day, as if there were a problem, although for all we knew, this official surveillance could have been the case all the time.

The Western Wall, called the Wailing Wall because faithful Jews weep here in lamentation for the loss of the Temple, was built in King Herod's time from the huge, edged stones that were Herod's trademark. Herod's temple was built on the site of the restored temple that was re-established after the Jews returned from their Babylonian exile in the sixth century before the Common Era. That restored temple, in turn, was built on the site of King Solomon's great temple, built in the generation after King David obtained the property of the Jebusite threshing floor on Mount Moriah over three thousand years ago. We were walking in the midst of a very old tradition here. For Jews, this is the central locus of the faith. For Christians, this was the wall that was part of the Temple when Jesus visited it. For Muslims, it was the place from which the Prophet Mohammed began his night journey. No one was unmoved by this experience, even though it was a little distracting to have so much security on hand.

We mounted the ramp beside the Western Wall to the courtyard outside the Dome of the Rock and Al Aqsa Mosque. The Dome building was called Al Borak in Arabic, the name of the horse who, in Muslim tradition, carried the Prophet Mohammed on his mystical night journey from the Rock in Jerusalem to the presence of Allah. This whole complex, including the Western Wall and Temple Mount, was the most sensitive spot in the Middle East. During our visit, we were told of riots after an inflammatory sermon in the mosque, and in the years since our visit, the site again became a flashpoint for the events that became known as the Al-Aqsa Intifada. But even prior to that, in the riot that we heard about in this visit, there had been Palestinians killed.

While we were outside the Al Aqsa mosque, a group of young Israeli army trainees was there, taking off their shoes and getting ready to enter the mosque as part of their orientation. Rachel, our Israeli guide, had immigrated to Israel at the age of twenty-two, which was considered above the age for the national draft. Rachel told us that the draft in Israel generally applied to young people of eighteen years of age, and their army service comprised three years for men, two years for women. The option for civil service was at this time available to women and to young men from religious families; *yeshiva* students were exempt. The debates at the time were around the possibility for a recruit to refuse to go to the Palestinian autonomous areas for their service time. Whatever the present controversies, few forms of refusal were available at that time.

It was always a struggle in Jerusalem, and the Temple Mount itself typified that. The Mount had been formerly under Jordanian rule until the Israelis took it over. Then, at the request of Moshe Dayan, the day-to-day custody, if not official sovereignty, was given to the Palestinians. This was an affront to the Jordanians since King Hussein had had the dome re-covered in gold after the peace conference in Madrid, at a reputed cost of 80 million US dollars. The whole thing was unacceptable to certain groups of religious Jews, who would only find acceptable the rebuilding of the Temple. Pleasing everyone was a delicate, impossible dance.

On the plaza of the Dome of the Rock, which the Muslims called Haram es-Sharif, we viewed the area of the Golden Gate, which all three of the monotheistic religions of Jerusalem associated in some way with their messianic or apocalyptic expectations. When the Temple was still standing, the Temple doors would have opened out onto the Golden Gate: not the one that is there now, but a previous incarnation of the Golden Gate, now buried underneath the present one. But now the Golden Gate was bricked up, and all you could see are the outlines of the two arches that formerly led in and out of the city wall. Inside the city walls and up the cobbled street, we had a tea stop at a little café in the Muslim Quarter—Turkish coffee and Arabian sweets, including the ever-present *boorma*, the little nests of toasted shredded wheat filled with honey-drenched pistachios.

The Stations of the Cross on the Via Dolorosa marked a traditional route of procession for the hundreds of thousands of Christians who visited Jerusalem. Our group was not expressly a pilgrim group, but there was great interest in following this traditional "way of sorrows" that commemorated the day of Jesus' execution. We began in the courtyard of the Omariyye College, a Muslim school on the Via Dolorosa that was probably the location of the Antonia Fortress in Herod's day. That was where the procession usually began, with the first Station of the Cross: "Jesus is condemned to death."

The two thousand year old stone pavement under the Chapel of the Condemnation, the Chapel of the Flagellation, and the Ecce Homo Convent, was the Second Station, "Jesus takes up the Cross." These places were likely outside the Antonia fortress in Roman times. The large stones of the flooring were called the *Lithostrotos*, meaning the stone pavement, and the New Testament story in which that Greek word appears is in the gospel of John 19:13, where the condemnation of Jesus is recounted. There on the pavement, right inside the church, and extending into the excavations under the Ecce Homo Convent next door, we could see an engraving made by Roman soldiers—a chequered board game and a portion of the Game of the King. These were games with which the Roman soldiers amused themselves, the latter being associated with Jesus' crowning with thorns. From our position in the courtyard between the Condemnation and the Flagellation churches, we could look through the arch in the wall and into the exit point of a contentious tunnel, running from this point in the Muslim Quarter to the Western Wall. The tunnel had been the subject of much attention in the news just prior to our visit. A large contingent of soldiers was on hand guarding the doorway and patrolling the street; they were possibly more numerous than the pilgrims and tourists, and I reflected that if this were the place that Jesus was standing when he was condemned, he would have been surrounded by soldiers at that time also. But the soldiers surrounding Jesus had been Romans, the frightening representatives of Rome's foreign military machine. The soldiers that I saw were Israelis, and from Jesus' perspective they might have represented a friendlier sight. In any case, the infamous tunnel conducted visitors, including many Israelis, along an archaeological walkway from the Western Wall plaza to the opening across from these two churches within the Muslim Quarter, and on a subsequent visit I discovered it to be a very worthwhile excursion.

The third station, "Jesus falls for the first time," was located at the Polish chapel at the corner of the El-Wad road and the Via Dolorosa. A patch of the Roman paving stones survived in front of this chapel, still forming part of the street. Most of the people hurrying by were Arabs shopping or going to and from work, but there was also a sturdy representation of tourists, soldiers, and the occasional religious Jew hurrying to study at his *yeshiva*, or to worship at a synagogue or at the Western Wall. Palestinian children, the girls in their aqua and white striped smocks that were their school uniform, passed here on their way to and from the Omariyye school.

Nearby was the fourth station, "Jesus meets his mother, Mary," in a little Armenian chapel with a stone relief of Jesus and Mary over the door. The El-Wad road was part of the Arab bazaar, so in between the various Stations of the Cross were shops touting their souvenirs of woodenware, books and religious items.

The fifth station was associated with an interesting modern legend. Over the door of the Franciscan Oratory is written in Latin "V: Simon the Cyrene carries the Cross." On the wall of the same building was a blotch a bit larger than a human hand, where many pilgrims believed Jesus put his hand on the day of his execution. That spot is now itself a place of pilgrimage, where people like to put their hands and remember Jesus' passion. What is interesting is that the house is only about 300 years old, and the pavement from Jesus' time is about twelve feet below the present level. We found this kind of folk piety in Jerusalem unhelpful as it diminished the dignity of the sites and evoked scoffing and scepticism.

The sixth station, "Veronica wipes Jesus' face," is the door of the chapel of the Little Sisters of Jesus, at St. Veronica's church located in the Souq. Since the St. Veronica station is stuck within the bazaar, we were dismayed to see also a St. Veronica's souvenir shop nearby, a reminder of the commercial opportunities that pilgrims bring. St. Veronica is not mentioned in the Bible; in fact there was probably no historical St. Veronica, unfortunately. The name Veronica is a conflation of the words "vera ica"—true picture, and refers to the picture of Jesus that is said to have appeared on the handkerchief that she used to wipe Jesus' face—all part of an apparently later tradition. The story reminds us that we see the true face of Christ when we reach out a hand to the suffering.

The seventh station, "Jesus falls for the second time," was a Roman pillar inside another little Franciscan chapel that seemed only to be open on Fridays for the Stations of the Cross. Most of the week, it was just a door in the covered bazaar, but on Fridays, a Franciscan in his long, brown habit stood at the door and ensured orderliness for visiting pilgrims. The eighth station, "Jesus consoles the women of Jerusalem." was a Latin cross on the wall of the Greek monastery, still in the Arab souq. The ninth station, "Jesus falls for the third time," was identified with a Roman pillar on the way into the roof area of the Church of the Holy Sepulchre.

We had now arrived onto the roof of part of the Church of the Holy Sepulchre, a part shared by two communities. Rachel emphasized how the different Christian communities had staked out their territories within this church, and the roof of the St. Helena chapel epitomized these divisions. The Egyptian Coptic and Ethiopian communities each claimed a right to this roof, and they begrudgingly shared it. While we were there, we saw priests and brothers from both sects keeping watch over the roof area. A fellow from our group began chatting with one of the Ethiopian priests, whose face lit up with delight at this opportunity to converse with a pilgrim. The poor little cabañas that were these fellows' cells were lined up along the side of the roof area, and these dark men in their long, deep-coloured clothing and black pillbox hats seemed quite happy, despite their apparent poverty.

The dome in the middle of this rooftop court was, when viewed from inside the church, the dome of St. Helena's Chapel. Helena identified the holy sites at the request of her son, the emperor Constantine, and we all wanted to know how she reached the conclusion that these were the actual historic spots of the crucifixion, entombment, resurrection. Perhaps the information came from spiritual resources, or from some resources that no longer existed, such as the library at Caesarea, or perhaps from interviewing local people to hear all the tradition around it. Helena's real reasons for choosing these particular sites were, alas, now lost to us.

The last five Stations of the Cross were in the Church of the Holy Sepulchre, and all were associated with the execution of Jesus by the Roman soldiers. There was the Chapel of the Stripping of Jesus' Garments, the tenth station, the exterior of which faces onto the courtyard in front of the main church entrance. The eleventh station, "Jesus is nailed to the cross" was the main Latin shrine. It was next to the place of Crucifixion, the twelfth station, which was the main Greek Orthodox shrine. To see these chapels, we entered the church and had a moment to look at the many glass-globed lamps hanging above the Stone of the Anointment, which was the thirteenth station, "Jesus is taken down from the Cross." Up a narrow flight of stairs from there was the place of the crucifixion. The Greek Orthodox chapel was rich and beautiful. It was all built over the rock that Helena identified as Calvary, and parts of the natural rock itself were visible under glass beside the altar. The paintings of Jesus on the cross and of the two Mary's were decorated such that their clothes are made of sheets of heavy silver. Rachel presented the crucifixion story very respectfully, but there was no sentimentality, excessive piety or unhistorical material in her presentation.

Our group was very interested in the Calvary chapel, the place where Jesus was crucified on that first Good Friday. Some were even awe-struck; we gazed in wonder. It was a very secular group, a mixture of people who were clearly Christians and who talked about it, as well as people who appeared to have no faith, but who must have been drawn to these places in some way. I wondered what was going through their minds. It appeared from their keen but serene faces that something was happening to them. They may not have been able to articulate it at that moment, but undoubtedly even the hardest skeptics were moved by the sight of these places so deeply part of the faith of Europe and the Americas. Maybe they were beginning to be transformed, just a little.

Next we descended the stairs to the Stone of Anointment on the main floor level, the stone where tradition states that Jesus' body was placed in preparation for burial, although the tradition concerning this stone likely dates from later. Then there was the tomb, or rather the stone "structure" over the tomb, and the lengthy queue of people waiting to go into the tomb, the fourteenth station:

"Jesus is laid in the Tomb." It was so busy that it seemed practical to wait until the line-up had disappeared.

Behind the tomb was the Syrian chapel, a very sad, dreary place in need of improvement, where it appeared there may have been a fire at one time and no restoration following. As there was a *status quo* on the church, in fact no improvements were allowed. Within the Syrian chapel were two small tombs, or rather one family tomb that resembled a pair of little ovens hollowed out along the floor. It was part of an old Jewish graveyard that pre-dated the church, and other parts of the burial yard were apparently accessible behind Zalatimo's bakery and other shops in the bazaar next door to the church. This ancient Jewish graveyard was there when the Romans came, and was at that time outside the city walls near a quarry. Now, it was well inside the Old City, as the present day configuration of city walls was quite different from those in Jesus' time.

Down some stairs, at a level far below the main area of the church, was St. Helena's chapel, a beautiful little chapel with a lively mosaic floor, and surrounded by paintings of Helena and the clergy bringing the true cross to the world. All along the wall of the staircase leading down to the chapel were hundreds of little crosses, carved into the wall by centuries of ecstatic pilgrims who had finally arrived at their destination. Down more steps and very deep inside and below the church, in a cavern right in the bedrock of Jerusalem, was the place where tradition says that Helena found the true cross. The spot was commemorated with a bit of wrought iron work, very restrained by Jerusalem standards.

On the other side of the Jewish Quarter, and outside the Zion Gate that faced Mt. Zion, was the so-called room of the Last Supper. The room actually had been built by the Crusaders in the Middle Ages, now part of what was called the Cenacle, which was situated beside the Dormitian abbey. Although the building housing this Last Supper room obviously dated from many centuries later than Jesus' time, the meal with the disciples may have been very close to this spot. This was the former Essene quarter of the Old City, and there was evidence from the gospels to suggest that the Last Supper took place in the Essene district. In Mark's gospel, for example, Jesus instructed his disciples as to how they would locate the appropriate room for their Passover, "Go into the city, and a man carrying a jar of water will meet you; follow him…" This is an important passage, as Mark is generally considered to be the earliest of the three synoptic gospels, and so it was set down closer to the actual events. Matthew, Mark, and Luke, by the way, are called the synoptic gospels because of their parallel structure. The watering jars were the key to the argument. As it was normally women's work to carry water jars, except in the more gender egalitarian Essene community, scholars have suggested that the Last Supper took place in an Essene milieu. This would be in keeping with the traditional location of the Last Supper room at the Cenacle near the Zion Gate. Although this building was not here in Jesus' day, some kind of building was here, and as this was the old Essene quarter, that Passover meal with the disciples was at, or very near, the space where we now stood. We took a deep breath and were very quiet. We were literally breathing the air of the impending redemption at the core of Christian belief.

From the wall near the Zion Gate, we looked out over the City of David and Pool of Siloam. The Pool of Siloam was in ancient times a significant part of the feast of Tabernacles, or *Sukkoth*. When the Temple was the centre of Jewish worship, each day during Sukkoth the priests would go down to Siloam and obtain water in a golden vessel, which they carried back, along with wine, to the altar in the Temple to be poured out as a sacrifice. Nowadays, it is on the feast of Rosh Hashanah that the pool is a destination. On that day, it is possible to see religious Jews march down to the pool with their pockets turned inside out, shaking out the crumbs, to express their "emptying out" or "casting off" of sins. This ritual is called *Tashlikh*, which actually means "casting off," and can be practised on Rosh Hashanah by Jews throughout the world, at the edge of any body of water, even a bathtub. The Pool of Siloam is also significant for Christians as the site where Jesus healed a man born blind.

On our free day, Melanie and I decided to visit Yad Vashem, the Holocaust museum. The word *holocaust* is increasingly considered to be an incorrect word for the event that is referred to in Israel as the Shoah. This is because the word *holocaust* is used in the Bible to denote a burnt offering lovingly offered to God as a sacrifice. The events of the Shoah arose from evil, and clearly have nothing to do with the Biblical idea of a holocaust.

We took the city bus to the area near Mount Herzl, burial ground of Israel's heroes, and entered the grounds of the museum. Yad Vashem surprised us; we had thought the museum was a building with artifacts in it, but no—not exactly. It was an entire park with various features and different buildings. Inside the entrance to the site was a treed walkway called the Avenue of the Righteous, dedicated to Gentiles who helped Jews escape the Shoah. Along the gardens were plates with the actual names and home countries of these people. A marker for Oscar Schindler had attracted some attention, and a lot of small stones had been placed before it by visitors to the site, as a memorial. Oscar Schindler had become much more famous since the making of the movie *Schindler's List*.

In the Hall of Remembrance were an eternal flame and a memorial where the names of the ghettos and camps were inlaid in brass letters on the floor. It was silent, dark, and solemn. We had a quiet moment to contemplate those dark, horrific events that were remembered here. Next door was the Historical Museum where there were a few artifacts, but mostly big photos and an extensive progression of information plates telling the entire story of the Shoah, all supported by an audio-visual presentation. The tableaux included personal stories as well, and photos of the people whose stories were told. These were to me the most heart-breaking, the most difficult to encounter, and the most valuable part of the exhibit. This part of the museum took a long time to go through, as I moved from one photo to the next, carefully reading the full account of the Shoah history. It was horrific, of course, but profound, and the information and memorials have been presented in a most dignified and respectful way, a way that makes it possible for people to encounter this massively cruel atrocity without being overwhelmed. Sometimes people have said to me that they do not want to go to Yad Vashem because it is too heart-breaking, and they do not want to come face to face with that tremendous grief. I believe, however, that a visit to Yad Vashem is a must for visitors to Israel. The displays are designed to help the visitor to face up to this dark time in history, and to come to terms with it.

When I exited the Historical Museum, it was dark and raining outside. I descended the walkway into the Children's Memorial, a building and grounds designed by Canadian-Israeli architect, Moshe Safdie. A room containing large, tragic photos of children was connected by a passage to a room in which the light from a single candle was multiplied into thousands by mirrors. Throughout this pavilion was broadcast over the sound system the names of children, a million and a half of them, being listed in English and Hebrew, telling where they died and, in some cases, their ages. There is more to the museum that we did not see that day, including some of the boxcars used to transport Jews to the concentration camps. The museum area takes a long time to see—more than one visit—and so the outdoor exhibits would have to be for another day. As it was, the experience of that one day of Yad Vashem gave us enough to ponder and lament for many years to come. At that moment, it was night and starting to rain, and we needed to find our way back to our group.

That evening at dinner I discovered the local vegetarian specialty called "corn schnitzel," a delicious cutlet made of a vegetarian base mixed with sweet corn, fried crispy, served with the best chips I have ever eaten, and a salad, plus guava juice and much coffee. There was not much spare time on these organized tours, but there was at least an opportunity for a late night laundromat visit. It was midnight by the time I finished all my chores.

The next day, Melanie and I set out to spend a full day at the Israel Museum, a huge institution filled with items so ancient, and so important to western culture, that many of them were mentioned in the Bible. The Shrine of the Book was part of the museum consisting of a separate little building especially constructed to house the Dead Sea Scrolls. It was our far and away favourite exhibit. The little building was round, built in the shape of the top part of the ancient jars in which the scrolls were found. The most exciting artifact was the Isaiah scroll, an almost complete scroll of the Biblical book of Isaiah; it was not the real scroll that was on display, but rather a very well presented copy. This Isaiah scroll was considerably older than any extant prior to the discovery, and yet was the same as our previously existing versions. This tells us that the Hebrew Bible changed very little during those years when it was recopied over and over, so exacting was the Hebrew scholarship that went into preserving the text.

The other items in the Shrine included the Temple Scroll, the Psalms Scroll, and several letters written by Bar Kokhva, leader of the second century Jewish revolt, in his own hand. This shrine and its contents were as wonderful to us as any antiquity could possibly be. Also outside the larger building is the art garden, a large outdoor area where sculpture is displayed among rosebushes and shrubbery: the works of Henry Moore, Rodin and plenty of others—a wonderful collection.

The interior of the Israel Museum was vast, and we had to pick and choose what to see. One delightful surprise we discovered at the museum was the numismatics gallery. I thought this exhibition of old coins would be boring, but the different forms of money on display comprised a fascinating history. There were some very ancient forms of payment, such as cowry shells, as well as imitation cowry shells carved from bone; ancient hoards of coins; Roman coins that were not too different from modern coins; kosher shekels and counterfeit kosher shekels. The kosher coins did not have images of people or animals on them because of the commandment against graven images. During Roman times, local people would not be able to pay their tithe to the temple, or to purchase animals for sacrifice, using Roman coins because the emperor's image appeared on all the coins, and images or pictures were forbidden by Jewish law. The Roman and other foreign coins would have to be changed for coinage acceptable to the Temple authority. These kosher coins are of interest to Christians because that was the business of the moneychangers whose tables Jesus overturned as a protest against the commercialization of Temple worship, told in the gospels of Matthew and Mark.

The Judaica gallery was extensive, and I spent a lot of time looking at Shabbat items; items for Jewish holidays; a wooden *sukkah* or Tabernacle with rustic designs painted on the interior; two entire synagogues that had been dismantled and put up inside the museum, one from India, one Italian; costumes; Torah cases, and on and on. There were period rooms, including a beautiful French salon with lovely porcelain on display. It was amazing how much European art was on display: lots of Pisarro, Renoir, Seurat, Monet and plenty of Old Dutch Masters. There were works such as Merchiesi who painted the scenes of San Marco Square in Venice. Of course, because of the prohibition of depicting humans and animals, there was very little in the way of a Middle Eastern tradition in the same sense as in Europe, but the extensiveness of the European collection, surely something of a peripheral item at this museum, was impressive. There was also Pre-Columbian and Ethnic Art. We were amazed to find Iroquois masks, Pacific Northwest native artifacts, and Australian aboriginal pieces!

The local archaeology was certainly one of the main features. In the Canaanite gallery were huge pottery sarcophagi, with comical faces baked onto them by their Philistine makers, as if the artisans were trying to caricature the portraits painted on Egyptian mummy cases. In the Israelite rooms were artifacts of the First and Second Temple periods. Included here were the seals and bullæ, which were the impressions made by seals, and other written and scribal goods. There were lots of ostracæ, which were potsherds used to write upon as a form of ancient recycling, and there were plenty of funerary goods. I wanted to see the Baruch seal, personal seal of the personal secretary to the prophet Jeremiah. In addition to writing the book of Jeremiah in the Bible, many scholars believe that Baruch was also the final redactor of Deuteronomy, and possibly other writings as well. I was psyched up to see this wonderful Biblical artifact, but it was not to be; the seal had been taken elsewhere on loan.

On the wall of the museum's seating area was the recently found Victory Stela from Tel Dan that contained the only extra-biblical reference to the House of King David. Besides such distinctly Hebrew artifacts, there were items from ancient neighbouring cultures: Egyptian goods, and a special exhibit of items making reference to the Mesopotamian flood myth of Gilgamesh. A charming part of the museum was the Youth wing. Children from around the world had contributed wonderful, vigorous artwork depicting their ideas of Jerusalem, art that was greatly endearing. A Canadian child had drawn a Quebecois winter scene with a lumberjack sort of fellow, a cabin and lots of snow. Over the lumberjack's head was a thought balloon containing a fantastic and colourful rendering of the Old City—a young Quebecker's dream of Jerusalem! There were usually temporary exhibits also on display, and that day there was an exhibition of the drawings and architectural models of Leopold Krakauer, a painter and architect from the period 1890 to 1954.

It was about five when we came out of the museum. The Knesset, the Israeli parliament building, was nearby, but required an appointment and advance planning in order to tour it. To do so might be a bit much in tandem with the museum, as we were very tired after touring that huge institution. We both stared in wonderment, however, at the barbed wire surrounding the Knesset. How very different from the parliaments of Canada and Australia, and much as we loved Israel and all that we saw there, we gave thanks for the peace we enjoyed in our home countries.

At the farewell dinner for this leg of the tour we all said goodbye, and some people went out for evening entertainment. Some would still be around for breakfast, but Wally and Mary were leaving at three in the morning to catch their flight home to Colorado.

◆   ◆   ◆

Some of my old comrades stayed on for the next tour, and that morning a few of us went to the citadel in the Old City. Although it had been built much later than the reign of King David, the citadel was known as the Tower of David and contained a complete history of Jerusalem. Organized tours were offered at the Tower, but on this occasion the group was so big that it was hard to hear the guide. As our next road tour operated from a different hotel, we moved our baggage from the hotel in west Jerusalem to a modest hotel in East Jerusalem not far from the Damascus Gate into the Old City. Our Israeli cab driver was not happy about this trip and charged us plenty for his pains. Although there was no longer at that time any closed boundary between West and East Jerusalem, many local Israelis had great fear of going into Arab East Jerusalem. It was as if that old white line dating from the Jordanian administration were still painted down the middle of the road.

Across from the Damascus Gate of the Old City was the Nablus Road, and some distance up that road was the Garden Tomb. This was a large first-century tomb carved into a rock cave, surrounded by beautiful gardens maintained by a British evangelical society that owned the property. Many of the people associated with the society believed this to be the tomb of Jesus. The Biblical evidence for that was slim, but the tomb was from the period and would have been the resting-place of a person of some status, a person similar to Joseph of Arimathea, the man who donated his tomb to be the resting place of Jesus. The side of the rock face nearby resembled a skull, and in the gospels Jesus' burial place was called Golgotha, the place of the skull. Yet even our guide at the site, a member of the society, said that this hillside would not have looked in the first century as it does today, and the general feeling of our group was that it was likely not the historical site of Jesus' entombment. Each person must make up his or her own mind about such places, and the important fact was that as a visual experience, it was superb. The tomb with the surrounding gardens gave us a sense of the place described in the gospels, and it was pleasant and wondrous to sit near this tomb and reflect upon that.

West Jerusalem's Ben Yehuda Mall in the evening was a lively scene of outdoor cafés, shoppers, noisy young folks, and people just out for a stroll. It was a popular spot, and there were usually hundreds of people in the street. We sat at one of the cafés for a falafel supper, then the next morning we set out for the walking tour of the Old City. Rachel was once more our guide. We entered at the Lions Gate, also known as the Lady Mary's Gate since the "Birthplace of the Virgin Mary," now a Greek Orthodox Chapel, is right inside the gate. Entering the city this way put us on the farthest end of the Via Dolorosa.

This time when we viewed the Stations of the Cross I consulted a photo guide booklet that clarified the traditional stations of the Via Dolorosa. The lads from the army were at the exit of the contentious tunnel again, although they did not seem to have many customers coming out of the tunnel today. This tunnel allowed visitors to walk along the exterior of the Temple Mount from the Western Wall plaza to the Via Dolorosa. It sounded intriguing, but was still such a bone of contention with the local people that I thought it best to come back later in life.

Rachel varies her presentation each time she guides, so it was not repetitious for us to retrace these steps; in fact, we were able to notice new details that we had not previously noticed. At the Church of the Holy Sepulchre, for example, we seemed to have more time to view the chapels as the church was not so crowded, and it was a good time to view the tomb of Jesus as there was hardly any queue. When we first entered that strange old nineteenth century structure built over the first century tomb, a priest was standing beside a slab of rock that was held up by a pedestal. This was said to be the rock from the door of the tomb. The inner part was very small, so the priest directed traffic, ensuring that only four people went in at a time. The interior was very ornate, and contained the lightly polished yellow stone sarcophagus from an early tomb. Three to four people at a time could kneel comfortably within the little space beside the sarcophagus. Candles were available, and several tapers were already burning inside the tomb, propped up in vases as if they were bouquets. Small icons and pictures were also on display. It was a solemn and mysterious place, really lovely.

Yet even surrounded by such profound holiness, human behaviour could be appalling. Besides the division of communities that shared the Holy Sepulchre, another sad thing concerned the slab of rock where Jesus' body is supposed to have been prepared for burial. The rock that used to be shown was really underneath. Another slab had to be placed on top of the original one to protect it from the ravages of pilgrims chipping away bits for souvenirs.

After the visit to the Holy Sepulchre, Melanie and I decided to visit one of the restaurants near the citadel that was decorated with especially oriental ambience: oriental rugs, embroideries and fabrics in deep reds, blues and browns. This was the area where the Armenian Quarter met the Christian Quarter, and in that district several nice sit-down restaurants compete for visitors' custom. We walked so much in the Old City that such restful interiors were a welcome respite. Afterwards we began to explore on our own.

Circumnavigating the Old City from the outside was next to impossible as there were places along the wall that could not be approached. Our curiosity led us, however, to two points of interest along the wall. The first was the Dormition Abbey. We went in to view the church and discovered that the sanctuary was not the only item of importance. There was an excellent coffee shop and clean restrooms for visitors, and in the crypt were displayed the Byzantine foundations of the church, now excavated and visible. The large chapel in the centre of the crypt housed a resting effigy of the Blessed Virgin at the moment of her dormition—her "falling asleep." The present church dated from 1910, and the Byzantine part was much deeper. The church itself was quite modern, with beautiful side chapels decorated with colourful and interesting mosaics. We also visited a second interesting place, the former Institute for Holy Land Studies, now called Jerusalem University College. It was an evangelical Christian institution that offered regular degree programs, as well as short-term study and the opportunity for field study groups to stay in residence. The programs enjoyed an excellent reputation.

Because of the difficulty in walking all around the outside perimeter of the city walls, Melanie and I started walking into a valley. As a result, we walked far out of our way, on a road then under construction, through a ravine below Mt. Zion. I suggested we climb the hill, but Melanie declared it to be a hill for mountain goats, and she trudged back the way we came. I began up the hill, triumphantly congratulating myself for being adventurous. As it turned out, she had been right—and I was no mountain goat! I got stuck halfway up the incline. It was very hot and the hill very steep. There was a secure-looking root, a possible hand-hold or foothold, projecting out of the ground a couple of feet above my reach. I spent a long time analyzing the problem, worrying and baking in the hot sun. I was becoming dehydrated. I knew I was very vulnerable, and if I did not do something soon I would either be picked off by dishonest passers by, or I would pass out from the sun. Like Winnie-the-Pooh, stuck in the door of the rabbit hole, I spent a good twenty minutes of wondering what to do. Eventually I flung my bags high above me on the hill and started to dig out footholds for myself with a rock. I made it up the hill at last, but I must have looked rather the worse for wear, because when I finally got to an Armenian shop to buy water the proprietor said, "What happened? Did you slip and fall? Your shirt is all dirty!"

I spared him the details, other than the fact that no accident had befallen me, but I knew that I was lucky not to have had a heart attack while perched up there.

The next day we headed for the Dead Sea. This meant heading back along the road to Jericho, only about twenty miles away, but yet so much lower, hotter and drier than Jerusalem. As we passed through the Judean desert, we could see along the roadside the camps of Bedouin, still trying to live their ancient lifestyle, although it was a greater challenge now than ever. The establishment of the state of Israel and other modern political entities had made it too difficult for them to continue roaming and seeking pasturage, as they could not cross borders with flocks of sheep and goats. Many of the Bedouin had had to abandon their traditional lifestyle and settle down. The process of settling, Rachel told us, followed a predictable pattern. First they would put up four walls with no roof, and the animals lived in with them. Then the roof would go on. Finally, the animals were put out of the house. The Judean Desert seemed to us an inhospitable dwelling place for those who were still living as nomads, but it was not a true desert like the Jordanian desert, because here it did rain. The winter's bits of dried vegetation turned into tufts of green with the first spring raindrop, after which there were several weeks of exquisitely lovely wildflowers.

We drove to the hilltop fortress of Masada, King Herod's mountain palace. It was a rugged climb, so we decided to take the cable car up, with the idea we would walk back down. From this vantage point, we could see miles of desert hills all around us, and the beautiful turquoise blue of the Dead Sea some short distance away. After viewing the huge cistern that supplied water to the palace residents, we wound down a staircase complex along the side of the mountain to where Herod had had his winter palace. Here we were, standing in the private apartment of the terrible King Herod. He was a quite a case, Herod—a very horrible, cruel man, who was only called Herod the Great because of his great building projects, and not because of his heart. Herod was paranoid of everyone; he feared the threat of the return of Hasmonean power so much that he killed his own wife and two sons because of their Hasmonean lineage. Herod's father had converted to Judaism, but his mother was Nabatean, and as Jewishness is matrilineal, Herod was never accepted by the Jews as a real Jew; it was only the Romans who considered him a Jew. When it became clear that he was dying of cancer, Herod ordered that on the day of his death forty rabbis and Jewish scholars were to be put to death so that the Jews would be in mourning, even though their grief would not be for him. What a dreadful man! Some of the pillars and wall paintings of his palace were still *in situ*, which evoked some of the original appearance of his rooms. He certainly chose a spectacular vista—the view over the Dead Sea and the mountains was awe-inspiring—but how did they get all the building materials up that hill?

The sights at Masada also included a Roman Bath House with some of the mosaics still in place. As it was a Jewish fortress, there were no pictures of gods, people or animals depicted in mosaics, but rather geometric designs only. There were huge storerooms as the fortress was originally intended to feed an army, and the rooms eventually held food to keep the community going in the face of the Roman siege. The Roman ramp that had been built to conquer the fortress was visible below. In addition to technical and engineering methods, the Romans used a terrible form of psychology in their warfare. They brought Jewish prisoners from the destruction of Jerusalem, family members of those inside Masada, and forced them to work, unprotected, on the siege ramp. If the prisoners did not co-operate, they were made into human burning catapult ammunition. The length of the siege was in dispute. Three years was the conventional story, but there were 10,000 Roman soldiers outside, all requiring food, water and supplies—and there were only 967 Jews inside. Our guide suggested the siege might have been three months. Masada was the last stronghold against the Romans to fall, in 73 CE; Qumran fell in 68, Jerusalem in 70.

The theory about Masada was that when the Romans arrived, the Jews who were residents of the site committed mass suicide by lots. This theory was supported by the fact that ostracæ, the recycled potsherds used as stationery, were found at the site. It is hypothesized by many historians that these were "lots" that were cast to determine who would be the ones to kill the others, and who would be the last remaining person. That person would then commit suicide. Yet if they were faithful Jews, including remnants of the Qumran community, to commit murder and then suicide would surely have defied their ethic. It was a mystery. It was significant that most of the data came from the historian Josephus. He was not an eyewitness but was in Rome when it happened, and he claimed that the information came from eyewitnesses that he found: a woman and some children.

The Ein Gedi Spa was a wonderful and healing experience at a beach beside the Dead Sea, and we stopped in there as a group. We donned our bathing suits and covered ourselves with the salty black mud from the Dead Sea that had been collected into vats for visitors' use. After taking photos of ourselves covered with the black mud, we let this "masque" dry, and we showered first with salt water, then fresh water. The heavy salt content in the rich black mud made our skin feel wonderfully soft for a few days afterward. After the mud treatment, a wheeled transit resembling a children's amusement train picked us up on the beach and drove us right down to the shore of the Dead Sea. We floated in there for a while, in fact, one was so buoyant in the Dead Sea that floating was the only thing we could do. If we accidentally lifted our feet up while walking out into the Dead Sea, we had a hard time getting them back down onto the bottom!

Near the spa was Qumran. In 1947, a Bedou shepherd boy found the pottery jars containing the Dead Sea scrolls inside a cave near here. In the 1950s, Père Roland de Vaux of the Ecole Biblique in Jerusalem excavated the Qumran site, and theorized that the site, inhabited for several centuries, was ultimately an Essene community, a first-century group of back-to-basics communards who wrote the scrolls and hid them in the caves. Since then, numerous academic disputes have arisen. One theory is that the Qumran folks were unrelated to the scrolls, and that the scrolls were mainstream literature brought from Jerusalem and hidden there from the pagan invaders. Recently, a new archaeological site near Qumran had revealed another community that seemed much more likely to be the first century Essene colony. There were other details, too. Huge amounts of water had been stored at Qumran, and some scholars pointed to this and said that ink was manufactured here. Others pointed up the Qumran mikvas, or ritual baths, which surely would have required plenty of water. The debate raged on.

◆   ◆   ◆

We set out for a two-day visit to Tiberias, and visited the coast on the way. The drive through the north part of Jerusalem and the Judaean hills took about an hour and forty-five minutes, and we headed west toward the coast. There, we stopped in Caesarea and sat in the ancient theatre of the old Roman city overlooking the seemingly vast and deep blue Mediterranean. Although the theatre itself was not as impressive as Bosra or Ephesus, the view from the seats was wonderful. The theatre had been partially restored, and concerts were once again being performed on its stage.

Not far away was Akko, the old Crusader port of Acre. The Ottoman Empire was still using part of this Crusader fortress as their main prison into the 19th century, but there were a few signs of relative modernity. A beautiful esplanade had been built along the seaside so residents and visitors alike could walk around the old port and enjoy the crusader walls built beside the blue Mediterranean Sea. The was not calm along this shore, and wonderful white waves were rolling in and crashing on whatever rocks jutted out of the water. Locals and visitors strolled up and down, taking in the vigorous sea air. I would return to this crusader city another day to explore the fortress interiors.

Forty-five minutes away was Nazareth. The main attraction in Jesus' hometown was the Church of the Annunciation, where the angel Gabriel was said to have announced to Mary that she would bear a child and name him Jesus. You can enter the church either on the main level, or directly into the lower part containing the grotto that was traditionally held to be the house of Mary's family. Behind the grotto, and outside the present church, were the remains of tunnels that used to lead into the grotto. There had been churches on the site since 356 CE, although the present church dated from 1969. The walls of the upper sanctuary, which seemed much larger than the lower part, were decorated with huge wall panels donated by the Roman Catholic communities of various countries. Each panel was different, and represented the artistic culture of the donor country. The one from Canada was a natural terra cotta abstract piece, but some of the panels depicted the Annunciation in folk art traditions, as in the case of Mexico, with the Lady of Guadalupe in her colourful array. In both the lower and upper churches, Mass was being said for pilgrim groups who had their own priests with them.

At the time of Jesus, Nazareth would have been a one-clan village of perhaps 150 people, all vaguely related to one another. The word *Natzrat*, according to Rachel, meant *the offspring*, and might have referred to the offspring of King David who returned and settled here after the Babylonian exile. The church was a busy place, and was a large and interesting monument, but it was a modern church where very little of the first century was visible. It was possible also to see some other sights in Nazareth, such as the Greek Catholic Synagogue Church, which may have been built on the site of the synagogue where Jesus preached, or perhaps one could view a conception of what the town was like in Jesus' day. Instead, we drove immediately to Tiberias to view the Sea of Galilee.

Our headquarters in Tiberias, essentially a resort town, was the Hotel Restal, a Jewish hotel that kept a kosher kitchen. Mezuzahs were affixed to the doorframes of all the rooms: little miniature house-blessings, each containing a verse of scripture. The practice of affixing a mezuzah to the door arose from one of the 613 commandments contained in the Torah (in Deuteronomy 6:9) to "...write [the commandments] upon the doorposts of your house and upon your gates." A proper kosher mezuzah consisted of two paragraphs from the Torah written on a parchment by a scribe, and would be contained in a case fixed to the upper right-hand doorpost of each door in the home. As a hotel was a temporary home, the commandment, or mitzvah, was also carried out on hotel doorways.

My dinner here was the best I had had on the trip, perhaps because it was a kosher hotel and the chef was better prepared for dietary restrictions. I had a soy patty, fried potatoes, cooked veggies and salad, and a green lentil soup, delicately spiced. After supper, anyone wanting coffee had to go to the bar to order it. The others had had a meat meal, so no coffee was offered with dinner because someone might want milk with it, and that would violate kosher dietary laws. After the meal, the group went down to the waterfront where I sat by the Sea of Galilee with Jenny, an Australian veterinarian, and had coffee at a restaurant with a "Fishermen's Wharf" atmosphere. Later at night, visitors strolled along the boardwalk to view the lake, to stop in at the brightly lit restaurants and cafés that lined one side of the boardwalk, and to breathe in the clean night air. The nights here could be cool but clear. We looked up at the starlit sky, and across the lake we could make out the black, hilly outline of the opposite shore, dotted with lights. The people here still fished for a living, and many of them moored their boats beside this esplanade, modern day descendants of the fishermen disciples.

The next morning we drove along the western shore of the Sea of Galilee to the excavated town of Capernaum. Unlike Nazareth, Cana and Tiberias, there was no modern town of Capernaum: just the ruins and the Franciscan monastery. After Jesus moved away from his hometown of Nazareth, he stayed in Capernaum with Peter the fisherman. One ancient little house, which the friars identify as the house of St. Peter, has been set apart on exhibit and a church has been built overtop of it. The site must have been revered centuries ago, as an early church had been built on top of the remains of the little house, and within that ancient church, the little house had been enclosed by a protective wall. The simple mosaic floor of the little Byzantine church was visible to us.

The synagogue was the most intact building there. It was late fourth century, but built on the remains of the first century synagogue that probably was the site of Jesus' early preaching. The earlier courses of basalt stone foundation were still visible, parts of the synagogue of Jesus' day. Other interesting items on display were hand mills, and an olive press: the equipment for making food in Jesus' time. Capernaum was one of the most exciting places we saw, partly because of its connection with the gospels, and also because there was no modern habitation at the site, so it was as it had been. The surrounding countryside was very unchanged, and the lakeside was mostly undeveloped, so there was an ambience of what it was like in Jesus' time.

It was a hot day. We drove up into the Golan Heights for an easy hike. The area was a national park, and as it happened, the concession was shut, but we set out anyway, and the concessionaire later very kindly drove up the trail to bring us big bottles of water. It was late in the year, but it was still very dry, and so the bottled water was a welcome sight. We hiked along an area that had been minefields, where it was important to stick to the marked trail. The fields were used only for cattle grazing, and occasionally a poor cow would manage to blow herself up on a forgotten land mine. We sidled along a canyon with interesting basalt natural pillars lining the sides, and we passed sad little abandoned villages that were destroyed in the war in the Golan Heights in 1973. Occasionally we saw abandoned weapons, such as burnt-out tanks stopped in their tracks, or an overturned tank, rusted out. When we got back from the hike a couple of hours later, and took the coach farther along the road, we saw other abandoned villages where the shells of the little houses were completely peppered with bullet holes.

Kuneitra was a completely abandoned village that was now in the No Man's Land of this north end of the country, and the UN installation beside Kuneitra kept its vigil between Israel and Syria. Above us on the hill was an Israeli army installation, and we were told not to photograph it as the military would come down and destroy our films. This area was only 60 kilometres from Damascus—so near and yet so "other." The hostilities with Syria were another problem apart from the Palestinian situation. After the First World War, Syria came under the French mandate but gained independence in 1946. Under that agreement, Syria obtained the Golan Heights. After 1948, when Israel became independent the Jews living along the border reported that life had become unbearable. In 1967, on the last day of the war, heads of the border settlements went to Jerusalem to get the government to do something, threatening to abandon the settlements if things did not improve. Israel pushed Syria back in 1967. After the Yom Kippur War in 1973, the Golan Heights were annexed by Israel. At the Madrid peace conference, Syria made return of the Golan Heights a condition of their participation, contending that this territory had been given to them, it was theirs, give it back. But Israel contended that the struggle for the

Golan Heights had been fought and won, and at the time of our visit, Israel still viewed return of the Golan Heights as a threat to their country's peaceful existence.

Our lunch stop was a Druze café where large, excellent falafel was offered for eight shekels, a bit more than two U.S. dollars. The group then decided to proceed to the Mount of the Beatitudes, the site traditionally associated with Jesus' Sermon on the Mount in the gospel of Matthew (chapters 5 to 7). It was a beautiful setting, with a lovely little round church, wonderful gardens, exquisite views of the lake, and a view of the red-domed Russian church near Capernaum. Our short time at the Beatitudes was a lovely respite. Surrounding the little church, monastery, and guesthouse, with its beautiful and serene gardens, were undeveloped fields. It gave us a very good impression of what the terrain was like in Jesus' day. Whether or not this was the actual site of any particular sermon was left up to the individual to assess, but in any case, it was very likely that this whole area had been the turf of the historical Jesus and his companions. We were delighted to be there, to tread where those saints had trodden, and to contemplate exactly what it meant in our time to walk in their footsteps.

The next visit was to Kibbutz Nof Ginosar, an agricultural kibbutz right on the Sea of Galilee. The kibbutz, as a system, was a communal enterprise where people lived together and work in a common source of revenue. Many of the kibbutzim were farms. On this kibbutz, the residences were fairly small, but communal buildings such as the dining room were very large. There were family homes and a home for the elderly. It used to be that kibbutzim had children's houses separate from their parents, as families had to be ready to bear arms at any time. Now that security was the responsibility of the large standing army, the trend was for children to remain at home with their parents. This kibbutz also had a museum that housed the "ancient boat," known to some as the "Jesus boat."

In touristy Tiberias, we had a free night for dinner, so the group walked down to the waterfront and split into smaller groups. I joined the group headed for an Italian place for spaghetti, minestrone and coffee, and then we took in the "Galilee Experience," a multi-screen slide presentation on the history of the Galilee area. This presentation gave an overview of Biblical and other history, but entirely from a Galilean rather than a national perspective, and with no mention of the large Arab-Israeli population of this region, which seemed to me a rather significant omission.

Later that evening, I was walking along the esplanade beside the Sea of Galilee, and very suddenly, in a mere instant, a great, strong wind came up. The wind was so strong that signs and shutters crashed into one another and were torn off their hinges. Boat-owners at the marina tried to rescue their equipment, and I was sprayed by water as I walked by. I was reminded of the story of Jesus calming the storm, so quickly did this high wind make its appearance. That Biblical event likely happened very near here on the Sea of Galilee. What a gift it was when a moment of nature brought close to us one of the Bible's stories! It made us instant participants in the action.

Back in my hotel room, the television was blaring out an old Star Trek episode. There had not seemed to be much Star Trek in Turkey and Syria, but Star Trek was certainly present in Israel. I wondered to myself if Middle Eastern cultures generally disapproved of science fiction, and if it were only North America's influence on modern Israel that brought such mythologies as Star Trek to Israeli TV screens.

Throughout this part of the north of Israel, signage was in Hebrew, Arabic and English. The situation for Palestinians was different here from in East Jerusalem and the territories, as many Arabs in the north had been Israeli citizens from the time of independence in 1948, and were entitled to Israeli passports and other rights of citizenship. Relationships changed with the coming of the al-Aqsa Intifada, but at the time, there was calm in the region. We departed Tiberias at seven-thirty the next morning and drove along the Sea of Galilee, passing on our way the newly built baptismal site of Yardenit. Pilgrims could not at the time be baptized in the old baptismal place in the Jordan River because it was a military zone, so they congregated here. As our group was not officially on a pilgrim tour, we left this site to explore another day.

At some distance from the Sea of Galilee was the ancient tel of Beth She'an, including the excavations of the beautiful Roman city of Scythopolis. We stopped first at the forum where gladiators fought lions, in a sport rather similar to bullfighting, and then we viewed the huge Roman town site. Beth She'an was mentioned in the Bible in connection with King Saul. On Mount Gilboa near Beth She'an, King Saul's sons Jonathan, Abinadab and Melchishua, were killed by the Philistines, and King Saul committed suicide: he fell upon his own sword, the Bible says. According to the Biblical narrative, the bodies of King Saul and his sons were nailed to the walls of Beth She'an by the Philistines in a grisly display of triumph, but the valiant men of Jabesh-gilead removed the bodies and burned them in Jabesh (2 Samuel:31). The town was deserted in Hasmonean times and was later rebuilt by the Romans, who renamed it Scythopolis and considered it to be the capital of the Decapolis, the "ten cities" of the ancient Near East. Visible today are the pillars in the gymnasium, and the mosaic floors in the shops—in fact, even the footpath in Palladium Street was tiled with mosaics; it must have been a very rich town. There were sewers under the roads, precursors of modern civic sewage systems. A bridge led up to the town's fortifications, and there was a temple, probably dedicated to Dionysius. Later the Christians took over, but a devastating earthquake in the year 749 led to the city's abandonment. It remained abandoned until archaeologists recently undertook the ongoing excavations. The ancient tel, which may contain Biblical Beth She'an, is now a grassy mound right beside the Roman city, and excavations of this tel had just begun at the time of our visit.

Our next stop was Jericho. The country was so small that we had already gone around the entire of the arable regions. This time our explorations of Jericho were very different from the first, as we started with a tour of Hisham's Palace, desert estate of the Umayyad caliph Hisham in the 8th century C.E. On approaching the site, we passed a large wheel carved in stone that has become the emblem of the site. The palace must have been lovely in its time, so beautiful were the mosaics and stonework. The most famous mosaic is a floor depicting the tree of life surrounded by animals. The visual representation of animals was strictly against Muslim tradition, and according to legend, the creators of the mosaics were sternly warned that this was idolatry out of which no good would come. Maybe they should have listened. It is thought that the palace was destroyed by the 749 C.E. earthquake before it was even completed, and the excavation visible today lay for centuries below the debris of the quake.

On the way through Jerusalem to get to Bethlehem, we glimpsed through the window the Kidron Valley tombs. I had been looking unsuccessfully for these earlier in the week, but had been unable to find them because I had not taken the correct exit from the Old City, the Dung Gate, that would have enabled me to get into the valley easily. The tombs were Second Temple period crypts dating from the first century, two built as a façade over a cave and one built freestanding. The cave tombs were associated with the Hezir family, or the family of James; the other is associated with Absalom, son of King David, although it was certainly built about a millennium after King David's time. Farther up the Bethlehem road we passed another significant burial place, "Rachel's tomb," just at the entrance to Bethlehem. The tradition of this site as the burial place of Rachel, wife of Jacob, was a longstanding one, but the present building over the burial dated from around 1620, and was built by Ottoman Turks. In later times, Rachel's tomb was to become a significantly contentious site during the al-Aqsa Intifada, and fortifications and walls went up to protect it. At this time, however, it was much more approachable. Bethlehem itself was a West Bank town that had at the time of our visit a Christian majority, and because of the important Christian shrines, derived eighty percent of its income from tourism. At the time of our arrival, it had been less than one year since Bethlehem's inclusion in the new and partially independent Palestinian Authority.

The Greek Orthodox Church of the Nativity was the centrepiece of Bethlehem, and was one of Christianity's most important shrines. Once a large and grand church, it seemed to us very sad and quite strange. The nave was empty except for groups of tourists, and it was sparse in its decoration. We found the church quite decrepit, featuring rather shabby and tawdry decoration in the chancel. The tiny nativity grotto was under the main altar, down some steps accessible beside the chancel. It was all so built over that it was hard to tell it had ever been a cave. The little spot with the star on the floor, traditional site of Jesus' birth, did nothing to evoke the Christmas moment for us; the atmosphere was simply weird. We found that reminders of the Incarnation were more likely to come from encounters with the local people outside the church. These folks were struggling to make a living, but were always ready to engage in a friendly talk.

Back in Jerusalem, Jenny the Australian veterinarian and I were planning for the end of the tour, and we went over to the Ecce Homo Convent to arrange for accommodation for our few nights in the country after the tour ended. I had arranged for this in advance for myself, and there was no problem as there was plenty of room at the convent to house Jenny. We had dinner in the new city where the café's proprietor had placed a long table outside along the street. I had, predictably, another meal of falafel and salad, with Turkish coffee, all for 15 NIS (New Israeli Shekels). On the way back to the room we passed small souvenir shops, and I bought fifty olive wood Christmas tree ornaments to take home as gifts, as they were small, very portable, and the price was very good.

I was just about to retire for the night. I had the light out and was adjusting the window when a young woman of our group, Colleen, came to the door to show me, as a traveler's helpful hint, her little water boiler. Colleen was an Australian woman who had taken a year off her teaching job to travel the world, and I found her project to be very exciting. How I envied her this year of travel; I would have loved to do something similar, but could not at the time see how that would be possible, given my other responsibilities. It turned out, however, that sometimes these little seeds of ideas fall on fertile ground.

The next morning most of our group left Jerusalem, either to go back to Jordan, or to continue on to Cairo. Jenny and I were the only ones left, and after relocating to our new accommodations at Ecce Homo, we set out to see some more of the Old City. We had a veggie burger supper in the Jewish Quarter, which at ten U.S. dollars was much more expensive than what we had grown accustomed to pay. Near the restaurant, we bought a dual ticket for the Burnt House and Herodian Houses from the humorous old gentleman at the entrance. These houses were first century C.E. residences that had been destroyed in the uprisings after the destruction of the Temple, and they were very well preserved. The Burnt House was a small, average house, whereas the Herodian Houses were those of more wealthy urbanites of the time, and so a range of lifestyles was represented. We perused some of the lovely but pricey shops in the Quarter, and I bought a beautiful silk scarf hand-painted in blues and greens, and depicting a large dove flying over an idealized Jerusalem.

A popular walking tour in Jerusalem was the Ramparts Walk around the top of the walls of the city, and this we undertook, first from the Damascus Gate to the Jaffa Gate, then from the Jaffa Gate to the Zion Gate. This worthwhile perspective wais a mixed blessing, as it offered an overhead view of the city, including into the properties enclosed by walls that shut out the view from the street level. But it also included less picturesque views, such as rubbish heaps, hundreds of rooftop clotheslines, and the occasional dead cat.

We wandered exhausted through the Jewish Quarter and headed back through the confusing streets of the bazaar. We were lured into a Christian shop by a woeful but persistent merchant who sold us each an olive wood crèche, that is, a nativity from Bethlehem with freestanding figures, for U.S.$35, and we considered it to be an excellent bargain. Because we were so tired, we decided to have dinner at the convent instead of going out. My dinner consisted of lots of cooked vegetables and a pleasant conversation with Sister Anne, a down-to-earth Sister of Sion originally from England. As she began to recount to us the history of the Sisters of Notre Dame de Sion, Sister Anne could not possibly know how very profoundly she was altering the path of my life. The congregation of Notre Dame de Sion, the house of Ecce Homo, the Old City of Jerusalem itself: all these would become my beloved, and the context for the greatest deepening of my passionate love affair with Jerusalem.

The congregation of Sion, as it is familiarly called, was begun in the nineteenth century by Theodore Ratisbonne, a Strasbourg Jew from a family of bankers, who scandalized his family by not only converting to Christianity, but by becoming a priest. Although the Ratisbonne family was not observant of the Jewish traditions, the family was appalled by Theodore's decision to become a Christian. His momentous decision had not been undertaken lightly. Theodore had studied in the salon of a Christian woman of Strasbourg named Louise Humann, a self-taught philosopher who took in students. After Theodore thought long and deeply about the question, he was baptized by Mademoiselle Humann in 1827, when he was twenty-four years old.

The person most angered by all this was Theodore's much younger brother, Alphonse, who could not accept his brother's conversion. Yet Alphonse himself became a Christian after a rather dramatic mystical experience, in which he was visited by an apparition of the Virgin Mary in 1842 while he was visiting the church of Sant'Andrea delle Fratte in Rome. He encouraged his brother Theodore in the founding of the congregation of Sion as an outgrowth of Theodore's work as a parish priest in Paris. Alphonse himself became such a devotee of Mary, the mother of Jesus, that he changed his name to Marie, and after his own priesting was known to the Sisters of Sion as their dear Père Marie—in English, Father Mary. The name Sion is the French spelling of Zion, the Biblical name for Jerusalem, and it was the good Father Mary who brought the Sisters of Sion to Jerusalem and established their convents there. The convent of Ecce Homo had grown considerably since Father Mary's arrival in Jerusalem, but amazingly, there seemed at the time of my visit to be only around a half-dozen Sisters running the huge house.

In the morning Jenny and I glanced at the ruins of the Lithostrotos under the convent, but there was a pilgrim group seated there and we felt we were intruding on their prayers, so we decided to return later for a closer look. On our way out of the Old City, we stopped at St. Anne's basilica, which turned out to be a wonderful surprise and highly significant as all through the gardens of the church are the excavations of the Pool of Bethesda. It was not merely a pool, in fact the pools were now dried up, but it actually had been a whole complex of medicinal baths that were in use in Jesus' time. A lot of Christian groups were around, many reading the passage in the fifth chapter of John's gospel about the healing of the man who had lain ill by the Pool of Bethesda for thirty-eight years. I quietly sat down beside an Italian group and eavesdropped on their reading of the gospel account. We learned that there had been a Byzantine church built over the pools, but it was replaced by the crusader church next to it, and the crusader church was turned into a Quranic law school by the Muslims. The rebuilt crusader church was the present church of the Missionaries of Africa, called the White Fathers, whose residence adjoined. This site had a particularly authentic feel to it. Pilgrims from all over the world were also visiting there, drawing themselves closer to the history of the site, and to the miracle that had taken place there. I counted the visit to be a highlight of the trip. As in Ephesus, I felt that I was glimpsing a living scene from the New Testament. A miracle of healing had taken place here, and it was possible that healings were taking place at that very moment: invisible healings, healing the heart.

Next we bought bread rings in the street, and I had the delightful experience of having my pocket picked by the same two fellows with the postcards, who harassed me as I passed, and then one flapped the postcards in my face while the other stole my wallet. Fortunately, the crime was seen and the wallet intercepted by a kind young Palestinian fellow who returned it to me intact. The local people themselves seemed to be fed up with these two thieves.

Across the valley we came upon the "prophets' tombs," actually a Byzantine period catacomb on someone's private property. The landlady opened the catacomb and gave us a kerosene lamp, telling us where to find the putative tombs of Haggai, Malachi and Zechariah. The tombs were the little hollowed-out "ovens" along the ground, like miniature caves that were used by the Jews for burial since Bible times. The lady that kept the place also made tea and coffee so we stayed for a while to enjoy the view of the Old City, then went on to the Mount of Olives viewing point. We wandered around the dusty streets of this Arab district looking for the "Ascension Chapel," the little place where pilgrims are shown the footprint in the spot where tradition holds that Jesus ascended to heaven. The little chapel was now owned by the mosque, but was at this time an extremely sad place that was not kept holy, and it smelled terrible.

We went to two churches that had a claim to be the Garden of Gethsemane. The first was the Church of All Nations, situated in a beautiful olive grove that included some very old trees. The church had been built right over the bedrock with parts of the rock exposed, considered to be the rock where Jesus prayed in agony on the night of his arrest. There had been churches on this site since the fourth century: the first around 380 C.E., then a twelfth century crusader church, and the new basilica was begun in 1919. The church was truly beautiful inside. We first entered through a wrought iron screen depicting olive branches. The mosaic floor was really wonderful and beautifully kept, and the chancel incorporated the natural rock on all sides. One of the nuns later told us, however, that she had once been expelled from this church by a member of the basilica community who operated it, when she was there with a group of Canadian priests. The man interrupted their Mass, pointed at the women involved, who were all nuns, and told them to get out of the chancel as women were not allowed in that part of the sanctuary! The group of Canadian priests then rose, and they all walked out together, shocked by this display. I also visited the strange old cave that was now the Orthodox Church of the Assumption, the site of the supposed tomb of Mary. There were literally hundreds of sanctuary lamps in there, and the antiquity of it was very impressive, but like so many traditional sites in Jerusalem, it seemed very shabby—really very tawdry. The condition of many of the holy sites in Jerusalem was shocking to pilgrims, but we found it helpful to bear in mind that there was a greater significance in what was being revealed at these places. The physical memorializing of an event was not always successful. I reflected that it was how the event was memorialized spiritually that really counted.

Adjacent to this church was another part of the Garden of Gethsemane associated with the night of Jesus' arrest. That site had a good foundation in tradition, since it was identified in 333 by the anonymous traveler called the Pilgrim of Bordeaux. The word *gethsemane* comes from the Hebrew words *Gat Shemanim*, an olive oil press. In attendance within the grotto was a Franciscan friar, who very quietly and politely remained in the background and advised us that it was fine to take photos, or to remain in the chapel for some time if we desired, and he otherwise left us alone to read, contemplate, or pray. On our way back we went into the Kidron Valley to take a closer look at the old tombs. The first one, the free-standing structure with the pointed roof, was locally called Absalom's Pillar. Tradition named it as the tomb of Absalom and Jehosephat, although it was certainly constructed very much later. Some Jews of the Old City, still outraged by Absalom's rebellion against his father King David, used to throw stones at the old tomb to display their indignation. The other tombs are the B'nai Hezir, who were the family of the sons of St. James, and the tomb of Zechariah—another Zechariah tomb, but this one dated to the first century B.C.E., quite a bit older than the other Byzantine one where the landlady served the tea and coffee. The Kidron Valley tombs were very decrepit and sad, but a new road was being built through there, and when I returned a few years later, it had become a tidy, splendid route through the valley.

The cobblestone walkway outside the Zion Gate was the usual venue for "King David," the brilliant and beautifully dressed street busker with the harp. He was a hale and handsome bearded man, wearing a gold crown and a long green satin garment painted with beautiful lion heads. He later confided that he had made the costume himself, and painted the beautiful lion faces down the front of it. As we passed by him, he noticed that Jenny was wearing a sweatshirt with "Australia" emblazoned across the front of it, and to our delight he began playing *Waltzing Matilda*. It was a strange number for King David, very different in style from the rest of his Psalms, but we learned the reason for this: he was from Brisbane. He and his family had come to Israel from Australia, and in fact his son was now in the army. We took our leave of the "king" and went to see King David's Tomb, another strange old monument inside a crusader building.

When we saw that the tomb was covered with a green cloth embroidered with a gold harp, altogether more Irish than Jewish in appearance, I thought for one crazy moment of that theatrical "king" outside: green cloth, gold harp—it all seemed a bit Irish. Well, of course the historical King David had not been Irish, but our dramatic looking King David the street musician surely piqued our interest in things davidian. King David's tomb was near the "Last Supper Room" that we had previously visited, which was itself adjacent to the beautiful Dormition Abbey. We went quietly into the church where a group was just beginning their Mass and singing the lovely Taizé chant of *Veni Sancti Spiritu*. Everywhere that we witnessed visiting groups singing and praying, it was impossible not to notice the deep joy that these pilgrims were experiencing, singing and praying in the Holy Land.

We grabbed a falafel on the way back and ate it at the convent before heading out to visit my old friend Ben Lubelski on Zionist Street. I had met Ben in Britain while touring with my family some years earlier. It took a long time to navigate to his apartment by bus, and I even had to make use of my now rusty Biblical Hebrew in order to read the street sign. Ben was very pleased to see us and fussed making tea and biscuits. He said he was used to having visitors as he was connected with a society that took people to the homes of local Israelis to see how they lived. Finally, after all this kitchen fussing, Ben began to talk. There was no need for us to make conversation; he did it all. He read us excerpts from his three published works, and proudly flashed about the rave reviews as well. He also told us how he had survived the concentration camp during the Shoah, when he lived in France, through the good fortune of having been transferred with the other intellectual activists and communists to Algeria, which was sufficiently out of the way that they were able to survive. All his compatriots who remained imprisoned in France proper were eventually transferred to the death camps and killed. After 1967, Ben and his wife Judith moved to Jerusalem. One of their two sons was killed in the struggle for the Golan Heights in 1973, and now that Judith also had died, and Ben's remaining son was working in Japan, Ben was on his own and really valued having visitors. He was enjoying his present career as a writer, and showed me the room where I would stay when I came to Jerusalem to write my book! Alas, it was not to be, as I did not see him again, and he passed away shortly before my next return to the country.

After the visit we tried to get back to the Old City, but went a bit too far on the bus, and a local busybody, the colourful but woeful type of old lady with the turned down stockings and frizzy hair, told us to get off the bus and she would tell us how to proceed. She put all her many bags onto the sidewalk around her and started to tell us how to get back to the Old City. It did not get far. Every time she asked us where we wanted to be, and we told her the Old City, she just said "Oh, my God! Oh, my God!" and occasionally "Why do you want to go there?" A man at the bus stop was becoming completely exasperated with these antics, and kept saying to her "Just tell them!" Or occasionally "That's none of your business! Just tell them where it is!" Finally we realized, no thanks to the lady's unhelpful guiding services, that we were near the King David Hotel, a landmark known to us, and near enough to the Old City that we could actually walk home—and this we did.

I woke up in the morning feeling that my system was out of sorts, due to travel and inappropriate diet, and I really needed (1) more protein, and (2) no sugar. In the circumstances, however, this was just too hard to accomplish. Jenny and I set out for the Nablus Road, first stopping at the Post Office to cash some travellers' cheques. The East Jerusalem Post Office was near the Garden Tomb, so it was convenient for me to go in and see that whole site, and to reflect on it some more. The Anglican cathedral of St. George, with its college and guesthouse, was also in this district. The cathedral and its grounds were very lovely, very English, very tidy compared to the surroundings, and had an air of aloofness. The college offered study programs for visitors. Near St. George's was a place called the Tomb of the Kings—nothing to do with any kings but rather a Persian noble-woman had had these catacombs built. The tombs were carved into a rock face and the opening faced into an excavated area. The site was in quite disgusting condition, but if tidied up it could have been made into a lovely garden, much more inviting to visitors. Disappointed, we trekked back into the Old City and to the Jewish Quarter where Jenny could buy coins from a specialty antique dealer.

That afternoon Jenny went out to follow the Stations of the Cross with the Franciscans from next door, and I decided to attend Mass within the Ecce Homo church downstairs. It was a simple but lovely liturgy in the nineteenth century basilica. The assembly consisted of the community of sisters, the residents and guests, and as far as I knew it was all very inclusive, although due to the acoustics in the basilica it was impossible to understand anything the presider said in his heavily accented South African English.

My homemade picnic dinner was interrupted millions of times by negotiations over the telephone with Betty, one of my dear Romanian ladies in Haifa, and Samer, the brilliant and flamboyant Ecce Homo male receptionist. Finally Samer re-organized my life such that I was to leave Ecce Homo a day early to go to Haifa the next morning, all necessitated by the problem of no transport on *Shabbat*, and no one home Sunday as the Haifa ladies worked that day.

One bonus of staying at Ecce Homo was the site of pilgrimage, the Lithostrotos, right in the house. This was formerly reputed to be part of the Antonia Fortress where Pilate lived, and where Jesus possibly was condemned, although in recent years the wisdom had become that these were the Antonia's paving stones, but they probably had been moved around during Emperor Hadrian's rebuilding of Jerusalem. On the pavement below the house was a very good example of the Game of the King played by the Roman soldiers. The soldiers would play these board games so frequently that they would actually etch the game onto the paving stones. In the Game of King, they would select a condemned prisoner, dress him up as a king, and torment him while throwing the dice and following the action of the game that always ended in the death of the prisoner. It was thought that this game was in the background of the accounts of Jesus' Crowning of Thorns in the New Testament (Matthew 27:27-31; Mark 15:16-20; John 19:1-7). As the Lithostrotos, or "stone pavement," was part of the Way of the Cross, millions of pilgrims had come through here. But tonight, after the Lithostrotos was closed and everyone gone, we went down to the ruins and had the whole thing to ourselves. It was a profound privilege.

Two of the people living at Ecce Homo were a Canadian woman volunteering on a three-month stint, and Pat, an Irish woman who was an associate of the Sisters of Sion working there on a three-year assignment. They were sitting out on the rooftop terrace enjoying the evening and the view, and it was from them that I learned about the possibility of volunteering at Ecce Homo. In those moments of sitting out on the terrace, I knew I wanted to come back and stay longer. I looked out from the terrace across the roofs of the Old City. The convent was very near the Dome of the Rock, which dominated the horizon at night, illuminated and glowing in gold. From our table on the terrace, the Dome seemed close enough to touch. The Mount of Olives was visible beyond, offering a different history and a different witness of God's redemptive work.

The next day was Saturday. After a hearty breakfast, I packed my bags and said my goodbyes. I obtained an application form from Sister Anne to become a volunteer at the convent for a three-month period, and told her I would think prayerfully about that. For many of us working full-time in the world, it would be difficult to imagine dropping out and allowing ourselves to go away for a long time. How could I leave my family or my career for that time? It seemed an impossibly bold suggestion.

Samer had my journey all arranged. I was to take three *sherutim* to get to Carmel, plus the taxi to get me to the sherut in the first place. He had instructed me what to pay for each leg of the journey, and warned me not to pay more. After all these cautions, I was terrified to get into the taxi outside the convent as I had no idea where my Arab driver would take me or what he would charge me. I got into the taxi with all my baggage and sat very quietly in the backseat, afraid to speak. After we were out in the main road, I could not stand the silence, and said to the driver, "So you know Samer?" The driver laughed out loud, and then I laughed, too. Samer was a colourful, effusive and apparently well-known character in the Old City, and the mere mention of him broke the ice. The friendly taxi driver dropped me off at the place near Jaffa Road where I was to get the sherut. After several minutes, I realized I was in the wrong place and should actually be standing around the corner. I moved all my baggage around there, and presently my cab driver came by to check on me. He said he had later thought he left me in the wrong place so he came back to see if I was all right. The local Palestinian people were often very kind like that. It was most heart-warming to see this kindness in action; the daily lives of these folks were very hard and very competitive.

When I arrived at Rehov Maian in Carmel, a suburb of Haifa, I went into the only place that was open, an old folks' home, and the young lady attendant telephoned the ladies whom I was there to visit. Although the girl could understand no English or French, we managed to communicate, and presently my friend Dorina appeared. She started talking to the young lady, and it turned out that the girl, like the ladies, was Romanian.

My three ladies were well into their seventies, and all three were still working. None of them had any intention of retiring, and they expressed their gratitude that they could still work. Dorina's shop selling purses and satchels was next door to Razila's toyshop. Betty ran a news and confectionary kiosk in a nearby park. None of the three ladies spoke English, but they spoke French in various degrees: Betty the best, Razila fairly well, and Dorina not at all. It was another time when it was good to be Canadian.

A nephew of the ladies, Dan, arrived in his car to take Razila and me on a tour of Haifa: the beautiful Stella Maris monastery, the panorama view of the beautiful city and the harbour. In the evening we attended the sixth birthday of a little grandnephew in his family's beautiful new town house. All the extended family was present, and there was a simple but very nice buffet dinner, with the typical Middle Eastern snacks of chicken, eggplant dip, humus, and chips. Everyone was speaking Hebrew, so I could not follow the conversation, but the niece and her husband spoke English to me, although their two little boys could only speak Hebrew. Many of the relatives also spoke Romanian, and the niece's husband referred to the assembly of old ladies as the Romanian Mafia. The new townhouse was lovely, but housing in this area was scandalously expensive, and the three old aunties speculated that the couple may have spent as much as a million U.S. dollars for this house. Later, back at Dorina's flat, I went with Razila and Dorina to walk their dogs around the neighbourhood, and they talked about Romania. Although they all loved Romania and spent a month out of every year in Bucharest, they also deeply loved Israel and were thrilled to be able to live there.

This was my last day in Israel. My flight for Amsterdam was to leave in the wee hours. I spent most of the day with Razila, and visited both her toyshop and Dorina's satchel shop. They told me that business had been very bad, but no matter: they were glad to be working. Razila's husband tended her shop while she took me on the bus to show me the town. The highlight of the day was the Bahai centre, a beautiful domed shrine with perfectly trimmed and extraordinary gardens. From the Bahai centre you can see the entire seaport of Haifa. The ladies were all proud of the city; they loved it there and would never move, not even to their beloved family home in Bucharest.

That evening we had dinner and Dorina packed my bag for me. Betty said, "You are not going to pack your bag; Dora will pack your bag. Dora is an expert!"

I looked at Dorina, who was standing defiantly with her arms folded over her chest, daring me to protest. Her hair was wild—she looked absolutely ferocious, so there was no arguing with her. She packed my bag and locked it with a miniature padlock.

Razila had arranged for a taxi to take me to the airport sherut, and she had paid for it in advance on her credit card, so there was no arguing with this either; it was part and parcel of Middle Eastern hospitality. I left the house at around nine in the evening, and the flight was to leave at three a.m., so I was very early. Because of this, and because I was travelling alone, I attracted the attention of airport security. I received a very thorough going-over by one young lady, then another, then a third. I patiently answered all their questions and showed them the receipts for everything I had bought or done, and responded from my diary. My bags were completely unpacked, and there was stuff all over the counter. I was reading aloud to them from my notes, and showing them every sales slip. There was one slightly tense moment when the security lady asked me, quite predictably, "Is this your bag? Did you pack it yourself? Are you aware of its contents?"

I have been a Customs Officer all my adult life, and I should have predicted this question. Instead, I must have looked horrified, and thought to myself, "Oh, no! Dora packed my bag!" And indeed it contained small, harmless items of which I was unaware: toiletries and various little gifts that she had included for my mother. I said that no, my 76-year-old auntie from Haifa had packed the bag, but that she was fiercely pro-Israel and would attempt no sabotage! Alas! I was doomed to endure another thorough interrogation. In the end, the security women had me so paranoid I was afraid to get on the plane, and I told them so. I said that I was convinced the plane would blow up and I had changed my mind, I didn't want to board. They were a bit more reassuring after this, and said that no ma'am, the plane would not blow up, but that Israel was simply a country with a lot of problems. Please go ahead and board.

It was late November when I arrived home. Throughout the following months there was a lot of upheaval in my life, inside and out. Externally, I was simplifying by moving into communal living, and it was time for my only child, an adult daughter, to move out on her own. Within me, there was some kind of change taking place, and I knew it had something to do with the journey into the landscape of the Bible. I could not have adequately stated what this meant, but there were a few clues. I was unusually inarticulate about how the experience of the Holy Land had affected me. Once, when my friend, an Anglican priest, asked me if I had felt closer to Jesus while in Jerusalem, I was at a loss what to say. I replied, "Not in Jerusalem—it's too much, too intense. But in Galilee, yes; you can feel closer to Jesus there." Yet at some level I did not really mean it. I had no language to describe how I felt, if I knew myself how I felt. It was as if I were inwardly protecting myself from the intensity of the experience of walking in the places where events from the Bible happened, and I was not allowing myself to encounter it in my depths. I had had such a short sojourn in the Holy Land, and I knew there was more to it that I wanted to explore. This feeling that my journey was incomplete spilled out into everything I did. It urgently called me to return. It was not finished. I needed to go back.

Small medicinal pools in the ruins of the Pool of Bethesda, now on the grounds of St. Anne's Church.

View from the roof of Ecce Homo Convent

Excavations of Herod's palace within the Citadel.

Police vehicles at the Western Wall, Jerusalem.

PART II

5

Nativity, a New Life

During my year of waiting to return to the Holy Land, this time as a convent volunteer, the Israeli-Palestinian situation began to show unrest. There had been a period of relative calm since the signing of the Oslo accord in 1993, but the delays in sorting out a final status to this agreement were beginning to produce a reaction. A couple of serious bombings in Israeli shopping districts in Jerusalem made me wonder if my proposed journey were wise. I phoned the convent and Sister Anne answered.

"Are you still expecting me? Is it a good idea to come?" I thought my voice must have sounded high, tense. Anne, on the other hand, sounded very gentle, very English, and she had a soft, angelic voice.

"Oh, Bonnie," she said. "Yes, I'm so looking forward to your coming. You won't recognize the convent. We've remodelled the whole reception area, and it's very beautiful."

In my imagination, bombs were dropping all around the convent. So what was the matter with this woman? Didn't she know there was a war right outside her door? It seemed rather moot to be talking about redecorating the hallway!

"Hello!" I began again, even more urgently. "Are you all right? Isn't there a war over there?"

There was a slight pause, and then her gentle voice was almost ethereal in its assurance.

"Oh, yes, there have been a few incidents," she said, "but there is also a lot of peacemaking going on, too. You probably don't hear about that. I hope you are still coming."

No question about it. A little more than a year after my first departure from Israel, I set out once again for Jerusalem, on the day after Boxing Day. After a long wait in Amsterdam, I approached my airport departure gate and was surprised to see an Israeli soldier toting a huge gun and walking up and down in front of the seating area. About eight security stations were open for business. I was a little stunned, but I am from a busy film-making city, and I naively wondered if they might be making a movie.

"What's going on?" I asked the soldier, and I am sure I sounded confused.

"Are you going to Tel Aviv?" he replied.

"Aha!" I thought. "Now I get it!"

Security in the Tel Aviv airport was also intense when I finally arrived there. I was sent to secondary security, and even questioned by the police as I exited the terminal. By now it was close to 2 a.m. of the second day following my departure. I went to the taxi stand and had a thoroughly unsatisfactory conversation with the driver of the sherut. Once I told him that I was going into the Old City, he did not want to discuss it further, but wanted to drop me at the Jaffa Gate or the Damascus Gate—at 3 a.m. with a pile of baggage! After an exasperating dialogue he left me at an East Jerusalem hotel that I knew of and from where I could phone Ecce Homo. The hotel was closed up and appeared deserted, but I pounded on the door repeatedly until the rather alarmed Palestinian night porter, who was obviously expecting no guests, staggered forward, pulling on his trousers. I explained my plight and he very kindly invited me in, called an Arab taxi for me and waited until I was safely on my way.

The Via Dolorosa was deserted except for my taxi driver and me. Ecce Homo at three in the morning seemed an impregnable fortress of the nineteenth century, and my anxiety level may have been a bit high. The taxi driver patiently waited to ensure I was safe while I pounded on the thick door and rang the bell until Fakhri, the night guard, finally opened the heavy old door and looked at me sleepily. What kindly and cordial treatment I have had from many Palestinians in Jerusalem! At the time of my arrival, I had been hearing only the worst possible things in the media, really only the activities of a few extremists, and we never heard news of the kindness and hospitality of the Palestinian people. I reflected that if people abroad had only ever heard about the violent events in our Canadian and American cities, they might never come and visit us. Now, at last, I was inside the house that in the months that followed would permanently capture both my imagination and my heart.

On my first evening I attended Mass in the Ecce Homo basilica attached to the house, where a Canadian priest named Jim B presided at an inclusive and friendly service. Sharing this Eucharist with others in the house grounded me and gathered me in, and I felt more at home. There were two Jims in the house; the other was a layperson, a Canadian volunteer, and the next morning I went into Agron Street in West Jerusalem with him. We were to meet Sister Rita to take her passport to her so she could meet the Prime Minister that afternoon in connection with her community work. While on this outing I perused the supermarket to see what vegetarian groceries were available. Since kosher regulations are fairly normative in Israel, there were many soy and other vegetarian choices, but I found the items to be very expensive.

Throughout that week I learned the volunteer jobs, which consisted of working at the reception desk, preparing the breakfast buffet for the guesthouse visitors, and performing one outdoor job per week, such as washing the church steps or sweeping out the garden terrace. In exchange for these duties, the volunteers received free room and board in a spacious flat within the convent, plus we received a small spending allowance. We were three volunteers in the house, all Canadians; besides Jim and me, there was Melanie, an attractive blonde in her thirties, with whom I shared the volunteers' flat.

The Ecce Homo convent is a very complex building, begun, raised, added onto over and over, and actually spanning some of the little streets by way of bridges at the upper levels. The upper terraces overlook the Via Dolorosa, which the house faces, and from up there we could see the constant processions of pilgrims trudging up the street, many bearing crosses, retracing the steps tradition says were taken by Jesus on the day of his execution. From the terraces we could also hear the sounds of hymns sung in every language. The dome of the Ecce Homo basilica, attached to the house, dominates the terraces, and on the rear side of the terrace we could look down on some of the inner courtyards and gardens also forming part of the house. We referred to the six Sisters and one Associate who ran the house as the Community. Of those, two were French-speaking, one spoke Portuguese, and the rest spoke English: it was a tower of Babel. There were also we three volunteers; twenty-four anglophone students who were all clergy and religious on sabbatical; about thirty Palestinian employees who spoke Arabic, English, and some French; and a fluctuating number of guests. The Biblical school also included around fifty additional students who lived off-site, and half of those were French-speaking. The Biblical program itself was available in French or English. The convent incorporated the guesthouse with its rooms, dormitories and youth hostel; the community's flat, which was called St. Mary's; the "old community," meaning the rooms for the francophone sisters; and the basilica. The place was huge.

On the day of New Year's Eve I had almost recovered from the terrible jet lag, so I tidied the flat, and Issa got my little stove and kettle going for me. Issa is Fakhri's son, and to describe this family's relationship and importance to the Sisters of Sion, and the responsibilities that they took on at Ecce Homo, would be difficult indeed. They were like family to the sisters, and were vital to the running of the house. I made my own dinner, one of my soy cutlets from the Supersol, fried crispy, and it was delicious. After the regular six o'clock evening Mass there was a festive New Year's dinner, followed by an hour of prayer for the New Year. The salon, a large room with deep cushioned seats, was decorated with a few potted plants and a table covered with an antique cloth. Anne, the sister who had made it possible for me to be there, led the prayer. It was a candle-lighting liturgy in which everyone had an opportunity to state something for which we were thankful in the past year, and to say a prayer for the coming year. Something for which I was thankful! Here I was, living the dream of being in Jerusalem, living in the house of the Crowning of Thorns, and surrounded by so much that is holy. Indeed, I had a great deal for which to give thanks.

The students' New Year's Eve party was held in the student coffee room, a large and comfortable lounge. The students hosted the party, and the volunteers and religious community were invited. We had to wear a silly hat to get in, so various expressions of what could be done with table napkins, greeting cards and ribbon were perched on people's heads. I was desperate; I had nothing with me that I could use to make a hat and I was not really settled in enough to know where to find materials, so in the end I wore an inverted plastic planter decorated with a rose made from a dish cloth and held on by clothes pins. A chiffon scarf kept the hat in place. It was hard to balance my chapeau, but I received a lot of compliments on the thing. There were party songs and Irish coffee; an African sister did a traditional dance of her culture, and everyone had a grand time. After the students' party, the entire household went outside, where the Old City of Jerusalem was spread out all around us, and church bells bonged out the New Year. Then the volunteers plus Anne and Pat, the same Irish woman who had been there during my first trip, came to our flat to celebrate further. After Pat managed to cut her finger on a kitchen knife some time after three in the morning, we decided it was time to turn in.

New Year's Day was a day off for us, so the staff ran the convent while the volunteers lolled around. I wrote a lot of letters in the morning, and in the afternoon we watched video movies in St. Mary's until late at night. Then I wandered out into the garden and got lost. I opened all kinds of upper story doors that led to other locked doors, and all the doors at the garden level seemed to be locked. I even checked out the rooftop solar hot-water system—God knows how I got up there—and I stood on the roof trying to figure out where I was. Lost again! I can even manage to get lost within one house! After a few minutes of slight panic, I eventually found my way back to the main terrace by way of the one and only unlocked door on the garden level.

Soon after I arrived, the month of Ramadan began. Faithful Muslims would fast during the day, and eat or drink only after sundown. It was fortunate this year that Ramadan fell during the shortest days of winter. The month of fasting falls according to a revolving lunar calendar, and sometimes it falls during the hotter weather, when it is especially difficult for workers to get through the workday without so much as a drink of water. As it was, our Palestinian neighbours would eat and drink only after sundown, and would get up at intervals during the night for further meals, roused from their slumbers by a boy with a drum who paraded through the streets to wake people up for their meal. One night the other volunteers and I waited up to see the boy herald pounding his way through the little streets of the Old City, expecting to see a picturesque little drummer or some other romantic scene. Instead what we saw was a young lad pounding a stick against a very large, empty plastic bottle, such as might be used to package liquids for restaurants. The window of my bedroom was immediately above the kitchen court of the neighbours below, and it acted as a funnel for noises and smells. As I had not eaten meat in twenty years, the strong smell of the all-night cooking of lamb and mutton was quite sickening to me, and closing my window did not help much.

Fridays during Ramadan were the times for the special prayers in the mosques, and thousands upon thousands of people crowded into the Al-Aqsa Mosque on the Haram es-Sharif, the old Temple Mount. We could hear the prayers from our terrace, and when prayers ended the worshippers poured into the streets and tried to go home. For hours afterward the streets were congested and it was impossible to go anywhere. By the end of the month, our fasting staff members were starting to be worn down and tired, although they never complained; in fact, some of the women were delighted with how much weight they were able to shed during Ramadan! At the end of the month of fasting there were three days of feasting and celebrating, the Eid al-Fitr, when everyone was decked out in fine new clothes.

But that came later. Now it was January 2, just the first Friday of Ramadan, and thousands of people poured out of the mosque into the streets of the Old City. The great crush of humanity made it very difficult to move around in the streets. There was immense security at the Western Wall, and at the Dome of the Rock we could see a sea of white scarves of the women outside the Al Aqsa mosque, and if we stood on our terrace we could hear the sermon from the mosque, although it was in Arabic and we could not understand it. Things were quiet at the house, so Melanie and I, together with one of the students, a nun from Australia, took the opportunity to do the Ramparts Walk on top of the Old

City walls. Later that afternoon I had a lesson on the important volunteer duty of washing down the basilica steps and sweeping up the bird droppings around the basilica dome. After this busy day I tried to join Sister Anne's guided tour of the Lithostrotos that she was presenting for a college group from Minnesota, but I was still somewhat jet-lagged and tired; I kept falling asleep and had to slip out of the tour to go to bed early.

On Saturday, I bought a bread ring and walked up the Mount of Olives with Jim. It was a bit of a hike and pretty tiring as it is so steep, but the postcard view of the Old City of Jerusalem never failed to deliver that thrill, that jolt of incredulity that I was actually there. I loved this scene from the Mount of Olives, and Jim was so fond of this particular walk that he did it every day. Although the view of the olive gardens was obstructed at the lower levels of the hill by the walls of private gardens belonging to churches, farther up we could see plenty of olive groves, just as there had been in ancient times. A bit farther south of the road are the thousands of tombs of faithful dead awaiting the final trumpet. In the afternoon I sat with Jim in the Lithostrotos reception, welcoming pilgrims to the stone pavement of Jesus' crowning of thorns.

On Saturday evenings at Ecce Homo, the Sunday Liturgy was celebrated, usually presided by someone from outside the house, and afterwards the volunteers and the visiting priest all had dinner in the community's suite, St. Mary's. The first guest presider of the New Year was Stéphane, a young and very funny White Father, a Missionary of Africa, originally from France but more recently from St. Anne's Basilica down the street. Stéphane joined us for dinner, as did the young guest Oscar. Oscar was a young American fellow whose parents were in diplomatic service, so he had actually spent very little time in the United States. Oscar was contemplating attending seminary in St. Paul, Minnesota, so everyone was teasing him about the cruel arctic weather, bears, wolves and other wild animals said to be the hazards of Minnesota. Jim and Stéphane were particularly outrageous in their descriptions of the ice, snow and savagery poor Oscar would encounter. I think he believed them.

Sunday was a day off for Christians at Ecce Homo. Most residents either went on excursions or to special Masses, and Muslim employees, whose holy day was Friday, performed the jobs. Sometimes I would sweep and wash the floors of the flat, fix up the kitchen, and make myself a hearty soup that I dipped into throughout the day. As the cuisine in the dining-room was very European and favoured meat and dairy dishes, I always had to have a vegan meal strategy.

That first Sunday of the New Year, I went for a walk with Anne through the Jewish Quarter and parts of the souq, or bazaar. Whereas on Friday there had been thousands of people in front of the Western Wall including about 50 army and police vehicles, today it was quiet and there were few people about. We went into the Holy Sepulchre church and lit candles, and we talked about the weird decorating within that old church. The traditions of the Holy Sepulchre represented a form of piety that was strange to us; it was an oriental church, and we were westerners. We talked about a new role for Mary in our lives, too—the mother of Jesus who has been so burdened by past traditions in art that we often lose sight of her humanity and nearness to us. I longed for Mary to be more human, motherly, and approachable.

I read in the late afternoon and listened to all the church bells of Jerusalem bonging out their joy, and I took delight in the scene from the terrace, including the golden Dome of the Rock picturesquely illuminated so near to us. After supper the community and volunteers gathered in St. Mary's to watch a television retrospective about Princess Diana. The availability of international news was fairly good as there were CNN, BBC and TV5, the international broadcast from France, but it was difficult to hear news of Canada. Meanwhile, my learning curve was flattening out, as by now I could make the guesthouse breakfast by myself. We had the group from St. Olaf's in Minnesota, plus the twenty-four resident students and the community, which meant a total of eighty-seven people at breakfast—a typical number for us to expect for breakfast. Days like this, then, were the pattern of our lives.

The next day was my first experience of the moneychanger. I had been very nervous about going to the moneychanger as I was afraid that I would be taken advantage of, or perhaps robbed on the way out. I had worried for nothing. The people who ran these businesses were our neighbours, and it was a very competitive business, all above board. I managed to change $100 at Victoria Money Changers at the Damascus Gate. What was more hazardous by far was my lack of familiarity with the streets, and after visiting the shops and winding far out of my way around the little warrens of the Old City, I made my life easier by buying a map for a few shekels.

As our house was part of an important shrine and incorporated a church, the Ecce Homo Basilica, worship was an important component of our week. The students in the Biblical program at Ecce Homo were people normally in ministry but now on sabbatical, and most of the men in the class were Catholic priests. While it was usually someone from outside who presided at the Sunday liturgy, the priests who lived in our house took turns saying the daily Mass; they planned their liturgies on teams, and music was provided either by Anne on her guitar or flute, or else one of the students would play the organ or piano. If the church itself was too cold, which often happened during the winter, we moved to a salon that could be heated.

We in the pews received a great variety of presiding and preaching styles. One evening early in the year, the presider was a Jesuit professor from Japan whose English was very difficult to understand. He anticipated this, and to get around it he made his message very accessible by adding some drama: turning out the lights, having verses of scripture read that talked about the coming of the light, and had each of his assistants carry in larger and larger candles. Another evening, one of the students preached a hilarious homily on being able to discern the signs of the times, and recounted how God had had to spare his life many times. He had literally knocked himself out—falling out of the car, out of a tree and so on—but he felt God had saved him from injury and death so that he could become a priest. That same evening in the reception area of the convent, some of the young convent employees were also discerning. They were engaged in a quiz as part of a Bible competition, and they had some really obscure questions. How many people did Jesus raise from the dead? (I make it three: Jairus' daughter, the son of the widow of Nain, and Lazarus). What does Bethphage mean? (house of figs). What does Emmaus mean? (warm wells). What was the name of the man whose ear was cut off on the night of Jesus' arrest? (Malchus). These were really hard questions!

Some of the students played board games in the evening, and once, after dinner, there was a slide show of the various class outings. Generally, though, evenings were quiet, and the streets were possibly not as safe as I was accustomed to, so there were very few late evening strolls outside the convent walls. Whereas at home I tended to stay up late, I got into a much healthier sleep rhythm while in the Old City. Even while Oscar was in the house, and we enjoyed late evening theological debates in the library, I still managed to get to bed before eleven. The house was very cold as there was no central heating, and I used my down sleeping bag throughout the winter, even with the radiator on.

Iskander, the maintenance man, insisted that he had fixed the shower, but I still felt as though I got a shock from it every time I touched the metal knob—not a real jolt, but a mild sensation of shock, especially in the area of any cut or irregularity on my hands. It turned out that a wire was touching some of the plumbing somewhere within the building. I had never heard of this problem in North America, but it seemed fairly usual over there and provided the basis of a number of in-house comedy skits on the electrified shower of the volunteers' flat. I stopped using it and started going to the other side of the house for a bath. Besides the bathroom with electrified shower, my spacious flat that I shared with

Melanie contained a washing machine, an outdoor terrace with a clothesline, a living room and a large kitchen. There was also a picturesque closet in the hall, with a door made from an old confessional door. We joked that it was our private confessional, but when we opened the door to look inside the closet, it contained an ironing board, some old Christmas decorations, and a case of toilet paper. This was recycling of the most offbeat kind, and it created a peculiar flavour of antique churchiness in an atmosphere of modern pragmatism.

My bedroom was the larger of the two as it had once contained two beds but now only contained one, plus a large double armoire and a couple of night stands. Iskander brought me a table and chair that I could use as a study desk, and I managed to obtain a tablecloth to go on it. The effect was quite homey, and the only drawback to the room was that it was very noisy. The principal noise pollution came from the neighbour, who hollered abusively at his wife and son, and had visitors pounding on the metal door at all hours of the night. I did not want to know what business brought them to the door so late. Another thing that kept me awake was the call to prayer, broadcast over a loudspeaker from the minaret across the street, and it was very, very loud. This was, however, a part of the culture that had existed long before I arrived in the Old City, so I accepted my lot and wore earplugs to bed every night that I was there.

One morning I was sitting at the Lithostrotos reception desk with Anne when, by excellent coincidence, Rachel, my guide from the previous year's tours, came in with some Anglicans who were getting ready to host a pilgrim group. Rachel and I exchanged numbers, and I took her pilgrim leaders up to the roof to enjoy the wonderful view of the Dome of the Rock and the Old City rooftops. Unfortunately, when they inquired at Sister Marie-Lise's guesthouse office, they discovered that there would be no room at the inn for the period they sought. Disappointed, they went to our patio for a coffee break. We would not be having Rachel staying with us, but this interlude at least gave me the opportunity to reconnect with her.

At least once a week we had an after-hours evening tour in the Lithostrotos. People come from all around the world to Ecce Homo because it is believed to be connected with Jesus' crowning of thorns and condemnation; thus, for Christians it is a very holy place. The actual historical location of the Crowning of Thorns is still debated, and it is acknowledged that the Herodian palace, where the citadel is now, has a better claim to being the actual place of Jesus' trial than does the Lithostrotos. This knowledge may be very important to historians and archaeologists, but it is of little consequence to faithful pilgrims. They want to have an experience of the passion of Jesus, and maybe also to walk where Jesus walked.

Down in the Lithostrotos, and beside the smooth pavement, are striated paving stones that had been part of a Roman period public road. As it is very likely that Jesus used the public road at some time, these striated stones are good candidates for stones on which the historical Jesus actually trod. In any case, what is now the Lithostrotos is the place that Christian pilgrims have revered and prayed over as the place of the crowning of thorns for many centuries, and that in itself makes it a holy place.

Most of the time, the receptionist in the Lithostrotos was the learned, and still very studious, Sister Isabelle-Marie, a French Sister of Sion who had formerly been in charge of a girls' school in Turkey. At the end of her long teaching career, she had continued to work in the ministry to pilgrims at Ecce Homo and was very happy still to be able to work. Impatient and opinionated on the outside, she was kind and appreciative on the inside. To compensate for her limited spoken English she illustrated her conversations with large, grand gestures that gained for her the reputation of being dramatic. One morning after breakfast, I heard the news that Sister Isabelle-Marie had had an accident the evening before—she had been visiting other sisters of the congregation at another house, and had tripped on the stairs and broken her arm. This injury was not good news; the woman was in her seventies, which meant that the healing of broken bones could be difficult. This necessitated that the volunteers and Anne would do extra "Lithos" shifts while Isabelle convalesced. On that first day, for example, I did receptionist duties in the convent in the late morning, then in the Lithostrotos in the afternoon. It was a good thing that we had been trained to take this over; we did not want Isabelle-Marie to be worrying about missing work, nor did we want her returning to duties before she was ready.

I spent the entire next morning sweeping the enclosed garden area and hosing it down. Our life in Jerusalem consisted of the performance of such ordinary household tasks in an attitude of service to one another, all against a completely extraordinary background. Serendipitous meetings occurred on a regular basis, as when I met, while sweeping the garden, a nun from Korea who had lived four blocks from me in my own neighbourhood half a world away, but whom I had never met in that more ordinary life back home.

Throughout my time at Ecce Homo I often sat at my makeshift desk in my room and wrote letters to people back home and elsewhere. Waiting for the post was one of the great activities of the day, and we soon learned that in order to receive mail we had to send some. The convent had e-mail, but it was for use of the guesthouse and community; others could receive e-mail, but we had to find some other way to respond, and at that time internet cafés were just catching on in the country. Letters sent by regular post took at least two weeks to arrive from either direction. We did feel rather cut off from our homes and from the rest of the world. Given this limitation, it was just a bit alarming when I received an e-mail from my young adult daughter telling me her phone had been cut off, and that my cat, whom she was babysitting, seemed depressed. This was not good news. For one thing, if I could not phone her, it would be at least two weeks each time before any communication from me would arrive. More importantly, this message was a strong clue that it was my daughter, and not the cat, who was depressed. Apart from remaining in touch with her father, who took action on the matter immediately, I tried not to worry too much about this, as there was very little I could do from such a distance. I had to go about the rhythm of life and trust that the matter was in God's hands.

In early January the Baptism of Jesus is celebrated. That Sunday, I was chosen to lead the procession in our basilica, carrying the huge paschal candle, and Pat came behind me with a jug of water, then came the presider, Father Frank, the Australian. After Frank blessed the water, Pat and I splashed the people in the pews to remind them of their baptism. At the Gospel procession, our dancer, Adelina, picked up the Bible from the aisle, and held it high while dancing up to the chancel, African-style, while everyone sang Alleluiah, and Frank received the Bible from her hand and read us the Baptism story. Anne had spent the entire day preparing for this liturgy, and even composed a little antiphon to be sung during the psalm.

Worship like this was wonderful: it was created in-house; it deepened our spirituality; it deepened our understanding of our faith. In celebrating Jesus' baptism in the Jordan River, not so very far away from us, we were brought up close to the Biblical event, and to the special meaning of our own baptism. Now often treated as a photo opportunity by the proud parents of little baptismal candidates, baptism is actually a momentous occasion for Christians: the initiation into the Christian faith community, including the undertaking of vows. I sat surrounded by other faithful and contemplated what this meant. Baptism is an enormous promise, and the baptismal vows are no less important in a Christian's life than the marriage vows. If taken seriously, these vows can be very challenging: the task is no less than to do the work of Christ in the world, and to treat everyone else as if they were Christ, particularly those who are rejected, marginalized or in need in any way. Some of these people are very different, very hard to love. To be a true Christian, then, is not just a feel-good thing; it is a very, very difficult task, and we all thought very seriously about that task as we celebrated the Baptism of Jesus.

By the following Sunday, it was the seventeenth of January and we were entering what is known in the church as "Ordinary Time." Ordinary in this context means that Christmas and Epiphany are over and it is the time of year when worship remains the same day after day, from the Ordinal, the daily prayer book. The feasts are over, and daily and weekly Mass goes back to an ordinary pattern. Of course, it is also a play on words, because the "ordinary" meaning of the word "ordinary" is that it is plain and unexceptional, and that is significant because the Bible consistently upholds the humblest and the least exceptional. Neither King Saul nor King David was the oldest or most distinguished brother in their families, but both of them became king. Moses himself was a rather ordinary, unexceptional fellow for a leader as he was said to be a very poor speaker, and he certainly had troubles with keeping his flock on task, but he led his people to the Promised Land. And of course, Jesus followed in this tradition as he was the small town man, born in a humble animal shelter, but whose program for life so many people are still following two thousand years later, and in fact find their salvation through bonding to him. That God works through the ordinary to do the extraordinary is at the core of the faith.

January 20th is the feast day of the Sisters of Sion, and on that day we attended a Mass in the chapel—not so much magnificent as humble, and in keeping with the ongoing sense of Ordinary Time, when we could be especially aware of the divine by our contact with the ordinary. We processed with candles, each representing a different branch of Sion. I carried the candle for the Contemplative Branch, an almost laughable irony as I had absolutely no vocation as a contemplative. Social and garrulous, I was destined to inhabit a noisy world. Suska, a Jewish friend from the Compassionate Listening group staying at the house, graciously came to the service with me, as a living example of the interfaith co-operation that Sion fosters. Our friend Father Don of the White Fathers was the presider, and he encouraged the congregation of Sion and upheld its ministry. Each member of the community had a role in the service, and a student, Rennie, a man with an exquisite tenor voice, sang his incomparable Salve Regina to the great delight of all.

There was a festive dinner and wine on the table compliments of the Sisters of Sion. Afterward, about six or eight of us walked Don home to St. Anne's where he was the superior of the White Fathers' community beside the pool of Bethesda, and Don opened the basilica for us before he retired for the night. It became for all of us there a mountaintop experience. We sat in the huge, dark Crusader church with only three candles burning beside a bouquet of flowers on the altar. In the barely illuminated darkness, Anne stepped up to the altar, between two giant stone pillars, and began to play her flute. The three candles created a dark, mysterious glow, and under the dome, each silver note from the flute rang for a full ten seconds after it was sounded, haunting us with its beauty. Anne played around twelve to fifteen songs, starting with a few hymns, then moving to soft ballads such as *Let It Be* and *Bridge Over Troubled Water*, and then, by request, *Jesu Joy of Man's Desiring*. The music was exquisite and thrilling, rolling off our every nerve ending in an ecstasy of sound. The man sitting behind me could not believe the resonance of the building, and I heard him muttering behind me "It's incredible. It can't be. Ten seconds of resonance!" It was a performance to which you could not buy a ticket anywhere on earth.

◆   ◆   ◆

The Palestinian staff of Ecce Homo were my guides to the unfamiliar culture and terrain I was inhabiting, and my relationships with these people were warm and rewarding. One night a few of us emerged from the Lithostrotos to find that our young part-time receptionist, Nabil, had managed to obtain some hard-to-find Islamic philosophy books, and he was cheerful and delighted with his purchases. He was sitting at the reception desk with his big pile of forbidden booty, gleefully reading and holding forth to a small audience on the restrictions imposed by the hard regime that had prohibited this literature. Nabil was constantly reading all kinds of material in various different languages. His huge project to document the families of Jerusalem, and to publish his findings, was a lifetime work. Once, he showed me some of the vast collection of archival black and white photos that many Jerusalem families had entrusted to him, and they were marvellous. In one historical photo that he showed me of the Western Wall depicted the houses and buildings that used to be there before they were bulldozed to create the Western Wall plaza. The Moroccan quarter of the Old City was among the casualties of this decision, and there it was in the photograph. Pictures of people's forbears, of their homes and neighbourhoods, and of the homes that they fled during the different conflicts, were all there. Nabil had hundreds of these pictures. He was a walking museum.

One evening I was privileged to visit the home of another staff member, Jiries, the receptionist and theological student who had invited me over for coffee. After his shift in the reception area, Jiries took me to the place in the Christian Quarter where he lived. We followed the cobbled Via Dolorosa until it became St. Francis Street, and we ducked through a half-size door in the stone wall and down a corridor that opened onto the courtyard of an old monastic community with a chapel of historic significance. Jiries occupied a small room, sharing the kitchen and bath with his aunt who lived on the other side of these facilities. As she was the senior, her suite was about three times the size of his. Jiries put on some soft Greek music after very thoughtfully offering me Neil Young or something that he thought would be more familiar; he made me wonderful Arabic coffee and brought in some Epiphany sweets that his mother had made. He asked me a lot of questions and revealed a lot about himself and his journey to the Orthodox priesthood, presently on hold, as he wanted to marry prior to his ordination. He gave me an interesting impression of Palestinian life by stating that people in Jerusalem were living without goals and that their success in life depended purely on luck. He, for example, had been educated in America only through a series of happy coincidences. Not everyone has such lucky breaks. The Palestinian people were pretty despondent about this situation, and Jiries himself was certainly dispirited as he was working at minimal part-time jobs, even with his six years of university education.

Afterwards he walked me home and we knocked and rang, knocked and rang for some time until Fakhri came and let me in. We were well into Ramadan, and although the Muslim staff members enjoyed the profound spiritual benefits of their daytime fasting, the rigours of it were taking a toll. Some seemed very tired and worn out. I finished the breakfast set-up and, thanks to the Arabic coffee, tossed around fitfully until five, when I had to do an early breakfast for the Minnesota college group who were on their way to an early outing.

The staff members enjoyed warm relationships with the community, especially as some had remained on staff for decades. Sister Trudy, director of our house, was to return from her home visit to Australia that night, and Fakhri was getting excited about this; he wanted to put up an Australian flag in the reception area. I managed to scurry up five small tabletop flags from the dining room, and arranged them on blue napkins on the reception desk. The next morning Fakhri told me how delighted he was to have his boss back, and how happy Trudy was to see the flags when she arrived in the wee hours.

Everyone loved Fakhri, and he was the convent's closest friend. He still slept there six nights a week, and had originally come to the house more than fifty-five years ago as a child, when he used to help the sisters with their groceries and garbage disposal. He grew up as an Ecce Homo staff member, and one day, as a young man, he pointed out to the Mother Superior a young lady who passed by each day on her way home from school. The two unlikely conspirators observed this lovely young girl among her peers and agreed: the girl was great. Fakhri brought his bride to the convent, where they shared a flat within the walls until shortly before the birth of their fourth child, when they moved to their own home on the Mount of Olives, and four more children followed those. That fourth child was Issa, who was now himself an important member of the Ecce Homo family.

The Ecce Homo hotel guests were always interesting, and I spend considerable time with some of them, especially if they were on their own and not caught up with the timetable of a group. We had Australian guests in the house at this time, and in the evening I met up with them: one fellow on his own, and a couple. The lady of the couple was an academic, finishing a Ph.D. in religious studies, which is a discipline that takes a comparative perspective on religion. Now, however, she now found that this study did not allow her the depth and growth that she craved, and she began moving more toward theology. Her growing spirituality and understanding of theology had begun to change her understanding of her own discipline. She spoke candidly about her struggles between her church life and her academic life, and as for so many visitors to the Holy Land, this trip was part of a deepening of her spirituality.

On my day off I rounded up young Oscar and we went to the Israel Museum. I would have taken the bus, but the weather was fine, and Oscar was concerned about every shekel, so we went on foot from the Old City, past the Knesset and into the museum, about a half-hour's walk. The museum is huge and the visitor has to set priorities. We both liked Biblical exhibits, so we began with the Dead Sea Scrolls, which of course I had seen before. We stood before each unrolled scroll, silent and too awestruck for any intelligent response. Whenever I have the honour of viewing such artifacts, I have the strange feeling that I am in the presence of something both mysterious and holy. The old translations of Psalm 96 used to include the line *"O worship the Lord in the beauty of holiness,"* and whenever I am in the presence of something so ancient, so mysterious, so dignified and so *beautifully holy*, I think of that psalm. In the Canaanite galleries I saw again my old friends, the big Philistine pottery sarcophagi with the funny faces. Poor country cousins of the Egyptian sarcophagi, these items were found buried in the ground standing up, and containing the non-mummified bones of human beings. To my delight, I saw the seal of Baruch, scribe to the prophet Jeremiah. I knew that I was looking at the personal stamp of the man who had written a significant amount of the Biblical text, and I was speechless. We toured some of the taken-apart-and-reassembled synagogues brought here from various places in the world, and our new discovery within the museum was a little carved pink ivory pomegranate scarcely two inches long. It was thought to be the only remaining artifact of King Solomon's Temple from the 8th century B.C.E. This exhibit made worthwhile the entire trek, and we exited the museum happy and thinking about what we had seen. Oscar was so happy with his outing that on the way home he very sweetly bought flowers for Anne.

Sometimes volunteers had an extra day off, and on one of these I went to the citadel with a guest, another Frank, a priest originally from Minnesota but who had been working in Copenhagen for twenty-five years. The tour offered at the citadel turned out to be so thorough and so very long that we abandoned it partway through in order to be back at the house in time for lunch. The day became more picturesque that afternoon when Frank and I accompanied Evan, a gentle and eccentric Bible professor who seemed to get lost easily, to the Western Wall. It was the afternoon before the third Friday in Ramadan and military personnel were already starting to pour into the plaza in front of the wall, intending to have a parade that night. Frank left us in the Jewish Quarter and Evan and I sat down to a coffee—a silent experience as Evan seemed to slip into a trance rather easily, very prayerful I'm sure, and would frequently shut his eyes during conversation. Off he went on his own, his slim frame wrapped in a rumpled raincoat, like a skinny and religious version of Columbo weaving his way through the Quarter. I had to trust he would eventually make his way back. He never returned on his own, however, and Jim had to go out and look for him, and brought him back.

Frank said Mass that evening in our small chapel, with a dialogue homily on Jesus' healing of the paralytic man, from Mark's gospel (2:1-12). There were only nine of us, including a family of three from Minnesota; surely it could not be a coincidence that everyone in town seemed to be from Minnesota: these folks, the college group, Frank, and maybe eventually Oscar. This family was of great interest to me as the couple was successfully sharing one part-time job and trying to live simply—reducing their need for income and getting off the consumer carousel. Because of the intimacy of our little gathering, Frank opened out the homily so that everyone did some reflection and contributed some insights—except Evan, of course, who had his eyes shut through the whole thing.

Our most high profile guest during this time was Joe, a former Ecce Homo volunteer, who arrived at the house from Canada with Jean-Guy, a French-Canadian organ builder who was there to assess whether or not the ancient pipe organ in the loft high above the basilica could be repaired. These two were quite an amusing pair. Joe was a mover and shaker, as witnessed by the fact that he had stayed six months volunteering at Ecce Homo, then returned to Canada and began mobilizing the local Knights of Columbus to raise money for the restoration of this instrument in faraway Jerusalem. He also proved to be a fascinating raconteur, and the sisters delighted in his company. Joe told us the story of how he had selected Jean-Guy to come and look at the organ at Ecce Homo. He had advertised in Ontario for an organ builder, and Jean Guy came to see him in the Knights' catering hall. Joe showed Jean-Guy a photo of the decrepitly beautiful pipe organ.

"Ah yes," Jean-Guy mused. "Nineteenth century French, sixteen hundred pipes, *this stop, that stop, etc., etc.,...*" Jean Guy continued rattling off particulars of the instrument in the picture.

"You can tell that from a picture?" Joe asked in astonishment.

"Oh, yes," was the matter of fact reply.

"Well, to tell you the truth," Joe confessed, "I had wanted to get Casavants to do this. They're supposed to be the best."

Casavant Frères was the renowned organ building firm in Quebec, and their reputation was formidable.

"Casavants trained me!" came the reply. "I was with Casavants for twenty years before I decided to go out on my own!" It was looking good, according to Joe.

"Just where exactly is this organ located, anyway?" Jean-Guy asked.

Joe pointed to the panoramic photo of the Old City of Jerusalem that he had put up over the bar. Jean-Guy took one look and slumped over onto the table, his face buried in his arm. A long time passed.

"Now I've done it," Joe thought. "I've killed the guy."

When Jean-Guy looked up again his eyes were filled with tears, and he choked out his response.

"I have almost died five times," he said, and he recounted to Joe the accidents, war service, and other brushes with the hereafter that had almost ended his life. "And I believe God has preserved me in order to do this job!"

He might have been right about that, because in the short time following the restoration of the Ecce Homo organ under his direction, Jean-Guy suffered a stroke, and although he survived, the Ecce Homo organ was the last big job of his career.

On the first Sunday morning of Joe's visit, a few of us went to the Garden Tomb to a Sunday morning service. Pat and Melanie enjoyed it more than I did. There were a few good songs, but most of them I did not know, and none of them featured what you would call inclusive language. The homilist was funny, engaging and pretty good, but there were major theological points of departure for me, and it was, on the whole, not my cup of tea, although some other Catholics in our party really enjoyed this worship. You certainly could not beat the atmosphere as the tomb, situated in the lovely garden, is right in front of the assembly during the service, and that was very inspiring. It is easy to imagine Jesus' resurrection appearance in that garden; it is so beautiful and the people in the joyful assembly are so happy to be there.

At the Austrian Hospice after the service, I learned that during Joe's time in Jerusalem he had actually trained the people in the café to make him a special, extra-large cappuccino—they even had some special name for it. Afterward, we lay low: Sunday afternoons at Ecce Homo were pretty quiet, and we spent time reading, writing and resting. In the evening, the two guests from Canada joined the volunteers to watch "The English Patient" in the community. There is a scene in the movie in which the *muezzin* announces the call to prayer. There is nothing funny about this, in fact it is an act of reverence, but we were very irreverent, and started to laugh because the sound tickled our familiarity. With the loudspeaker of the main mosque right across the street from our rooms, the call to prayer was a strident part of our daily lives. Every morning the call was so loud that, between the muezzin and the neighbour, I still had to wear earplugs in order to get through the night. Joe asked us if it were not enough that we had this coming in the windows at four-thirty in the morning—did we have to watch movies about it, too?

Next day, as a result of Joe's influence, a reporter from the Canadian Broadcasting Corporation came to Ecce Homo with her film crew, and started taping interviews in the organ loft. Joe had arranged for her to speak with Jean-Guy and to do a spot on how a group of Canadians was revitalizing this important part of Ecce Homo's music ministry. Joe invited the CBC people for coffee, and I made a coffee and tea service, but it became so late that the production people were anxious to leave. Jim, Joe and I drank the coffee on the terrace and basked in the light from the illuminated Dome of the Rock. The interviews had been a great success: the interest piece was later broadcast on the national news in Canada, which brought images of Ecce Homo into living rooms that had never heard of the place.

We had the group of Compassionate Listeners in the house, and while I was on reception next day, a Listener named Marv came by and started chatting. We decided we would go for a walk, and I thought it was no wonder he ended up in the Listeners' group: he was an excellent listener! Marv was a counsellor in San Francisco and must have been a very good one. We went through the souq to a place we could get Turkish coffee and talked there for a time, then moved on to the Holy Sepulchre. On the way, I started to tell him about the day my father died, when I was seventeen years old, and I suddenly found it very hard to get the story out, even though I have told it hundreds of times. That day, I found myself stammering and close to tears, as if I had formerly told it in a robotic way but was now connecting for the first time with my own pain. Instinctively, Marv moved closer and put his arm around me. This helped, and I found it not only a very comforting gesture, but I must say that he was more sensitive to that story than anyone I had previously met. This simple but deeply empathetic gesture was most comforting and touched me greatly, as did the rest of our conversation.

Marv was very candid about his own history, including talking about past events that must have been humiliating for him. He was honest and trusting—valuable qualities rarely found. He was Jewish, but Marv was still interested in exploring the points of interest in the Christian Quarter, and we sat and talked by the tomb inside the Holy Sepulchre church, and later in the Lutheran Church of the Redeemer. Then we went to the Western Wall and Jewish Quarter. There Marv told me much about his own spiritual quest, beginning with the American Jewish experience of our era of growing up, with some degree of observance but with a sense of being more in the mainstream of American culture than outside of it. Then came the awakening of the '60s, and the arrival on the Jewish scene of Shlomo Carlebach, the popular singing rabbi who was a revitalizing influence on so many young Jews. What followed for Marv was a lifetime of personal search. Even though he had lived in Israel before, this two-week trip appeared to be doing more to answer his questions than had the period of actually living there. The process that the Listeners were going through—interviewing ordinary people who had had painful experiences of conflict and extraordinary experiences of peacemaking—appeared to be propelling him along his path of discovery in a profound way.

We went to the only shop that was still open that evening, Shorashim of the Old City on Tiferet Square in the Jewish Quarter, where the two engaging Canadian-Israeli proprietors, Moshe and Dov, sell beautiful Biblical items and live for the moment when a customer will start up a lively theological conversation. Their clientele included people who just wandered in, as well as Jewish and Christian visitor groups who came specifically for the conversation. It was now after seven and Marv and I walked back. I suggested I cook at our flat, and he bought a few things to supplement the poor meal. Ziad, the convent cook, had made me some fresh vegetables, so I took that plus bread, humus and my own soup. Marv blessed the bread and I prayed before the meal, then he prayed after. This was very simple ritual but it drew us immediately closer. We drank wine and talked into the night.

The next day, the CBC was back filming the students' final Mass, and later in the afternoon two of the Listeners were having trouble getting a taxi as the police had blocked access to the Old City. I helped Suska to the Lions Gate and loaded her into some kind of conveyance, then helped Marv get to Notre Dame so he could go to West Jerusalem for a Shabbat celebration. We knew it would be impossible to get out of the Old City the next day, Saturday, as the buses would have shut down for Shabbat. Marv told me as he departed that the last two days had been just delightful, as they had been for me. I had thus a brief glimpse of what life is like for the Sisters at Ecce Homo; they just start to become attached to their travellers when the pilgrims, visitors, volunteers, or students depart. There are always farewells.

At Ecce Homo there were always opportunities to meet people and to get into immediate and deep theological conversation with them. Not only were there the guesthouse and residential school, but interesting people would actually just drop in at the door. They were not always Christian pilgrims, but because of the inter-faith orientation of the Sisters of Sion, Jewish visitors came as well. One day a couple from Atlanta came in requesting to see one of the sisters who was not there, and who in fact did not live at Ecce Homo, but I offered to show the guests around the house. I led them to the top terrace, the basilica top and bottom, the Lithostrotos, and I made them coffee in the dining room. The husband was an ordained rabbi who taught Judaic studies in the university at home, and the couple was in Israel for their son's wedding. They were eager to see everything and arrived with the characteristic curiosity that North Americans display when they come to the Near East. Interested in the Christian rhythm of the house and the relationships with the Palestinian staff, this delightful Jewish family gave me great hope for the future of interfaith dialogue.

Awareness of Judaism was a constant in our house, and as part of the Biblical program, an evening Shabbat meal was planned, to be conducted by Rabbi Michael, the teacher of the Judaism course. The Shabbat, or Sabbath, lasts from sunset on Friday until sunset on Saturday, and is officially observed in Israel. This means that public facilities, such as buses and institutions, do not operate during those hours; in fact, they close down well in advance of Friday sunset so that operators can arrive home in advance of the Shabbat siren. The Bible is very clear in its intention that human beings do not work, but rather rest, during the Shabbat. The arrival of the Shabbat on Friday evening is honoured with a prayer time for the congregation, and with a special meal together, either with the family, or with friends. Before our Shabbat dinner, the students and volunteers were to attend the evening service at the synagogue where Michael and his family worshipped: a liberal synagogue, very unusual as most Jewish congregations in Israel are Orthodox. Michael was an ordained rabbi but was not in congregational ministry at the time, and another fellow was in fact the presiding rabbi of the synagogue and conducted the service. The trip to the synagogue turned out to be a great challenge. At the midday prayer this second Friday of Ramadan, there were reportedly a half-million worshippers in the Old City, mainly at the Al Aqsa mosque where we could see from our terrace an absolute sea of white head-coverings of the women. The other mosques were also full, so when we left the house at 2 p.m. to go to the Damascus Gate, the streets were packed with people, including the army, and all we could do was to shuffle along slowly. An American student was in the lead, a tall fellow so we could all see him. Jim B was behind him with a hand on the leader's back the whole way. I was behind Jim B with my hand on his shoulder, and when we got temporarily separated, the Muslim people in the big crush could see that we were trying to stay together and moved aside to help us. When Melanie got a bit lost some distance behind me, I reached back and clasped her hand, and people made way for her the best they could. Everyone was very kind, and except for a few aggressive matriarchs, it was as orderly as could be expected. Still, it took us forty-five minutes to go from the house to the Damascus Gate, a walk that usually takes less than five minutes.

We had to make up for lost time so we hiked quickly down King David Street and finally found the synagogue. Michael told the history of the congregation, and of how they had received their original little building as a gift from the former mayor of Jerusalem, Teddy Kolleck, following an attack by a small group of Orthodox Jews on Simcha Torah night. The attackers and their rabbis later apologized. Liberal Jews were still a very tiny minority in Israel, where the Orthodox were the establishment under two Chief Rabbis, one Sephardic and one Ashkenazy. As the national religion, Michael informed us, the Orthodox received government funds for buildings, rabbis' salaries, and Torah scrolls, whereas liberals had to fund everything themselves. In America, of course, the situation was much the reverse, where liberals were the vast majority, and the Orthodox in the minority. The service was lovely—a Friday evening service to welcome in the Shabbat, so there was no Torah reading, but we all enjoyed the singing.

After the service we took the sherut back to Ecce Homo, where the Sisters and staff had prepared a beautiful Shabbat meal, presided over by Michael and his wife Sally, with their two little boys. There were white damask tablecloths on the tables, and all the appropriate prayers and blessings were said. Sitting across from me was Frank, that most quintessential Australian, who entertained us with funny stories, and beside him was Anne Catherine, a Sister of Sion who was also a very respected teacher of Jewish-Christian studies. The two Filipino priests, Romeo and José, were beside me, and when the point of the meal was reached

when we were to share the Aaronic blessing, Romeo turned to José and pronounced the familiar blessing from the Book of Numbers: "The Lord bless you
and keep you; the Lord make his face to shine upon you, and be gracious to you;
the Lord lift up his countenance upon you, and give you peace." When it was my
turn to give Romeo the blessing, he automatically went into his priestly role and
put his hand on my head, so I said, "No, Romeo, I'm the priest here!" Romeo
was delighted and, laughing, received this reassuring gesture of friendship. I also
gave José my blessing while I was at it. There was plenty of food and wine, and
everyone enjoyed the Shabbat liturgy and our gracious presiders. After the meal
we quickly restored the place to its usual configuration, and Melanie and I set up
for next day's breakfast.

One weekend in January, after a big outing, I returned to Ecce Homo and
shut myself in to do some writing. When I went outside to go and have dinner,
there was snow everywhere. What a shock! I had no idea it had been snowing,
intensely buried in my correspondence as I was. I deliberately live in a part of
Canada that is relatively free of snow, only to go to the Near East and encounter
this! Slipping and sliding around on the shiny paving stones, I tried to make my
way to the terrace. The Dome of the Rock was spectacular in the snow, so I slid
back to get my camera. Jim B was having a wonderful time pelting people with
snowballs, particularly me because I hate the stuff so much, and also particularly
Eymard, the Sri Lankan student, because she had never seen snow before and
didn't know how to fight back. Later, while sipping wine in my room and trying
to warm myself, I realized I was getting a cold, thanks to all this up and down
weather, and the absence of central heating in the convent.

On the next morning after the snowfall a lot of the staff could not make it in
to work. As well, something had happened to the phones so that only one line
was working. It is unusual for it to snow in Jerusalem, and apparently when it
does everything slips to a halt. We were a bit busy because two groups were
checking out—the American "Compassionate Listening" group went to Gaza,
and St. Olaf's College of Minnesota went to Galilee. Guests were trying to get
transportation, but the *sherutim* were not running in the snow. Meanwhile,
Fakhri kept going outside and standing on the doorstop, bundled up in his
kufeeyah and waiting to see if any deliverymen would make it to the house in this
weather.

Despite the snow, I ventured out to the bazaar to buy chocolate—no problem;
you can buy anything in an Arab bazaar—and Anne and I took advantage of a
new feature of the Via Dolorosa, a new coffee shop called The "Caffine Station,"
right by the Fifth Station of the Cross. There was a nice Bedouin atmosphere, but

I thought it a bit pricey. One cappucino, one double espresso, and two miniscule pieces of baklava for twenty shekels seemed high, especially when the surrounding local restaurants were so cheap. It was, however, likely a very high-rent district as every pilgrim in Jerusalem had to trudge by that spot. While we were there, two other Ecce Homo students came in, then Melanie. The Caffine Station seemed sure to turn into the Old City meeting place.

I had really done very little exploring of the Old City since I had been there before, and expected to be there for some time, so I was not in a hurry to see it all at once in the manner of highly motivated tourists. One time, I actually did go out for a walk into the main streets from which I felt securely that I could get home without getting lost. The closest route was a walk down the souq and a visit to the Holy Sepulchre where I sat contemplating for quite some time in front of the tomb and at the rock of Calvary. The Orthodox priests were preparing for Greek Epiphany, as theirs is later than the Latin one, and were bringing huge floral arrangements into the Calvary chapel. After they left, there were very few people around so it was a good time to reflect. While I was seated beside the main Latin shrine, a dark mysterious person came into the chapel and sat near me. It was a chunky person, but I could not easily tell if this was a woman or a man, nor could I easily tell the colour of the person's skin, so covered up was he or she. The apparition was wearing a long, black robe with a black cowl pulled over the face as if to obscure identity, and carrying a number of bags. This was so very unexpected that I became scared of this person and I wondered why she, or was it he, was sitting right beside me when the Church of the Holy Sepulchre, a building that seemingly covers several acres, was completely empty. Another bench would have been equally available. This was making me nervous. On the other hand, the visitor may be completely harmless, and I did not want to hurt his or her feelings by getting up and running away. All efforts at meditation were now ended in favour of a heightened state of awareness and readiness for alarm. I felt isolated and vulnerable. After a few minutes of polite and nervous vigilance, my previous contemplation the farthest thing from my mind, I slowly left the chapel.

To get away from it all, we sometimes went to the quieter of the Sion houses at Ein Karem, traditionally held to be the birthplace of John the Baptist. Anne would pack up the three volunteers and Pat and we would drive across Jerusalem to Ein Karem village. It was normally a short drive, but seemed like a long way if the traffic was bad passing through the busy area of Mount Hertzl behind Yad Vashem. Ein Karem was beautiful in summer, but the first time I visited was very wet and cold, and the sisters there had a simple but scrumptious vegetarian meal ready consisting of an eggplant casserole and a thick soup. The Sisters represented a wide citizenry, including three Canadians: Sister Donna, the director, was Canadian, and there were two Canadian volunteers; the other sisters were European and Australian.

The rooms at Ein Karem were spare but beautiful, and appeared to have been recently refurbished. Almost every window looked out on some part of the gardens, which were very extensive and included flowers, shrubbery and food plants. The next morning was still rainy, and I slept a bit, then went down to the quiet dining room where the breakfast was still out on the buffet, but there were few people around. Indoors, the house was silent and serene; outdoors, the weather was so bad that it even hailed during the morning. Ages later, after my return, I would tell stories of all this snow, hail and bad weather, and people hearing me would be astonished because many North Americans had in their minds that Jerusalem was a blistering hot desert all year.

Despite the rain and hail, I enjoyed touring the grounds with Anne, especially Father Mary's little house and the cemetery where he and some of the sisters are buried. Father Mary was Alphonse Ratisbonne, brother of Theodore Ratisbonne who founded the Sisters of Sion. It was Father Mary, or Alphonse, who had been instrumental in the establishment of Sion's ministries in Jerusalem. The simple little house where he lived out his last years and finally died is now kept as a memorial, although sisters and friends who are visiting often actually stay in the house, and even sleep in the saggy, uncomfortable bed where he died. We also went all through the big Ein Karem house, including both the large and small chapels. The grounds and garden were breathtaking and lovely—so quiet, and we could see the Church of the Visitation and the Hadassah Medical Centre from outside the dignified buff stone monastery and guesthouse. The surrounding terrain was the hill country of Judea mentioned in the New Testament, where Mary of Nazareth went to visit her cousin Elizabeth before the birth of the child Jesus. I fantasized retiring in that exquisite place.

◆   ◆   ◆

One afternoon a Palestinian woman who was teaching at the university delivered a lecture in our large salon. She talked about the situation of Palestinian women, with emphasis on marriage customs and law. Sadly, many Muslim Palestinian women are unaware of their rights under Islamic law; they marry very young and their families often are themselves unaware of everything to which their daughters are entitled. This reality is changing only very slowly, mainly in the cities and main centres, so the situation for Palestinian women was, accordingly, quite oppressive by western standards in some villages. Sometimes married as young as thirteen, most of them depended on their husbands' good will for their security and happiness. Family values were strong and young men were taught responsibility, but there were some casualties of the system, and for those women there were few options.

Eventually came that sad time at the end of the term when our students were leaving. As it was still Ramadan, transportation out of the Old City was a problem and we often had to assist departing students to get to the airport sherut with their baggage. One afternoon during that time I entertained Addie, an elderly Dominican nun with a flair for survival and constant crisis, by serving her soup and tea at our flat before Mass. Later, it took an entire delegation of volunteers plus Anne to get the intrepid Addie to the Notre Dame Center to catch her sherut, she was in such a flap and had so many suitcases, bags and boxes. She and Melanie were a picturesque pair—Mel bundled up in her winter coat and looking like a kind of thin, blonde Canadian lumberjack with a navy blue toque pulled down over her head, and Addie in her traditional black and white habit, leaning on Melanie as they struggled arm in arm toward the Damascus Gate in the cold, dark and inclement weather. We had coffee with Addie in the café where she was waiting for her transport, then left her around ten. We pitied the staff of Notre Dame Center who would have a long shift of entertaining Addie, who was not given to sitting quietly but enjoyed attention and making a fuss. Addie's great triumph was that the director of the Biblical program had been reluctant to accept her as a student because of her age, but Addie had been one of the few students who had not become ill during the term. Constantly chuckling to herself, Addie continually proclaimed this victory, asserting that she was seventy-five but healthier than most of these young ones of sixty-odd!

Adelina, our African dancer, was leaving to go back to Africa that day. We volunteers all clattered down the Via Dolorosa with her enormous bags and piled her into the Joe vehicle at the Lion's Gate. Joe was taking Jean-Guy and Jim on an excursion to the Negev, so he could drop off Adelina at her taxi. Now the only students left were Mary, Marie and Eymard. I joined these last three remaining students for a cup of tea in the students' lounge, where we felt like tiny creatures lost in an enormous guesthouse.

On the Saturday evening, Stéphane came down from St. Anne's to say Mass, and afterward the three students in the class joined us at St. Mary's for a prayer and a meal. They began recounting some of the stories that had become Ecce Homo classics. One of these was "Marie and the Camel".

At the Christmas party Marie received a little olive wood camel from her secret Krist Kindle. She wanted to find out who was her Krist Kindle and she surmised, since the camel came in a box that had contained large tensor bandages and featured a picture of a very hairy leg, that the donor had been a man with a sports injury. Marie decided to see if any of the men appeared to be limping. They got wind of this, however, and the next morning at breakfast, all of the men in the class came in limping, some with great bandages wrapped around their legs. When Marie spoke to anyone without a bandage, in an effort to eliminate the person as a suspect, he would roll up his trouser leg and show the hidden bandage underneath. Vic, a quiet and seemingly serious Canadian fellow, rolled up his trouser leg to show the fake incision and stitches he had drawn on his leg!

Camel references and limping went on and on. At Epiphany, Marie allowed her camel to be used at the Cradle with the Wise Men in the basilica, and after the Mass, she noticed that the camel had a bandaid around its knee! The next morning at breakfast, she began questioning everyone as to whether they had any bandaids. One of the students called for a show of hands as to who had bandaids in their room, and 99% of the class raised their hands. Vic leaned over and said sincerely "I used the last one yesterday."

The class continued the camelmania and limping jokes to the last. As the students were preparing to leave, Marie received an early morning knock on her door, and a penitent confessed in all seriousness "I'm sorry to have had you on, Marie, but I am your Krist Kindle." Marie was very touched and thanked the person for this revelation. A few minutes later, however, another penitent came to the door and said "I'm sorry to have had you on, Marie, but I am your Krist Kindle."

"What?" she cried.

When the third penitent arrived at the door and said "I'm sorry, Marie, but I..." she just said, "Oh, get out!" and slammed the door shut.

So when her fellow student Trish came to Marie and produced a photo of Trish whispering into a camel's ear "Who would have thought, Mr. Camel, that we could keep Marie guessing for so long?" and the camel in the picture laughing, Marie was not about to fall for this so-called evidence, and she so indicated to Trish. Accordingly, Trish went away and returned with the inculpatory evidence: the other half of the tensor bandage box! It had been a great bit of fun and was typical of that class's wonderful collective sense of humour.

Just as the Marie story was winding up, Joe came in and began to tell his story, with grand gestures, of the great trial of parking the rented van at Notre Dame Center in a grand display of ingenious networking. Joe had had to pass at three levels. The gate-keeper and reception levels were attended by Palestinian men, so Joe dropped Fakhri's name, claiming that it was Fakhri who wanted him to park there. Since everyone in the Muslim Quarter knew Fakhri, this seemed to do the trick. The next level was the phone call to the Father Abbot, and Joe dropped the name of Sister Trudy. This also seemed to do the trick: the receptionist stopped fussing about it, and Joe left the van there. All this drama was in aid of our plan to go to Galilee the next morning. Joe would go up to Notre Dame to get the van, and then pick us up at Damascus Gate at 08:30. We made hearty picnic lunches the night before; there was no danger we would starve.

6

Ordinary Times, Divine Places

The Christian year begins early in winter with the season of Advent. Advent begins four Sundays before Christmas, and ends on December 24. During that time, Christians anticipate the coming of Jesus, in fact the word Advent means "coming". It is a good time to reflect on our human state, and on our need for light to come and enter our darkness; hence, candles are a central theme of this time. Unlike the retail season in the consumer world, the Christmas Season just begins on Christmas Day and lasts through the twelve nights afterward until Epiphany on January 6. The season officially ends with the Baptism of Jesus the following week, and Ordinary Time begins. Then, after the long season of Lent, the holy weekend of Good Friday and Easter, called the Triduum, followed by the time of Pentecost, interrupts the long course of Ordinary Time, which again lasts until the following Advent. It is a different rhythm from the secular year, but for Christians this ebb and flow between the major feasts of Christmas and Easter, celebrating the birth, death and resurrection of Jesus, is the basic framework of our spiritual life.

So we were an ordinary tour party assembled and waiting in the van at Damascus Gate by eight-thirty the next day, including my former guide, Rachel—nine of us in the van, with Joe driving. It was a mini-pilgrimage to the northern part of the country. We followed the Jordan Valley route, through the checkpoint into the territory known as the West Bank, passing by the Dead Sea and Jericho. The drizzly weather cleared up and became sunny. The Jordan valley was wide and spacious, even if the river itself belied the old song—the Jordan River was not chilly and wide, but in some places is just a trickle. We arrived at the Yardenit baptismal site in about two hours. This stretch of the Jordan River was at this time about the size of a good-sized creek back home, but it was very picturesque. Greenery grew along the banks, and tall eucalyptus leaned toward the centre, creating a holy tree tunnel. The baptismal site was a development for pilgrims: modern, and with very good facilities for people to congregate and to enter the water together. The footpath led onto a ramp, and there was a sturdy handrail for pilgrims to hold as they entered the water. Above the riverbank wais an esplanade with shops, a café, changing rooms, and a very large gift shop. Few people were around that day, wintry and rainy as it was—too cold to be baptized in the Jordan that day! After we read out the baptismal vows and renewed our baptism, we proceeded around the eastern shore of the Sea of Galilee, seeing a different perspective of the lake with dark clouds and overcast sky. By this time it was raining again. What inclement weather those fisher disciples must have had to endure in order to make a simple living!

Near the site of biblical Capernaum was the beautiful Russian church with its red onion domes, and we drove up the road to the gate. A flock of chickens and a few peafowl met us at the locked gate, and we rang the bell but no one answered. It was Sunday and it seemed that the community was shut down for their Sabbath, with only the fowl out and about. We toured the Capernaum site, where the church over St. Peter's house was open and we almost had an opportunity to go inside, but the custodian stopped us and would not let us in, even for prayer. We were advised that the church was built through a bequest that stipulated it be used only for Roman Catholic Masses, and so it is impossible even to go into the church for prayer, much less to view the architecture.

At the little lakeside church down the road, the Primacy of St. Peter, the events of the twenty-first chapter of John's gospel were remembered, when the resurrected Jesus appeared to the disciples on the beach and cooked fish for them for breakfast. We stood on the same beach huddled under umbrellas, and went into the little church where I read John 21 aloud to my companions. The Franciscan custodians of the site had done a wonderful work of preserving the natural surroundings and the ambience of the stony beach where Jesus and his close followers once walked.

By now we were tucking into our picnic lunches, so we stopped at the Galilee Inn, a restaurant where Jim knew the proprietor, who was called Ben. We were soaked through, and very glad to see the excellent fried potatoes, wine, and coffee that Ben brought us as we sat around the pot-bellied stove, chatting with Ben while his dogs basked in the warmth. Near Ben's establishment, we came to the Mount of Beatitudes, where I had visited so briefly with Rachel's group the year before. This time, we were at leisure to explore the grounds of the beautiful little dome-shaped church, the convent and guesthouse that commemorate Jesus' famous Sermon on the Mount. The Beatitudes themselves are the blessings, found in Matthew 5:3-12, and we selected someone to read the passage aloud:

"Blessed are the poor in spirit, for theirs is the kingdom of heaven.

Blessed are those who mourn, for they will be comforted.

Blessed are the meek, for they will inherit the earth.

Blessed are those who hunger and thirst for righteousness, for they will be filled.

Blessed are the merciful, for they will receive mercy.

Blessed are the pure in heart, for they will see God.

Blessed are the peacemakers, for they will be called children of God.

Blessed are those who are persecuted for righteousness' sake, for theirs is the kingdom of heaven.

Blessed are you when people revile you and persecute you and utter all kinds of evil against you falsely on my account. Rejoice and be glad, for your reward is great in heaven, for in the same way they persecuted the prophets who were before you."

The little Italianate church was built under a dome, with seating in the round, and with a cupola featuring the Beatitudes in stained glass, the text in Latin. Outside were expansive and well kept gardens—drooping shrubbery and bougainvillea—with a panoramic view of the Sea of Galilee. We were blessed indeed to be able to be in this serene place, so redolent of Jesus' teaching ministry on these hillsides. We were blessed also to have Rachel with us, as she is a professional guide and although she was with us to relax, she was always generous in sharing her enormous knowledge of these places of interest.

The next place along the shore was Tabgha, the place of the multiplication of loaves and fishes. The Benedictine church was modern but incorporated features of the thirteenth century church on which it had been built, including the rock that tradition says Jesus used as a table for five loaves and two fishes. This church's most famous feature was the beautiful mosaic floor, remnant of the old church, depicting the basket of loaves surrounded by two fish. This motif was very familiar as it was repeated on souvenir goods and book covers everywhere in Israel. The Benedictine custodians of the church ask that visitors remain quiet, and thus the interior of the church always seemed a prayerful space. On either side of the altar and its mosaic floor stood icons surrounded by a bank of votive candles. The entire effect was one of prayerful communing with God. The loaves and fishes theme, of course, is the entire background of the eucharist or communion, the central ritual of many of the Christian churches. In this act of worship, the eating of bread, symbolically incorporating into oneself the very body of

Christ, is another instance of "ordinary times". Through these ordinary earthly elements of bread and wine, sanctified into celestial food, the worshipper comes into close communion with the divine. Again, the ordinary is made extraordinary.

Our drive home was very long, six hours, including going out to the coast and getting stuck in a traffic tie-up in which the police appeared to be looking for someone specific. We had a stop at a McDonald's at Afuna, and sang hundreds of songs on the way home: old chestnuts such as *By the Light of the Silvery Moon, Moon River, Waltzing Matilda* and every familiar folk song that we knew. It was Robbie Burns night, and when we arrived back at Ecce Homo, the volunteers and Anne went to Jim's room for a modest celebration. It was not your traditional Burns night, but the kind of Burns night one might expect in a Jerusalem convent: instead of addressing the haggis, Anne was asking us our favourite Bible passages, and reading them out! We did toast the immortal memory of Scotland's bard, however, then Jim kicked us out as he had the St. Olaf's group getting up for an early excursion the next day, and Jim had to make their breakfast.

At breakfast, the talk of the town was Sister Emmanuelle, a Belgian Sister of Sion of 89 years of age who had lived many years with the rag pickers in Cairo and had become quite renowned. She had already complained of the tepid tea water the night before, stating that even the rag pickers have hot tea water. She had foiled the plans of the sisters from Ein Karem, who had waited two hours for her at the airport, only to have her say she was not going to stay with them she was staying at Ecce Homo so she could pray at the Holy Sepulchre. She got up and went to 7 a.m. Mass at St. Anne's, refusing to use a walking stick because that would make her appear old. The woman was a terror. She made her way back from St. Anne's and I had the chance to meet her briefly and to chat. She was very approachable and kind, although I have seen her on television spots in which she gave the interviewers a run for their money. Later she told the sisters that she would be turning ninety that fall, after which she intended to go to Paradise. She had it all planned. I felt that I was in the presence of a living legend, although it seemed that if she had her way she would not be living all that much longer. As it turned out, the Lord had a somewhat different schedule for her; the ninetieth birthday was passed without incident, and she was still going strong, working in her office and doing TV interviews a couple of years later.

While extraordinary things were commonplace in Jerusalem, the smallest everyday things were often impossible. Sometimes Anne would go for a walk with one or more of the volunteers, either within the Old City, or venturing outside to Jaffa Street. On one such trip I decided to try the bank, but it was obviously going to take me forever to do anything in there. All the signage was in Hebrew and people were waiting about in chairs, but I had no idea for what or for whom, and I could have potentially waited ages before anyone ventured out of their sacred little offices and assisted me. English does not seem to be spoken as much in banks as it is in retail stores. Jim showed us an internet bar very close to the Old City, in case we ever needed the internet; it was a novelty at the time, although by a year or so later there were hundreds of such facilities. Once, on finding ourselves alone on our walk, Anne and I had Turkish coffee and Arabian sweets at the Jerusalem Star Restaurant, twelve shekels for the two. The new café had charged us twenty for the same thing, only with tinier bits of baklava. The "Star" was around the corner from our convent and it was very charming. The restaurant was decorated with wood panelling and lace tablecloths, which gave it a very cosy interior, and photos of British and Jordanian royalty were the featured decoration. The menu was very limited for vegetarians, to be sure, but omnivores fared better.

The Sisters had gone to Ein Kerem to prepare for their Chapter meeting, and the St. Olaf's College group had gone to Petra. Once again, the convent was almost empty. The following night at supper, Jim told the students that we were going to tell ghost stories in the Lithostrotos. The remaining students were shocked that we would do such a thing at a holy site, and the more scandalized and quiet their response, the more outrageous Jim became. Finally someone relieved the moment by saying, "We're not going to tell ghost stories in the Lithostrotos, folks. We'll be in the cistern".

Joe gave us the ghost story performance of a lifetime. The volunteers, Pat and a houseguest were seated on the ancient stairs below our house, where no external light could enter, and Joe was on the bridge platform with just two candles and a cigarette burning. The rest was darkness. King Herod's cistern rang with Joe's voice, water was dripping down, darkness and damp antiquity closed in around us. Joe was brilliant. The story was quite long. Only a tiny glimmer of light entered the cistern from somewhere, and when, during the performance, Joe extinguished the candles, it was so scary that it was all I could do to force myself to remain there, and only the fear of falling back down the uneven steps in the dark glued me to my place. Joe relit a candle and finished the tale.

Afterwards, Joe confessed that it was a story he had heard years ago as a boy at Scout camp, but we apparently were not very sophisticated, and it certainly did its magic in terrifying us. We celebrated this Thespian success with a congenial gathering and a movie in the community. On our way back to the flat we could hear some disturbance in the street outside, and the next morning, as I was washing the floor of the front corridor with the front door open, Father Don walked by the house and said there had been a fight the previous night between two families. He believed that knives were involved and there could have been a stabbing. The police and army broke up the fight, but the talk was that they would be at it again, only with guns. Fakhri said he believed he knew who the feuding families were, one from our street and one behind us, and we would just wait and see what developed. Issa was warning me never to interfere with such a battle because it is always the people trying to help that actually get hurt. The people involved in the ruckus get into a fighting frenzy and have no idea whom they are hitting. Issa knew of a situation in which a group of young men were beating up on another, and it turned out to be their own brother, but they were in such a rage that they did not even recognize him. There is a conventional Palestinian way of sorting out these differences, very civilized according to Issa, but sometimes, young men simply do not use this traditional method. Without bothering to find out the facts or determine who is responsible, they just react, with the impetuosity of youth.

We were undergoing a commissioning of the disciples, in the sense that the few remaining students who had become our friends were leaving the house and going back to the places where they had responsibilities. Marie was leaving to go back to Britain that evening and I made an arrangement with her that we would help her get to Notre Dame on foot to avoid the uncertainty of the taxi service in the Old City. Although taxi operators were quite willing to come right to the front door, sometimes the police closed the gates during Ramadan and no one would be able to bring a vehicle within the city walls. To celebrate, I bought some *boorma*, the Arabian sweets made of shredded wheat; a pound of Turkish coffee; some terrible peanut butter and some humus to supplement what I received in the dining room. Throughout my time in Jerusalem I wished I had brought more peanut butter and other foods to supplement my protein intake. The cooks did their best to provide something for me, but as they were all Palestinians, raised in a herding culture, it was not easy for them to come up with vegan menus. Sometimes I would simply store up legumes and other vegetarian leftovers in my fridge in the flat and make soup out of it later in the week.

The next departure was a sad one for us: our dear Joe, with his companion Jean-Guy. Our little group of sisters and volunteers gathered in the community after dinner to say goodbye, and at nine, when Joe and Jean-Guy's taxi was supposed to arrive, it was evident that no taxis were getting into the Old City, due to security during Ramadan. Anne and Joe went out to get the convent car from the car park at the end of the street. They got stuck in a miniature traffic jam caused by an emergency vehicle oncoming, as the street is only wide enough for one very small vehicle at a time, and this little white one with its flashing blue emergency light obviously had the right of way. Joe and Jean-Guy made their sherut with not a minute to spare.

Next departure was Marie, who claimed she had to clean her room up first. As her room could not have been eight feet by ten feet, I wondered what on earth she could be doing to it that took so many days to accomplish. She had made an appearance at lunch wearing a camel shirt with the face on the front and the rear end on the back, a reference to the camel antics. It was evident that Marie did not want to leave, and as the day progressed she became increasingly comical, mainly to console herself. By the time she was ready to go she was ostentatiously pretending to dribble Scotch into her tea and generally acting humorous in order to mask her misery at leaving Jerusalem. We left the house at eleven, Jim, Eymard and I dragging the bags and walking to Notre Dame Center. We sat for a few minutes with Marie, and I had given her a very hefty novel to read since she had to wait until almost four a.m. for her airport sherut. We all knew that she was grief-stricken at having to leave, but she was putting on such a brave face that I felt sad to leave her there, so tiny amid her baggage and books.

There were different kinds of groups who came to Ecce Homo. The most engaging type for us were the groups who stayed in the guesthouse and who featured discussions and study sessions as part of the group experience, as in the case of the Listeners and the St. Olaf's College class. Sometimes church groups and pilgrim groups would also stay in our guesthouse, and so they would usually be present for breakfast and the evening meal. Other groups might only come to the Lithostrotos on pilgrimage and would arrange to have lunch at Ecce Homo as part of their visit. Tour groups in the Near East are very often served chicken and rice, so the Ecce Homo lunch was a popular choice as it usually included such comfort foods as mashed potatoes and roast beef.

On my days off I would make myself available to show people how to get around the Old City, taking them to places of interest. Sometimes I would have more than one such outing in a day. Occasionally, I would be the one receiving the orientation, as guests would tell me about their life journeys or their projects. One day I walked to the Jewish Quarter in the pouring rain with the soundman from the Listeners' film crew, the last of his group to remain after the others had gone. We had some dinner and Turkish coffee in the Bird of Paradise Café and I learned about some of the interviews the Listeners had done for their project—extraordinary interviews. They had, for example, spoken with a rabbi whose son, in the Israeli army, had been killed by a Palestinian during an incident. The son's army companions had then immediately gone after the young Palestinian and killed him. In an act of compassion, the rabbi had contacted the family of the Palestinian young man to console the family on their loss. This must have been one of those peacemaking events to which Anne had referred when I spoke to her on the phone about whether or not to come to the country. It means not only peacemaking from the heart, but also in spite of the heart, and with such divine love that it eclipses our natural human tendency to hold grudges and seek revenge.

Beyond the house, I was not able to guide people as adequately as I could in our own ruins, since I had not ventured out very much to explore the Old City in detail. This was partly because I had seen it before and also because I had been putting a lot of energy into meeting with the people who came and went at the house. As it was now the Ecce Homo school interterm, I had more time to take people out on walks and to do some exploration of my own. I first made arrangements to go on an exploratory walk with the remaining students, Mary and Eymard, and I had a good idea of what I wanted to learn. The major markets of the City converged in a small area where there are three parallel streets, and I wanted to learn the Arabic names of all these and of the other markets, and the types of merchandise you could expect to find there both now and in Crusader times.

We began near the busy marketplace of the Damascus Gate and entered the Suq Khan-es-Zeit, the old Olive Oil Market. This street was built atop the Roman street, called the Cardo, that stretched from one end of the walled city to the other, and essentially still does. It was called the Malcuisinat by the Crusaders—Street of Bad Cooking. Apparently Middle Eastern food never really caught on with the Crusaders! There was not much cooking there today, as the street—really just a narrow walkway—offered a wide variety of shops selling CD's, clothing, shoes, toiletries, souvenirs, sweets and all kinds of household goods.

When we arrived at the steps leading toward the Coptic Patriarchate, we went up and found ourselves on the roof of the Holy Sepulchre, where are all the backs of the little cabañas in which the Ethiopian priests and brothers live. We did not actually go to the Ethiopian monastery but rather explored some of the details of the roof, such as the quaint old bells, and the old water pump. When we went back to the street from the roof, we found ourselves at another door, and thus entered the precinct of the Coptic Patriarchate. The parishioners were getting ready for a party, perhaps their Epiphany, and as there were only three of us, and we were quiet and respectful, they allowed us to view their church, even though it is not normally open to the public. It appeared to be quite modern, or modernized, with only a few decorations: a painting of Our Lady—and a Christmas tree, although it was near the end of January. The church was otherwise spare, but a single and very beautiful chandelier was suspended from the ceiling, as if it were the only concession to ornamentation .

On our way back toward the souq, we decided to view the excavations at the Russian Orthodox church. Although this display is mentioned in the guidebooks, it is not visited very often by groups, so that most pilgrims do not have the opportunity to see it. The two usually in attendance, Vera and her daughter Anna, had invited me there one day when they came to the Lithostrotos for prayer. The two women were not in, but Jibril, their employee at the door, was very hospitable. He showed us the lovely chapel of St. Alexander, very orthodox in its ornamentation, and allowed us to explore the remains of the Judgment Gate and the other Hadrian's Arch of the Cardo besides the Ecce Homo one. A sign posted in the ruins warned that women wearing trousers would not be admitted, but rather women were to wear skirts. As we were all wearing trousers, this was a bit alarming, but Jibril assured us that this warning applied only to Mass times, as women were to wear skirts and dresses to attend the liturgy.

The Russian excavation was one of the truly authentic remains of first century Jerusalem. A portion of the Herodian city wall was extant, with the threshold stone of the Judgment Gate still in place. This gate was believed to be the exit from the city through which soldiers would have led prisoners on their way to the execution area outside the city. It was highly likely that Jesus walked through this gate to his crucifixion, and that made the Russian excavations one of the most profound sites for Christian pilgrims. The excavations also included the remains of the old steps up to the Holy Sepulchre dating from later Roman times, when the church was the Temple of Venus. An interesting feature of the wall segment was a small portal beside the Judgment Gate, large enough only for a human being to squeeze through, but not a horse or camel. After the city gate was closed at night, a person could, for security reasons, still be admitted through this portal. It was called the Eye of the Needle—hence the aphorism told by Jesus: "It is easier for a camel to go through the eye of a needle than for a rich person to enter the Kingdom of God."[1]

We returned to the Triple Market. Another of the side branches of the market was the Suq el-Lahammin, the meat market, which eventually bent into the Suq el-Hussor, the old basket market, then suddenly rejoined Chabad Street in the

---

1.   Matthew 19:24; Mark 10:25; Luke 18:25

Jewish Quarter. The meat market was pretty ghastly, with carcasses hung near the walkway for easy inspection by customers. The smell was terrible. The central corridor of this Triple Market was the continuation of the Suq Khan-es-Zeit, called the Suq el-Attarin, or Spice Market. This market had been roofed over by the Crusaders, and if you remained on the street it became the Cardo, then Chabad Street. The third branch was the Suq el Khawajat, or Kissaria, which became Jewish Quarter Road, and then ended at Tiferet Square. The centre of the Triple Market was also the crossroad for the Suq el-Bazaar (David Street) and the Bab el-Silsileh (Street of the Chain), which ran perpendicular to the Triple Market. It was a terrible plan—well, there was no plan, it just "growed," like Topsy.

In the Jewish Quarter, we noticed some beautiful doorways of buildings, each one a modern work of art created after the 1967 war, and we visited the War of Independence Memorial, the Hurva Synagogue ruins and the ruins of the hospice of St. Mary of the German Knights. This latter hospice resembled the ruins of a church, as it was a Gothic style of building, and very large. Now, it was open to the air, and visitors could just go in, sit on a bench, and read or meditate. The shops were shut for Shabbat, and while we were there the Shabbat siren sounded. People were hurrying off to their homes, to the Western Wall, or to synagogue to begin their prayer. Through the Cardo, we were able to wind back to the Via Dolorosa, our own street. The street was usually so crowded one could not really appreciate any details of the architecture. Now, with so few people in the streets, we were able to notice for the first time the sign on the side of the Melkite church, St. Veronica's. The sign denoting the church to be the place of the 6th Station was high above the streets. On busy days, such details become invisible, and part of the charm of staying long-term in the Holy Land was the privilege of being able to notice these little details.

A side street led off the Via Dolorosa and up some steps. It was usually unwise to enter such streets unaccompanied, but as there were three of us, which made it relatively safe, we decided to explore. The side street was called el-Beriaq and it led to a long, steep street called Aqabat, which descended back to the El Wad Road in a big arc. Along Aqabat we saw several Mameluke-style doorways, dating from the fourteenth century. There were also a number of doorways decorated in the style of painting that the local people applied to the door fronts to celebrate pilgrimage to Mecca: stencils of stars and pictures of the Ka'abah, the holiest site in Mecca. The neighbours did this as a congratulatory gesture to the family that has made the *hajj*, the pilgrimage to Mecca that faithful Muslims are required to make once in their lifetime.

When we arrived back at the house, it was around five-thirty in the evening, and six of our students who had just returned from a side-trip to Egypt were there, telling us stories of their journey. José had been among them. He was a Filipino priest working in Ethiopia, and throughout his time of study he lived in Bethlehem with members of his congregation. On the trip to Egypt, José became the subject of everyone's teasing when the belly dancer got him up on the floor and tried to get him to dance. When he just stood there, confused and not responding, the dancer grabbed him by the hips and started to show him how to dance the traditional Middle Eastern belly dance. José had had no idea that this was the plan and, mortified, he panicked and ran back to his seat. After that the group kept teasing him about the belly dancer, and claiming that they had even heard him calling her name in his sleep. So when José cheerfully bounced up to us and said, "Did you hear?" we all started laughing. He was certainly a good sport about it. At that moment two of his travel companions came by and José said accusingly "You told them!" They replied, ever so innocently, "No—no more than about ten times!" To make him feel better, I promised to take José on a walking tour in the Old City, including the Russian excavations.

When the day of José's walking tour rolled around, I started to realize that despite his four months in the country, he had not spent the time in Jerusalem that I thought he had, because he did not seem to know his way around the very small space that is the Old City. We went first up the steps to the Coptic area and I was hoping to get into the actual compound where the priests and brothers lived. Instead we ended up on the roof again, and José asked the priest in attendance, in the Ethiopian language of Amharic, where St. Michael's chapel was. The Ethiopian priest kept shushing us and indicating the door into the upper part of the Holy Sepulchre, so we went in. The ancient Ethiopian Mass was underway, brimming over with beautiful chant and tons of incense. We stayed for some time in a meditative mood, enjoying the chanting and viewing the interior of the chapel. There is, for instance, a large painting of Solomon entertaining the Queen of Sheba, the event from which Ethiopians date their relationship with Israel. The congregation was just beginning the readings, and I shut my eyes and started to enter the mood, when José leaned over and said, "Their Masses last at least an hour and a half," so we departed.

We tripped through the Holy Sepulchre, the marketplace of the Muristan, and the Lutheran Church of the Redeemer, and then took the shortcut into the Jewish Quarter. Our object was to find the remains of the huge Nea church, built by the emperor Justinian but subsequently lost when the city was destroyed. Historians knew that it had existed, however, as there was a large church other than the Holy Sepulchre pictured on the Madaba map that I had visited the previous year in present-day Jordan. Even though we are now aware of the Nea, it was still very difficult to find. After searching all around, we finally found two bits that had been excavated: a small part of the apse, now embedded in the City Wall, and a part of a wall including the entry into a vault. The portion of the apse is marked, but is a very small remain, and almost invisible. The vaults are larger, but are not visible from the sidewalk, and people hurry by without knowing there is a historic site right beside them. The level of the church is considerably below the modern level, and all remains of the church were actually lost until the 1967 war. Shortly after the war, during construction of one of Canadian-Israeli architect Moshe Safdie's projects, a great empty underground space was opened up and was found to be part of the vaults of the Nea.

Near the marked remains of the Nea church was the Batei Mahase compound, where 19th century houses for Jewish refugees are alongside modern buildings built by the Rothchild family, all forming part of a vigorous community. We entered the neighbourhood from Batei Mahase, the street that ran alongside the city wall near the Zion Gate. There we saw tidy housing and public buildings where schoolchildren played outdoors in their playground, bordered all around by row homes and community buildings, all built in the same buff stone that is visible everywhere. No one seemed to mind our visit, and we were able to view the historical display in one of the community halls.

At the Russian excavations, our friend Jibril was again in attendance and I enjoyed showing José the bit of the Cardo, the steps up to the Temple of Venus which later became the Church of the Holy Sepulchre, the City Wall, including the "eye of the needle," the threshold of the Judgment Gate, and Hadrian's great arch. Again we had missed Anna. As photography was prohibited in the Russian excavations, I bought some of the poor quality slides on offer, to use in future Bible studies, and we took our leave. At the exit, José missed the stairs and took a flying leap. He landed on his feet but had scared himself, so was out of sorts, and shortly afterwards he returned home to Bethlehem. It had been a grand day out, and very typical of how much could be viewed during even a short outing in the Old City. The space was so tiny that a lot of history could be packed into a day.

Throughout the following week I continued to explore the little side streets with the student, Mary, but could not find the elusive feature known as the Small Wall. This gave us an opportunity to view the Arab housing, built tightly in little enclosed warrens not usually accessible to the visitor. We located an alley that appeared too dark to explore, and I had a feeling the Small Wall was down there, but it seemed to be in an area that outsiders could not enter. The so-called Small

Wall is a part of the Western Wall that is not in the Western Wall plaza, but is actually incorporated into someone's house, an Arab family who was said to welcome their Jewish neighbours to pray at the Small Wall by leaving the light on outside. If this is true, it is another extraordinary little peacemaking effort that we will likely never hear about on the news. We would have to find it another time.

That Saturday, Jim B, the Canadian priest, asked me to read the gospel at the evening Mass. After the reading, as is my custom, I held up the book and proclaimed "This is the Good News: the Gospel of Christ." These words are slightly different from what is written in the Mass book, and I noticed Jim smiling broadly to himself and mouthing the words "the Good News." I was a little puzzled as to why he thought this so odd, since the word "gospel" means "good news" and is a very usual term for the gospel. I was a little hurt and thought he might consider me quaint. From that day forward, however, Jim B did the same thing himself, so I managed to figure out that he was actually pleased with the words. I was very touched by his particularly nice gesture of imitation, and counted it as an affirmation.

There were plenty of opportunities for study within our convent walls, including two libraries. One was the theological library for use by the students. The other was a more general French library in the area of the house occupied by the remnant of the francophone nuns' community. We referred to this area of the house as the "Old Community" and I spent many hours within those rooms. There was seldom anyone there, and there were hundreds of interesting books and periodicals. It was in the Old Community library that I came upon a huge bonanza—a stack of old issues of "*Le Monde de la Bible*," an excellent magazine published in France with beautiful photographs of Biblical sites and articles by well-known scholars. I indulged myself in reading my new booty, especially savouring an issue completely devoted to the journeys of St. Paul.

Meanwhile, we had a guest in the house who was a French journalist-photographer, and he had wanted to interview an Israeli woman and a Palestinian woman to see what their typical days were like. As he did not know anyone in the Old City, I had begun asking around in order to find some women who might consent to these interviews. On one of my walks I ran into my French journalist, who was on his way to the Western Wall. I had already spoken to a Palestinian lady who had graciously agreed to invite him into her house. This seemed like a good time to seek help with the Israeli part of it, so we went to Moshe's shop. Moshe said his neighbour, a Jewish woman who was the hard-working mother of five children, might agree to it. When I phoned her I discovered that the lady was actually a bit shy, having been misled in the past by an American news crew.

They had had something of the same idea as my French fellow, but the news item they produced would have depicted Moshe's neighbour in a negative light, and she took this pretty personally. She felt that the story would have suggested that every Israeli woman wore designer clothes and fed her children bon bons all day, while the poor Palestinian woman did not even have soap to wash her children's clothes. While there are great differences in the daily lives of much of the populations of the two groups, this was an unfair portrayal. There are certainly people on both sides really struggling to make ends meet; but fortunately the network did not use the item at all. This had been a relief for the lady, and when I also learned a bit later that the French journalist had decided to abandon the photo project in view of the sensitivity surrounding it, I phoned Moshe's friend to tell her she was off the hook, and she was again relieved to hear it.

On February 3, we celebrated St. Blaise's day with the blessing of the throats. It is a strange old ritual. Blaise was a bishop who performed miracles in fourth century Armenia. He had at one time miraculously saved a boy from choking to death, and in commemoration of this, Blaise became the patron saint of throat sufferers. For his pains, however, he was martyred, beheaded by the authorities, in what was ironically a major trauma to his own throat. In the unique St. Blaise's Day liturgy, the officiant blesses the throats of the people by placing crossed candles on either side of the throat and saying a healing prayer. The form is unusual, but is a traditional expression of the healing ministry of the church, and I found it both reassuring and charming. It was a practice that I had not come across in parish life at home.

During the time that Isabelle-Marie was still convalescing with her broken arm, I was attending the Lithostrotos reception in her place, when an elderly Sister of Sion came through and told me that care of the Lithostrotos had always been her job. She went for a bit of a walk among the ruins, and came back to give me some tips on what needed to be done. She said that she used to enhance the Game of the Kings with tempera paint or cocoa so that visitors could more easily make out the etchings on the pavement, and that the archaeologists had told her that this was temporary colouring that would not seep into the stone. As there could be some risk to the sacred stones, I brought the matter up to the community, who felt it was better to be safe than sorry when dealing with an ancient treasure. More research was necessary before we started painting lines on the Roman stones. As it turned out, some weeks later an archaeologist from the University of Palestine came to the ruins to view them, and had no comment on the question of sprinkling cocoa on the holy site. He left a number where we could contact the experts whenever we needed them, but ultimately we carried on as we had been doing, showing the stones *au naturel.*

We had a little Brazilian sister named Wanda in our community. She was a very tiny, quiet little thing, who tiptoed around like a little bird, always smiling, and was generally held to be the sweetest person who had ever been born. She maintained that angelic persona only because she could not speak English, and her French was also fairly limited, so most of the household had very little discourse with her. She spoke French to me, her third language after Portuguese and Spanish, and entertained me with some hilarious stories that revealed what a naughty little thing she had been as a young sister.

Wanda told me stories about the wise old superior with whom she used to work in Sao Paolo and who, alas, had now left this world. Between the Sisters of Sion's Sao Paolo convent and the church was the bordello, and there were three more bordellos along the other side of the street. Often there would be disputes that Mother Superior would be called upon to settle, and whenever Mother arrived at the bordello, all the men would disappear. On one occasion, there was also a lot of noise from the seniors' residence, a 100-bed facility next door to the convent on the other side—the non-bordello side. Mother went in, satisfied herself that the patients were not cold or hungry, and ordered them back to bed. On further investigation she discovered that farm products such as milk and cheese that were being donated to the facility were actually being sold by the woman who ran the place, and the woman was pocketing the money. The residents were suffering from insufficient nutrition and probably from other forms of abuse. With police assistance, the purposeful nun took over the nursing home, ensured that everyone was being fed properly, and ran the place for two years before handing it over to secular caregivers. After she had been administering for only one month, however, and the residents had had one month of proper nutrition, they all started working again! Another funny story was the objectionable neighbour, a priest who was afraid of Mother, mainly because he had some under-the-table activities going on. Late one night he was caught sneaking around the grounds, and loading Mother Superior's pig onto a cart so he could use it to breed his pig. She caught him and put an end to the scheme, telling him the pigs were too young to be bred and he was to put her pig back where he found it!

Wanda had been a bit of a "baby nun" in that she had entered the convent as a teenager. She tried to enter when she was fourteen, but was told to go home and wait, and if she still felt called to the convent in a few years, she was welcome to return. She entered at sixteen. During her novitiate, she had been warned by Mother Superior that she was not to go out riding on her own. That was all

Wanda needed to hear, and at the first opportunity, she crept out to the stable, bridled her favourite horse, and rode off away from the barn. Something spooked the horse on the way, and Wanda ended up being thrown off, and dragged through the mud for a good many metres. Far from being remorseful, she was still laughing when she appeared, coated in mud, before her superior for the forthcoming scolding.

New students were arriving for the opening of the forthcoming term, and some of them were fellow Canadians. One of these was Raymond, who was the priest in the beautiful and historic little Canadian town of Niagara-on the-Lake. He joined the group who played cards and backgammon every evening and any other possible time. Another was Paul-André, a Jesuit father from Quebec who was living and working as a missionary in Brazil, and who would be staying not in our house but with the Jesuit fathers some distance away. The number of Canadians among us was increasing rapidly, and it was both reassuring and a bit odd to be surrounded by so many of my fellow citizens so very far from home.

The first Saturday of the term we had a special dinner to welcome our new-comers. Gleaming white tablecloths were used instead of our usual deep-toned coloured ones, and instead of individual tables for six, there was one large table set up in a horseshoe. The students were made to feel special, and they were very excited, although they were all tired from their journey to Jerusalem.

During this time, the household was preparing for the special dinner to be held for Fakhri for the fiftieth anniversary of his employment at Ecce Homo. He had actually been at Ecce Homo for around 55 years, but his time there as a child before being placed on payroll was not included in this statistic, and it was the "official" career that was being celebrated that week. I went out the day before the party to try and find a gift for him. Of course, in Arab souqs, the proprietors stand outside their shops and encourage customers to enter. On David Street a shopkeeper lured me into his shop, a young fellow named Sameer, which is an Arabic name, but he was blond and blue-eyed and actually looked more Finnish than Palestinian. I was looking for a pen and a blank book and he could not help me, but he managed to convey that he was urgently looking for a wife. He was so woebegone, and pressured me so much, I said that I knew some women and I would send them by his store. Poor Pat and Mel! I thought he was not likely their type, but who knows? I took his name and address, and hurried on to the book-store at Jaffa Gate, where I managed to buy a gift. I stopped for coffee with one of our students, and on the way back Sameer waved at me cheerily but conspiratori-ally. The young fellow had told me he was twenty-five and about to graduate in civil engineering, but our student had a bad feeling about the young man, purely an intuitive thing, and warned me to be very cautious of this chap.

The party for Fakhri's jubilee was a grand occasion. As many of the Sisters who could possibly come to the party did so, and thus it was a good opportunity for residents to meet some of the sisters who are normally scattered throughout the Mediterranean. All of Fakhri's family was there—the eight children with their spouses and little ones, several nephews—including Ziad and Rassem, our cooks, who had cooked the whole feast, staying overnight at the convent so they could get an early start. It was all Palestinian food, and there were speeches in Arabic, French and English. Fakhri received an inscribed gold watch and a thick sweater from the sisters, plus tons of gifts and cards from so many people who had worked with him. The little children all got mylar helium balloons and were as cute as a swarm of bugs. The whole family was gracious and charming. Some of the younger women had their hair covered and wore the traditional dress, whereas others dressed in western styles with their hair uncovered. Either way, it was for each lady her own choice. I learned that Fakhri, who seemed to us to be such a sage patriarch, was only sixty-four and his wife certainly much younger, but they were the heads of a bustling clan of descendants. With the family, the Sisters and the volunteers there must have been about eighty people there. As with any Middle Eastern occasion, there was an enormous abundance of food, and all the foods were traditional Palestinian dishes, but a few guests were disappointed there was no wine, as his is a pious Muslim family. Issa took videos, and everyone was excited, especially the youngsters. After the party the volunteers and sisters moved the decorations into the staff room where the staff would be honouring Fakhri in a further celebration the next day.

To wind down after the party, Melanie, Pat, Jim and Anne joined me in my kitchen for coffee and tea, and to reminisce, but the high point was when I tried to recruit Pat and Mel as visitors to the shop of their potential suitor, Sameer. I gave them Sameer's address, but they seemed not at all excited about their forthcoming wedding and new husband, and in fact were a bit alarmed, but said they would go by his shop. This was all that I had promised to him, and satisfied with myself, I went off to help Trudy take flowers around to the new students' rooms so that there would be fresh flowers there when any more newcomers arrived.

Always at the beginning of the new school term there was an opening Mass for the students, partly in English and partly French, with a visiting celebrant from down the street, followed by a festive lunch reception for the entire student body, a lovely affair with wine on the table and speeches by the directors of the school. The volunteers attended this affair, and we were introduced to the students as their potential helpers during their sabbatical in Jerusalem. At the opening luncheon, our table of naughty volunteers managed to pinch an extra bottle of wine so we became fairly tiddly, and an afternoon siesta seemed like a good plan.

One of the new students was an ebullient young Irish priest named Paul, and he and I sat on the terrace in the freezing cold drinking Turkish coffee in the evening. Although the weather was still cold and wet, we tried to sit out on the terrace as much as possible to enjoy the view of the Old City and the Dome of the Rock. The roofs of the houses were visible as well as the domes of all the churches, and we could see from our privileged location the Mount of Olives spread out to our left.

On the same day, I was guiding a new guest around the house and decided to explore some unused rooms adjoining the ancient Lithostrotos. A little chapel has been built beside the Lithostrotos for the convenience of pilgrims. In the corner of that chapel, we found a little door. Like two Alices in Wonderland, we went through the little door and discovered a large excavation or undercroft, including a round structure that I later learned was part of a Roman silo. It was a very exciting discovery, but the next evening at dinner, when I revealed to the others that I had found the little "cave" with the Roman silo, Sister Isabelle-Marie threatened to have it locked up as dangerous, and I started to protest this, quite theatrically I must admit. We got into a dramatic pseudo-argument, really hamming it up, but she did believe it should be locked so that pilgrims could not wander in there and hurt themselves. I conceded that this was prudent, and the next day a padlock appeared on the little door, which cut off any further exploration.

A new guest from Alsace, Jérôme, was at breakfast, a very young man of very few words, and with bright red hair—perhaps there were Viking raids even in Alsace. The students complained that Jérôme never spoke, and also never seemed to go out. He told me that he had no real plan for his Jerusalem sojourn, and was there mainly to sort out some of his thoughts about religion. He never spoke to the students because he had little or no English. I took Jérôme and another French guest, Giselle, to the Lithos, including the controversial "cave" before it was locked up. While it seemed that Giselle really enjoyed the experience, and after reading the Bible passage about the crowning of thorns, actually went on to read the entire chapter aloud and to borrow the Bible for the remaining week, I got the impression that Jérôme didn't enjoy all this Bible reading very much as he practically ran away afterward. There was a big moon that night; perhaps that had a bearing on his behaviour.

Giselle was very keen to experience the Old City, and in the morning she and I went to the Western Wall. It was *Shabbat* and I did not approach the wall, but

Giselle prepared a prayer and placed it into a crack in the wall. She suggested that we go up the ramp and try to enter the Al-Aqsa mosque and the Dome of the Rock. Until that moment, the entrance fee had kept me out of the Dome, but this visit was Giselle's very gracious gift to me. The Dome of the Rock is a 16th century improvement on an older, 7th century building, completely covered in a variety of peacock blue ceramic tiles, and roofed in gold. Inside the building, which is not a typical house of worship but which has the stature of a mosque, a circular walkway surrounds an enormous, prominent rock that juts out of the ground, several metres across. This rock is so high, so very prominent, that it certainly seemed logical to conclude this was the focus of the Temple of Biblical times. If so, then this rock surely must have been an important part of that worship, maybe even the altar of sacrifice itself. Today, it is in the custody of the Waqf, the Islamic religious trust of Jerusalem, and is particularly revered as the place from which the Prophet Mohammed commenced his mystical Night Journey. It is a very holy place, the third most important site to Islam after Mecca and Medina. There is a line in the old hymn St. Patrick's Breastplate that mentions the "old, eternal rocks." While it may be argued that even rocks are not eternal, seeing this particular rock made us feel we were given a glimpse of eternity itself.

We went home by way of the little side street that is usually accessible only to Muslims, but on this day the gate was open, and we were able to go through this way and to see what very few steps it actually was from our front door to the Dome of the Rock.

I decided to accompany Giselle and Jérôme to the Israel museum on my next Sunday off. There were tours offered of the collection, and we split up so that they could take the French tour and I the English. My tour consisted of archaeology with a bit of Judaica, and theirs was more varied, but in any case when the tour ended Giselle took the bus somewhere and I walked home. By that time we had lost Jérôme, but that evening he joined me in the old community room, where in the course of our talk I discovered more about what he was doing in Jerusalem. Jérôme mentioned a book that he had recently read: Le voyage de Théo, by Catherine Clément. This book, which has been translated into English under the title Theo's Odyssey, is a fictionalized account of a journey taken by a young boy to introduce him to world religions. The boy, Theo, meets various world peoples and has the opportunity to encounter their understanding of God. There is a parallel fiction by Norwegian author Jostein Gaarder, Sophie's World, that seeks to teach the history of philosophy to young people. After reading Théo, Jérôme came to Jerusalem on a quest, the nature of which he could not really articulate and with which he struggled all the time he was there. But he *was* there, so the book must have had a deep effect on him.

One morning around that time, I was working at the reception desk when I heard the most wonderful singing. Not that it was grand opera or anything, but the quality of it was prayerful and sincere. It was the Frères Maristes, a group of French brothers who were staying in the house and who were at that moment participating in their morning prayer. They were the most spiritual, and perhaps also the nicest, people we had ever met; they even managed to impress the hard-boiled Jérôme. In the midst of this serenity, the temporary residents were going through the process of registering at their respective consulates in Tel Aviv in response to the escalating situation with Iraq. I actually had a conversation with Anne about gas masks and where to go in case of attack. I started to plan what I would take with me into a shelter, if it came to that, and remembering my terrible experience in Syria, I started hoarding toilet paper!

That night our flat was the scene of preparations for St. Valentine's Day. On one side of our sitting room there was a small party in progress where some visitors were chatting, and on the other Melanie and Pat were cutting out Valentines for the Valentine lunch the next day. The students' Valentine's Day party was under way in the salon, all decorated by Pat and Melanie. The staff had made "upside-down," a very popular Palestinian chicken and rice dish, and a festive atmosphere prevailed. In actual fact, the students' lunch was in the salon because the dining rooms were full of 140 people from tour groups. Rennie sang "*The Rose of Tralee*" and a Schubert *lied*, "*Roselein*," for Pat. Everyone was delighted, especially Pat, although the performance was partly spoiled by some of the students who did not seem to understand that this was a rehearsed performance, and they decided to sing along with Rennie.

I had agreed to conduct a tour of the Lithostrotos in French for the Mariste brothers. French is my second language and I seldom speak it at home. Until this moment, my French language tours were for individuals and were very informal, so this was a bit daunting, but in keeping with their character, the brothers were both appreciative and supportive. Eventually, we were all sitting on the Roman pavement, and one brother, Jean, was selected to read all of John 19 because, they said, he was the *real* Frenchman. I expressed shocked surprise that he was the only *real* Frenchman, and they laughed. After his reading they fell into a profound meditation, a silence that looked like it was going to last. "Now what should I do?" I thought. These fellows were completely blissed-out, and I thought I would be stuck there for some time unless I beat a graceful retreat. So after a few words of closure, I invited them to go down there to that deep and inspiring place whenever they wanted, and I fled.

That evening I was bringing Turkish coffee on a tray to share with a new Canadian student, whom we called Brian the Younger, when the other students sitting with him in their "prayer group" doing their "meditation"—cards and backgammon—started to behave rather mysteriously. I later learned that I had barged in on the secret production of Valentine cards for the volunteers by the students. They quickly put the cards under the table while Brian and I obliviously had a grand time enjoying our Turkish coffee. Mary mentioned vaguely that she and Dominica had gone out to do a little job, so when the Valentines cards later appeared in the volunteers' mailboxes, Mary naturally became the chief suspect, and Dominica her accomplice. The cards were in the mail rack by dinnertime, hand written with a number of different messages. These were kind and thoughtful students.

Jerusalem was, is and ever will be full of Holy Eccentrics. These are not only those afflicted with Jerusalem Syndrome, the tendency to identify with figures from the Bible, but are people who start out as pious individuals but who become weird or extreme. Some of them are simply picturesque and sincere characters. My mystery person in the Latin chapel of the Holy Sepulchre was a good example. After my alarm on that occasion, I had not mentioned the visitor to anyone. But some weeks later Eymard, the student from Sri Lanka, was telling Mary that she was going to see her friend Paraclete at St. Anne's.

"Paraclete!?" I exclaimed.

"You mean the Holy Spirit!?" Mary exclaimed.

Eymard laughed and told us that that was her friend's name. When Eymard described her friend, I knew that Paraclete had been the stranger that I had seen in the Calvary chapel, and Mary said she, too, had seen Paraclete. We learned that Paraclete had been a Rosary sister from Nigeria but had left her congregation to become a holy hermit. She asked the Latin Patriarch for his patronage and he told her she could be part of his diocese but she would have to be self-supporting. She prayed rosaries for people in order to earn a bit of money, and Eymard believed that Paraclete actually slept in some nook or cranny of the Holy Sepulchre that the bishop had provided for her.

Some days after this, I was sitting at the Lithostrotos reception when a young Brazilian man named Heinar arrived at my counter, trying to decipher the Via Dolorosa folder. I asked him to come back at three when I would be free to help him and to introduce him to Wanda, with whom he could speak Portuguese. Heinar had a grand time talking to Wanda and enjoying the Ecce Homo terraces and basilica, and I said I would point out for him the Stations of the Cross on the Via Dolorosa. As we approached the last stations, it happened that the Franciscans were singing the Latin office at the Holy Sepulchre, and we sat surrounded by beautiful singing and lots of incense. Heinar was very moved by the experience, falling to his knees during the prayers. We were at the Calvary chapel and I suggested he go right up to the altar of the main Orthodox shrine and place his hand in the indentation where the cross is reputed to have stood, while I sat at the side of the Latin chapel. When Heinar returned his face was shining, as Moses' face was after meeting God on Mount Sinai, and his eyes were full of tears. He sat by me, placed his hand on my arm and whispered "It's wonderful!"

At that moment Paraclete plopped down beside us. It was an instance of God's profound sense of humour, pitting the sublime against the ridiculous in a shrine whose décor was over the top. Overcome with this, in an aura of incense, I tried not to burst out laughing as it would surely destroy the young man's experience, and Paraclete would no doubt be offended. We looked at some other features of the church and departed.

Our own little holy eccentric, and surely the sweetest of the lot, was Sister Bernadette. She came to Mass at our house every night and ensured everyone was settled in and had the necessary books or handouts. French-speaking, and universally addressed as Ma Soeur, we did not know whether or not she was a real nun, but her clothes certainly gave the impression of religiosity. She was a tiny thing who would never again see seventy, and dressed in a grey duffle coat and a hood that looked like the under-cowl of a knight's helmet. She lived at the community of the Syrian church where our accountant, Roger, was a deacon, and in fact if anyone ever phoned the Syrian church, Sister Bernadette generally answered the phone. I was told that she had taught philosophy at a respected university and had been known as a philosopher of some eminence. She now lived a life of simple piety, trailing around from one Mass to another, and I have speculated that the reason for her slight physique was that she probably ate nothing but communion wafers, and likely did not weigh eighty pounds.

During this unsteady time when we did not know whether or not war would break out, we had a thoroughly lovely English group in the house, a parish pilgrimage from Warwick. I had enjoyed some great theological debates with their wonderful priest, Canon Edward Stewart. Most of the group were well into retirement and could even be called elderly, but they were absolutely intrepid, marching off daily to their latest excursion. Canon Edward remarked that these people had been waiting all their lives for their pilgrimage to Jerusalem, and they were not going to let a little thing like the threat of war spoil it for them. They had already survived lots of war, including World War Two. This Middle East sabre rattling was nothing to them; they were absolutely fearless, and so deeply appreciative of being in Jerusalem at last. Now, however, this charming group of octogenarians in running shoes was leaving us, and we all felt sad that we would no longer be meeting them on their way to their outings. They had had a great time. The Brigadier was a natural leader within the group, and he and his wife thanked Melanie and me profusely, as did all members of the group, especially the gracious Canon Edward. We said our good-bye to the joyful band of folk.

While groups were leaving, the newly arrived students were by now starting to encounter the holy places that they had so long desired to see, and they were not joyful, but appalled. The Irish student, Paul, celebrated Mass that evening in the salon, and he talked with great candour about his shock in discovering the holy shrines of Jerusalem and how profane they actually seemed—how different from his expectations. We all knew exactly what he meant, as very many of us, and a huge number of our guests, experience shock and loss when we encounter the strangeness of the Jerusalem shrines, so foreign in ornamentation, and tawdry in their presentation. And yet, Paul went on to say, it is not the shrines that are holy, but the people who live here; it is human contact that is holy.

I decided to go to Christ Church, the church near the Jaffa Gate and the citadel that claimed to be Evangelical Anglican, although the Archbishop of Canterbury has apparently denied that the place is connected with the Anglican communion. In a country where it is illegal to try to convert the Jews to Christianity, Messianic ministries such as this teeter on the brink of impropriety. Still, the lovely old Christ Church is a very beautiful sanctuary. There is a large guesthouse, fairly pricey, with enforced rules. Their brochure reads plainly, *"As an Christian Guest House, we do not permit non-married couples to share."*

I began chatting with the gatekeeper, Meir. He was a Jew from Iran who had come to Israel in the '50s, then converted to the messianic movement. He showed me the guesthouse and dining room, including some pillars which were the remains of a Byzantine church and which were now visible within the house. There was also a large painting of Jerusalem in 1864, very interesting as it was possible to make out most of the monuments, but some places had not yet been built at that time. Meir promised to come and visit Ecce Homo, although he was living in the West Bank near Jericho and commuted to work, so it would be difficult.

In the evening, Anne called me and invited Melanie and me to the community. Melanie was sure we were in some kind of trouble and mused, "I wonder what we've done!" My guess was that it was to talk about our strategy during this political crisis between Iraq and the U.S. Since the continental U.S. was too big an opponent for Iraq, a U.S. ally such as Israel would be the likely target. I was right; the meeting was about what we would do in an emergency, and about gas masks. We stated our preferences—Melanie and I would both stay at Ecce Homo, and Jim would wait and make a last minute decision. Anne said she would collect our passports and go to the appropriate ministry and see if she could obtain gas masks for the volunteers. Sister Trudy, our director, said she wanted to ensure we had the right materials if we had to seal off a room—one in the guesthouse, and one in the Community. The right materials were polyethylene sheeting and cello or duct tape, all of which were in top demand and short supply throughout the country.

I had a glass of wine to ensure I would not be haunted by this conversation or the macabre hilarity that followed it. The previous night I had dreamt that my bed was in the alley outside the Lithostrotos door, and that because I had decided to stay there instead of in the empty and available apartment beside it, I ended up getting locked outside. If there was going to be a war, I did not fancy being locked *inside* Israel, but in such times you have to make a decision and stick with it. It was scary, but we all took our chances.

Many of our neighbours, including the elderly man who brought our morning newspapers, were supporters of Saddam Hussein. My dealings with our wrinkled, toothless paper carrier were quite formal. Every morning he would come into the reception area, nod and shake my hand, give me the papers, then wait while I marked the number of papers on the calendar, shake my hand again and depart. During these times, he became quite animated in his conversation, and without a word of English managed to express his displeasure with President Clinton and his great admiration for Saddam. There was, of course, very little I could say, as I still had not learned Arabic, so I just said "Oh?" and "Ah" at the appropriate times.

Although nothing seemed to work properly here, including household appliances, I decided to try to make banana cakes in the community. This was a challenge considering I could not read most of the Arabic and Hebrew labels on ingredients, but the community's oven sure beat trying to use the funny little oven in my rangette in the flat. Rassem the cook pointed out some of the things I needed from the kitchen. The community's oven had its idiosyncrasies as well, and Anne said that when the team first arrived in Israel they were completely regressed. Formerly professionals and thoroughly competent women, they suddenly could not use the phone; they could not use the oven or the stovetop; they could not use the bank. They turned into children again. In the end I did produce two cakes with icing that in no way resembled chocolate—in fact the icing sugar in the Near East in no way resembles icing sugar. At any rate, they made it into the category of edible by a slim margin in my opinion, but since, due to my vegan lifestyle, I had not had cake or pudding for a couple of months, I was very glad to have them.

I was very sad when the Frères Maristes left, and I vowed I would write to my new friend Frère Richard, who would be finishing his study in France then returning to Africa. They had all been wonderful guests. I did hear again from Richard, a very sad letter to say that his family in Congo had lost everything in the war in that country, his father had been killed, and the rest of them had become refugees. He subsequently wrote to everyone he had ever met in the world, in an appeal for help. The day that the brothers departed, I was so sad that I spent my breaks from work sitting moping in the Condemnation Church in the Franciscan monastery next door. How could the Sisters stand these constant departures? I was always in a state of grieving for the never-ending leave-takings.

That night the Community took the volunteers out for supper so we walked down to the Jerusalem Star. At the corner was a small demonstration—no, it was a collection of curious neighbours, police and army, a Cadillac with the drapes drawn, and blocked traffic. We hypothesized that Ariel Sharon, the hawkish cabinet minister who subsequently went on to become Prime Minister, was visiting his controversial house near Damascus Gate in the Muslim Quarter. The house was inside an arch over the bazaar, and he had suspended from the top of the arch a gigantic seventy-foot Israeli flag. At the restaurant I had falafel and Arabic salad, the usual choice for vegetarians when there was no specifically vegetarian menu; several others had steak. Afterwards we went to St. Mary's for a piece of the funny cake I had made, and we watched the news of the events unfolding between the U.S. and Iraq.

By now Isabelle-Marie had the soft cast off her arm, but the arm was still swollen and black and blue. During the next week or so we all checked on her periodically at work, as she insisted on going back to work in the Lithostrotos because she was so bored with being sick. There was time for me to do a bit of housework, and I put on some washing, hosed down our terrace in the flat and got ready to go to Ein Kerem.

Anne was already at Ein Kerem, having already spent another morning queueing up for gas masks. Trudy, Rita, and I went to the village by car, bringing with us a Christian Brother from Australia who was an Ecce Homo student. In the car we started telling stories of picturesque guests we had met. When we talked about the perennially lost Professor Evan, without actually mentioning his name, the student said, "Sounds like dear old Evan."

'What? You know him!" We could not believe this coincidence. Our companion told us that, incredibly, Evan used to be a large, football type of guy; then he decided that nuts and milk were the perfect diet. He lost a huge amount of weight, collapsed and went into an almost irreversible coma. The doctors were able to pull him out of it and he changed to a more sensible regimen, but from that time it was as if he were a different person. I was delighted with the fellow's descriptions of Evan as they were so true—he even mentioned Evan's hallmark habit of sitting with his eyes shut during a conversation, even when at dinner and surrounded by people!

At Ein Kerem, we wandered about the quiet property—gardens, cemetery, Father Mary's house—then we went to the Contemplatives' chapel to sing the evening office in Hebrew, followed by supper. After this our friend, Brother Jack, gave a presentation on the Exodus passages immediately following the decalog, including the splashing of blood on the people. When a volunteer to be presenter at next month's colloquium was called for, everyone in the room looked intently at their toes, not wishing to make eye contact. While intensely contemplating my own toes, I sat thinking I would not be able to do it all myself, but maybe with a partner. At that moment, another woman, Gemma, said "Well, I wouldn't be able to do it all myself, but maybe with a partner." It was destiny; I volunteered. Gemma and I were to get together the first week in March to talk about our plan for the following month's Torah study. After our group arrived back home, I looked at the passages we were going to be talking about and I almost died. It was Exodus 35-40, with the instructions for the building of the Tabernacle. To me, this was the most boring part of the Bible, and any time that I tried to read the Bible from beginning to end, this was the part where I always gave up. It was going to be a challenge.

The staff and students coming in early in the morning to the reception desk told me that there were hundreds of police and army at the Damascus Gate and people were being questioned. It was suspected that there was a bomb in the Arab street market outside the gate. After work, we had a prayer meeting for peace since everyone's attention was somewhat diverted to the current political event, and afterward Mel and I had a few of the others over to our flat. Anne was playing "*I Don't Know How to Love Him*" on her flute while I tried to open our bottle of wine.

At that moment Jim came in with one of the students, who grabbed Anne's guitar and started playing something else, his aggressive musical intrusion steamrolling right over her song. At the end he received some words of appreciation from the group, and I said "Didn't you like what Anne was playing?" He suddenly realized what he had done, and he said, "Oh, I was trying to accompany her," which of course was not true, but from that moment he did try to accompany her. He played a lot of songs and we sang along and finally he asked everyone for their favourite hymn, and played them. I like a lot of hymns and couldn't think of a favourite, so I offered "Draw Us in the Spirit's Tether," and I sang the first two verses.

"Who wrote that?" the fellow demanded in disgust, and I said I didn't know but it was called the Union Seminary hymn. To this he snorted contemptuously "Oh, God!" and did not comment further.

I think that moment was the end of our relationship, I was so hurt, and so shocked at his insensitivity. I withdrew from the scene and as the others seemed to be having a good time, I went to the far-off library and read until I felt sure everyone had gone. After living throughout this time in a house that so untiringly promoted religious tolerance, I was stunned into silence whenever such narrow-mindedness was expressed. When I returned to the flat, only Pat and Mel were there, and we talked about something else for a while, to change the subject before we turned in.

One afternoon the community and volunteers went up to St. Mary's for a gas mask demonstration from Issa. In the event of an emergency, you go to your polyethylene and duct tape shelter and listen to the radio. When the Israeli government has analysed the chemicals used in the attack, they would let the public know which packet to insert in the gas mask. There is also a syringe in the box that one might have to inject into one's hip if so instructed. Issa took all the parts of the gas mask kit out of the box and showed us how to use them. He had lived in Jerusalem and the West Bank all his life and to him this was routine. To us it was terrifying and bizarre. Now we three Canadian volunteers were really nervous and resorted to macabre humour, since we had no gas masks and had had very little joy obtaining information or assistance from our government, apart from their advice to return to Canada at once.

I sat out on the terrace and tried to write in my journal. It was a sunny, warm afternoon, and Jérôme of Alsace joined me at my patio table. He peered over the edge of the balustrade and joked that despite the troubles there were still pilgrim groups on the Via Dolorosa, although they were all wearing gas masks. Melanie was making a special dinner for the community, so I helped her chop a few vegetables then hurried off to worship. In his sermon, Don talked about peace; it was a message we all needed to hear. Melanie's pasta dinner was excellent and we lingered afterwards, chatting with Don, then we walked down the road to the Old City car park and Anne drove us to Ein Kerem.

It was a wonderful night. I developed a secret retirement plan to go to Ein Kerem and to stay there for the rest of my life! In the morning we sat outside with the Ein Kerem volunteers and discussed our respective plans in the event of war with Iraq—try and obtain a gas mask was the only thing that popped to mind. Despite these worries, at Ein Kerem I felt I was at the most beautiful spot on earth. This was like being one of the Romantic poets, transported away by the exquisite beauty of the surroundings. Life consisted of a walk around the gardens, a conversation with my friend Hugo, the cat, whom I had met the previous Thursday night, and a visit to the cemetery to chat with Father Mary. The view from the garden was spectacular, taking in what in Bible times was called "the hill country of Judea," the Hadasseh medical centre on the hill, and the olive grove and almond trees that surrounded the monastery. Ein Kerem is the place traditionally associated with Mary's visit to her cousin Elizabeth. If Mary were to visit Ein Kerem today, she would surely still be transported by the beauty of it: the sights and the fresh smell of the gardens, with the almond trees in blossom. We snoozed for a time and played with the cat, ate a huge lunch out in the sun. After dark we walked down to the bus shelter in the village and took the bus to King George Street, and from there walked home.

Earlier, I had had my first organ lesson from the lovely little Korean sister, Dominica. The lessons took place in the freezing cold basilica, and were based on my very minimal ability to play the piano. We used the electronic organ, not the ancient pipe organ that was destined for restoration. I found the technique a bit tricky but fun. From Dominica's Korean hymnbook I was to practise *"Nearer My God to Thee," "Silent Night,"* and another familiar sounding hymn to which Dominica did not know the English name. On my return from Ein Karem, Dominica came flying out to remind me I have to practise every day. She was right, of course. There is only one way to get to Carnegie Hall: practice, practice, practice!

The newspapers implied that the situation surrounding the U.S.–Iraq standoff was pretty good. At the same time, Anne phoned me to say that in my hours off I could go up to the mall and buy myself a gas mask and the house would pay for it. In Canada, we go to the mall to see movies and to buy fashions; here in Jerusalem, you go to the mall to buy gas masks. We received a fax from the Canadian Government advising all Canadians and Americans to go home unless you had essential business in Israel—the same message that both governments had published in the newspaper throughout the week. Still, on the other hand, the streets were full of pilgrims; we had over a thousand people through the Lithostrotos that morning, and forty Canadians came for lunch. A tour group of forty-five Austrians was staying in the house. People did not seem to be rushing home because of the news.

After my duties on Reception, I practised the organ until noon. It was really getting me down practising *Silent Night* two days from Lent. Tourists visiting the basilica from the viewing platform outside could hear me playing, and I was sure they were wondering why we were playing Christmas carols at Ecce Homo such a long time after Christmas. The previous day I had told Dominica that I would not practise *Nearer My God to Thee* with all of this war crisis going on, as it reminded me of the Titanic. Dominica was completely confused by this, and told me that in Korea this hymn is used at communion; no one would associate it with funerals, as we do. Without *Silent Night* and *Farewell Titanic*, I was left with only the familiar-sounding hymn with the unknown title; I asked Dominica for some new pieces, and she thought a moment, then said "Number 61 in the Korean hymnbook." The woman knew the book by heart!

At dinner, there was a Benedictine abbot from Provence at our table who was entertaining his old comrade from St. Emilion, and they were two very French, hale good fellows. They had a bottle of wine and shared it with us, and they also shared their considerable insights on viticulture. Paul was also at our table, and he and I both promised to bring wine to dinner on the following night; it would be the last chance for a party as that next night would be Mardi Gras.

7

Into the Wilderness—a Lenten Diary

Mardi Gras

In places where the Mardi Gras festivities are a tourist attraction, the event of Mardi Gras can last a week or even two, but in the Christian calendar Mardi Gras is just one day. It is the Tuesday before Lent. It used to be the last opportunity to use up all the sugar and fat in the house before Ash Wednesday, when the lean days of fasting would begin. For this reason, it made culinary sense to use up these materials by making pancakes, and in some places Mardi Gras, which means literally Fat Tuesday, is called by its other name: Pancake Day.

We were in a festive mood because it was a birthday for two people in our house, a man and a woman, so at lunch we had a huge pink and blue birthday cake, and although the two were unrelated, they did a theatrical bit of holding the knife together to cut the cake, as if it were a wedding reception. That evening gifts and cards were given to the two birthday people, and a few of us had a little dinner celebration with the Benedictine abbot and his stocky, picturesque friend who was the owner of a cuvée in St. Emilion. Paul joined us as promised with his bottle of wine, but this was to be our little group's last hurrah. For my own part, during the forty days plus Sundays of Lent, I maintain a strict prohibition as part of my personal discipline, and so by tomorrow I would be tea-totalling. The students invited us to their Mardi Gras party, and everyone had a grand sing-along—and for a few brave ones a dance-along. Anyone with any kind of talent did a little party-piece or played guitar, and we all had fun.

Ash Wednesday

At lunch on Ash Wednesday there were a couple of complaints from students about the meager fare, to which the dining-room waitress replied, "You're fasting!" and kept on humming as she worked. A vote was taken among the students as to how Lent would be observed, and it was decided that there would be meatless Fridays; no change for me as I live a meatless life. On Ash Wednesday, Christians specially observe the day by having a cross of ashes marked on their foreheads. On that day we are reminded that we are dust, and to dust we shall return. It is all quite sobering and grim, but we cannot party every day, and sometimes we have to come face to face with our sins. Our household and a few guests had our Ash Wednesday Mass in the salon with deposition of ashes, as it is called, and a homily about the traditional Lenten observances of prayer, fasting and almsgiving, which can be tailored to suit the spiritual needs of the individual or community. In many ways, I have a hard time disciplining myself to certain kinds of piety, so during that time I have a predictable plan. I increase my vegan discipline to eliminate wine, which I normally love; that is my way of fasting. As a prayer discipline, I make a list of forty people and pray for someone off the list each day of Lent, and hold that person up in my thoughts. To give alms, I find a worthy cause to whom to give a bit of time or money. It's not huge, but it is the sticking with it that counts.

The next day I attended Rabbi Michael's class on the Jewish festivals. He talked about Passover, so a lot of it was study of Exodus. This was good background information, considering I was going to be doing a presentation on Exodus at the Torah study at Ein Kerem. Michael showed us a lovely little miniature Torah scroll that had been a gift from his congregation in the U.S., and which had in turn been a gift to the congregation from David Ben Gurion when he was seeking financial support for the new state of Israel among Jews in the U.S. As the little scroll was, ages later, still in the box and stored in the attic, they hoped that Michael would be able to make better use of it, and he has made excellent use of it indeed in teaching. I was inspired by this, and managed also to do some study in the Biblical library for my Exodus passages on the construction of the Tabernacle.

February 27: Commemoration of the Crowning of Thorns—Ecce Homo's Special Day

When our classes and chores had ended, everyone in the house started to get ready for the Mass of the Crowning of Thorns, which would be celebrated in the basilica by the Latin patriarch. The liturgy was very traditional, in keeping with the conservatism of Jerusalem. The patriarch was His Beatitude Michel Sabbah, a Palestinian very quiet in demeanour who, despite this absence of modernity, was a solid and inspiring pastor to a people undergoing such crisis. It was mainly in French with a smattering of Latin thrown in, I suppose for old times' sake, and the patriarch and his entourage gave it an air of formality. The Our Father was supposed to be in Arabic, but the old fellow apparently forgot this and automatically plunged into the prayer in French. Despite the dustiness of the celebration, there were a few good parts. One was the offertory, which consisted of a procession of about a half dozen Ecce Homo employees, who were Palestinian Christians and who thoroughly enjoyed their role in the liturgy. The music was good, too; Anne played her flute, Paul played the organ, and Rennie, the student with the beautiful tenor voice, sang the psalm. I sang the gospel acclamation. There was a variety of hymns, ranging from very contemporary ones to that old favourite *How Great Thou Art*. Some friends of the house and community came to the service, including members of other religious communities and some local laypeople. After the Mass there was a tea, then we dispersed until dinner. The whole thing was counted a great success.

That weekend, Anne and I finally found the Small Wall, that bit of the Western Wall that is separated from the public gathering area, and that comprises the lower part of a later building. The "wall" consists of one or two courses of the huge Herodian stones along the foundation, but the rest of the building is made of much smaller stones erected much later. I felt triumphant on finally finding it, and a bit awed. Once again I experienced that feeling of being in the presence of something of great antiquity that is holy; yet it was now being used for a very ordinary purpose—someone's house. We spent only a few minutes there as we were intruders in someone's respite from the world, but took some pictures as a souvenir and to illustrate the enormous size of the stones. There is an epilogue, unfortunately. The next time I visited the old neighbourhood, a couple of years later, the Muslim residents no longer appeared to be there, and in the courtyard formerly welcoming visitors to prayer, there was a yeshiva, a religious school. I wondered what had become of the previous residents.

We still had the taciturn Jérôme with us, and I occasionally sat with him and tried to get him to chat. He was a quiet lad, who didn't seem to have the knack of small talk. Lucky for me some new guests arrived at the house, who were easier to engage in conversation. Joel, for example, and his mother, Joan were very interesting. Joel lives in San Francisco and Joan in Pennsylvania, and both were doing things in the world, but in very opposite spheres. Until a short while before, Joan had been the dean of an academic institution but was now doing something entirely different. She identified that change is now a career expectation of most people, so to facilitate the process she was setting up what she called the Change Agency. Joel was not an academic, however, and I thought him a very good candidate for the Listeners' group, or another kind of activism. He was, for example, a bicycle-activist, vigorously advocating the bicycle as a green alternative to the motorcar for urbanites. These two were Jewish by tradition, but were interested in hearing about various spiritual disciplines of the Christian life, and seemed to be quite interested when I talked about such practices as Ignatian or Augustinian forms of prayer. They expressed a range of spiritual interests, and Joel gave me a most interesting syllabus from a group called the "Guild for Psychological Studies," a spiritual academy based in San Francisco and inspired by various religious traditions; they brought groups to Jerusalem as part of some of their courses. It was an intriguing syllabus listing courses loosely based in tradition, but with a distinctly west coast flavour.

Some nights the evening meals were more vegetarian than others, and occasionally I would spend some time later on cooking my own dinner. Sometimes I was able to make myself a simple chickpea humus to have on hand as a protein supplement, spread on toast. After supper, I would often make Turkish coffee for myself and invite someone else to join me in the "old community" as it was always a quiet refuge, and socializing in a library is a comfort. I began to feel a connection with these rooms, and eventually to feel a deep sense of sharing in the life of the house and its ministry. I have never felt that I had any vocation as a sister; I could never be obedient, and I have not discarded the possibility of one day remarrying. Religious life was, for many reasons, not for me; but gradually I knew that I wanted to carry on the work of the Sisters of Sion in some way. I would join the congregation as an associate.

A group of students from the English-speaking class was getting ready for a trip to Mount Sinai as part of their program, and I had been quite slow in realizing that the trip was being planned and that it might represent an opportunity for me. I was at that moment completely penniless, but in an incredibly gracious gesture, Sister Rita called me and said that if I wanted to go to Sinai with the group, the sisters would lend me the money. As it happened, the trip turned out to be quite hard to put together on short notice, and as well I was simply not psychologically prepared, so I let the opportunity pass me by. I had a reprieve a few days later when I became aware that the French-speaking class was also going on the Sinai trip, so I approached their director, Bernard Geoffroy, about possibly joining in. He could not possibly have been more gracious. Not only was the Sinai trip open to me, but I was also invited to join the class in their weekly Biblical outings. He said there was a special price for volunteers. The special price for volunteers turned out to be free, just pay entrances, but most entrances were in any case covered by the National Parks cards purchased by the school. I was given a student card, which could be used anywhere in Israel. This was the most splendid generosity, and I bubbled with anticipation; my first school outing would be the following week—to the Negev.

During my time in Jerusalem, the Vatican published its fourth statement on relations between Christians and Jews, *We Remember: Reflections on the Shoah* (Holocaust). As this paper was of particular interest to the Sisters of Sion in their ministry, a member of the congregation who was coming from Rome to teach a unit on Jewish prayer of the High Holidays brought with her the text of the statement, and within twenty-four hours of its release, we were studying it in the classroom. It was a document that I never thought I would read in my lifetime. It represented a change in Christian thinking toward taking responsibility for the antijudaic strand of Christian tradition. The document talked about repentance and actually used the word *teshuva*, the Hebrew word for repentance that is used in connection with Jewish rites. It was deeply satisfying and highly appropriate that we were listening to Sister Lucy's lectures about Yom Kippur and the *teshuva* leading up to it, and then shortly afterward hearing this statement. Lucy's work in Rome includes consultation on *SIDIC*, a journal of Jewish-Christian dialogue, as well as maintaining an interfaith centre and library. Her teaching on a post-holocaust hermeneutic of Jewish prayer was well received by the class. We were all delighted to meet her and to hear the very helpful ideas of this thoughtful teacher.

The same afternoon I went off to the Ratisbonne Institute to meet with Gemma, my volunteer partner for the Torah study, as she had an office within the institute, although her principal ministry was directing coursework at the Center for Holocaust Studies. Jim's girlfriend Darlene was visiting from Canada, and she was originally going to come to Ratisbonne with me, but changed her mind at the last minute as she wanted to do some shopping. I walked into West Jerusalem by myself.

The Ratisbonne Institute, later known as the Christian Center for Jewish Studies, is located very near the Great Synagogue of Jerusalem. It was established by the Fathers of Sion in the nineteenth century, but now is a Vatican jurisdiction. The building and grounds of the institute are truly beautiful, and I spent a bit of time looking at the early roses and other flowers surrounding the old fountain and statuary. Gemma met me at the gate and gave me a brief tour, including the well-appointed theological library, and I did not want to leave without picking up information on how to apply for studies. We bashed out a workable plan for our presentation on the Torah readings on the tabernacle, which were the portions to be read that week in the synagogue, then walked to Gemma's home at the convent of the Sisters of St. Joseph for tea and a chat. Apart from the eastern branches of Christianity, the Franciscans were the first Roman Catholic, Christian order to have a presence in the Holy Land, and they arrived in the thirteenth century; the Sisters of St. Joseph were the next, and they arrived in the nineteenth century. These were, in some ways, the old guard. The Sisters of Sion arrived in the 1850's.

Darlene should have come with me to Ratisbonne. When I arrived home I found her with an ice-pack on her face—she had fallen on the terribly uneven cobblestones in the souq and broken her nose. She was in good humour, but it was evident that the poor lady was in pain. Later I sat at Mass, in a half-listening state. I was brought abruptly to a start by an amazing comment at the beginning of the sermon. Raymond was speaking of his illness with tuberculosis when he was a young seminarian, and the words that flew out to me like a giant neon sign were, "…and my life was saved by Dr. Dean Macdonald." Some few years before that time, my own father's life had been saved by this same surgeon, Dr. Dean Macdonald, in St. Catharines, Canada, near Niagara Falls. Dr. Macdonald performed the pioneering duodenal ulcer surgery on my dad and prolonged his life for 19 years. I was catapulted back to my childhood, when we often drove by the local sanitarium. It was a dark and mysterious place to me, mainly because my parents spoke of it in a hushed tone. They were afraid of tuberculosis, and associated it with death. I now thought what a coincidence that during some of those drives past that hospital forty years ago and half a world away, Raymond had been in there! And fortunately, he had not died, but was here before me, looking hale and well. It is, of course, a very small world, but Jerusalem seems to make it even smaller. It is astonishing how many coincidences happen there, and how many people with whom one is somehow connected somehow appear.

I started to assemble some items for the Negev trip on Monday with Bernard's class, including maps and a Jerusalem Bible in French. Between my shifts as receptionist, I also tried to prepare ahead some vegetarian meals for myself, some of which worked and some of which didn't. The vegetable pasta soup was always a great success, but I had no success with making tortillas out of the peculiar kinds of flour whose labels I was unable to read. I made refried beans out of a large bean that might have been halfway between a pinto bean and a fava bean. The resulting paste was practically edible, but I was desperate, and ate it as a protein supplement anyway. The taste was very strong and not at all similar to the refried beans we put in tortillas at home.

My Alsatian friend Jérôme had gained a reputation among the resident students for his aloofness, although he spoke very little English and was a quiet person anyway, so there was not much chance of finding him partying among the English. He and I spent considerable time together and would always speak French. Sometimes we walked someplace specific, but mainly he spent long hours sitting outside on the terrace, writing in his journal. One morning I walked up the Mount of Olives with Jérôme. We visited the Greek Orthodox shrine in an underground cave that the Eastern churches revere as Mary's tomb; the Church of All Nations with its adjoining Garden of Gethsemane; Dominus Flevit where the Lord wept over Jerusalem; and we took in the view from above the cemetery. Once he was no longer in a group, Jérôme could be very funny, and so we talked and laughed throughout our excursion. Walking backwards up the road, and of course not knowing where he was going, Jérôme quipped to me, "Jesus is my guide." I said that if he kept walking backwards up the middle of the road he might be seeing Jesus, his guide, a lot sooner than he expected because he might get hit by a truck. Gradually Jérôme came out of his shell somewhat, and the residents of the convent noticed this with pleasure—they had thought him to be too stand-offish and were delighted to see a glimpse of the real Jérôme.

It was still very cold out at night, but I often sat out at the patio tables on the terrace and enjoyed the night view, my flask of Turkish coffee at hand to warm me up. One evening the Canadian student Brian the Younger joined me and brought a little portable tape recorder. He had turned it on at six o'clock Sunday morning to record the sounds of Jerusalem from his window next to the garden, and he wanted to play the tape for me. A wild symphony of hundreds of birds fairly roared from the little speakers, punctuated by the occasional call to prayer and the bonging of church bells. It was glorious, the sort of thing you hardly notice when it is actually happening. Playing such loud birdsong must have confused any birds that were roosting near us, however. It was hard enough for poultry to figure out the rhythm of life in the Old City as there was always illumination, and confused roosters crowed at all hours, unable to get their job right. Now we were messing up the poor songbirds.

Then there was the mystery of the Cow Pie Liturgy, which, happily, achieved its final dénouement. One day of the same week I arrived at the convent reception desk where my roommate Melanie said "Why is the basilica full of cow pies?" I trotted around the corner of the hallway to view the basilica. Indeed, in front of the altar was a board with several round, flat objects, which to my imperfect eye appeared to be made either of mud or pottery, arranged on it. It was a new one for me. I could not imagine with what obscure rite it could be connected, and I thought it odd that the cow pies were not arranged as a cross, but in a straight line at uneven intervals, perpendicular to the altar table. Through that day and the days following we were reluctant to book Masses in the basilica, thinking that visiting groups would do something to upset the arrangements for the forthcoming cow pie liturgy. A few groups did go in there and celebrate Mass, making no comment about the cow pies arranged in the chancel. I came to the conclusion that these people knew what the cow pies were for even if I did not, and they were not bothered about them.

At last all was revealed. Now it was well known throughout the house that at Midnight Mass on Christmas Eve a student tripped up the chancel steps and broke a bowl of burning incense all over the carpet. It was a terrible event for the poor man, and a terrible event for everyone in the pews as they thought the poor fellow had had a heart attack and might even be dead. He was not dead but only terribly embarrassed by this radical invention of a new rite, and the chancel carpet was full of smouldering holes. The board with the arrangement of cow pies, actually flat lead weights, had been placed there by Rita and Issa who were trying to make the unruly new carpet to lie flat, all to no avail. This might be the way a lot of new rites and traditions come into being—nothing theological about it at all.

The Negev

The Nablus road in the early morning was a bustling scene of traffic, buses and mainly Arab pedestrians, picking up their breakfast of sesame bread rings or mini-baguettes from the stand at the corner. Sheruts were dropping off workers, commuters from the West Bank, some of whom were queued up outside the Ministry of Interior to obtain their permits. My instructions for Monday morning were to be outside Mahfouz' bus garage in the Nablus Road at 0700. It was a sunny morning and I arrived in plenty of time, with my backpack full of lunch, water, mountains of snack food, a Bible that weighed a ton, plus several maps. I was in the wrong spot, of course, until another student arrived and showed me the meeting spot a few metres up the road. About ten of us set out from this spot in our large and luxurious Mahfouz tour bus, nothing like what I had imagined we would take. We picked up other groups of students near their residences. My French-Canadian acquaintance René sat with me in the bus—a charming gesture since there were plenty of window seats available. René was a personable companion. Originally from Quebec, he had been working in Chile for many years—a cheerful and dedicated guitar-playing priest whose whole life represented an option for the poor.

The bus drove around to Ein Kerem and picked up Bernard, who immediately went on the microphone and started his tour-guide talk. As a licensed guide, Bernard was very comfortable with this role and always did a talk along the way, usually with a Biblical perspective. As well, when we would arrive at the sites we were to visit, Bernard would do the guiding, give the Biblical history and often do also a lovely close reading or exegesis of the Biblical text.

We took the road through Kiriat Gat and eventually to Beer Sheva, the "capital of the Negev". Beer Sheva is both an ancient site and a new city, of which a large percentage of the population are Bedouin, and where one of the great places of interest is the Bedou market. The city is home to 150,000 people, and to the beautiful new Ben Gurion University of the Negev, founded in 1969. The university is a striking, modern building with a soaring façade and a huge front garden of date palms. The ancient site of Beer Sheva is associated with Abraham's pact with Abimelech, purchasing the right to dig a well some four thousand years ago[1]. The very name Beer Sheva means "well of the seven" in memory of the seven lambs that Abraham paid to Abimelech for the well. In Bible times *Beer-Sheba* was considered the southern boundary of the southern kingdom of Judah[2], and there was even an expression "from Dan to Beer-Sheba" which denoted the entire nation.

The treed hills of Ein Kerem had given way to fields of green wheat, the product of specialized desert agriculture. Now heading south of Beer Sheva, we were entering a more desert terrain—plenty of dust between the sparser vegetation, yet persistent wildflowers everywhere. The soil in the Negev was a greyish colour, punctuated by bits of green. The modern Israelis have worked hard to revive the ancient Nabatean technology of farming the desert, and this form of agriculture has been so useful to waterless countries that the methods are being taught in the

---

1.   Gen 21:22 and 26:26-32
2.   2 Kgs 23:8 and 2 Chr 19:4

Ben Gurion University to plenty of young agriculturists from Africa and other dry regions. In the farming areas we saw fields of yellow flowers, and in the desert red poppies as well as other purple flowers and white.

Here and there alongside the road were Bedou encampments, some in the traditionally shaped wall tents, and some in white cone-shaped military tents supplied by the government. At each camp there were women dressed mainly in black, men with the red and white kafeeyahs on their heads, several carefree little children, and plenty of goats and donkeys. At the bottom of a hill, on which was perched a fortress dating from King Solomon's time, we passed a boy driving a flock of sheep, still living the lifestyle of Solomon's subjects.

All of the Negev is the domain of the Bedouin, and they still gather to trade at the market in Beer Sheva. Although some of the Bedouin are still nomads in their tents, others now live in houses or semi-permanent buildings. The Israeli government was at the time trying to bring education to the Bedouin while still allowing them as much as possible to follow their traditional ways. This schooling was being delivered through the building of modular schools throughout the Negev, and school buses picked up the school children anywhere they stood along the highway.

Our destination was the walled city of Mamshit, the now excavated desert-farming centre of the Nabateans. It was developed from an old caravan saray and flourished in the Mid-Nabatean period. It was later rebuilt by the Romans and appeared on the Madaba Map thanks to its two churches, the Nile church and the Eastern church. We approached the walled city made of warm yellow stone and examined its cisterns, homes and churches. As the Nabateans were also horse breeders, there were beautiful equerries. Unfortunately, the still extant mosaics on the church floors, which I had seen in photos, were covered over with stones to protect them from the ravages of visiting Bedouin who often settle down in excavated sites and live there. Bernard recounted the history of the resistance to "images" in the church, as well as describing the technique of water-gathering. There is usually a lot of night condensation in the desert, in fact if you sleep outside in the Negev at night, you can wring out your sleeping bag in the morning and extract litres of water from it. The Nabateans successfully gathered this condensation by means of stone terracing and little basins. The water that they gathered in this way was then used in irrigation. After our visit to the ruins, we had our lunch in the shade of the rest area at Mamshit, and then got back in the bus for the next drive.

We carried on to Newe Zohar (Neh-veh-zoh-HAR) near the Dead Sea and the region traditionally associated with the destruction of Sodom and Gomorrah in Genesis 19. When we got out of the bus a student read the chapter aloud that recounts the story of the destruction of the two cities that God punished for their wickedness. Bernard spoke about the history of the region, the salt geology, and did a beautiful exegesis of the text. There are many rock pillars in this region, and the major component of the soil is salt. We passed by the curious salt formation known as Lot's wife, a pillar of salt that is especially suggestive of a human being and redolent of the woman who disobeyed God by looking back at the city as she was escaping its cataclysmic end;[3] hence the expression: *never look back.* At another lookout point we could see the Dead Sea, and beyond it the mountains of Moab. We drove through the Biblical towns of Hebron and Bethlehem, but these were explorations for another day, and we made our way into Jerusalem. As each group was dropped off near their dwellings, I said goodbye to my companions and I trudged home from Mahfouz' garage.

The next day after my grand day out was a working day. I made the breakfast then did receptionist duty. Issa helped me to get the stove going in the Old Community, so after lunch I put some banana cakes into the little oven, then ran down to the basilica to repair hymn books with Anne. This task consisted of checking the contents of each one of sixty folders filled with photocopied music, and it was such a frustrating job I ended up packing the hymn books into a box and taking them to the flat, along with a hot banana cake with chocolate icing. Anne came for the cake, and Rita arrived at that moment for our meeting. We ate lots of cake, drank coffee, went over the documents for the Associates' program, and Rita said she would recommend me for the program. I had a feeling this kaffee-klatch was going to change the direction of my life.

After our meeting I recalled that I still had a cake in the oven with the heat reduced to ultra-low. I arrived in time to rescue the cake, ice it with chocolate icing, then to visit with Isabelle-Marie and her school friend Monique, so I invited them up to have some cake in the Old Community. The two lovely French women did not even bother to sit down but started in on the cake while standing up in the kitchen. They looked like a pair of school kids enjoying a forbidden snack.

That evening Sister Polly, one of the students, played some meditation improvs on the guitar. Polly was an interesting old girl. When Polly first arrived she wore a brown Franciscan veil all the time over her lovely long, white, thick wavy hair. One day she appeared with her hair down and it was gorgeous. After a time, the veil appeared on fewer and fewer occasions; at first she would wear it for

---

3.   Genesis 19:26

"official" purposes only: for Mass, to do the Stations of the Cross, and so on. Eventually we hardly saw the veil at all. The rest of her attire was selected for comfort, and generally consisted of an Arran cardigan, a skirt, bobby socks and runners, all variously with or without the veil. Polly was a delightful holy character and a good sport. One day she asked the men at our dining table what the little red switch was in the bathroom, and they replied it is to turn on the outlet for the electric shaver. Polly said she has been turning it on and off religiously each day, thinking it was to heat the hot water for her shower!

In a convent where we were constantly surrounded by exciting scholarship, perhaps the most amazing course of study was Sister Wanda's English lessons. As a Brazilian, Wanda's first language was Portuguese; she was also competent in French and Spanish. Wanda needed English in order to function well at Ecce Homo so she was enrolled in a structured American English program. Wanda studied very hard and took this study most seriously, so she made progress in spite of the strange nature of the curriculum. The content of this course was so outlandish that it became the subject of jokes, and Wanda was always being asked what new words she had learned. One lesson taught the expression "nudist colony" and everyone asked where she would ever use this information. By incredible coincidence it was used at Mass the following evening when the homilist used the expression "as welcome as a mosquito in a nudist colony"! Wanda learned words like "voluptuous" and "willowy" before she had learned "fat" or "thin". The living end had been reached when Wanda come home with a lesson on drug words of the 1960s, and learned that "snow," "horse" and "acid" had meanings other than their surface significance, and we really did wonder where sweet Sister Wanda might use such language.

I was awake at 04:00 waiting for the muezzin's call to prayer at 04:30. As if it was not enough having main minaret across the street, a new mosque had also been opened across the street, just as loud as the original one, so now we were getting it in stereo. The francophone class was planning their Sinai trip, and I hurried to Bernard's office to give him a down payment. It was the Jewish feast of Purim, and I had a busy workday, but I had made arrangements to meet Pilar, a retired Spanish sister in the French program, at her lodging with the White Sisters so we could go to the synagogue to hear the reading of the book of Esther. Traditionally, the entire book of Esther, "the whole Megillah," is read at Purim. Some others from the house wanted to come along, but it took a few of them so long to get ready that I suggested Rita lead the English ones to the Great Synagogue by way of Akhron Street and I would trot over to the White Sisters to get Pilar, and the French speakers could follow another way. Wanda came with me, as it was easier for her to speak French than English. When we crossed at the light in front of the Damascus Gate, we saw Pilar and her friend Rose Marie coming up the street. The three Latin ladies had their own speed. They linked arms, and three abreast, they swayed slowly up the street, unable to manage the hills any faster. We met up with René and he tried to hurry us all, but the three were not to be hurried. In the end we made it in time before the service began—saved by the fact that the sisters knew a shortcut through the park.

When we arrived at the Great Synagogue of Jerusalem there were hundreds of people arriving, and queuing up for a thorough security check including baggage search and metal detectors. No airport had ever done a more thorough search on us, and I began to wonder if going to the synagogue were not a more dangerous activity than I had ever suspected. I was asked if I had a gun or even a plastic gun and my daypack was searched. We later learned that the prime minister, Binyamin Netanyahu, and his wife were at the service, and undercover police and security were throughout the synagogue. There were lots of little kids on hand in their costumes, and the prime minister's son was a small cowboy. Wielding his plastic guns, he was riding on the railing near Mr. Netanyahu and was talking to the prime minister from time to time during the service. We were separated from René, of course, and were up in the women's section. I could see members of our English-speaking group, as well as the Sisters of Sion with their students from Ratisbonne. Pilar was between Wanda and me, and Wanda and I could barely keep from laughing as throughout the service, while the pious were following along in their *megillot*, Pilar was openly reading a travel article about Mount Sinai. Throughout the reading, children were ready with their noisemakers, and whenever the name of the villain Haman was spoken, there was a great din of noisemakers and of people banging their hands on the reading desk. It was great fun. Afterwards, outside the synagogue, Anne Catherine met us and was giving out the special Purim cookies called *Hamentaschen*, the "ears of Haman".

There was a great crush of people outside the synagogue, and René had said he would not wait afterwards so the four of us ladies went down to Ben Yehuda Street to see if there were any festivities. There were a few people in their costumes but in the main it was quiet—most of the public festivities had been the night before. I grabbed a falafel as we walked back to the Old City, and Pilar and Rose Marie left Wanda and me at the Damascus Gate. It was dark but the walled streets of the Arab quarter were illuminated. As we walked, a group of young Israeli men overtook us, singing loudly and running down the El Wad Road in a provocative demonstration. When we arrived back at Ecce Homo we found the rest of the Purim group in the dining room having a late supper.

The next morning we heard there had been a bombing on the Nablus Road in front of the White Sisters' convent where Pilar and company lived. Everything was blocked off and even pedestrians could not get through, so they did not come to school that day. We heard that a number of people were taken to hospital, four of whom were wounded. It had happened in the Arab district, and the wounded were French pilgrims—it didn't seem to make sense, as these French had nothing to do with the local situation. During the day I visited the Jerusalem Pottery near the sixth station of the Cross in the Via Dolorosa, an Armenian pottery work, whose wares were more expensive than the regular tourist wares, but certainly more lovely. The pottery was owned by the Karakashian brothers, who were the purveyors of the street name tiles embedded in the walls of the Old City. The most delightful of their items for sale were tiles with colourful scenes of Bible stories; Noah, Abraham, Adam and Eve, the Nativity, and so many other stories were depicted as simple but colourful and lively drawings.

I had made arrangements to go with René to St. Stephen's Church at the Ecole biblique, near where the bomb had gone off, where we believed we would be able to get a ride in diplomatic vehicles to Beth Shean. I was to meet him the next day, Saturday, outside the Damascus Gate at 08:40 hours. The program was an outings and sightseeing arrangement organized by the Ecole biblique to give diplomatic staff an opportunity to do some sightseeing, and the public were invited to take part if there was room in the car. René and I were placed with a couple called Oys and Jeanne from the South African government. The fifth passenger was Dominique, a young French researcher doing a paper on some facet of Palestinian history. None of the passengers was terribly diplomatic by vocation, so it was very sporting of Oys and Jeanne to go through with the trip. We had a beautiful drive up the Jordan Valley, the garrulous Dominique doing most of the talking, and he was very bright with a great range of interests.

When we arrived in Beth Shean we had only to flash our National Parks cards and we were admitted free into the site. Our guide was Marcel, a personable Frenchman and a scholar at the Ecole biblique, who gave a very general talk about the site, and then took us on a very detailed inspection of the Roman city and the ancient tel. We took special notice of the mosaics, and climbed the tel for a splendid view of the surrounding valley. Archaeological excavation was just beginning atop this tel, and somewhere under the upper strata was the town on whose walls the body of Saul, ancient Israel's first king, was displayed by his Philistine slayers[4] around 1000 B.C.E..

---

4.   I Samuel 31:10

A wonderful carpet of wildflowers was spread all over the hills and fields, and I was shocked when a callous woman in our party grabbed a handful of the beautiful red anemones and idly tore them to bits, strewing the ruined petals on the path as she went. Some people might have called her a Philistine, but out of respect for the poor Philistines, I thought to myself, *"Quelle vache!"* As I knew from my previous visit to the site, the Roman habitation of Beth Shean was a beautiful city of the Decapolis called Scythopolis. The road leading into and out of the Roman city was in modern times colonnaded by a neat double row of palms, but in some places excavations showed the Roman Cardo two metres below, and that road had been colonnaded with beautiful Roman pillars. Scythopolis had been an especially beautiful Roman city, and is still renowned for its mosaics. The most famous of these was the Tyche mosaic, which has a central motif of the goddess Tyche as guardian of the city.

We piled back into our convoy of five or six cars, all bearing CC or CD licence plates: *corps consulaire*, and *corps diplomatique*. The next stop, very nearby, was the Hippodrome, which had been excavated and exposed to view, and was at some distance from the rest of the ancient ruins, so there was no tollbooth. We could not find a suitable place to eat nearby, so the convoy set out for Jericho to a restaurant familiar to them. René was very insistent that he and I would remain outside and eat our picnic, even when the others insisted they would buy our dinner. René is a minimalist whose life decision has been an option for the poor, and he allows himself few things that his parishioners would be unable to obtain. Had he not been there, I would likely have caved in and joined the group, but in view of his firm philosophy, we parked ourselves on a tile step beside a Jericho road and consumed our picnic lunches in the warm sun. A very young woman, just a girl really, went by pushing her baby in the stroller, and she would have walked past us frowning except that I engaged her eyes, smiled and said hello. She was delighted and spoke to me in English, a limited conversation, but a friendly one. Two local men were parking their car across from the restaurant, and they also were most friendly to us, wanting to know where we lived and enjoying the best conversation we could share given their limited English and non-existent French, in the presence of my completely non-existent Arabic. After their meal, the diplomatic corps returned to the cars, and Oys dropped us off at Lion's Gate, after which René walked me to the convent door and carried on home. We had had a grand day, without spending a cent, thanks to the great generosity of the Ecole biblique and the volunteers who do the driving on their days off.

Mass was just about to begin in the basilica so I hurried down to the church. John, our Dominican friend from the Ecole biblique, was the celebrant and he did a charming talk on the parable of the fig tree[5]. In this story, a vineyard owner wants to cut down his fig tree because for three years it had not borne fruit, but his gardener offered to dig around the root and put manure on it if the owner would give the tree one more year. John used to do quite a lot of gardening at the Ecole, so this story really engaged his interest. He pointed out that the fig tree was a symbol of the leadership of the day, so the people listening to the parable would have been roaring with laughter at the image of piling manure all around. Later, at dinner in the community, John continued talking about gardening, giving Rita all kinds of advice on plants and soil. John also said that he had been meeting with a group of lay people who were trying to become involved with the apostolic life of the Dominicans without joining and taking vows. As with other religious congregations, they were trying to establish a new lay level of membership—and one of the people meeting with him was Oys. What a small town! Clearly, this was why Oys was involved with the outings program at the Ecole biblique.

The next day I was offered another outing. Jim had rented a vehicle and after breakfast he, Darlene, Anne and I set out for Galilee by way of the Jordan Valley. It was a beautiful, sunny and warm day. The wild flowers were absolutely at their peak. We had heard that Switzerland is the country with the most wild flowers in the world, but Israel comes in second. This must have been the best day of the year for wild flowers in the Jordan Valley. The meadows on either side of us were thickly dotted with an exquisite carpet of these beautiful flowers: red, yellow, purple and white, all arranged on a background of intensely green grass. The usual stopping point on these trips up the Jordan Valley was the crocodile farm, and we stopped there briefly for a coffee and to buy petrol, then enjoyed the rest of our drive to the Galilee region.

We took Darlene to the Baptismal site, her first encounter with the Jordan River. Along the shore of the Sea of Galilee we stopped at a lovely spot and told stories about things people had said when they came to the Holy Land. My favourite was the story of a participant at a retreat in which the question for reflection was "Who is Jesus for you?" This fellow wrote only "Jesus is the one who sets the prisoners free." Very long before, as a young man, he had been a prisoner of war in Vietnam, and it was so terrible that he could stand the torture and ill treatment no more, and decided that he would commit suicide as soon as possible. But first he prayed "Lord, if you are there, set me free." The next day the Americans came into the camp and rescued all the prisoners, and the young man was set free. Later he became a priest and dedicated his life to the gospel.

---

5.   Luke 13:6-9

On a high hill there is a church that commemorates Jesus' exorcism of the demons into a herd of pigs, called the Miracle of the Swine church at Kursi. In the New Testament story[6] the pigs went over a cliff and into the sea, but today the cliff associated with the event is very far from the water; in fact, the highway is between the water and the cliff, so very much has the Sea of Galilee receded. We stopped the car at the side of the highway below the ruins and Anne read the story aloud to us. A short while later, we passed over the little bridge on the Jordan and saw that the little trickle we had seen the last time we were here had swollen to a much greater torrent, and thus was not so disappointing for Darlene. We stopped at the Russian church with the red domes near Capernaum and rang the doorbell at the end of the drive, but it was again Sunday and only the chickens and peacocks came to the gate. We visited Capernaum, then Jim's favourite picnic spot, and Anne and I sat down on the beach and ate our lunches, while Jim and Darlene went into the nearby orchard to pick themselves a grapefruit. At that particular spot you can hear the conversation of fishermen out in the water in their boats, but as if they were talking in your ear. It is an acoustic phenomenon, and Jim is convinced that that is the spot where Jesus, as reported in the gospels, taught from a boat so that people could hear him. Everyone on shore would have been able to hear his teaching.

We went to St. Peter's Church, associated with the primacy of Peter, where there was a noisy gang of Arab schoolgirls visiting with their teacher, an equally noisy nun who was at a total loss to control them. Jim could not enjoy the spot with all of this racket and we left shortly after arriving. At the Mount of Beatitudes, Jim came out with a friend, Lawrence, who said he would call Sister Carmelina to meet us. Lawrence seated us in the dining-room and brought coffee, and Carmelina, dressed in the brown Franciscan habit, joined us. She was Maltese, a very gentle soul, and she was the gardener responsible for much of the beauty of the gardens surrounding the little dome-shaped church. We went back to the Galilee Inn. Here Jim's other acquaintance, Ben, had his restaurant bar. We had perfectly fried chips and beautiful lemon tea flavoured with fresh herbs. The last time we had been there Anne remarked, tongue in cheek, that Ben was probably short for Benedict, so we had been secretly referring to the establishment as Benedict's Place ever since!

Jim had made a commitment to pick up three of the students at the Lion's Gate at twenty past seven to take them to a concert, so it was a wild drive back to Jerusalem and we counted ourselves lucky to get home in one piece. Anne and I

---

6.   Matthew 8:28-34

tried to eat in a restaurant but it was too late—the Jerusalem Star had no falafel, and a nearby restaurant gave us stone-cold chips and falafel, squashed down by the filthy hands of the little boy who waited on us, and we did not fancy it. We trudged home and searched the dining-room for food, to no avail. I made my own dinner in my little kitchen.

The next morning was the Monday outing of the francophone class to Megiddo. I had regretted missing Megiddo on my sight-seeing trip the previous year, because of its importance in the Bible and in the development of Judaic worship, and hence of Christian worship. The day was slow starting. I left the house late, at 06:55, running against the clock to be at Mahfouz' garage at 07:00. I had been kept awake by a tremendous wind crashing everything together, and when I went out in the morning I saw that there had been a spring sandstorm. The air was a dusty golden soup, and sand had been deposited everywhere. As I ran to the meeting place I was, of course, breathing sand and crunching it between my teeth. I felt a bit sick for some time, but I had plenty of time to recover because for over three-quarters of an hour nothing happened anyway. There was some mix-up about the driver, and when we finally departed nearly an hour later the people we were supposed to meet at Notre Dame were gone. Meanwhile, there was some activity in the Nablus Road, up the road from where the bomb had been the previous week. Our group witnessed the violent arrest of a young Palestinian man who was kicked four times with tremendous force by the arresting soldiers. We picked up the few members from Ratisbonne and then, at Ein Kerem, our teacher, Bernard, who was in a fury. He got on the cell phone to the bus company and it was decided that the rest of our group would be transported at company expense in a sherut and meet us in Caesarea. We saw little until we got farther north as the air was so thick with dust, and Bernard told us that the temperature typically would now fall and it would rain.

We passed by one small town after another, including Lod, the village that is the address of Ben-Gurion airport. Lod was biblical Lida, one of the places associated with the apostle Peter, along with Caesarea and Joffa. The population in this area is mainly Jewish. Life here is a mixed blessing as sandstorms are regular in spring and enrich the soil, but they also deposit sand and dust all over the villages and in the houses. This combination of alluvial soil, sand and mountain run-off produces a fertile mix in the region west of Jerusalem. Petah Tikvah, "village of hope," is a new city dating from the new birth of Judaism after 1967. North of Petah Tikvah is the Plain of Sharon where the Philistines regrouped before returning to Gilboa to defeat King Saul. There were big oak trees in the plains of Sharon until the Middle Ages; the Crusaders compared them to the forests of

Europe. Now they are all gone, swept away by Europeans and war. Throughout the region we encountered road works and terrible traffic tie-ups.

We were still choking on dust and sand as we drove through Pardes, a village whose name is a Persian word that has the same root as the word Paradise. The ancient sage, Rabbi Akiva, who was martyred in the Jewish revolt against Rome in 136 CE, said that to enter into Pardes is to enter into Paradise. This is one of those wonderful gems of Hebrew wisdom that is built on word play, and that in itself illustrates the principle it seeks to describe. It is actually about studying the Bible. Biblical Hebrew is basically a consonants-only language, and so the words for Pardes, which means "garden," and Paradise are spelled the same way. They consist of the letters *peh, resh, dalet* and *samech*. These four letters are also an acronym for the different steps involved in a Jewish tradition of Torah study used in the kabbalah, the mystical tradition of Judaism. *Peh* is for *pshat*—the literal level of meaning; *resh* is for *remez*—the metaphorical or "story-telling" meaning; *dalet* is for *drosh*—the level of further inquiry; and *samech* is for *sod*—the hidden or esoteric wisdom of the passage. To "do" pardes is to begin with the most obvious meaning, the most mundane layer, and to ask of the text, "What are you saying?" Other meanings will reveal themselves. Thus the name Pardes, in addition to suggesting Paradise, is also suggestive of the love of Torah study.

In Akiva's day, Pardes was a little, insignificant village, and to compare it with Paradise is very consistent with the entire endeavour of the Hebrew Bible, in which the poor, lowly, or humble are held up as being especially beloved of God. So what Rabbi Akiva meant was that this activity, this "pardes," is the key to scripture, and it is like saying that the divine is revealed in the most ordinary and mundane of things. Talk of Pardes and you will enter Paradise; Paradise, like the essence of the Torah, exists in simplicity. A hundred years before the time of Akiva, Rabbi Hillel stated the principle in an even more radical way. There is a famous story about a student who came before Hillel and asked Hillel to teach him the entire Torah while the student stood on one foot. To this, Rabbi Hillel replied, "What is hateful to you, do not do to your neighbor. That is the whole Torah; the rest is commentary. Now go and learn it."

At the rendezvous near Caesarea we met up with our missing fellows and set out for Megiddo. It was a savage atmosphere when we arrived at the Iron Age ruin of Megiddo with its walls dating from Solomon's time. The dust storm swept through the open plain surrounding the site, the air was soupy with sand and dust, and the palms swayed furiously. We entered the now excavated city and viewed the altar, a circular raised platform made of stones. So this was Armageddon, the Hellenized rendering of the Hebrew words Har Megiddo, or Mount

Megiddo. Here was the stage whereon the final battle between the forces of good and evil would be fought.[7] This sanctuary, formerly Canaanite and later Israelite, is the nine-thousand year old ancestral cousin of our own worship. The configuration of this early altar, and the rites and animal sacrifices practised here, provided the pattern for later Jewish rites in King Solomon's Temple in Jerusalem, which in turn contributed much to Christian worship and came down to us in the sacrifice of the Mass. We descended into the great underground tunnel that King Ahab built three thousand years ago as a hidden water conduit to ensure that fresh water would flow into ancient Megiddo even if it were under attack. The tunnel was enormous: 183 steps down and quite a long way to the spring and to the hidden exit beyond.

When we emerged it was beginning to rain. The Bible calls this rainfall after a dust storm the Rains of Benediction, because it is the source of replenishment of the soil. This area is still farmland. The Plains of Yisreel, the biblical name for this central plain, is now occupied by kibbutzim, the great communal farms established there in the early part of the twentieth century, very difficult to see at that moment because the air was too thick with sand.

Our next stop was the spring of Harod[8] where Gideon selected his army to fight the Midianites. First Gideon allowed whoever was trembling with fear to return home, and twenty-two thousand returned home. Then Gideon separated those who lapped water like a dog from those who carried water to their mouths with their hands. God promised to deliver Gideon's company from the Midianites through those who lapped, which was only about three hundred men, and surely the most unsophisticated of the assembly. The spring emerges from a cave at the foot of Mount Gilboa, and we all inspected the stream. Jean-Claude knelt down to see what he could see inside the cave, and someone shouted "Look! Jean-Claude is lapping like a dog!" We were still chuckling about poor Jean-Claude as we sat down to hear a lecture about the story, which illustrates how in Hebrew tradition God chooses or saves the smallest, the weakest, the humblest, the least likely in every case. This concept was not new when it appeared in the New Testament and upheld Jesus of Nazareth, the poor man from a small town. It was already a very old Hebrew idea that was recounted in some of the oldest parts of the Hebrew Bible.

Mount Gilboa was the hill where King Saul died around 1015 or 1010 B.C.E.[9], and it is still natural and undeveloped. Wild flowers bloomed every-

---

7.   Revelation 16:14-16
8.   Judges 7:1ff

where, including a variety of deep purple iris that grows only here and nowhere else in the world. The panoramic view spread out below us included large farms, kibbutzim settled immediately after the Russian Revolution. It is possible that the hill has remained wild and untouched-looking because it was cursed by King David.[10] The sky was sombre now, and we learned that it had begun to rain all over the country, cleaning the air of its golden burden of sand and dust. After a couple more stops in the coach, we set out for home, under greatly improved weather conditions. When we arrived back at the Old City it was dark.

On St. Patrick's Day the Irish were out in force—not a military force, but a party force. After the day's chores a large group, consisting of everyone in the house except for a few, left to go to Notre Dame Center just outside the Old City for Mass at 6:30, with one of the students as presider. Wanda and I stayed home and prepared the dinner for the faithful remnant of eight or so who were not going to the party. I was unfamiliar with the big steam oven in the kitchen, and as a result I overcooked the vegetables. In the candlelight at our dinner table, the food didn't seem so bad if you didn't inspect it too closely. The people who went out to the party had a more gala St. Patrick's Day, but sometimes it is good to stay home. For one thing, the weather at this time of year was unpredictable. We had just finished sweeping up the residue of the big dust storm when we were hit by a great hailstorm. The sunroof over our reception area was a kind of heavy plastic that sounded as though it were being bombarded with boulders. I had said I would join the others at Notre Dame for coffee and for the social part after the dinner, but in this weather there was absolutely no way I was venturing out. I put together the breakfast for morning, and Wanda did most of the tidying up.

The next morning there was snow! I could not believe my eyes. After the beautiful weekend with all the wild flowers, then the sandstorm, then hail—now this! Spring was slow in making inroads. I was on Lithostrotos reception duty, and since by now the power was out, I thought we would have no visitors. In fact, we were busy with pilgrim groups who were fleeing inside the buildings and not wanting to be outside in the inclement weather. The sisters scurried around with emergency lamps trying to make the excavation hospitable, although the cistern was simply too dark for us to allow entry to visitors. After about an hour the lights came back on and things gradually returned to normal. When the sun came out the snow began to melt rapidly, and people returned outside.

---

9.   1Sam 28:4 & 31
10.   2 Sam 1:21

Jerusalem comes to a halt whenever it snows. There is simply not the equipment to remove snow quickly and easily, so people cannot get around. As the staff had not come in, except Ziad the cook and Iskander the maintenance man, Ziad cooked the lunch and Pat did all the dining-room duties by herself. The students, who had a day off classes because their instructors could not make it to the convent in the snow, helped clean up the lunch, including doing the dishwasher. I did some office chores then went to relieve Isabelle-Marie at the Lithostrotos reception. At that moment, a fellow came to the door and said to us, "My mother was a Sister of Sion…" and with that, Isabelle-Marie began to laugh! The fellow, ignoring this, launched into his story, but the greeting had struck Isabelle as funny and it was several moments before she recovered from the joke. It turns out that the American gentleman's stepmother had been a Sister of Sion for 20 years, including a term as Superior in Kansas City, before she left the convent to get married. At the outset of her career, she had been in love with a wealthy young man in college and her parents had not approved of the match so she entered the convent and was quite successful in religious life but later left to marry a widower with a son. That son was our visitor. He and his wife were with another couple, and they asked me to give them a tour of the Lithos, so this I did. Fortunately, they seemed oblivious to Isabelle's mirth and instead were awe-struck by their encounter with the Lithostrotos and with our house. They were thrilled with the place and told Isabelle and me that it had been the highlight of their trip.

The next day was the Torah study that I was to lead in concert with my study partner, Gemma. It was late afternoon when our study group drove out to Ein Kerem, five of us squashed into the tiny vehicle. We reviewed the evening office first so we would be prepared for it, since the service was in Hebrew, then we went to the chapel at La Solitude, the home of the Contemplative Sisters of Sion. After the prayers, there was a simple dinner, then the Bible study.

The passages included the instructions for building the tabernacle and the Ark of the Covenant[11]. I began by telling the story of the wonderful liturgy that I had attended in Vancouver as part of the World AIDS conference a couple of years earlier. The liturgy had been an interfaith service at Christ Church Cathedral, whose interior walls had been completely draped with large panels of the AIDS Quilt. The Quilt was a portable collection of large memorial panels that, like the veils of the tabernacle, had transformed the cathedral into a giant temple of healing and a dwelling place for God. The text that we were studying starts out with a reiteration of the Shabbat mitzvah, the commandment to observe the sabbath,

---

11. Exodus 35:1 to 40:38

and Gemma read this part of the text in Hebrew and English. The group then was invited to discuss sabbath observance. Participants offered insights as to whether or not it is appropriate for Christians to observe Shabbat, that is, to observe, in some way, Saturday as a day of rest. There was great sensitivity around this, as participants did not want to appropriate anything that would be considered a discreetly Jewish sign of identity, or to do anything that could be seen as cultural theft. The group members pointed out, however, that the Sinai covenant has never been revoked, including the Shabbat mitzvah, and that Sunday celebrates the resurrection, whereas the Shabbat celebrates creation. So Saturday and Sunday, they concluded, serve different functions in the Christian week. The early church observed Shabbat into the third and fourth centuries, so it would be in keeping with liturgical reform, which seeks to recover some of the patterns of the early church, to observe the Shabbat in some way. Participants mentioned books on "Shabbat" and the "tabernacle" and gave brief reviews of what they had read.

In addition to its role in the personal human journey, the Exodus is the national foundational epic of Israel. As part of the study, I talked about the Star Trek episode *"Birthright,"* in which Worf tells the young folks why we tell these old stories, that is, to "tell us who we are". I wanted to illustrate that the Exodus story, like Worf's ancient epic, tells Israel who Israel is. Later in the week Anne showed me the Ents' story from *"Lord of the Rings,"* in which the tree talks about how trees, or Ents, say their name. It takes a very long time for them to say their names as their entire story is their name—but one has to take the time to say who one is.

It was the evening when the clocks were to go ahead an hour—in Israel only! It would be another week before Palestine would put the clocks ahead, and as the Old City spans the two cultures, the week in between promised to be the reign of chrono-chaos. I was the victim of baking chaos also, as I bought what I thought was baking soda to make a cake, but the resulting cakes were a total disaster. The baking ingredients in that country are never what you expect them to be, and I had the additional challenge of having to throw the ingredients together while scurrying around the main kitchen trying not to get in the way of the cook. Someone suggested there may be a gracious way of throwing the cakes out to the buzzards, but I thought better of it as the prospect of having buzzards flying overhead was unappealing. I suspected that buzzards produce very large excrement with fragments of undigested bone sticking out of it. The cakes went into the bin.

That spring I made friends with a guest from New York, a retired lady named Mary, who had come to the convent as a pilgrim. I promised her I would show her the streets of the Old City, and over breakfast I drew her a map. I hoped that when I am Mary's age I will be as active as she is, and as fiscally responsible. Although she lives in one of the most costly areas of the U.S., Mary stretches her dollar as much as she can so she can enjoy her retirement, such as by being a museum volunteer. Mary and I set out for the vicinity of the Zion Gate with the intention of visiting the Dormition Abbey, but that day it happened to be temporarily closed as the community was celebrating the feast of their patron, St. Benedict. While we waited for the celebration to finish at the Dormition, we visited the ruins of the Hurva Synagogue. It was a sunny day, and we were sitting on a stone bench inside the old ruin when a young man wandered in and began looking around. It was obvious from his attire that he was from a religious Jewish family as he wore the dark suit and large, creased black fedora of the Sephardi Haredim. He spoke no English, but in our efforts at communication we deduced he was visiting Jerusalem from Tel Aviv, and we were surprised by the open warmth that this fellow showed to us, since more often the Haredim have no interest in speaking with Christians. This lovely young man could only manage a very little bit of English, but his beautiful face and kind demeanour very effectively conveyed the depth of his greeting. He not only shook our hands, but when I managed to convey I was from Canada he kissed me on both cheeks! This was so unexpected, so very welcoming to us as foreigners, and especially as we were women, that this charming young man's absolutely extraordinary gesture made my day!

When we arrived back at our Jerusalem home, Mass was just starting, but I was called upon to escort two Palestinian archaeologists who were viewing the Lithostrotos. They were researching the area from Herod's Gate to the Via Dolorosa during Ottoman times, and even though they knew a great deal about the history of this little area of land, they were nonetheless surprised at the extensive Roman excavations below the Ecce Homo convent. Many people had remarked to us from time to time that the Ecce Homo ruins were under-promoted, and encountering the Lithostrotos is often an unexpected pleasure.

When I trotted into the basilica, late, the gospel was being read and it was the parable of the Prodigal Son[12]. Father Don's sermon was about reconciliation, and he included an opportunity for the Mass to be stopped and resumed tomorrow so that we could meanwhile be reconciled with one another. No one raised a hand to request such a recess, however, and it was a good thing since Don later confessed that he really had no plan of action in the event that someone took him up

---

12. Luke 15:11-32

on the offer. Reconciliation was a fertile topic, though, and later on as we went up to the Community for dinner, we were still talking about the intriguing story of the Prodigal Son. In the story, one of two brothers demands his inheritance from his father, then goes off and squanders the money on prostitutes. He drifts down in the world, until the point is reached when he is working at a job tending pigs. For a Jew, this was indeed hitting bottom as pigs are considered ritually unacceptable. When the young man realizes the pigs are eating better than he is, he is jolted into going home again and seeking his father's forgiveness. His father is overjoyed to see him, and kills the fatted calf for a celebration banquet, but his brother, who has been faithfully at his father's side all that time, is jealous and grumbles about this. His father says, "this brother of yours was dead and has come to life; he was lost and has been found." And what does the word "prodigal" mean, anyway, as we seldom hear it except in connection with this story? The word, I found out, means lavishly extravagant. Other questions about the story were tossed around: Where was the mother? Why did the brother feel like a slave or a captive? The story poses so many intriguing questions to explore further.

Melanie, Pat and I made ourselves prodigal lunches for our next day's journey, but we dilly-dallied so much and set out so late that Sunday to rent a car that it was well into the day before we got started. I had already had my first disaster, which was that I laundered my wallet and everything was wet, including my now half-dissolved student card. Melanie drove our little red rented runabout up the Jordan Valley, and we stopped at the Crocodile Farm for a snack—not of crocodile, but of chips. Our circuitous route through the country included Nazareth, and we reached Akko in the afternoon, parked in the street, then walked to the seaside and along the promenade toward the old Crusader city. The actual entrance to the Crusader city was elusive, and we wound around the Arab residential streets. The population seems mixed as you hear both Hebrew and Arabic spoken in the street, and signage is in Hebrew, Arabic and English. People were friendly and no-pressure, and when Pat would start playing football with little kids in the street, they were all delighted with their new playmate. The highlight of the day was visiting the bat colony inside the Crusader fort and we spent some time trying to communicate with them. There is a culture of seaside cafés where we could order chips and humus, and we sat and watched from the sea wall as the sun went down beyond the Mediterranean, where the waves crashed against rocks in the water and created a beautiful spray.

The drive home was pretty grueling as it was dark and mostly freeway. We got a bit turned around in Haifa as we ended up driving in the little neighbourhoods before we figured out how to find our way back onto the highway. Our one stop was at McDonald's, where we could get a coffee, and next door to that was a sex shop. How the righteous had gone down the slippery slope! At the beginning of the day they had been asking if anyone had brought a Bible, proclaiming that they liked to have one wherever they traveled. Now, at the end of the day, they were keen on perusing videos and toys at the sex shop—but they were shy, and pushed me through the door first. Hah! I scoffed at their decline.

We arrived back at the Old City car park before it closed, but only because the attendant was on Palestinian time and had not yet put his clock ahead. Our house, however, for practical reasons, had put the clock ahead on Israeli time and so it was after our household's eleven o'clock curfew when we got in, but we managed to get Fakhri to open the door.

The Jewish season of Passover was almost upon us, and throughout the world, Jews were preparing for the ritual seder meal at which the story is recounted of Moses and the exodus from slavery in Egypt. Our Biblical Program was presenting an instructed seder meal that week, hosted by Ecce Homo and presided over by Rabbi Michael. Because of my schedule of chores, the seder was half-over when I arrived and there was a choice of two seats: one right beside the rabbi, or else Elijah's seat, a chair that sits empty in case the prophet Elijah turns up with the Messiah in tow, on his donkey. I sat beside Michael as I am not Elijah, and I have absolutely no messianic pretensions or connections, and thus the Elijah seat implied responsibilities that I did not care to take on. Michael was a great character, always funny and lively, and it was a lovely seder, interrupted by my need to rush back to work.

After dinner I managed to produce a more successful cake in the little oven of the Old Community, and Isabelle-Marie joined me for a cup of tea while it baked. We had had a little get-together for Jim and Darlene as they would soon be returning to Canada, and I reflected that someday I would be the one leaving, and it was not going to be easy. I was not finished absorbing the exquisite reality of living in the Biblical landscape. New levels of understanding presented themselves constantly, just as in the rhythm of our worship the daily readings were always catching up to our geographical life. That very evening one of the students had shared with us a wonderful reflection on the healing at the pool of Bethesda, which was just up the street from us at St. Anne's. The reading was the healing of the paralysed man beside the pool of Bethesda. Theresa, the speaker, first affirmed, by talking about her personal experience, that there is more than one way to be paralysed. Paralysis might mean simply an inability to move forward. From there, she went on to tell her story of her own ever-growing understanding of salvation. Just as there is no way that we can save ourselves, there is also no way that God can stop loving us. We human beings have a tendency to try to save ourselves, but there is no point. We must just trust that God will do that for us. As well, we can just trust that God will continue loving us no matter what we do to separate ourselves from God's love.

Jim and Darlene were leaving at two in the afternoon the following day, and they had wanted to tour the crypt of the Ecce Homo basilica before they left. Issa had told us that we probably would not like it down in the crypt as there was a terrible statue that he did not like, and he kept it covered by a sheet. That made us all more curious than ever, so as soon as lunch was out of the way, we pressed Issa to open the trapdoor and to take us into the crypt of the Ecce Homo Basilica. Mary, my new friend from New York, was at hand so she came along with us on the tour. When the trapdoor near the chancel of the basilica was opened, a narrow staircase was revealed, leading to the undercroft below. The stairwell opened onto a dusty and sparsely decorated chapel, and on a deep ledge we saw that something was covered with a bedsheet—surely the controversial statue. Issa hopped up onto the ledge and pulled off the sheet. We were absolutely aghast. What we were looking at was a figure from the past; we were experiencing an encounter with the spirituality of our European faith ancestors, and it is a spirituality to which some people today still adhere. The statue is called "Ecce Homo," Pilate's words as he presented to the crowd the flagellated Christ. What was so shocking about the statue was that it was so overdone, with its hundreds of ripped-open wounds and its torn-open flesh. This version of Ecce Homo represented a form of macabre piety that we acknowledged, but could no longer say was our own. Yes, I know there was a Good Friday, but I prefer to be more cautious about how I remember the events of Good Friday, and how I understand their meaning for me. This statue was a reminder to me that if I get too hung up on the literal details, I might very well miss the theological point.

Immediately after the tour of the crypt, Jim and Darlene posed on the front steps for photos, and Rashid's taxi pulled up to take them to the airport for their trip back to Canada via Rome. The brother of Rassem the cook, who is also Issa's cousin, was the taxi driver, and so Jim and Darlene felt even more that their visit was a community event.

Mel, Pat and I went to the Caffine Station for a coffee, then shopped in the souq for paper goods. We were back to the subject of reconciliation and began to talk about confession—namely, what sins we were going to confess before Easter, and to whom. This was a good exercise. For one thing, simply sharing with one another the burden of our wrongdoings did a lot to diminish their weight. For another thing, it gave us an opportunity to discuss our personal theologies of repentance and of sacramental confession. This same conversation was to go on for a long time as each of us struggled with the reality of sin, of our own wrongdoings, and the meaning of repentance and reconciliation.

8

Renewing the Covenant: Mount Sinai

We were going to Mount Sinai, modern-day Israelites on their way to meet with their God and to receive the Law. At four-thirty in the morning my friend Joseph from St. Anne's up the street met me at our door and we trudged off, Joseph carrying my bag—I could easily have carried my own bag, but these French can be very gallant. Others joined us outside Damascus Gate, and a small bus pulled up.

Once we had left the city and entered the desert, Bernard started the morning office over the speakers of the coach. We were a group of seventeen students, and the participants joined in the singing of the psalms, and took turns reading the daily scriptures. It was a gentle event that helped us all to be calm and to focus on the forthcoming journey. We drove through the desert of Sin mentioned in Exodus and Numbers, and slowly the day dawned over the desert. Out the coach window, we could see the desert installation of a holy eccentric, a messianic Jew who has become quite well known and lives in an abandoned barracks. After a rest stop we continued along the Wadi Paran, the dry valley south of the Dead Sea, where the Jordanian mountains were very close by. There were kibbutzim along the way, all practising a very protective form of desert agriculture. After Ketura, date gardens began to appear in place of the fields of sunflowers and tomatoes that we had seen earlier. As we passed the wildlife preserve, ostriches lined up along the fences and watched us all zoom past in our cars, and Bernard amused us by describing the life cycle of the ostrich as it was at that time the mating season. After we passed the place known as "Solomon's Mines," we at length came to the border where the long process of leaving Israel and entering Egypt took place. We met our official guide, apart from Bernard, Ahab (pronounced *Ah-HAB*).

The terrain began to change colour from grey to the redder, pinker hues of the Sinai. We passed the Timna mines where copper is produced, and where underground galleries were quarried out ages ago by slaves small enough to manoeuvre in the tiny places. The landscape was inhospitable with high, red granite hills all around, and little or no vegetation. We stopped at a viewpoint on the Gulf of Aqaba to view a fortified island with an intact Crusader castle, taken by Salah al Din in the 15th century. Here Egypt, Israel, Jordan and Arabia all converge, and the granite hills of all three are visible in that spot, and surround the Gulf. Most of this region is inhabited by Bedouin, who still live their traditional lifestyle, and who were made Egyptian nationals by Anwar Sadat. We went to the town of Nuweiba, Egypt's most important port, not only because of its commercial transport, but also because from here many people embark for the hajj to Mecca. We had seen a sign near the border that said "St. Catherine's Monastery 220 km.," and another "Jerusalem to Eilat 230 km.," so our journey was to be a little over 450 km., or 270 miles, each way.

Ahab got on the microphone and apologized for his French, which was perfectly fine although he was better in English, and he said that the only time he would ever guide in French was for Bernard. He talked about Egypt and its main industries, the Suez Canal, petroleum, and tourism. And as we were on our way to Sinai, Bernard then talked about Moses: of his 120 years, Moses spent 40 years in Egypt, 40 years wandering in the desert, and 40 years in the service of his father-in-law Jethro, priest of the Midianites. It is through being a shepherd—a "pastor"—that Moses learned patience.

We stopped by the beach for our picnic lunch and put our toes into the Red Sea. Besides me, there were four French women in our party, plus Jill, an English nun temporarily residing in the monastery at St. Peter in Gallicantu. The men were my two friends René and Joseph, French-Canadians Paul-André and Igino, four other fellows from the class, a young Italian priest named Andrea, plus Bernard and Ahab. We stopped to have tea with a Bedouin family who were in the business of receiving guests in their tent enclosure. This enclosure was surrounded by woven camel hair, and the family's two camels were parked beside their shiny, new yellow jeep. The husband made us tea, which I did not drink, and the wife made sesame bread and displayed some beaded jewellery that she had made. One of our group, a family man from Africa who was missing his wife and six children, picked up two of the Bedou children and hugged them, and one of the nuns picked up the baby and made him cry, after which everyone gave her a bad time. The toilet at this place was dreadful: a piece of ground about two and a half feet square with a broken piece of K3 board in the center, and screened by flour and rice bags tacked onto a wooden frame. This was the worst affair I had seen in a while and I could not bring myself even to enter it, but I took photos to show the folks back home.

The next stop was the rock of inscription, although I was not aware that that was our destination and I left the camera in the bus. We began trekking across the desert and I began thinking about my bladder. If this was going to last a long time I could be in trouble. We examined the rock with its ancient inscriptions carved by ages of pilgrims, then set out for a rock shelf where we would be able to hear Mass. Now I was really miserable. There was no way I would survive Mass. I trudged along, grumbling and looking for potential hiding places behind the rocks that I could use as a loo without getting too far separated from the group. To top it all off, the priest who was celebrating the Mass came trotting along with the communion bag and said, "Here, hold the bag; I'm going for a pee". And with that he slowed to about ten or twelve feet behind me and began to leave his mark in the desert. Now I was really incensed. "What!" I cried out, and thought to myself "I hate men."

Joseph began to point out potential rock hideaways. "Maybe you could go there." Everything he pointed to seemed to me to be a hundred miles away. At length we came to a small hill in the desert with a little, round ruin of a stone hut perched on top.

"Do you think that is my cabaña?" I said to Joseph.

"I think that is your cabaña," he replied, and the patient Joseph stood guard for me on the path below.

All along the way, young Bedouin fellows walked alongside with their camels and tried to get us to engage them, saying repeatedly "Chameau, chameau, chameau," meaning 'camel'. All through our lovely Mass, up on the rock platform with a natural stone altar, our young Bedouin businessmen waited nearby, chattering loudly throughout. They followed us back to the bus, again encouraging us with "Chameau, chameau, chameau," even though it was quite clear that none of us was interested in renting a camel. I later remarked that if they had been saying "Toilette, toilette, toilette" they would have had more business.

We arrived at our St. Catherine's hotel, the Es-Salam adjacent to the military airport. I was sharing a room with Jill, the English nun from Bury St. Edmonds. She spoke limited French and we were placed together so we could speak English. I had been a bit concerned about the availability of vegan food, but I had a very good supper. Once the dining room discovered I was vegetarian, they came almost at once with vegetable soup, tahineh, pita and vegetables. Jill and I chatted briefly after dinner then we went right to sleep as we were to gather at one-thirty in the morning for the drive to the mountain, and then the trek up Mt. Sinai. We went to sleep around eight at night.

At one-thirty, Jill and I were the first ones ready and we began to wonder if we had the wrong time. There actually had been a great deal of confusion over what time everything would be, since Egypt is an hour different from Israel, which as you recall is an hour different from Palestine. Some people changed their clocks and some did not, and both time zones were announced for each event—it was ridiculous. In this instance, Jill and I were correct and everyone else was sleeping it out. Bernard appeared presently, thoroughly put out because no one was awake. Finally, we were all present and our coach set out, in the darkest time of night, for the holy mountain.

I was feeling a bit ill on the bus and fighting nausea, but it did not diminish the excitement of what was to happen. Some of the group decided to ascend on foot, but Bernard had engaged six camels and their camel-drivers at twelve dollars each: ten for the camel and two for the boy. Jacqueline was a little confused on this, so when the boy took her arm and started pulling her to the camel, she started yelling "Bernard, Bernard!"" and thought she was being kidnapped. My camel's name was Sem-Sem, my boy, Hassan. It was absolutely exhilarating, the six of us plodding slowly up the holy mountain on our camels, the others braving it on foot. The path wound back and forth up the mountain, and the lights from the flashlights of the many pilgrims wound back and forth up the trail like an illuminated string of pearls. This was also the first time for Bernard to ascend the mountain by camel, since he had always to take care of others in the past, and this time we had a separate guide and the group was small enough for him to relax. Igino and Jésus started out on foot but engaged camels partway as they found the trek too rigorous. One of them tried to negotiate a discount because he had already walked halfway, but the young Bedouin camel-driver said, "No discount, because you are fat."

At first all was well, but eventually I was freezing. It was still dark and it was foggy and windy, and I could not tell if I was cold because of the weather, or if I was chilling because I was sick. Oh, well! I was having a great time ascending the holy mountain of God, the lights from the flashlights of other pilgrims winding back and forth, and away up high, like strings of lights winding around a Christmas tree lot, except there were no trees for a hundred miles. I thought "I'll bet Moses wished he had a camel like this when he went up the mountain!" When we reached the end of the portion of the trek that camels can travel, I realized that I had no photo of myself on the camel, and I began to holler "René, René, René, get the camera!" Poor old René began desperately digging in his packsack, and then maneuvering back and forth trying to get a picture. He took the picture. The flash went off. He said "I've got you, but not much of the camel!"—and at that moment the camel sat down! When the boy started pulling me off the saddle, I stood my ground and gesticulated madly that I wanted a photo, so the boy got the camel back on its feet, behind first and then the front legs, slowly, and René danced around some more and took a picture that we hoped included the camel.

The next part of the journey was the walk up the path to the summit. The weather was terribly inclement: blowing, raining, freezing. I began to trudge along beside Jill, wondering if this venture were wise. Jacqueline was unable to breathe in the rarified air and was assisted back to the rest stop, a hut where hot and cold drinks and packaged snacks were available. Marie-Geneviève went with her and did not venture back again. After about 500 metres I decided this was not wise and that I would be sick if I continued. I went back to the rest stop and waited with the half-dozen others. After a few cups of sweet tea and a quiet rest I began to improve and by morning I felt fine.

When the intrepid others returned from the summit it was daylight. We ate our picnic breakfast and went slowly down the mountain, everyone on foot. I took my time, as did Huguette and Jacqueline, while Joseph, Jean-Claude and a few others lingered behind to ensure everyone was alright. Jacqueline particularly had trouble with the terrain, and at one moment Joseph was waiting for her, his hand outstretched, and she said "*Le bon pasteur!*[1]" He replied softly, "*Il va avant.*[2]"

When we had all arrived back at St. Catherine's Monastery we found a modest corner of the garden, and we celebrated a simple but beautiful Mass on a theme of remembering. René, the presider, was very cute in his vestments and alpaca-hair toque. This get-up, plus the Chicoutimi accent—*très charmant*, and oh, so *québecois*! We had a bit of time to view parts of the monastery, mainly the church and the icon museum, the most extensive in the world. Bernard mentioned that the tradition of icons was that we are not so much looking at them as that they are looking at us. I thought of all those horrendous plastic pictures of Jesus whose eyes follow you around the room and I wondered if those hideous things are actually a decadent vestige of the icon tradition. What a terrible thought. Some of the icons in the museum are very famous and were familiar to us as works of art, or in reproduction.

---

1.   The Good Shepherd
2.   He goes before.

Our coach took us back through the desert and we were all sleepy and tired. We arrived at a posh hotel where we had a buffet lunch. We had no time for the beach, but somehow time for the gift shop. Everyone was talking about *papyruses*, pap-ee-roos in French, and I thought they were saying "papiers russes"! I wondered how it was that all these French missionaries could understand Russian newspapers—or were they wanting fancy Russian wrapping paper and stationery? We bought a few papyri as gifts, and we scurried back to the bus and went to our hotel in Nuweiba. We had lots of time to play on the beach by the Red Sea. The water was choppy and only Paul-André and Igino, both strong swimmers, really ventured out. Colette, Marie-Geneviève and I splashed around on the beach and a few others appeared, but did not get wet. The Egyptian army were nowhere to be seen, and the Red Sea did not part.

After I had showered and cleaned up we still had plenty of time before dinner to rest and recuperate, so I said to Jill "Would you like to read some psalms together?" She was delighted with this suggestion, and we selected several psalms that were appropriate to the occasion. She would read each one in English and then I would read the same one in French. We then had some quiet, sharing and prayer, and thus managed to put together a quiet evening office.

At this hotel I did not manage so well at dinner. I told Ahab of my needs and he said the hotel could give me potato, rice and pasta with my bread—four starches! I tried to protest but he waved my protests aside with a grand gesture, not understanding that I did not want this awful meal. He kept saying "No, it's alright!" as if my concern was that this was too kind, rather than that this was thoroughly unappetizing. The dining room brought out all this stuff at the same time as the soup so it all got cold and I sent it back untouched. They were a bit put out that they had, they thought, responded to my need but I was so thankless.

Sunday morning we were up at 05:15 or so, had breakfast at 6, and went to the beach for Mass. Igino celebrated the Sunday Mass on the beach with the Red Sea rolling behind him. I read the Hebrew lesson—my first time of reading the Bible in French during Mass. We departed and went in the bus through the bleak, red Sinai desert hills. I sat with Joseph and he told me stories of his very hard ministry in Peru, and of his motorcycle accident thirty years before, resulting in spinal injury and paralysis. It is only because of two rounds of surgery and seven months in hospital, plus the grace of God, that he walks today.

Going back through the borders was again time-consuming, and we were fortunate to have Igino with us, who speaks Arabic, French, Italian and English, and so was able to help everyone. I got a new one-month visa in my passport that would see me through to my departure date home. In Eilat we visited the Underwater Observatory Marine Park, an underwater nature reserve where you see all kinds of species in their natural habitat, facilitated by a superbly produced portable audio-guide. We ate our picnic lunch at a roadside stop nearby, then drove on to the Negev. After the Israelites had entered into the Covenant they wandered here in the western part of the Negev, then entered into Edom. They could not get past the Edomites so had to go back down into Arava, where phosphates are now mined.

We stopped at the Mitzpeh Ramon observatory to view the huge natural crater with its various strata and its wealth of fossils. Mitzpeh means viewpoint, and Ramon comes from a word meaning highest. It is the crater itself, a huge natural depression and quite wonderful, that is called the Ramon Crater; the town is Mitzpeh Ramon. We continued our desert journey and gradually vegetation began to appear and to get thicker. We passed the Ben Gurion College of Agriculture, an outpost of the university, where young African students and others learn desert culture, and we passed through the wilderness of Sin through Beer Sheva. It was around six when we were dropped off at the Damascus Gate and walked home, the faithful Joseph carrying my bag—it was impossible to stop him. After recounting my travel stories at the dinner table, I packed a picnic lunch for the morning, gave Pat and Mel their little gifts, then slept.

Next day the class outing was called, "The Way of the Passion"; it was an instructed excursion following the path followed by Jesus from the time of his arrest, to the time of his execution on the cross. As the four accounts in the New Testament differ somewhat, Bernard had decided to follow the account in the gospel of John. The class gathered in front of the Gethsemane Church, the grotto of arrest, at eight. As was the case in all our instructed outings, at each stop throughout the day we had the regular guide information and tradition, then scripture reading, then close reading and exegesis, then 10 to 20 minutes for prayer. People read in roles for the scripture readings from the gospel of John, and Bernard's lectures and interpretation of the story were wonderful. So profound was the impact of this presentation that I considered my entire trip worthwhile for this day alone.

We began at the place of Jesus' arrest. The grotto of arrest is maintained by the Franciscans as a chapel, but it is very minimally furnished, with chairs, an altar and a very few decorations. The entrance is slightly hidden from the road and resembles a very modest chapel entrance with the word Gethsemani written over the doorway. A stairway descends into the cave. The restrained decorating has ensured that an ambience of the grotto's original appearance is still available to the visitor today. It still looks like a cavity in the rock that probably would have opened onto the olive garden in ancient times. Now it is enclosed, but the rock features of the grotto form the walls and ceiling. We began our enactment of St. John's Passion in this chapel: reading the scripture, hearing a close reading of the story, and ten minutes of silent contemplation. We were sitting on the actual spot where the event likely happened, and it was easy to feel the presence of the terrible fear of the disciples, the betrayal of Jesus by his friend and follower Judas, the awful closeness of that powerful night. We were silent; we had no words to express our nearness to that moment two thousand years ago.

Afterwards, we briefly visited the tomb of Mary next door. There are two traditions of Mary. The Latin tradition is that she went to Ephesus with John, who is traditionally held to be the person to which the gospel of John refers as Jesus' "beloved disciple," and lived out her life there. The Eastern or Orthodox tradition is that she remained in Jerusalem. The present-day Dormition Abbey is Benedictine, uses the Latin rite, and springs from that tradition, but the Tomb of Mary is, of course, Orthodox. We did not go into the Church of the Agony, also called the Church of All Nations, as this scene is not part of John's passion story. We entered the Kidron Valley and viewed the tombs. At St. Peter in Gallicantu, the traditional spot of Peter's denial of Jesus, we not only had a role-play reading and prayer time in the chapel, but we also viewed the church, the ancient stairs and the ruins of the prison cell. We had our lunch there as well, in a little salon with an adjacent kitchen. This was more of a social time with other members of the class than a classroom time. We needed a break from the intensity of the day's program.

Our class trudged through the walls of the Old City by way of the Zion Gate, and into the Armenian Quarter to St. Mark's Convent for a similar program, including a long discussion of the text of St. John's Passion and of the trial and arrest of Jesus. Finally we went to the Holy Sepulchre for an analysis of the building and what the original site was like. We spent some moments in the Calvary chapel and then assembled on a bench at the foot of the rock of Calvary, under the stairs, for another lecture that included a gruesome physical description of the process of death by crucifixion.

Crucifixion was a cruel method of execution that the Romans practised only on foreigners and not on Roman citizens. It was typically used as a lesson to the entire community to prevent disorder, such as robbery or sedition. In this instance, the Romans wanted to make sure that others contemplating making a public disturbance or trying to develop a following would be completely discouraged. The condemned was made to carry the crossbeam for his own execution through the public streets to the place where it would be carried out. Then he was stripped naked, bound or nailed to the crossbeam and raised up the standing beam. The condemned was then helpless. He would become dehydrated, beset by insects and the weather, and taunted by cruel soldiers and passersby. The process was painful and prolonged; it might be several days before the person succumbed to death. Bodily needs and functions did not cease during that time, of course. Everything about crucifixion was calculated to humiliate the condemned, the family and the community. It was a sad discourse, but at first I did not connect with it, and it held only historical interest for me, until Bernard described the nails shattering the wrists of the condemned. Bernard said, "By this time, Jesus would have gone into shock."

In that second, the agony was made personal. I looked at the faces of my classmates, each one tormented by grief, each one seeing only the broken man who, with so many others, endured this torture near this very place. One student had been looking at the floor, but when he raised his eyes to look at Bernard, his empathy with the suffering Jesus was proclaimed by his pained expression. I began to feel sick. The suffering was too nearby. Good Friday lost its sanitized distance and I was assailed by waves of agony and grief and all that had been experienced in this very place, not only by Jesus, but by thousands of condemned local people who were executed by the Roman occupiers. In a few moments the class was ended. It had begun to rain outside, and we dispersed quickly to our various homes.

In the evening, Anne came over to our flat and she, Pat, Mel and I discussed the forthcoming Holy Week preparations, some of which were contentious. The group planning the reconciliation liturgy was having problems. Reconciliation is a sacrament of the church that formerly was always called confession and absolution. Nowadays, the trend has been to try to recover the original intent of this action. Unfortunately, it had become an ordeal in people's minds, the very idea propelling them back into elementary school where they would have to recount their sins to the priest. So many people had such bad memories of confession, that it has been rethought. The healing benefits of being reconciled to God and the community can be available to us if we confess our issues and wrongdoings, and show remorse for them. We can obtain a pardon from the church, on behalf of the entire Christian community. This is the idea, but the rite has much baggage connected with it, and many people in our household no longer believed in the necessity of private confession. They preferred what is called a general absolution to be granted, that is, that people would privately recall their own sins and recount them to God, and the priest, on behalf of the larger Christian community, would grant a pardon, or absolution, to the entire assembly. The priest responsible for the forthcoming reconciliation liturgy, however, did not agree with these folks. He held that general absolution was only to be used where there were not enough priests available for private confessions and, since many of the men in our neighbourhood were priests, there was plenty of opportunity for confession. We debated this point among ourselves, while Melanie made spaghetti. She, Pat and I had a late meal and continued talking about Holy Week. Ironically, it seemed that the Rite of Reconciliation, far from being a healing ministry, was actually causing people around us great pain.

This particular theological debate raged on all week. Our own group, planning the Holy Thursday footwashing liturgy, had much to discuss, although there was less contention in our group, and even a great deal of agreement. The footwashing liturgy takes place on Holy Thursday, also called Maundy Thursday. It is the Thursday before Easter, and it commemorates the Last Supper, when Jesus had his last meal with the disciples, and to teach them an important lesson, wrapped a towel around his waist and washed the feet of each of them. In doing so, Jesus taught the disciples, as he teaches us, that our task is to be a servant to one another, and to care for the most basic needs of each person. Our talks about what we were planning for the service sharpened our views of the theology of servant ministry.

The next morning after a long session of writing in my journal I went with Anne, Mel, and Pat down to St. Anne's to talk with Don about the Holy Thursday service, at which Don was to preside. Our conversation was far-ranging, however, and went not only into the theology of the foot-washing service, but also of the priestly charism, the sacrament of confession, what was to happen at the reconciliation service next Tuesday, and everything else we could think of. Eventually, we each chose what our role in the celebration would be. I volunteered to do a modern version of Peter's protest, and Mel would pose the traditional questions to the priests that are usually asked annually at the chrism Mass to invite them to renew their priesthood. There was a long theological discussion about whether we should do handwashing only and dispense with footwashing. Such a compromise might prevent embarrassment for people, and encourage everyone to take part. Usually the people that come to church on that evening are rather restrained in how far they are willing to take part. In the end we decided that Don would wash the feet of the twelve pre-selected participants, then a choice would be offered as to whether people wanted one hand or one foot washed.

The weekend before Easter is Palm Sunday, when we remember Jesus' triumphant ride into Jerusalem on a donkey, when people came out to lay palm branches on the road in front of him, shouting "Hosanna!" On the eve of Palm Sunday, Ecce Homo had its own Palm Sunday Mass, starting in the Lithostrotos reception and proceeding to the basilica. Our palms were olive branches gathered from our garden on the Mount of Olives. The presider was a friend of the house, a charming Jesuit from Oregon named Tom, who was a student elsewhere but often visited Ecce Homo. He was the same fellow who had once misunderstood Wanda's English and thought she was dying of a terminal disease. When he had said "Oh dear, is it serious? Is it cancer?" Wanda replied "No, I am from Brazil."

Palm Sunday

Some time before all this, an English couple once came to the house on holiday from their missionary work in Africa, and I promised them a late night Lithostrotos tour. That evening, when I arrived at their door, the husband was asleep, but his wife, Sue, really wanted to come along. Our Lithos visit turned out to be just as inspiring for me as it was for her. I used to start the visits with a discussion of the huge cornerstone at the bottom of the stairs. Previously, whenever I heard the words in Psalm 118 *"The stone that the builders rejected has become the cornerstone,"* a verse that is quoted in the New Testament[3], I always pictured the cornerstone in the modern sense. Modern cornerstones for me are the ceremonial plaques dedicated when a building is being constructed. Many are time capsules into which are placed newspapers and memorabilia of the day so that when the building is demolished, people can see what was going on when it was built. In the ancient world, the cornerstone was actually the foundation of two courses of pillars that go off at right angles to one another. Because the weight of the structure is concentrated on that point, the cornerstone has to be perfect; so the stone that the builders rejected must have already been perfect, else it could not have functioned as a cornerstone. The cornerstone in the Ecce Homo ruins is one of these massive foundation stones that was probably a part of the Antonia Fortress, or of another of the buildings associated with the Temple when it was extant. I loved that stone; to me, it was a pathway into the Psalms.

While we were still standing by this cornerstone, Sue seemed almost transported, and began telling me the story of how she was instantaneously drawn to Christianity by a vision that she experienced while looking in the bathroom mirror, of a man riding a donkey and people arranging palm leaves on the ground in his path. She had had at that time very little Bible knowledge and she did not rec-

---

3.   1 Peter 2:6

ognize the scene. She told her husband about it and he suggested that the fellow on the donkey in her vision was likely Jesus, riding into Jerusalem on the first Palm Sunday, hearing the cries of people shouting Hosanna. This vision led to Sue's conversion to Christianity.

Sue and I went down into the Herodian cistern and Hasmonean period excavations below the house, and onto the stone pavement, where we remained for about an hour and a quarter. During this time, we read all of John 18 aloud and shared a prayer time together. Although we had never met one another until that day, the deep meaning of the surroundings allowed us to go deep: in the spiritual sense, and in the sense of trust, as well. Afterward we left and I accidentally turned off the lights on Pat and Mel who, I learned, were down in the pitch-black excavations somewhere, but Fakhri knew they were there and rescued them. Fortunately, they were clever enough to have a candle with them, so they were not completely stranded in the otherwise totally dark regions below the house and the street.

Now that the actual day of Palm Sunday was upon us, we had the morning free, and we chose that time to remember the Holocaust. Thus, on the morning of Palm Sunday, Mel, Pat, Rita, a guest named Jeff, and I all met and set out for the address known as the Chamber of the Holocaust. In order to find it, we received directions from King David, the Brisbane street busker, and found the Chamber down a little street just outside the Zion Gate. An additional witness to that given at Yad Vashem, this one was not an official government museum, but rather had been put together by survivors. Not only was the museum absolutely horrific, which was entirely appropriate, the gentleman in attendance was absolutely obsessed with ensuring we heard his own entire saga of Jewish history. The man was interesting at first, but it did not end. He talked on and on, and did not even stop to take a breath, so traumatized was he by the events he was recounting. Whatever his past experiences had been, they now compelled him to tell the entire story. We stood motionless, helpless, too polite to interrupt his tirade, like wedding guests captivated by the Ancient Mariner.

At last we took our leave and went to the Protestant cemetery near St. Peter in Gallicantu to visit the grave of Oskar Schindler. The cemetery was undergoing improvements, and everything seemed new. The grave was a flat tomb in the European style, raised only slightly off the ground, and very plain. On the surface were a few words celebrating the twelve hundred Jews whom Schindler managed to protect during the Nazi administration. Visitors had placed flowers and memorial pebbles on the grave cover.

Later, on the afternoon of Palm Sunday, we all walked over the Mount of Olives to Bethphage, from where the procession would depart to follow in Jesus' footsteps on the day of his triumphal entry into Jerusalem. When we were leaving the Old City by the Lions Gate, some boys were already leading sheep up to the gate for tomorrow's Muslim feast of sacrifice, the Eid al-Adha. This was the first sunny weekend of the year, and it was a hard climb to Bethphage and very hot. I really felt that I might be sick in all this heat, but fortunately I eventually recovered. Melanie and Pat bought big palms for the procession, huge branches taller than themselves. The two were wearing their patch trousers and shades, and with their palm branches on end, they looked like they were standing beside big green surfboards. I started talking to René and Joseph, as well as some others from the French class, and so I got separated from Mel and Pat. There was a colourful array of scouts in their uniforms, with flags and banners. Some other groups had banners too; the Melkite church, for example, had a big red velvet banner with a painting of Jesus on it. There was singing in all languages. The Sisters and Brothers of the Beatitudes, beautiful in their simple off-white with brown habits and sandals, were singing long before the procession even started.

When the assembly began to move toward the Old City, I marched with friends from the Sinai trip, in between the Rosary Scouts of Nazareth and the delegation from the Melkite Church. Pilar, our Spanish student, was for some reason marching with the Melkites. There were hundreds of police and soldiers, including huge numbers of UN troops along the side of the road. The local police looked serious, but the UN troops were mainly taking pictures of the parade. The scouts from Nazareth seemed to be the best organized; they had printed song sheets with them and their song leader used a microphone to lead their Arabic hymns. We were a huge and colourful procession finishing on the grounds of St. Anne's monastery, where the Latin patriarch addressed the crowd. It was very difficult to hear or understand the Patriarch out of doors, and we went on home, exhausted but exhilarated.

On Sunday evening, Anne phoned me to say I could help Sister Vicky, the house accountant, with an important bank errand if I liked; all that was required was that I have a visitor's visa in my passport, and it would be helpful if I owned a money-belt. On Monday I went to Vicky's office with my money-belt. The task consisted of taking a huge amount of cash to the bank, concealed under my clothes. I wore the money belt under my shirt, and Vicky packed thirty thousand United States dollars in large bills onto me. I put my big sweatshirt over top. I looked ridiculous. Then Vicky made herself especially noticeable by packing five thousand one-dollar bills on herself and putting on her winter coat, zipped up, even though it was boiling hot outside.

"You're going like that?" I asked.

"Yes," she replied. I shook my head, completely convinced we were going to be mugged. As we walked through the little alleyways leading to Herod's Gate, I was in a heightened state, and eventually was so paranoid that when the garbage man's donkey moved over toward me on the path, I had visions of him crushing me against the walls and was sure my number was up. There were people in Jerusalem who would gladly slit your throat for a lot less than thirty thousand dollars.

When we arrived at the bank the manager, a young Scot named Ian, waited on us in person and I told him that I felt like a drug dealer. With that I pulled out the money-belt with the thirty thousand from under my shirt. For my pains he arranged a small loan of a hundred dollars for me as I was completely broke, and I estimated that that should about last until I was ready to leave the country. Later that day I went to the souq with my hundred dollars and priced the Hebron pottery. Large plates were sixteen shekels, small plates twelve, chalices sixteen, and the little lamps similar to ancient ones were two shekels. The streets were crowded as everyone was getting ready for the Muslim feast of sacrifice of the sheep the next day; but I was tuckered out from my banking adventure, and I slept for the rest of the afternoon.

In the evening I suddenly remembered that the very knowledgeable Sister Anne Catherine had invited the community and volunteers to her home, called Beit Ruth, where she would give an explanation of the Passover seder ceremony. I searched around to see if anyone else was going but apparently I was the only one from our house who would be attending. A group of eight sisters and volunteers had already assembled in the living room of Beit Ruth: the three who lived there, plus five from the monastery of Ein Karem. The Beit Ruth sisters offered us a lovely buffet supper, and they put together a humus and salad sandwich on a pita for me. None of us would have considered it appropriate for Christians to celebrate Jewish liturgies, so we did not actually have a seder meal. Instead, Anne Catherine went over the Passover order of service, the *haggada,* in detail, explaining each point.

The Jewish holiday of Passover celebrates the passage of the Israelites from slavery in Egypt, through the period of wandering in the desert, and the establishment of the nation in the Promised Land. Moses is the central figure of the Passover, and it is the national foundational epic of the Jewish people. The story is well-known, and there is even a major motion picture about it, but one of the most interesting things I learned that evening had to do with the destruction of the Temple. Lamb, Anne Catherine commented to us, should not be eaten at the Passover meal because the Temple is not in existence, so no lamb can be sacrificed in the Jewish sense. Furthermore, she pointed out that the Temple was the dwelling place of God among the people, but the Temple is gone. The good thing about that bitter fact is that to recognize the absence of God is to desire God's presence, to yearn for God. Oh, to get to the point of recognizing the absence of God! I am not even there yet.

When I walked home there was a festival atmosphere outside the Damascus Gate in anticipation of the feast of sheep. There was cotton candy and other party food, and young people were socializing on the steps leading up to the gate.

The next evening the entire household, including anyone who wanted to attend, assembled in the salon for the service of reconciliation that had been the subject of controversy for several weeks. The purpose of the liturgy was to give everyone an opportunity to be reconciled with God before the drama of Christ's passion and Easter began. The team planning the service had created a lovely little sand desert in the middle of the floor, with a pair of sandals and a staff placed in front of it, to allow us figuratively to begin our journey. Around the room were bowls of purple and white carnations and after the readings telling how the desert will bloom[4], an opportunity was given to make the miniature desert to bloom. There must have been at least sixty people in the salon, and each of us in turn selected a flower and "planted" it in the little desert. After all the discussion about private confession versus general absolution, the priest who had finally offered to help, Paul in fact, pronounced a general absolution to the assembly, and he also played the piano for the service, such a versatile chap that he was. Everyone was given an opportunity for peacemaking. The event was beautiful in every way. The participants felt uplifted, and several people took pictures of the little desert after the service because it was so picturesque.

After that exhilarating experience, our lives turned once again to the mundane. Melanie and I arrived at Pat's room where Mel planned to colour Pat's hair. Melanie held up the package to show me the colour. It was an unfamiliar brand, and the packaging was all written in Hebrew, but it was when I saw the picture on the box that I nearly fainted. It was called Flaming Red, but it actually looked deep neon pink on the box! Surely she wasn't thinking of doing this. It was too punk for words! I thought that possibly we could add a chancel drama of Moses and the Burning Bush to our Thursday liturgy with Pat's hair playing the leading

---

4.   Isaiah 35:1-10 and Psalm 126

role. It would be a kind of liturgical encore to the Footwashing with Guerilla Theatre we were planning! Pat's hair, I am thankful to say, did not turn out neon pink, but rather looked as though it was going to be quite normal. When Pat made a grand entrance the next day with her new Easter hairstyle, it looked very good. Mel had cut it quite short and spiky, and it turned out a deep auburn similar to her natural colour.

It was my day to visit the Ophel Archaeological Garden, which is the excavation of the old Temple Mount area, a place of ongoing archaeology. To begin with, I viewed the old steps up to the Hulda's Gate of the Temple by which Jesus, on his last day before his execution, probably left the temple. It was very hot and actually so bright that I could not look at the temple wall, so much light was reflecting off the stones. Passover and Easter were near, and the Temple was glowing.

It is always wonderful scrambling around the very stones where ancient people came to worship, and to walk in the very spots where Jesus taught. These were the moments of my Jerusalem life that I cherished. Right after the footwashing group had their rehearsal, however, I had to have a nap as the bright sun and lack of protein were conspiring to give me a headache. After my again minimal dinner, Mel and I put together the breakfast, and then my friend Marie-Antoinette came with me to the kitchen of the flat and we had a big theological discussion, in French, while I made myself a decent bowl of vegetable and bean soup. It was another late night after another full day, and it later dawned on me that in the midst of all this activity, I had even forgotten to go to the music practice for the forthcoming liturgies. Mea culpa. I could not think of everything!

Ancient altar at the Har of Megiddo: Armageddon.

The Jordan River.

St. Catherine's Monastery on Mount Sinai.

Buying our Palms on Palm Sunday.

The Ecce Homo Arch on the Via Dolorosa, with neighbouring merchants.

The Calvary Chapel in the Church of the Holy Sepulchre: place of the crucifixion.

Biblical waterwheel at Neot Kedumim.

The Ecce Homo Community, from left: Anne, Bonnie, Isabelle Marie, Trudy, Melanie, Pat, Marie-Lise, Christiane-Marie, Issa.

Ecce Homo Basilica.

Maundy Thursday

The house was packed with people in the lead-up to the Easter weekend. When my morning's duties were completed, and after a lunch of my own making, I started getting ready for the big footwashing service. If I was going to get my feet washed, I was going to have shaved legs and soft little baby feet, even though I had teased Don beforehand that I was going to sleep in my runners to ensure my feet were well ripened for the occasion.

As I was about to hop into the shower, Melanie phoned from Reception and said that Father Joseph from St. Anne's was here to see me. I was rather expecting Joseph as I had left a message for him at St. Anne's, and I asked if he could either wait or come back. After a brief consultation, Melanie informed me he would come back in half an hour. A little while later she phoned again to say Father Joseph had called to say he could not return in half an hour. Much later, surprisingly, Jiries tracked me down in the coffee room to say Father Joseph from St. Anne's was here to see me. I said "It's a French priest, right?" and Jiries said "No." Then he hung up.

When I arrived at Reception there was a lovely man whom I had never seen before, an African, English-speaking priest from Uganda. He was a student in the White Fathers' formation program—a kind and lovely man, but certainly not the Joseph for whom I thought I had left the message. I should have known something was amiss the moment Melanie started to report on her conversations with Father Joseph. My Joseph, as far as I knew, did not speak a word of English. And this other poor man had been tracking me down for two days! He had even come to the house twice. I felt terrible. The poor fellow had no idea who I was, but in case I needed his help, he was untiringly willing to be of service.

The exciting night of the footwashing liturgy was upon us, the night when we remember Jesus' Passover meal with his friends and followers, as well as his arrest in the Garden of Gethsemane after that last supper. People were now beginning to arrive for Mass and I visited with some of these guests on the terrace. I ran into Oys and Jeanne, my Ecole Biblique drivers, and gave them a brief tour of the house. I helped Pat assemble the pitchers, basins and towels for the service, then met with Don to go over our lines for "Peter's refusal". It was a good thing we talked about it, because he had had a very different idea from me as to what he would say. My plan was to imitate the protest of the disciple Peter, who did not think it right that Jesus should wash his feet, but I would put the refusal into a contemporary context relevant to the people in the pews. During the Mass, I sang the gospel acclamation and then the eleven of us went up to the chancel steps and waited for a few seconds; then we sat down on the chancel steps. There were eleven of us rather than the twelve that had accompanied Jesus. There was no theological reason for that, but we were a portly lot and only eleven of our derrières would fit along the chancel steps. As the reader read out the story, Don, imitating the actions of Jesus at the Last Supper, started washing the feet, and at the right moment in the story, the reader stopped and went away, and the drama began. When Don came to me, I put up my hand and said, somewhat breathlessly, "Stop! Stop! Stop! Wait! I know we are all in this, and that I volunteered for this, but I am not comfortable with it, for reasons that I perhaps cannot articulate, so let me ask you—are you intending to wash my feet?"

Don, still kneeling in front of me, replied "If you will let me."

Everyone in the basilica looked shocked. They sat upright in their seats, half of them thinking, "Oh, no! Now she's wrecked it!" Paul, who was sitting at the organ throughout all this, later told me that he was completely taken in and thought my protest was quite real. Whether or not this was true, it was most gracious of him to say it.

I said to Don, "You know, I would actually be more comfortable with this if I were to wash your feet than for you to be washing mine."

Don's reply to this was what he believed Jesus would say in the same situation. He began speaking to me as if I were the kindest minister in the world.

"You are always so kind," he said, "always taking care of others, giving of yourself." If only this were true. In his role now speaking as Jesus, Don asserted, "You are always doing for others, but never allowing anyone to do the same for you. But if you want to join me in my program, to minister to others in my name, would you let others—let me—minister to you?"

After a pause, he went on, "So let me ask you now: will you let me wash your feet?"

I smiled at him, and replied "Yes, alright, yes, please." And so he did.

The congregation all smiled and breathed a sigh of relief. They were delighted with this display and with the message. They all seemed to understand that it was really about them, and about their own reluctance to accept the ministry of others because they each thought that they were the ones who should be doing the doing.

Those eleven of us who had had our feet washed formed four teams, and Don then brilliantly wove into his talk the notion that the twelfth person missing from the "disciple" group was each one of the people in the pews. He invited everyone to come forward to have a foot or their hands washed. Now, under normal circumstances, Catholics are very often shy about this kind of demonstration, and particularly at the annual footwashing liturgy. But on this occasion, I believe absolutely everyone in that basilica came forward. Our team had a great many hands and feet to wash. The people who came to us were so happy about it, too. Some even came up and kissed me. It was very interesting how independent all these ministers and missionaries were; many of them wanted to grab the towel and dry their own hands, but I insisted on drying their hands for them. One said I would make a great masseuse. Several whispered that for the first few seconds they were taken in by my outburst—kind words to an amateur actor's ears!

Once a year, priests have an opportunity to renew their priesthood before the community, and Maundy Thursday, also called Holy Thursday, can be the occasion for this. This part of the liturgy is know as the Chrism Mass. Melanie, in a solid and confident voice, read out the chrism questions to the priests on behalf of the Christian community, and all the priests in the congregation stood up and renewed their priesthood. Then the people renewed their own ministries. Mel was an Anglican, who considered herself Protestant, and said that she felt very honoured to have been given this role. She took this responsibility very seriously, and carried it out with aplomb.

After Mass we had dinner, then at eight everyone in the house assembled at the door with flashlights, and we walked to the Mount of Olives and away up into the Sisters of Sion's beautiful olive garden overlooking the city—to Gethsemane. It was dark by the time we left the house, and an almost full moon was rising into the clear sky. The Old City was beautiful from the Mount, golden and illuminated, the golden Dome of the Rock brilliant behind the expectant Golden Gate. I stood up on a stone wall and read aloud the Gethsemane story from Luke's gospel. Then we were silent for a half-hour of prayer and meditation, all sitting along the stone wall of the olive grove overlooking the Old City, under the olive trees, under the full moon—in silence, entranced. Even the traffic seemed to be glowing on the road below us, and plenty of police vehicles shone their blue lights. There were hundreds of police on hand, their voices amplified and booming over their loudspeakers. I leaned over and whispered to Marie Antoinette "*Il y a toujours une atmosphère d'arrestation!*"[5]

After our meditation, we all stood up and descended the Mount, crossed the busy street in front of the Church of All Nations, and entered the Kidron Valley. Crowds of people were walking in both directions, and we saw numerous people that we knew. All of these pilgrims in the streets were walking in the steps of Jesus on the night of his arrest, remembering the events, remembering the terror. We

---

5.   There is still an air of arrest.

walked into the Kidron Valley and past the Kidron Valley tombs, which would have been there in Jesus' day, and which Jesus would have passed on that awful night.

We arrived at St. Peter in Gallicantu where, according to tradition, Peter denied Jesus three times before the cock crew. Incredibly, there was actually a rooster crowing, perhaps one of the neighbours' fowl, confused about the time because the city is always illuminated. Beside the church is the ancient staircase believed to be part of a larger set of steps that existed in Jesus' time, and may have been the logical path between the Kidron Valley and the house of Caiaphas, the high priest. It is believed that Jesus went up these steps on the night of his arrest, and may have been held in a prison now on display below the church. I waited outdoors on the ancient steps with many others, all seated along the wide, ancient stairs with candles lit. The whole town seemed to be out, and a lot of people familiar to us were on hand.

Once again, we read the gospel story of Peter's denial and after another half-hour of prayer and meditation we trudged home by way of the Temple Mount and Western Wall. The excavations on the south end of the Temple Mount seemed haunted this night, the ruined buildings like ghosts. Around midnight I went to sleep.

Good Friday

It was a short night. We were up early on Good Friday to do the Stations of the Cross on the Via Dolorosa, starting at six. Our order of service would follow the traditional stations established long ago by the Franciscans, but we would not use the traditional prayers. Instead we used a contemporary version, with reflections and prayers that talked about justice and peace. For so many people in our world today there is no justice and no peace, and in that regard, it is still Good Friday.

Good Friday is the day when Jesus was crucified. It is the day of the Via Dolorosa, but this early in the morning the streets were fairly empty. There were only a few workers, a few pilgrims, and a little Palestinian boy of about five years, huddled on the side of the bazaar guarding the bit of milk and cheese that his family was to sell that day. It was so early that the Holy Sepulchre was not yet opened for the day, so we had to remember, from the courtyard outside, the Stations that were inside the church. Anne led the group, and the participants in the group took turns reading the reflections. Perhaps fifty to eighty people were assembled outside the Holy Sepulchre, some very silent, contemplating the way of the Cross in the half-light of morning.

After breakfast I went down to St. Annes's to meet with Joseph—the right one this time—to go to the souq for a coffee before I started work. Work on Good Friday meant helping Issa to welcome pilgrims into the Lithostrotos. As the Lithostrotos is traditionally connected with the events of Good Friday, the place was open for silent prayer only, no groups and no charge, but we had to enforce that with some tour guides who still wanted to conduct tours. I was able to stand in the doorway and see all the Christian groups parading down the Via Dolorosa. There were hundreds of army, police, T.V. crews and pilgrims. Some were quite flashy, such as the costumed actors with the microphones, centurions with their red plumes and helmets performing the flagellation as they passed by, an outrageous floozy of a Mary Magdalene narrating and grieving over the loudspeaker. The scouts were on hand again, too, some of them no more than around five years old, some young adults. Two delightful young fellows from Alberta had come to the house to visit their former parish priest who was a student in our program, and these two were the coolest pilgrims imaginable. They had come down to Jerusalem from their kibbutz jobs to join in the pageant of Holy Week, fashionable in their bleach blonde dreadlocks and shades, pious in their faith, carrying their little wooden crosses, deepening their understanding. They were in the parade also, part of the spectacle.

The neighbours' little boys had their donkeys out on the streets and they tried to cross the Via Dolorosa during the parade, dodging the procession and having great fun. Several of our Muslim friends were also out and about, including Fakhri, all dressed up because they were still celebrating their feast. In the afternoon there was a Good Friday service right on the Lithostrotos, on the very stone pavement believed to be the site of Jesus' condemnation. Paul led the service and others from Ecce Homo participated and provided the music. Anne sang the incantations. A wooden cross had been placed on the stone pavement and surrounded by little candles, and veneration of the Cross continued for some time. On this very pavement Jesus may have walked on the day of his condemnation. It was an unforgettable scene—and what was its meaning? What brought me here to this place–the place of judgment? What was I to learn here? The rigours of the week were starting to wear on me and, to my mortification, I dozed off, just as the disciples did in Luke's account of Gethsemane, although their sleepiness was from grief, according to the gospel, not pilgrim-house exhaustion.

In the evening, many of the students and guests, including Marie-Antoinette and the Jesuit fathers, arrived home from a very long service at the Maronite church. They told me the liturgy had gone on for about two-and-a-half hours, during which flowers were given out. A few of our guests gave me their carnations and I had enough for a modest bouquet. I picked out a small vase from the dining room, helped MaryAnne with breakfast prep, and took my flowers to my room.

Nine: Jubilee Renewal

Holy Saturday

After breakfast on Easter Eve, I met up with my party that was going to Bethlehem: AnneMarie and Fred, the Canadian couple; a South African couple; and an elderly Irish nun whose fussing about threatened to drive everyone crazy over the holidays. We found a bus outside the Damascus Gate and paid two shekels each to go to Bethlehem, which meant into the suburbs and through the checkpoint. It was dusty and hot, and we walked the long distance through the narrow and crowded streets of Bethlehem, now nothing like the quiet scene on Christmas cards, but a bustling Arab town. At length we arrived at the Church of the Nativity. It was odd to be going to the place of the Nativity at Easter, although heaven knows, it is always Christmas in Bethlehem, where some people have Merry Christmas signs up all year round.

After a visit to the church we walked toward the Shepherds' Fields, an open area that is shown to pilgrims eager to remember the Christmas story. The fields were now alongside a residential district where a lot of new homes had been built, and we looked for the home of the wood carver that AnneMarie had met the previous week. It was wonderfully hot. We passed Palestinian schoolgirls in their mint-green striped school uniforms, and one of the girls recognized AnneMarie from before and started chatting with her. That was good; it meant we were going the right way. We arrived at the home of a woodcarver who had a workshop attached to his beautiful buff stone house, and who looked from side to side before he let us in, like the owner of a speakeasy looking for the police. We were fortunate that he allowed us to buy goods from him at wholesale rates as he was taking a big risk in doing so. If local retailers knew he was doing that, they would boycott his business. I bought a large nativity consisting of a stable and a dozen or so figures carved with detailed faces, and quantities of small wooden gift items. The fellow was even so kind as to drive us back to the sherut, although he had to make two trips as we could not all fit into his little car. We got one sherut to the checkpoint and another to the Damascus Gate, and this was only a little more expensive than taking the rattletrap bus. We dropped off our bundles at Ecce

Homo then ran down to the three-shekel falafel man for a Middle Eastern fast food fix, and while we were at it we all bought the recipe for falafel.

It was now around four and I began to get ready for the Easter Vigil. The Vigil began on the terrace roof. Fakhri, a faithful Muslim, lit the New Fire as he probably had done for the previous fifty years. It was a wonderful testimony to the kind of deep respect that is possible between adherents of the great monotheistic faiths. Jim B presided at the Mass in gold vestments that appeared to sparkle as he lit the huge paschal candle. By now it was dark, and we were on the top terrace with our fire, enacting the same ceremony that Christians have enacted every Easter eve for almost two thousand years. We moved down to the main terrace for the next part of the Mass and eventually filed into the basilica, where Jim B. stood on the chancel steps with the paschal candle. I thought he looked rather like an angel wearing the gold chasuble, and I later told him that if I had been an icon painter I would have used him as a model. There was definitely an air of mystery in this Mass that I had not experienced in previous years. The Roman ruins behind the altar were the ancient and silent witnesses to an ancient rite that had had its beginnings right here in this neighbourhood, very long ago.

It was a wonderful Mass. My part was the first reading, the first chapter of Genesis, the Creation story, which is one of my favourite parts of the Bible. One of the students had, unfortunately, been recalled to Ireland because her father was dying. Jim's homily began with a recognition of that, and went on to talk about reaching the moment of surrender in our relationship with God. The moment of surrender. Dear me. Here I am, still trying to save myself. Save me, Lord.

After the Mass there were tea, coffee and cakes in the Lithostrotos reception area. Mel, Pat and I drank wine on the terrace roof, my first wine since the beginning of Lent, and we laughed and revelled in the Alleluiah moment. We were up there until around two o'clock in the morning, celebrating the resurrection on the terrace with a view of the very Temple Mount itself, seeing in our minds' eye the Temple as it used to be, the Temple that had stood on that very spot. Now on Easter Eve, that Temple was in many ways nearer than ever, shimmering before our eyes, making known its presence even in its absence. The Lord is risen indeed. Alleluiah!

Easter Sunday

Another short night. We got up at four-thirty after going to bed at two-thirty, and those who were interested walked out of the Old City and up Mount Scopus for a sunrise Mass celebrated by Brian the Younger, the Canadian priest who had been my Turkish coffee friend. He was not a morning person and he was finding this to be a tough trek, in fact, he kept asking himself why he had volunteered for this. It was worth it, of course. Our Mass took place by a low stone wall in front of the Mormon college. A linen cloth and a few simple articles were spread atop the wall, and we could all watch the sun rise across the valley below. At first we were in the dark, but soon the burning sun showed itself above the horizon. There were around thirty of us in our group, and it was simple, but it was unforgettable. Many of the students were there, the household, several guests, and our two cool dudes with the blonde dreadlocks who had so much enjoyed the Good Friday procession.

Even all of this was not enough, and after breakfast I fixed myself up as I must have looked quite bedraggled by then, and MaryAnne and I went to another Mass, this one at St. Anne's. Church bells from all over the Old City had been booming out Easter all morning. The beautiful old crusader church beside the Biblical pool of Bethesda was bright and glorious, full of flowers for Easter, and ringing with the *a cappella* voices of the worshippers. The St. Anne's community, including my friend Joseph, was all vested in natural coloured albs with matching embroidered stoles. The song leader was very strong and it was a joyful celebration.

MaryAnne disappeared right after the communion, and Joseph waited for me outside the church. After he changed his clothes we set out for the Armenian restaurant near the Jaffa Gate, a place with charming, folkloric interior design. This lunch was to be his gift to me to thank me for making the cake for his reconciliation liturgy, although I was under the impression that he had already given me several bottles of wine and numerous outings for Turkish coffee in honour of that same cake.

I ordered the two vegetarian appetizers, which were very good, and Joseph had brought along a bottle of wine. He told me about the earlier part of his life in France, including military service and then the seminary, before going to South America as a missionary. I told him a bit about my early years as a west coast hippie, frivolous in comparison to what he had experienced. Our lives had been very different and lived within vastly different contexts, yet in the time that we had known each other we discovered we had actually become quite close. We were unlikely as companions—as if each represented the other's road not taken. I was not especially looking for someone to share my life. I believe I had been going through the motions of seeking, but it was not a very active search. Yet eventually we admitted to each other that we had become much more than just school friends.

But mission and culture both conspired against us. He was committed to a mission to which he felt God had called him, and he was both useful and needed where he was. He would not be able to work in the locale where I lived. He could not speak English, and where I lived you had to speak English or Chinese. Quit work? I could not see that happening; not to a person with a mission. That was it, then. But I thought at the time that if things were different, things would be different.

Still, we could have a delightful lunch together, and we could talk about the deeper meanings of events around us, and we could reveal our inner worlds to one another in safety. We had left the restaurant and were walking past Christ Church near the citadel, when I heard someone call my name. It was Meir, the gatekeeper at the church, calling and waving. "Happy Easter!" I replied, and asked Meir if we could view the church. We were the only people sitting in the dignified church, its interior proclaiming in Hebrew the resurrection of which we were in the midst. For my part, I appended an additional prayer, thanking God for my new friend, but also asking why I cannot have a normal life. This was a lovely man, but certainly not the one I had prayed to meet.

We encountered on the way back a parade of Orthodox priests, scouts and others dressed up and carrying the woven, flower-bedecked palms that are the symbol of the Orthodox Palm Sunday celebration. The Latins and others were proclaiming resurrection; the Orthodox and Ethiopians, still following the Julian rather than the Gregorian calendar, were just beginning the cycle. Joseph dropped me off at the end of our street, and I hurried up home while he went to the post office. To us, so accustomed to living in a country where Christmas, Easter and Thanksgiving are the major public holidays, it seemed funny to be going to the post office on Easter Sunday.

At the house I hurriedly got ready and ran down to the street, Melanie right behind me, and all the rest of the community, the seven nuns and three volunteers, were in the van with Issa driving. We drove to El Qubeibeh, one of the claimants of being the Emmaus of the gospel. There is a Franciscan church incorporating the ruins of a little house traditionally thought to be that of the Cleopas mentioned in Luke's gospel, although the house is possibly of a later date. We went to the lookout point and viewed the valley, then assembled in the garden. I read aloud the account of Emmaus[6], in which the disciples encounter the risen Christ on the road to Emmaus, but do not know who he is until they recognize him in the breaking of the bread. We had a half-hour to meditate or roam on our

6.   Luke 24

own, so I went into the church, looked around briefly, and sat in a pew near the back. In the chancel a tiny group of people was celebrating Mass in Spanish, so I closed my eyes and listened to their singing while I communed silently with God. After half an hour we piled back into the van and Issa drove us to the monastery of the Salvatorian Sisters. There, Sister Ursula greeted us and presented lovely tea and cakes in their garden overlooking the Judean hills. Most sisters in their community are German, and their ministry is long-term care for local women, in a healthy country environment.

We drove home and there was a beautiful Easter dinner for everyone in the house, with wine for the residents, and lovely white tablecloths and candles. We all helped with cleanup. After my shower I went outside for a rooftop drink on the upper terrace with Pat and Mel, who teased me about sitting outside in my nightshirt on the convent roof. The two outrageous women accused me of having the shirt seductively open to the navel, in an effort to seduce one of the guests. It was a preposterous accusation, given that the nightshirt does not open to the navel but only has a couple of buttons, unrevealingly located at the lower throat. I pretended to be miffed and offended, and told the women they were exaggerating. The constant retelling of the story, in the presence of their fertile imaginations, will no doubt transform this innocent tale into an Ecce Homo classic, and a completely apocryphal one at that. Harumph!

Easter Monday

The members of the francophone class were at Mahfouz garage before seven in the morning. The students had been asked to reflect on "What is your Emmaus? Where do you see Christ in the breaking of the bread?" We drove to a place at the top of a hill and took the gravel road on foot, walking in the general direction of the Emmaus tradition, to Motza. There are four or more Emmaus claimants, and Motza is the most recent in ascendancy. Most of us walked two by two, as the disciples had done in the gospel story. I was in a threesome, on one side of Hedwig, the elderly sister who kept slipping, with Joseph on her other side, holding her up. They began to talk about instances in their own ministry that were Emmaus for them. Joseph had already told me about having been arrested in Argentina and questioned for nine hours with a gun at his temple, but refusing to sign a confession, and having his name on a list of those scheduled to disappear so that he had had to flee the country in secrecy. Now he began to talk about the martyrs of South America, friends who had had their feet encased in cement and had been thrown from an aircraft. We arrived at Canada Park at the bottom of the hill, a nature park built on the ruins of three Palestinian villages destroyed by Israel in 1967. We all sat down and various people got up and spoke about their own Emmaus, powerful stories every one. Most of these people were missionaries, and all had encountered challenges that were Good Fridays in their lives. It was wonderful to hear about the Emmaus revelations that all of them had also experienced.

We divided into two groups. Half of us went to Newe Shalom on the bus, and those that wanted to do so walked the two-and-a-half hour trek. I stayed in the bus, and our party arrived at the White Dove guesthouse at Newe Shalom where we waited in the café. The others arrived some time later, Joseph limping after twisting his ankle. A woman from the Newe Shalom community gave us a presentation on how this intentional community of Arabs and Jews, living together in peace, came into being. The development resembled a European housing community in that there were individual family units, whitewashed and pristine, arranged rather like row housing. The units were beautifully kept, and each had shrubbery and flowers in the front garden. The Jews and Arabs living here were not religious, and that seemed to be the formula for success. The house of prayer was an open, quiet space, and no distinctive liturgies of either faith were celebrated. Rather, any prayer or meditation was to be of a neutral nature, something that could be shared. We received one of the community's newsletters, and read the very sad story of one of the first babies to be born at Newe Shalom, who had now grown up and, tragically, had been killed in an accident in the Israeli army.

Our next stop was Latroun Abbey, a soaring and beautiful country monastery and vineyard that was the home of Trappist monks living in a community setting. We viewed the church—very high vaults with a prominent statue of Our Lady above the chancel—and went to their shop where they sold their excellent wines and their own teabags. I bought chamomile tea flavoured with anise, and a bottle of Pinot Noir.

Next was the Nicopolis at Imwas, another Emmaus claimant where the remains of the twelfth century nave sat open to the air beside the present church. Here, in the ruins of the old church, the Latin patriarch celebrated Mass in honour of the traditional feast day of Emmaus. This was the home of the Sisters and Brothers of the Beatitudes, whose beautiful singing was a wonderful addition to the liturgy. They sang almost throughout the whole Mass, and I noted that they had songbooks of their own composition. Along the side of the old ruined church was a stone ledge, where I sat between Joseph and Andrea, the Italian priest from the Sinai trip, who had gone up to Imwas independently for this celebration. Our trip ran overtime and when I arrived home after seven o'clock there was no power in the convent, and the residents were in the dining room having an impromptu candlelight meal.

The next day was Tuesday, and with Holy Week and the Easter weekend over, the house started to empty. Marie-Antoinette left to go to her volunteer term at Kiriat Yearim. Jeffrey, AnneMarie and Fred had already left, and others would be following them soon. It was the second week of April and we were into an early heat wave.

At five in the afternoon, after work, I went to St. Anne's and suggested to Joseph we sit by the ruins on the St. Anne's grounds. We read aloud the story of the healing of the paralysed man at the pool of Bethesda, and I asked Joseph if he ever dreamed he would be living by the Bethesda pool where the biblical story took place. What did he think was the meaning of his sojourn in this particular spot? He said it reinforced him in his mission because this was the place for rejected people: lepers, the impure, sick people. Jesus went into the Temple, but Jesus also came here and shared his healing presence with the rejected. This affirmed Joseph in his ministry to the poor and rejected. That was where he was meant to be. Then he asked what about me. But I was not living in the place so it was probably not the same for me, although I love the place. Instead, I thought about the thirty-eight years that the man sat there and would not even answer Jesus' question, but blamed other circumstances for his immobility. That was where I fit into this story: thirty-eight years of paralysis, thirty-eight years of immobility. As Theresa had remarked during her talk on this story, there is more than one way to be paralysed. More significant for me was the fact that I was living at the Lithostrotos: the crowning of thorns—the humiliation—the reverse and inverse of glory—the place of judgment. Later on I worked on this same exegesis with MaryAnne, trying to discern in what way God calls me to be among the condemned, or to stand judged.

Melanie's and my departure days were drawing near, and Anne would in fact be leaving before me to go to England for her holiday, so after my morning duties next day, Anne and I met at Reception and we went to El Binad, the Arab Orthodox society. There we had coffee and a snack, and had our heart-to-heart. I told her my highs and lows of the time I had been at Ecce Homo—I had no secrets from her, anyway, so none of this could have been news. The number one highlight for me was the meeting with people and engaging with them at a very deep level. When people come to Jerusalem, they are open and seeking and ready to go deep. For me this had been was a treat, a spiritual treat, and wonderful.

The other wonderful thing was the privilege of having lived inside the Biblical narrative—of living the Sacred Story: ascending Mount Sinai, participating in daily worship within the liturgical calendar, especially going through Holy Week and Easter, all in the places where these Biblical events took place. The day when the story of the healing at the Bethesda pool came up in the lectionary was a good example of that, and Theresa's sharing of her insights had been rendered so much more profound and exquisite by our proximity to the actual place. In the evenings on the terrace during Holy Week I could look toward the Temple Mount and imagine the Temple where the Dome is now. It became an increasingly present vision, through which we were all resurrected and newly transformed. I said that the lows I had enumerated were not really lows at all, but only small losses: not having continuity of attending courses in their entirety, but only individual classes; friendships that would be interrupted or would end.

I had decided to give Joseph my Bible as a souvenir, so at the Al Binad shop where Palestinian women's crafts were sold, I bought beautiful bookmarks for him and for Anne. Back at the house there was lunch, "family only," and Joseph dropped by on the way to his lecture. In the afternoon I worked on my diary and rested. The "family" set out for Abu Shanab's for our farewell dinner as Anne was leaving for England next day, and Melanie and I would both be leaving soon. It was the "last supper". We had our dessert back at St. Mary's, and we reminisced with stories and photos. I began to think of my impending departure.

The next morning the new schedule was out, and it was set up so that I could not go on the outing with the francophone class on the following Tuesday, my last Tuesday in Jerusalem! I was devastated. I was glum making breakfast and pouted all morning. Fortunately there was only a small group in the dining room, so I could drag myself around but still finish the job. Joseph dropped by at breakfast and gave me a kit list for our Ein Gedi trip the following Sunday, then I went down to meet Rita, Pat and Melanie who were joining me for the Ecole Biblique visit in response to a lunch invitation from our Dominican friend John at the Ecole. There were hundreds of people in the streets for the Orthodox Good Friday, and Pilar came out of our house, after her class, at the same time as we did, so we all wove through the crowds together out the Damascus Gate. A vendor ran into Pilar with his cart and scraped her leg. The merchants seemed to have returned to the steps at the Damascus Gate, even though the police had insisted last year that they sell only in the newly developed permanent market place closer to the street. Now they were all over the steps, and it was a real maze.

At the Ecole, John led us into the dining room. It was a self-serve buffet with beautiful food. I chose deep-fried eggplant, tabbouleh, raw carrots, and Middle Eastern rice, with red wine, then bananas and Turkish coffee. The students, who were only about twenty in number plus externes, were away so that only the community, faculty and staff were around. We went down a beautiful corridor, lined with all kinds of plants and archaeological exhibits, to the community rooms. In the community are a huge Fra Angelico of the life of St. Augustine, a collection of antique photographic equipment, Roland de Vaux's own drawings of Qumran, and a model of the terrain below the Holy Sepulchre based on probes. This model represents what would be there if the present Church of the Holy Sepulchre were removed. The site of the Sepulchre is a former quarry and the rock of Calvary was a rock outcropping so cracked it was unusable. The tomb was cut out of the rock nearby.

Lord, I believe; help my unbelief! It was a useful piece of work, this model. Until that moment the Church of the Holy Sepulchre, site of pilgrimage though it may be, was an imposition to the site of such proportion, and so over-decorated, so built over, so tawdry, in fact so very profane that I could not get past it. Not that it changed my personal conception of what happened on the first Good Friday and the days following. I was pretty secure about that. This unbelief had more to do with skepticism as to the sites where these events took place. With that horrendous church occupying the site of the old first century quarry, it was impossible for me to imagine what the site had looked like before the church was built. This model was an archaeologist's conception of the terrain beneath the church, and it clarified just how this could have been the site of the crucifixion. Now that I had some visual idea of how the site probably looked before the Holy Sepulchre was built, I began to think of the traditional rock of Calvary as the best candidate for the site of Jesus' execution. It was a prominent rock jutting out above ground, outside the city walls. The rock was cracked and so would not have been useful as dressed stone; thus it remained untouched. An execution intended to teach a terrible lesson to the local people was very likely to have been carried out atop a prominent stone, the better to be visible to the town. This was much more visible on the model than it ever had been during my visits to the actual site.

Next John took us to the tombs on the grounds of the Ecole, which included a First Temple Period tomb complex, some units of which still had Byzantine burials in them. The modern crypt had been added to the ancient one and so the bodies of Père Roland de Vaux, who excavated Qumran, and other modern-day Dominicans were interred nearby. After the tombs we entered the main building and viewed a room with a ping-pong table in the middle and a display of historical and important photographs all around. Adjacent to that is the church. The basilica of St. Stephen is a beautiful sanctuary of warm red marble, very high, with paintings of various saints on the wall and stained clerestory windows. There are nicks in the walls left by bullets fired in the 1967 war, and one of those bullets had left its mark on a painting on the altar of a side chapel.

That same evening several of us attended a choir concert at the Brigham Young College. The young people who sing in this large ensemble are not in a choir program, but rather they participate on a volunteer basis, like joining a club; yet they were very well trained. Their choral music was beautiful and included several sacred classics, such as a version of Mozart's *Ave Verum*, and also some arrangements of folk pieces such as *Some Folks*. The audience consisted of people like us whom the college had invited, but it seemed sparsely attended, and we wondered cynically if they would have had a better response if they had charged admission. We had taken a taxi over to the place, and Fakhri picked us up in the van to go back. Many different kinds of entertainment were available to us, and concerts such as this were typical of my own choices. Some of the others who were more interested in city night life found that an occasional excursion to Tel Aviv was the best way to do the night scene.

There had been a virulent illness that ripped through our student population during the spring term, and a few of the students were not recovering as quickly as could be hoped. Although I have no medical skills, I wanted to help in some way, so I invited any of the sick people to come down to the Bethesda pool for a reflection and healing prayer. Two students, Veronica and Theresa, had been very ill, and there was some question as to whether or not Veronica was even well enough to go down the street as I was proposing, but she insisted she could. We sat beside the pool of Bethesda, now a dried-up ruin, and shared insights and prayer. Veronica, who had struggled with cancer prior to this, did not stay with the rest us but walked to the far end of the excavations by herself. She was very quiet and introspective, and had very little energy. Long after I returned to Canada, I learned that Veronica had died about four months after this visit to the Biblical site of healing. I think she knew, during those moments beside the pool of Bethesda, that her remaining days were few.

On Sunday morning I met Joseph outside and we set out for Ein Gedi. We missed the bus outside the Damascus Gate so walked over to Prophets Street and got the #1 to the Central Bus Station. I reflected that perhaps it was the last time for a while that I would be able to see the Judean Desert, and I drank in the dry scenery greedily, not knowing when I might be back. There is a concession in front of the nature reserve where we stopped for a coffee before setting forth along the trails. In the ladies' washroom was a young man, an apparently religious Jewish fellow, but limited, and who did not seem to know why the woman shouting at him was protesting. He stared at her without comprehension while she berated him, in English, which he apparently could not understand, for being in the wrong toilet. Pointing at the picture on the door might have served her better.

Joseph and I set out on the trail and some ibex, the tiny antelope of Ein Gedi, very tame, came right up to us along the path. They are like deer, but very miniature—no bigger than dogs. The trail goes up past four waterfalls, the springs of Ein Gedi, and we stopped and sat down for a while beside each of the pools. It was dusty and hot, and if I had been more brilliant I would have worn my bathing suit so that I could have gone into the water. The area near these pools is associated with the pursuit of David by King Saul, and when I saw all the caverns in the rocks above it was easy to imagine David cutting off part of Saul's garment while Saul was relieving himself in the cave[7]. The springs and waterfalls are also mentioned in the Song of Songs[8], and this was, of course, Joseph's inspiration for bringing me here.

After the hike it was a bit after noon and we stopped for another drink then headed across the highway toward the beach. We changed at the restaurant and sat on the beach for a while, then went into the water of the Dead Sea. It was extremely salty, much saltier than I remember it being at the spa the previous year, and the thick water stung my eyes mercilessly. Although I was only in a few feet of water, I started to panic, unable to find a foothold. There were plenty of other people at the beach—perhaps a few visitors, but mainly local people. It was very hot, and I saw a Palestinian woman, completely covered up in her long coat and headscarf, wade into the water with all her clothes on. A similar phenomenon occurred when a party of schoolchildren came by, the boys in swimming shorts, the girls in their mint green and white striped uniforms. After the boys had had their swim, the girls could either go into the water with all their clothes on or else remain on the beach. No swimsuits in some of the conservative families of Palestine!

There were showers on the beach where we could shower off the salt, and we dried ourselves in the sun. We changed and grabbed a plate of chips at the restaurant and got the bus back. The coach was crowded and we could not sit together. There seemed to be a lot of young army personnel, out and about on their time off. They have to keep their weapons with them at all times because the penalty for having them stolen is so great—jail time, period. It is tough for this constant parade of young people with their military weapons to manoeuvre in a crowd, and

---

7.   I Samuel 24:1-7
8.   Song of Songs 1:14 and 2:14

it always seems they are poking their guns into your flesh. It is unintentional, but it is a nuisance.

We walked from the central Bus Station to the Ben Yehuda Mall and had a glass of wine, in the place I had said I would never again go after the suicide bombing of the previous year. Joseph dropped me off home around nine and I waited for Isabelle-Marie to return from her Ein Gedi junket with Sr. Régine. They had taken what you could call the high-end outing as they were going to the Ein Gedi spa to pamper themselves and to relax. When Isabelle-Marie came in we had our re-warmed suppers together and she talked with great glee and relish about her favourite part of the spa—the sulphur-jacuzzi.

The next morning I had to pick up an envelope of program information at the Ecole Biblique, and when I returned, the receptionist announced that Sister Trudy wanted to talk to me, so would I please phone her. I wondered with dread what it could be about; guilt oozed from every pore. I was sure she had finally found out about my indiscreet display of bad language within earshot of a guest some time earlier and would surely send me away at once! I went into a quiet room and called Trudy from there. She told me that she had rearranged the schedule so that I could go on the class outing on Tuesday, and if the staff members were unable to fill in for me, she would do it herself as she felt it was important I go. This kind and unmerited gesture stunned me. At that moment, my love for that woman knew no bounds.

Although Rita had seemed quite ill the previous night, she decided that she was indeed well enough to go on the little trip to Cairo that she and MaryAnne had been planning. Rita had phoned to say good-bye to me the previous night, and MaryAnne left me a note in the morning. Anne was in England. I would not see these women again during my present visit. It truly seemed that the end of my sojourn was approaching.

The doctor told Veronica that it was best she go home to South Africa and be treated there by her own physician. She looked very ill indeed, and seemed detached. At our daily Mass she was anointed and all the participants laid hands on her in healing prayer. She was quiet but serene throughout this, and shortly afterward she requested that she be left alone to deal with her illness and sudden leave-taking in solitude. I was emotionally voluble myself, one minute feeling I was ready to go home, the next minute grieving my forthcoming departure. I also felt sorry about Veronica, and as well, it seemed I was saying goodbyes all the time. The last of the guests that had been with us over Easter were departing. It all had an air of finality.

Neot Kedumim

On the morning of the Tuesday outing, our first stop was Neot Kedumim near the airport.

It is called the "Biblical Landscape Reserve" and is a sanctuary for the many varieties of trees and plants mentioned in the Bible, a form of horticulture that the reserve calls "green archaeology." When you enter the grounds of Neot Kedumim, it appears to be simply a large area of parkland. On closer inspection, you notice that every little thing about that park is redolent of the Bible. Its beauty is deep and Biblical. I was completely enchanted.

Cedar, willow, hyssop, myrtle and exquisite wildflowers of every brilliant colour line the paths. Date palms, olives and other food plants flourish everywhere. The air is filled with the ecstatic fragrance of trees heavy with blossoms. The reserve is available year-round, so in their season follow pomegranates and almonds, filling the air with the musty suggestion of sweetness and ripe fruit. Ancient presses pour out olive oil and wine. Wheat and chaff are separated on the winnowing floor. Woolly sheep graze by their sheepfold. *The voice of the turtledove is heard in our land.* Here we could encounter the land flowing with milk and honey, whose terraces burgeon with produce, and whose wisdom is the balm of the soul. Here Biblical plants, ecologies and growing methods are preserved and presented. When we walked through that gate and down the path, we entered the landscape of the psalms: *"He makes me to lie down in green pastures."*

Despite the constant threat of drought in this land, the reserve is wonderfully green. The very name *neot* means pastures, places of beauty. True to Hebrew tradition, the reserve's name contains a play on words, for *kedumim* means ancient times or the past, but also suggests the root word *kadima*, meaning moving forward in time, and *kedem*, the East, redolent of the garden of Eden. The name *Neot Kedumim*, then, suggests "future growth from past roots," perhaps roots that go back to the beginning of time.

Its story is exciting. Neot Kedumim was established as a non-profit society in 1965 by Nogah Hareuveni, whose parents had been botanical pioneers in Israel from 1906 and later. To honour their work, Hareuveni set out to transform 625 unpromising acres of dry, rocky dust in Israel's Modi'in region into a model of Biblical ecology for visitors to enter and to experience, literally to bring the Bible to life. When the acreage was acquired the terrain was desolate, the soil eroded. The government workers who signed the property over to Hareuveni must have smiled to themselves; it was a mad project, and perhaps they were amused by his idealism. In spite of the skeptics, Hareuveni persevered. He created terraces identical to those built in ancient times, and olive trees were transplanted throughout. King Solomon had said, "*I built pools in order to water my garden,*" so Hareuveni did that also. Hundreds of trees were planted and eventually established. The once scruffy, inhospitable terrain turned into a Biblical landscape come to life. Now, Neot Kedumim is host to weddings, bar mitzvahs, educational and pilgrim groups, and in 1994 the site was awarded the Prize of Israel, the nation's highest recognition for contribution to society.

Sturdy almond trees were put in, that give produce twice: once when the nuts are furry, green, pliable and chewy, and then again when the nuts are ripe and hard. The little tree works hard to produce its fur, wood, and nuts, so it wakes up and blossoms in earliest spring in order to have its fruit ready in July. The terebinthe is visible at Neot Kedumim, the tree on which Absalom, the rebel son of King David, was hanged. Most trees did not have such a negative press in the ancient world, however; in fact, the diligent Hebrews loved trees and held them in high esteem. The *fistuk* (FIS-took), for example, first cousin of the terebinthe, is the pistachio, which is a faithful friend as it produces a delicious nut that is a staple in the Near East.

The image of trees becomes prominent in the book of Judges, where a parable illustrates to the people that they do not need a king. The tale recounts how each member of the society of trees was in turn asked to be the king of the trees: the olive, the vine, the cedar. Each one was too busy producing oil, fruit, or wine and had no time to rule. Only the spiny jujube—the Crown of Thorns—that produces mediocre fruit and prickly thorns, agreed to be king as he had nothing better to do. It is the Bible's wry comment on the task of governing!

The Dale of the Song of Songs within the reserve commemorates that exquisite song of Solomon that is the romantic poem *par excellence* of ancient Israel. The poem is in the form of a dialogue between lovers, probably a shepherd and shepherdess, all in the context of the natural world in which they worked and lived. In the poem, every beautiful image in nature is a reminder of the beloved and of the beloved's sensual ripeness. Each of the Song's images is represented at Neot Kedumim for the delight of the visitor. *The fig tree puts forth its figs, and the vines are in blossom*; even the doves and flocks of goats are present in the reserve.

Plants useful to ancient people as medicines are especially of interest at Neot Kedumim. According to the Mishnah, it is allowable to chew parts of the mastick, or *sopi*, plant on the sabbath. Perhaps that is because of the plant's life-giving properties: it smells medicinal and is used as a disinfectant. Mastick's other practical use is as a natural toothbrush; you just feather the sticks with your pocket knife—or your sword! Medicinal plants are mentioned in the story of

Joseph in the Bible: merchants brought *sopi*, as well as *lot*, the ancient equivalent of laudanum.

Fistuk, almond and mastick, and the sticky rock rose with its pine smell—these were part of the original forest of Israel. They are small and compact, grow in rocky, uneven terrain, and make efficient use of limited water. When Moses arrived at the borders of the Promised Land, the Bible says that he looked over and saw a land flowing with milk and honey. What he saw was a rocky terrain with low shrubs; but in the wildflowers and scruffy goat pasturage Moses could see the vision of potential milk and honey that could be. Nowadays, big pines are planted all around Jerusalem, especially near cemeteries. They establish very quickly and are allowed to grow very tall, much taller than the native plants. Yet these intruders are not indigenous to the region, and they require a lot of water in order to look good. As Israel endures a long dry season, the big pines often look brown and unhealthy while the compact native shrubbery is still green.

In ancient times, the number seven signified perfection and completion; hence, the Lord rested on the seventh day of creation, and all of creation was organised in sevens. The menorah, the seven-branched candlestick, was so important to these ancient people that Neot Kedumim has devoted a large area as a refuge for the moriah sage, the tall, branched plant that may have inspired the menorah. Another area is devoted to the seven species of Deuteronomy: *a land of wheat, and barley, of vines and fig trees, and pomegranates; a land of oil olive, and honey.* Also seen are tall reeds such as were used to write the scriptures. The reed is flexible and modest, not hard like the cedars. So also is the divine law: flexible, and not hard.

Still *in situ* along the reserve's trails are authentic archaeological sites that offer a further window into the ancient world. There is an ancient ritual bath or *mikveh,* that was used in purification rites. There are also pressing floors for producing wine, a threshing floor for separating grain, cisterns, a sheepfold, a Byzantine church, and even the remains of a village. As well, agricultural implements have been recreated and are demonstrated in hands-on exhibits: ploughshares, olive presses and grinding stones.

Having a clear picture of what the plants look like really enhances the reading of the Bible; so many plants are mentioned and they are all of special significance for the people of Bible times, as our Dominican friend, John, had pointed out in his sermon about the fig tree. Cedars and hyssop, olive, fig, pomegranate trees, grapevines and date palms—these were all a close-up part of ancient life. Here with the Biblical program group, throughout our pleasant hike through the grounds, Bernard lectured on the relationship between native plants and the Biblical narrative. Throughout his talk we heard constant gunfire, a sound effect that was not congruent with the gentle subject under discussion. There must have been military training nearby. We ate our lunches at picnic tables on the grounds, where there was also a concession. Some students were complaining that there was no coffee, but I went up and ordered a thick Turkish coffee and sat down with the complainers.

"Ah, but is it coffee, or is it mud?" one of them asked.

"It's mud," I replied, to her great disgust. "I like this mud."

After the picnic we went to Kiryat Yearim, the place where in ancient times the Ark of the Covenant rested for twenty years.[9] My friend Marie-Antoinette was now at the monastery in Kiryat Yearim as a volunteer and she had apparently been waiting for us. She had had a very bad couple of days when she first got there as the workdays were long by volunteer standards, seven hours, with only one day off per week and really nowhere to go in the little village. She seemed to have settled in by the time she saw us. After we had had our half-hour to view the church and monastery grounds, we got into the bus and went to Abu Gosh, the Crusaders' church of the Resurrection that is another Emmaus claimant, and Marie-Antoinette came with us. It was a beautiful and peaceful Benedictine monastery with a very well-preserved church and a lush, green garden. We sat on a wooden bench and inhaled the garden air.

That evening was my last Mass with the Ecce Homo students. Raymond was the presider. He had been one of the very ill ones and had become thin, but he was looking much better. He graciously made mention of my departure and Melanie's in the prayers, as well as prayers for Veronica and for the late father of the student who had returned to Ireland. This really seemed final. I phoned home to Canada to make sure someone would pick me up at the airport when I got there.

Pat, Melanie and I were a glum trio, sitting in the flat like three buzzards on a tree, and we put out all our bits that we did not want to carry home. I was still working on repairing those confounded hymnbooks, and we were eating walnuts by cracking open the shells under our feet, creating a huge mess. Any vestiges of refinement that we had possessed went out the window. Mel and I cracked open some wine, but were civilized enough to use a corkscrew rather than stomp it under our feet. I recalled seeing Kathleen's face when she left in the sherut in January, how happy she was and how ready she had been to leave. There was no way

---

9.   I Samuel 6:19—7:2

I was ready. I was going kicking and screaming to the airport. I loved this country, and if I could not stay, I vowed I would go back.

The students in the house were leaving for their Galilee retreat early in the morning, and Trudy was going with them as their spiritual director. Don would leave in a couple of days to join them also, but in the meantime he and Stéphane had invited me to St. Anne's for dinner on my last evening in Jerusalem. It was all goodbyes, and late in the afternoon I walked down to St. Anne's for my dinner with the White Fathers. I arrived early so we could spend some time together before the meal. Their cook had made me a vegetarian meal of raw vegetables with a spinach soup, after which we three sat in the salon with our wine glasses. The phone rang quite a bit as Don was on duty, but we talked about my experience of Jerusalem, and reminisced about our great footwashing night. Don said that the students had really pondered our message from that night, and that they mentioned it often. I was delighted and gratified by this. Finally when I was ready to depart, I asked Don if he had any sage advice for me. He encouraged me in my mission, encouraged me generally, and gave me a bit of free spiritual direction.

I said, "Anything else?" And with that, he stretched out his arms and started singing "Always Look on the Bright Side of Life," that most irreverent crucifixion scene from *The Life of Brian*. Here was a profound man and a gifted spiritual director—with a great sense of humour! If I ever returned to Jerusalem again, he would by that time be back in Africa. This was the last of the old neighbourhood as I knew it. Stéphane walked me home, and I thought how very much I appreciated these two extraordinary priests.

Thursday morning Melanie kindly relieved me at Reception so I could say goodbye to the francophone class. While waiting for the students, I spent a few minutes with Bernard, when the sirens started up and we observed the annual two minutes of silence in recognition of the Holocaust. Bernard then told me about an incident in class that morning in which a student, a French sister, had expressed irritation at this observance and said what about the Palestinian cause, and something to the effect that anyway, the Jews killed Jesus. This was an outrageous statement considering that the ministry of the Biblical program was to put an end to this kind of thinking. As well, that is not even church doctrine! Bernard said he had exploded at the time, but in the end it turned out to be an opportunity for discussion, to clear the air of some persistent anti-judaism, and to make inroads in confronting anti-Semitism.

I said my good-byes to the students one by one and some promised they would write to me. After these good-byes I felt I had a tremendous pain in my chest—heartache—and I hid in the flat doing departure chores so I would not have to go through that again. The volunteers were by now the only English speakers left in the house; it must have been like former days at Ecce Homo, when it was a French-speaking house. At lunch, our visiting sister, Christiane-Marie, was talking about the incident in Bernard's class as she had been there at the time. The other French women remarked confidently that it was probably a Canadian who made the offensive comments, but Christiane-Marie confirmed that it had been a French woman who said it, and added that it could have arisen more from French political leanings than from Christian anti-Semitism. Canadians vindicated!

When Mel and Pat came home we shared a pitcher of Sangria in the flat and were able to laugh, despite our sadness. I put together the instructions for the hymnbook repairs, and packed them all into a box. I also packed a box of other songbooks to send up to the retreat in Galilee. That evening at six, just before I left Jerusalem, Mel, Pat and I finally went to the controversial Western Wall tunnel, where an excellent interpretation of the site is presented—absolutely great. The tour took us along the old esplanade on the western side of the Temple Mount, now under the Muslim Quarter, and the wall was still in superb condition because it had been buried all those years. At the time of their departure, the Romans had been building a sidewalk alongside the Temple, and they left the cut and unlaid paving stones leaning up against the Western Wall. Everything was sitting right in the very place they had left it. The electronic moving model of the Temple precinct was a superb visual accompaniment to the commentary. We sat in a theatre while the guide described the Temple area during its various periods, and motorized variations of the esplanade made their appearance and retreat on the model at appropriate times during the talk. We ended up at the other side of the Struthion Pool, the side blocked off from the part of the pool visible under Ecce Homo, and we heard the story of how the pool was found in the 19th century during excavations for construction of the Sisters of Sion convent!

After we exited the tunnel, right across from our house, we went up the stairs to our door. The armed security guard who had been with the tour group, but whom we had never really noticed, motioned us to get back with the group. I said, "We live here". He still insisted we remain with the group. I repeated "We live here," and he said he was group security, were we with the group? Pat replied "No" so he went on down the Via Dolorosa with the group, the rifle slung over his shoulder, no longer interested in our defection.

I was packed and planned to leave the house at nine-thirty to get the sherut to the airport for my three a.m. departure. Joseph, whom Isabelle-Marie called my *chevalier servant*, was planning to go to the airport with me, and I persuaded him to arrive early so he could visit with us in the Community beforehand. Isabelle-Marie was delighted to see him and chatted away merrily. It was a pleasant evening, and everyone was conspiring to be upbeat so I would not fall apart. At length Pat, Melanie, Joseph and I said good-bye to the community, and as I went out the door, Wanda and Isabelle-Marie pressed an envelope into my hand as an extraordinarily kind gift from them. My three faithful companions dragged my baggage to Notre Dame and we sat in the café for a last coffee. When Nesher's *sherut* appeared, Joseph and I piled in, and he waved to Pat and Mel and said he would be back presently. My good-byes to Mel and Pat were hard to say. I was so distracted I forgot to thank them for carrying my bags.

Two days later, after a gruelling trip home and long delays, I woke up in my own bed. It felt strange. I thought, "Oh—I'm not in Jerusalem! It's over." No *muezzin* called me to prayer over the loudspeaker. It was terribly quiet. No need to make breakfast for a hundred and twenty people. No early morning Reception, and no washing the convent steps before the *externes* arrived. At first I had a profound feeling of loss. Of course, there is much to be said for being home, in one's own bed, surrounded by familiar belongings. While I missed Jerusalem, Ecce Homo and even the clamorous call to prayer, I felt embraced by my tiny room with its white walls and high, pine ceiling. The pottery I had brought from Turkey and Palestine hung on my walls as beautiful reminders of my life in the Holy Land. I went back to work, and life seemed to continue as before.

Yet although I appeared to adjust to life at home, in some ways it was as if my Ecce Homo life were still going on. My relationships with my new friends continued within me and I felt that in a way I was still communicating with Pat, Mel, the students and guests. Gradually the conception took shape that my time in the Near East was another life within, one that I was living concurrently with this one. As the weeks passed I increasingly saw the lessons of the journey in terms of the wonderful, sacred story set out in the Bible. The landscape of the Holy Land, in which I had delighted and where I gained such a rich experience, was now a landscape that I both carried inside me, and lived within. I was actually living the sacred story.

9

Jubilee Renewal

Moses instructed the Israelites to "count off seven weeks of years, seven times seven years, so that the period of seven weeks of years gives forty-nine years. Then you shall have the trumpet sounded loud; on the tenth day of the seventh month—on the day of atonement—you shall have the trumpet sounded throughout all your land. And you shall hallow the fiftieth year and you shall proclaim liberty throughout the land to all its inhabitants. It shall be a jubilee for you: you shall return, every one of you, to your property and every one of you to your family. That fiftieth year shall be a jubilee for you:…".[1]

Now that I am living the sacred story, inside and out, every event of my life seems to be embedded in a solid and ancient context. I no longer drift around in a formless, existential void, living within a vacuum, trying to discern the right thing to do without reference points for the decision. North American life is beset with excesses, meaninglessness, and a kind of malaise. I began to think of this as the Babylonian exile. After they were conquered by Babylon and taken captive, the Israelites were banished from Israel, the land they loved and the very stage on which the Israelite relationship with God was enacted. North America, also, has been conquered by harmful forces—greed, for example—and we who live there have been violently separated from the world-views that have been our context, our basic assumptions and our comfort in the past.

I thought of myself as one of the Biblical Israelites who first shaped the forms of our faith. Holiness began to spill over from the memories of my Holyland experience into the daily course of life. For one thing, my lifetime of neglecting the Sabbath no longer seemed right, and I began to long for the holiness and harmony that I could gain by keeping the Sabbath in some way. I thought often of the Torah readings at Ein Kerem in which we were amazed by the number of times the *Shabbat mitzvah*, the commandment to keep a holy sabbath, is repeated in the Bible: is it 140 times, or 160? The *Shabbat mitzvah* is given in the Ten

---

1.   Leviticus 25:8ff

Commandments; for that alone we can consider it to be of principal importance—one of the Top Ten.[2] I decided that one holy thing I could do was to
cease work on the sabbath, the *Shabbat*, and use the time for rest and renewal.
Proceeding along a cautious continuum, I gradually began to reduce my Saturday
activities to provide myself a rest. My own life was beginning to be enacted
within a Biblical scheme, but it was just beginning, vague and confused.
Increased clarity came with the approach to my fiftieth birthday.

In Bible times, there was concern not only for rest for human beings, but also
for the land itself. So, just as God rested on the seventh day and that became the
Shabbat, the seventh year was considered to be a Shabbat for the land. Fields were
worked for six years, and on the seventh the field lay fallow. It had a rest. After
seven cycles of seven years, forty-nine years, there was proclaimed a year of Jubilee. Debts were cancelled, wealth was redistributed, slaves were freed, and families
were eligible to redeem their lands that had been leased out. The concept of complete transfer of land title for all time did not exist because the Israelites knew that
the land belonged to God. The fiftieth year was the Jubilee year. It was a year for
renewal, freedom and justice. Just as the world needs a year of Jubilee, I acknowledged that I needed a personal year of Jubilee, and I proclaimed to all my friends
that I was going to have a Jubilee in my life.

On the Day of Atonement, Yom Kippur, just prior to my forty-ninth birthday, I sounded the trumpet. The Biblical word for trumpet is *yubhal*, from which
we get the word jubilee. But the *yubhal* was a ram's horn, not very vegetarian. I
dug around the house and came up with a lovely olive wood recorder from Israel.
It might not make much noise, but this was a purely symbolic gesture. I stood on
the veranda of our house and sounded the first strain.

There were some practical and tangible dimensions to my jubilee. Over the
years I had borrowed books and other items from people, and they had borrowed
things from me. I decided to go through everything in my possession, determine
if it belonged to someone else, or if it should belong to someone else, and to
return it or render it to the right person. I would start now paying off any remaining debts and do my best to acquit any such old business. If anyone owed me
anything, I would either call in the debt or forgive it outright. I could not think
of anything that anyone owed me, though; they might have a few books they had
forgotten to return, that was all.

There would also be an intangible side to my jubilee. I would deal with inner
and emotional debt. I would get ready to forgive others by working on my old

---

2.   Ten Commandments: Exodus 20:1-17 and Deuteronomy 5:7-21

issues, and to seek forgiveness from others by examining my own conscience and listening to others with open ears. When all this was done, I would go to sacramental confession and end it. These activities would go on during the year between my forty-ninth and fiftieth birthdays, that is, during my fiftieth year.

All these things I did. And at the end of that time, I sounded my little "trumpet," again, and my time of celebration began. It was an especially sacred time within the sacred story, the story that I am living. And now, my debts have been forgiven, and I am new again.

0-595-28320-9

p 92. Qumran --- & Dead sea Scrolls

Printed in the United States
16388LVS00003B/265-267